MW00699346

100
YEARS
SIMON & SCHUSTER

# Habitations

a novel

# Sheila Sundar

SIMON & SCHUSTER

*New York   Toronto   London   Sydney   New Delhi*

1230 Avenue of the Americas
New York, NY 10020

First Simon & Schuster hardcover edition April 2024

SIMON & SCHUSTER and colophon are registered trademarks of Simon & Schuster, LLC

Simon & Schuster: Celebrating 100 Years of Publishing in 2024

For information about special discounts for bulk purchases, please contact Simon & Schuster Special Sales at 1-866-506-1949 or business@simonandschuster.com.

The Simon & Schuster Speakers Bureau can bring authors to your live event. For more information or to book an event, contact the Simon & Schuster Speakers Bureau at 1-866-248-3049 or visit our website at www.simonspeakers.com.

Interior design by Lewelin Polanco

Manufactured in the United States of America

1  3  5  7  9  10  8  6  4  2

Library of Congress Cataloging-in-Publication Data is available.

ISBN 978-1-6680-1610-7
ISBN 978-1-6680-1612-1 (ebook)

*For my parents*
*And in memory of Nana Periappa, the family storyteller*

# Part 1

# 1

Vega had been prone to bouts of car sickness as a child, but she hadn't felt anything like this since then, when her well-being had been somebody else's responsibility and she could bend over and everything would be set into motion—her mother rubbing her back, her father plying her with sips of fizzy water. She rarely missed her parents these days. Her mother called too often to allow Vega the chance. But now, she wanted them next to her. She wanted her mother's cool hand on her forehead, the delicious *shh* of her father's Schweppes bottle. The train slowed and screeched. She burped into her lap and was relieved that nothing came up.

Suresh was waiting at the Morris Plains station. He had changed from his work clothes and was dressed in one of his standard evening outfits: a maroon Oxford University sweatshirt and black track pants. His copy of *The 125 Best Brain Teasers of All Time* was lying on the passenger seat. Vega had bought the book for him at a newsstand next to CUNY and she was both touched and a little depressed by how much he seemed to appreciate it, how little it took to make her husband happy. Sometimes, she wished she could be so simple.

"You had a good day?" he asked.

"Yes. You?"

"Yes. Quite fine."

It was nearly freezing outside, but she cracked open the window. "Did you solve any interesting brain teasers?"

He came to a complete stop at the parking lot exit and waited for

what felt like a full minute until the next car passed. "Actually, one particularly good one. The name of what nine-letter animal can be spelled
from the letters of 'inauguration'?"

She tapped the word with her fingers. "'Inauguration' has more
than nine letters."

"But the name of the animal does not need to use all the letters.
It needs only to be composed of letters found in 'inauguration.' If you
think about it for even a minute, it will come to you."

She wished he would stop talking. Her nausea was resurfacing,
and the mere thought of letters—shuffling them, reading them, puzzling through them—made her want to throw up. But she was aware,
too, that her reticence was the primary reason Suresh always tried so
hard. "I give up," she said. "Tell me."

"'Orangutan.'"

"I see. I thought of a few three- or four-letter words, but I would
never have come up with 'orangutan.'"

"You would if you used pen and paper," Suresh said. "That's the
best strategy."

Inside the apartment, Vega was comforted by the smell of onions.
Suresh had cooked dinner, as he always did on Tuesday and Thursday
nights, and they ate quietly. Afterwards, she joined him on the couch
and watched *NBC Nightly News*. They had bought the couch a few
months back, to replace two temporary lawn chairs unloaded by an
acquaintance—another Indian software engineer who had moved to
Houston. Vega still didn't know how to arrange herself comfortably on
it. Leaning against its arm, her feet eventually drifted over to Suresh's
side, sometimes brushing his thigh, and then she would begin the
awkward shuffle of pulling them back.

They sat rigidly and stared at the clip that had played the previous
two nights: Elián González, lying in a stretcher, his head tilted to the
side and eyes wide open, his body draped in a brown blanket. "Madness," Suresh said. "Such a small boy."

Vega, too, found it all quite mad. She was disturbed by the wretch-
edness of the situation, but also by the national obsession, the use of

a small child for political sport. In India, even floods and train derailments that killed hundreds held national attention for only a day or two before being demoted to small boxes on the third or fourth pages of the *Hindu*. She still wasn't used to this style of American coverage, this persistence of a single, terrible story. Four years earlier, when she arrived in the States for the first time as an adult, it had bothered her to see O. J. Simpson's face emblazoned at every Manhattan newsstand. Even her mother had been following the trial on BBC. "What kind of country is this?" Rukmini had asked. "Where men kill their wives?"

"It's sensationalist coverage, Amma," Vega had said. At the time, the call had irritated her. Her mother always shouted over the phone but held the receiver too far from her mouth, making her voice both deafening and barely audible. "There's plenty of crime in India," Vega told her. "Much of it unreported." She reminded her that Hindu fundamentalists had rioted three years prior, killing nearly a thousand.

Rukmini, to whom a singular crime was more terrifying than a sweeping disaster, was unconvinced. "That is different," she said. "Lock your doors and windows always. Don't go any place on your own. Ever."

The next afternoon, Vega sat in the office of her graduate advisor, Margo Fink. In all of CUNY—in all of New York, maybe—this was Vega's favorite place. It was tucked into a far, quiet end of the sociology wing. The floor was covered in a worn Persian rug, and it had a distinct smell Vega loved—some combination of dust, old books, and wood polish. A framed photograph hung next to the doorway, taken on one of Margo's annual research trips to Poland. It was the exterior of a synagogue in Kraków, an old woman resting her palm against the building's metal gate. Vega had stared at the image for what amounted to hours, and it always stirred something inside her.

That morning, Vega had gagged while brushing her teeth. Her saliva tasted salty, then metallic. Hours later, she purchased the pregnancy test at the CVS next to Penn Station and crouched over the stick in the sociology department bathroom. As she waited for the results, she stared at a photograph on the insert of the box. A white couple was smiling, staring down lovingly, the man's hands wrapped around the woman's shoulders. She had found the image ridiculous and held on to it with the intention of showing it to Margo, who had laughed and said, "Maybe it's not what you think. Maybe they were smiling because the test was negative." Now, Margo asked, "Have you told your husband?"

To Margo, Suresh was an abstraction. Vega had only spoken about him once, in the context of her green card application, and she wasn't sure if Margo even knew his name. "I don't plan on telling him just yet. Once he knows, then I've rather made the decision."

"I'm only asking because I want to make sure that you aren't navigating this alone. I know you have a lot of people in your life. I hope you lean on them. Me included."

The only person Vega could imagine confiding in was her childhood friend, Gayatri, but she was in Ahmedabad for the year on a research fellowship, sharing a flat and telephone with three other graduate students. If Vega had great or terrible news—a travel grant or a grim health diagnosis—she would have called her immediately. But this was news she did not know how to share. Her gynecologist had prescribed her birth control a year ago, shortly after she was married, and the disk sat, still unopened, in her underwear drawer. She and Suresh had sex so infrequently, she reasoned, that contraception wasn't necessary, but occasionally she would touch the plastic container and try to make sense of these dueling emotions: she did not want a child with Suresh, but she couldn't bear to remove the possibility of having one altogether.

That night, after Suresh went to sleep promptly at nine thirty, she retreated to her study, closed the door, and dialed her parents. Her mother picked up on the first ring, sounding, as she always did, as though she knew that it was Vega on the other end of the line. Vega didn't plan to tell her parents the news—certainly not in its tentative, uncertain state. But hearing her mother's voice, she wished that she could. She wanted to give them something to be happy about.

"We were thinking of you last evening," Rukmini said. "We had idiyappam for dinner. You remember that you used to love that."

"I still like it," Vega said. "Did you cook or did Vasanti?"

"I supervised. She puts too much clove, sometimes. It isn't good for Appa's heartburn."

Vega wanted to question the science behind this but changed her mind. "How is Appa?"

"Feeling strong. He's gone for his morning walk. You're studying late tonight?"

"Not too late. I have to transcribe an interview." Vega talked for a bit about her research, and she could almost hear Rukmini's body shifting, settling into place as she listened. Rukmini's own career had been spotty—she'd worked on and off as a copy editor for a few science publications, always part-time, and had quit fully after Ashwini's diagnosis—but she delighted in the professional satisfaction of her husband and surviving daughter. Vega was in the second year of her doctoral program, winding down her coursework and beginning her dissertation on unaccompanied child migration. It surprised Vega how invested her mother was in the content of this research. Rukmini had no sociological impulses of her own; she had grown up in an orthodox Brahmin family that was abjectly cruel to their house staff, so she prided herself in being a relatively progressive thinker, an upper-middle-class lawyer's wife who paid the housekeeper a fair salary, voted consistently for Congress Party candidates, and ventured out of their South Chennai neighborhood a few times each week to participate in what she called "poor feedings" at a temple in Tondiarpet.

"If you ask my brothers their opinion, they will tell you that I'm a card-carrying Communist," Rukmini had once declared.

"I'm certain nobody would make that mistake, Amma," Vega had responded. This was when Ashwini was alive, when there was still humor in the house. Vega recalled, distinctly, that her father had laughed.

For years, all she had wanted was to touch her sister again, to braid Ashwini's damp hair or pull her hand as they walked down the street.

Sometimes, for a split second, Vega was certain that she could *smell* her sister—her blend of coconut oil, sandalwood talc, and adolescent sweat. Then the smell would disappear, and she would remember with miserable clarity that Ashwini was gone. Now, she half listened as Rukmini rambled about the importance of cardiovascular exercise. She wanted to interrupt her, to say, "Amma. I'm having a baby." Instead, she sat in her dark study, mumbling in agreement.

Vega's family had never been religious, but they observed the customary thirteen-day mourning period following Ashwini's death. Rukmini's brothers and their families came from Bangalore with their enormous suitcases and booming voices. Vega's paternal grandmother arrived from Madurai and sat on the daybed, looking catatonic, gesturing to Vega when she needed a glass of water or to be helped to the toilet. A Hindu priest came to their door every day to walk them through another round of prayers. To make room for their relatives, Vega spent nights on a pallet on the floor of her parents' bedroom. She hardly slept, and neither did they, though none of them spoke a word. In the mornings, she and Rukmini bathed and draped themselves in stiff, white, cotton saris. This was the only time, during those two weeks, when Vega and her mother were alone together. It was when she missed Ashwini most acutely, when she realized how thin their lives had become.

Vega was seventeen years old then, in her final term at Rhodes School, and had been admitted to her two top-choice universities: Jawaharlal Nehru University in Delhi and University of Hyderabad. She had been leaning towards JNU, but she could no longer imagine leaving Chennai, so she enrolled at Sri Vidya, a women's college in Mylapore that she had passed countless times throughout her life. Had she attended JNU, she might have retreated more selfishly into student life. But Sri Vidya was all routine and no temptation. The lectures were easy and many of her classmates were girls she had known from primary and secondary school. She spent most nights at her parents' house, waking up early to have coffee with them before catching the 102P bus back to campus. She avoided anything recreational—sports clubs, rotary club, the weekly co-ed mixer. It occurred to her often, as she passed students clustered in the student center or canteen, how much Ashwini would have loved college.

Throughout the thirteen days of mourning, Vega had barely been able to look at her mother. But over the coming years, as she commuted back and forth from Sri Vidya, she observed that Rukmini—in her own slow and methodical way—seemed to be surviving. She woke up every day at five o'clock for morning walks and continued her volunteer work in Tondiarpet. She cried often, but always openly, sitting on the sofa with her head in her hands and her body rocking gently.

It was Vega's father who was slipping away. He had returned to his office at Iyer Law College just weeks after Ashwini died, but he no longer came home brimming with stories, repeating debates that had unfolded during his class or announcing which of his students had secured judicial clerkships. One evening, he quietly announced that he had stepped down from his chair as the head of the moot court.

"Let the younger fellows take over," he'd said. His tone reminded Vega of the way she used to play carom when she was younger, a game she never really cared for, pushing the coins idly across the board, not particularly caring whether or not they struck. Vega expected her mother to reason with him, but she just said, "Whatever you need, Gopal." Vega hadn't realized before just how much this quality of her mother's enraged her: the willingness to feign helplessness, as though every complex matter in the world was the domain of men.

Then a new semester began. Vega's father went to campus and came home. On Tuesday and Thursday evenings, when he would otherwise be at moot court practice, he sat idly in their living room, watching NDTV at a volume too quiet for Vega to follow, but just loud enough to be distracting. She was relieved when classes began at Sri Vidya.

His former classmate, Naren Uncle, came to stay for a week. Vega and Ashwini had adored Naren when they were small. He was unmarried and childless, had made his money through some dubious investments in the Gulf and seemed to be spending the rest of his years ostentatiously getting rid of it. He used to visit often, and on the nights before he left, would slip a five-hundred rupee note underneath Ashwini's and Vega's pillows.

This time, nobody seemed to enjoy his company. His presence made the house feel cramped. One night, he took Vega to dinner at Bay Leaf. They sat at a corner table, and he ordered excessively—saag paneer, malai kofta, some odd appetizer involving fried lotus root. Vega filled her plate and forced herself to eat.

"I wish we could have convinced them to join us," he said. "They need some joy in their lives. Even a meal in a restaurant would be good for them."

It was such an absurd notion that it made her laugh. "They're able to go through the motions of life, Naren Uncle. But joy is another thing entirely."

"That is my point."

"I don't know if I can fully explain this to you. They haven't been to a restaurant since Ashwini died. If they were here, they would be staring at the menu, thinking of what she would have ordered."

"It's painful for us all. I half expected her to open the door when I arrived."

Vega sliced into a malai kofta with the side of her spoon and mashed it into her rice. She didn't know how to express what she was thinking; you could miss somebody in a distant, far-off way, or you could miss them viscerally, wake up imagining their smell. But Naren Uncle seemed to move through life alone. He couldn't possibly understand the difference.

"I need a small favor from you, Vegavahini. Would you be willing to help out your old uncle?"

"I can try, of course."

"Good. There's a scholar exchange program with National Law College. I've told your father he should apply, but he isn't in a state of mind to take my advice. He's more likely, I think, to listen to you."

Vega stared at him, baffled. How could a child dispense advice to a parent? This was her father, a man whose wisdom she had never doubted, who had famously refused tenure at Iyer Law College and had written an editorial in the *Hindu* titled, "Returning Academic Inquiry to Indian Institutions." When she was young, she would sneak into his study just to open his notebooks and stare at his perfect, angled handwriting. She took a bite of kofta and said, "He isn't in a state of mind to take my advice either, Naren Uncle."

At Iyer Law College, her father dropped one class and then a second, until he was teaching only a single seminar. He seemed to be sliding towards retirement, though he never talked about it, or made plans for his life beyond the university. And then came the stroke. "It won't be life-ending," the doctor had said. "But it will be life-altering." He recommended hiring a full-time nurse, but Rukmini wouldn't hear of it. "Bathing him and changing him is a wife's job. Not the job of a stranger."

I n the first weeks of her father's recovery, Vega was embarrassed by her parents' bare emotional and physical need—the small rise of her father's skin where the intravenous needle pierced it, and the sag of her mother's breasts when she stood in the waiting room, crying, wearing no bra underneath her sari blouse. "I can't bear any more hospitals," her mother said, her head on Vega's shoulder, in a role reversal that Vega hated. *I'm the child*, she wanted to say. She had been alone with her father in the hospital when he gestured that he needed to use his bedpan, and she had simply exited for the hallway, waiting not only for him to finish but for a nurse to come and clear it. A full hour passed by the time she returned. By then he had fallen asleep. The air was thick with the smell of antiseptic soap.

Vega was in her final term at Sri Vidya and had been admitted to a master's program in Hyderabad. Ashwini had been gone four years by then, and Vega was both restless to leave Madras and resolved—by her own guilt over leaving—to make herself useful in the intervening months. After graduating, she'd moved her few belongings back into her parents' house. She set up a radio next to her father's bed and played *BBC News* during the day and Carnatic music in the evenings. She fielded phone calls from his colleagues and students. One weekend, Gayatri took the train from Bangalore, and she and Vega spent a full afternoon walking the length of the beach from Adyar to Fort George.

"What are you thinking about, these days?" Gayatri had asked.

"That's a funny question."

"It's a genuine one. Tell me."

"Hyderabad. My parents. Her, of course. She was *fourteen* years old, Gayatri. As I get older, I realize how young she was."

Gayatri put her arm around Vega's shoulders. She was the only one of Vega's friends with whom she'd grown closer, not drifted away from, after Ashwini's death. Gayatri had loved Ashwini like a sister, had been present for all thirteen days of the mourning period, and in their final term at Rhodes School, would come to Vega's front steps every morning and walk with her to campus, clutching Vega's elbow, the way they used to when they were little girls.

They stopped at Art Haus and wandered through an exhibit of photographs taken from a Kerala village. The pictures were simple: men hoisting nets from boats, women scrubbing and descaling fish. But one stopped Vega. It was of a young girl, nine or ten years old, holding a baby on her hip and looking directly at the camera, her lips pursed and her head slightly cocked. Vega stared at it until her eyes blurred.

# 2

Vega quickly fell in love with Hyderabad. She loved the teak-paneled library, the tiny seminar classes in which the students sat in half-moon formations around the professors. She loved the way new words came to roll off her tongue: *precarity, alienation, feminist methodologies*. Her grief over Ashwini was still lodged inside her like some heavy, unmovable object. Sometimes she woke up in the middle of the night, convinced she was choking. But now, for the first time, it seemed possible to continue living. She called home every week, and every week her father sounded stronger. "You're happy?" he would ask, over and over again. "Yes," she said each time. "I'm happy."

Unlike Sri Vidya, a women's college governed by a strict nine p.m. curfew, at Hyderabad, male and female students flitted in and out of the hostel at all hours. At night, a crowd gathered in the common room and tore into communal plates of biryani and potato chips. They passed around used books. "Keep it," her classmate Sanjay had said after giving her a worn copy of *The Wretched of the Earth*. He was a political science student, and though Vega didn't initially find him attractive, she liked how easily he laughed. They had a single class together, Quantitative Methods, and he began waiting for her afterwards so they could walk towards the library or canteen, or—once, with a larger group—to the Old City, where they ate massive thalis and wandered around a maze of book stalls.

She couldn't recall what happened later. Either Sanjay lost interest in her, or she in him. But she guessed that it had all fallen apart in her

second term, because that was when she'd enrolled in a course with
Sukumar Reddy.

Reddy was among the younger of the social science professors.
His book, *Colonial Subjects*, had won the 1992 Edinburgh Prize for
Contemporary South Asian Scholarship. He had been educated in the
States, and it was rumored that he'd turned down a position at MIT
to teach at Hyderabad. His lectures were oversubscribed, and he often
held them outside on the campus green, always dressed in his loose
kurta and jute sandals.

"I have a thing for Tamilians," he'd told her during their first meeting. "So much that I married a Tamil girl years back. I think I fell in
love with her because of the language. It's a beautiful language."

"Thank you," she'd said. It was the wrong response, though it had
been a strange comment to begin with. But maybe this was how people
talked in graduate school.

Reddy nodded. "In any case, tell me about your research interests."

Vega wished that she had dressed better for the meeting. She was
wearing a version of what she always wore in those days: a sleeveless
cotton salwar and large, fake gold earrings. Her hair was tied back in
a loose braid.

"My field is maternal health," she'd said. "But I would like to examine the subject through a sociological lens." Reddy was still staring
at her, so she kept talking. She explained that she had grown up surrounded by the ghosts of dead women and children: her father's brother
had died in infancy and her paternal grandmother had lost a sister in
childbirth. Vega didn't register these losses as tragedies—as profound
as the death of her own sister—but they surfaced in her mind throughout her years at Sri Vidya, where she'd read obsessively about prenatal
nutrition, breastfeeding, poverty, caste. She rarely spoke during class
and did not have a close relationship with any of her undergraduate
professors, so it surprised her, now, to describe her interests aloud.

Reddy nodded along, and Vega suspected that he wasn't actually
listening, but he'd asked to see her again, and at the conclusion of their

second meeting, he'd stared at her for a few heavy seconds, then said, "Forgive me if I'm embarrassing you. But it's rare to speak with someone who expresses herself with such clarity."

She was embarrassed, but she was also thrilled by the way he looked at her, then upset with herself for wanting to be looked at. When he'd offered to be her advisor, she'd agreed, even though she had planned on asking Professor Ramnarayan, a brilliant septuagenarian who had taught Vega's Global Inequalities course. "I accept two, three students per term," Reddy said. "Maximum. If you don't accept the spot, somebody else will by the end of day. I assure you." Looking back, Vega was astonished by the simplicity of this manipulation, how pliantly she had accepted an offer that she knew, even in the moment, she did not really want.

Their time together had become more languid. He'd usually skim her papers and spend the remainder of the meeting talking about himself: his ex-wife, his years in the States, his many funded research trips. One afternoon, in his office, he showed Vega the blueprints for a school he was designing with his daughter, Ambika, in mind. "It will be Telegu-medium," Reddy said. "Indigenous and land-based. A working coconut farm, so the operation can fully sustain itself. We have a team of investors from Bangalore." He had pulled Vega's chair next to his, and his arm brushed against hers as he spoke.

"He's divorced, no?" Gayatri asked over the phone. She and Vega talked every week, even though the connection from their respective hostels was terrible. Gayatri sounded as though she were speaking into a fan.

"It isn't a crime to be divorced, Gayatri."

"Of course it isn't. But does he spend this much time with all of his advisees?"

"He's very informal," Vega said. "It's his style."

"Are the teachers volunteers? How will the farm revenue cover the cost of their salaries?"

"I don't know, Gayatri." The questions had crossed Vega's mind too, but it annoyed her to hear Gayatri raise them. "I suppose that's why they have the investors."


Vega knew little about sex, but enough to anticipate a long seduction, a protracted period of looks and intimations and maneuvering. If she and Reddy ended up in bed, she assumed the whole thing would be made to seem like a wonderful accident. But one afternoon, he looked at her directly, then said, "I'd like you to come home with me."

He lived on a leafy street in Banjara Hills. She knew he lived with his parents and daughter, but she was still surprised to see that his house was scattered with evidence of multigenerational living. A child's red bicycle was propped next to the steps and a pair of slippers sat beside the door. In the kitchen, he'd fixed Vega what he called a green juice. "I drink it twice each day," he said. "Spinach, mint, green apple, and sweet lime." She sipped it—sour, raw tasting, bitter—and distracted herself by staring at a series of colorful drawings hanging on the wall.

"Your daughter drew these?"

"She's my artist, Ambika. An absolute creative through and through."

He stared at Vega until she finished her glass, then slid behind her and lifted her kurta just above her waist, running his fingers against her stomach.

Months later, after it was over, Vega mined her memories for the signs that had been so obvious to Gayatri. The way Reddy left his bed, unmade, the sheets stained and rumpled. "I have a house girl who comes," he'd said.

"Surely she doesn't need to see this," Vega said, trying to sound playful. It would have been so easy to strip the bed, to spare the house girl the embarrassment of seeing the mess. But Reddy just shrugged. "It's the girl's job. I pay her, don't I?"

And then there was his insistence on the verandah. "Come outside," he always said to her after sex. "I want to see you in the sun." Vega was conscious of the neighboring windows surrounding them.

She was conscious, too, of the clothesline that hung across it, draped with his daughter's uniforms and his mother's saris. It was not enough to conceal her body, but enough to remind her that she had no business being there. "Nobody can see," Reddy said. "And if they want to look, let them look."

He liked when she sat naked on the verandah floor and spread open her knees. He wanted her to touch herself, to tell him her fantasies. By then, Vega always felt drained of fantasies. What she wanted was to get dressed and leave. She wanted to go back to her sparse, dimly lit hostel and return to her thesis.

"Have you ever wanted to be with two men at once?"

"No."

"How about women? Are you attracted to women?"

"Reddy. Enough."

"Do you ever want to fuck me outside?"

"The thought has never occurred to me," she said, but she went along with it anyway, her head pushed against the verandah wall, her lower back pressed between the tile and the weight of Reddy's body. Back at the hostel, she filled the shower bucket with cold water and scrubbed herself clean, first with sandalwood soap, and then with the Dettol that she normally used only on her hands—the smell of disinfectant taking her back to her father's hospital room.

By the close of the term, Hyderabad had lost its shine. She didn't feel a sense of wonder when she stepped into the library or lecture hall. The friends she made had branched off into smaller circles. Sanjay had met somebody else and usually nodded to Vega when he saw her across campus.

In May, she submitted the withdrawal forms to the head of the sociology department—a stern woman named Dr. Das, who had been Vega's Quantitative Methods professor.

"You have decent marks," Dr. Das said. "Will you continue your research elsewhere?"

"I hope to." In some distant way, she did hope to. But what she really wanted was to go backward, not forward, to have another chance.

She wanted to be a student at Hyderabad again, enrolling in her fall-term classes, meeting Sanjay for the first time.

"If you've made up your mind," Dr. Das said, "then we can speak about some of the technical details. If you transfer to any other Indian institution, you will have partial credit towards a master's. And if you choose to reapply to Hyderabad, we will be very happy to have you back with us."

"Thank you," Vega said. "I understand that."

Dr. Das stared at Vega for a moment, then signed the paper and slid it to the corner of her desk.

For the next few days, as she floated through campus, she considered the possibility of staying in Hyderabad. She could speak with Dr. Das and tell her that she had changed her mind. She could pour herself into her thesis. But a few evenings later, she wandered past Nehru Hall and glanced into the lobby. Months earlier, at a post-lecture reception, she had come upon Reddy holding his signature gin and tonic, surrounded by a cluster of adoring graduate students. He was telling a story about his graduate school days in Michigan. "There was a custodian who worked in the social science building. African American man. Very decent man. Once a week or so I would bring him coffee. We would sit and talk about history, philosophy, science. On my final day, he said to me, 'You know, Professor? Of all the people who work here, you are the only one—the *only* one—who has ever asked my name. I told him, 'You and I are brothers.' I pointed to my skin and I told him, 'We've both been subjugated.'"

Reddy had told Vega this story before. Even then, in the haze following sex, it had seemed riddled with improbabilities. Listening to its retelling, she had seen Reddy in a new light: a man who contributed nothing to the world, who peddled false injustices and made his living by crafting false solutions. She thought of the homeopathic doctor Rukmini had visited years ago following some abdominal pain, who had massaged various pressure points on her foot, diagnosed her with something called mood imbalance, then offered to sell her a home-made remedy at a special price.

She sent Gayatri an email later that night. She wanted to avoid the back-and-forth of conversation. *I can't stay here, Gayatri. I'm too damn embarrassed.*

A few hours later, Gayatri called her anyway. "I want to make sure that you aren't sabotaging this because you feel guilty living your life."

"I said that I was embarrassed. Guilt has nothing to do with it."

"She would want you to be happy, Vega. If she were alive, she would want you to continue with your life."

"That is a very untestable theory, Gayatri. How can you know what she would have wanted?"

Gayatri didn't answer that question. Instead, she said, "One of my hostel mates keeps a cat. It's against school rules, but she keeps it anyway. And it just reminded me of Ashwini. It's something she would have done."

When Ashwini was ten or eleven, she and a group of friends had found a litter of kittens near the campus at Rhodes. There were seven of them, still hairless. Ashwini managed to procure a box from one of the cooks at the Rhodes canteen, and there was some level of fuss and school-level celebrity that she enjoyed on the day of the discovery. This ended as soon as they arrived home. Rukmini—who was terrified of all animals—determined that the kittens were rabid-looking and commanded Vega to take them to the veterinary clinic at the Theosophical Society.

For the next several weeks, Ashwini insisted on going to the clinic every day after school. Vega found these visits miserable. She hated the combined smell of sawdust and animal piss, the sight of the kittens tumbling blindly in their box—it was the same box in which they had transported them, but the clinic volunteers lined it with newspaper that they swapped every few hours and was always streaked with shit. Mainly, she hated the fear that they would approach the box and find that the number had dwindled to five or six, and Vega had wanted to spare Ashwini what seemed like a terminal and useless affection. "Maybe it isn't a good idea to name them," Gayatri once told Ashwini when she joined them for one of their clinic visits. "Maybe wait until they're stronger."

"I already named them," Ashwini said. "I can't un-name them."

One day, when the kittens were roughly a month old, the box disappeared. From what Vega could gather—the clinic director spoke a fast, colloquial Tamil that Vega sometimes struggled to understand—they had separated the male and female kittens and sent them to the clinic's outpost in Avadi, where they would be spayed and neutered and generally left to roam. To Vega, it seemed like the best possible outcome. But Ashwini was distraught. "I wanted to adopt one," she'd cried to Vega. "Amma promised me."

Years later, after Ashwini was gone, it occurred to Vega that the kittens—at least some of them—had likely outlived her sister. At the time, she'd simply let Ashwini climb into her bed at night and cry herself to sleep. "I liked the orange one best," Ashwini said. "I named her Limey."

What sort of name was that? Why would anyone name an orange kitten after a lime? But Vega just said, "I know," and let her cry.

Now, Vega held the phone and listened to the staticky sound of Gayatri's breath. She had a stupid hope that Gayatri would offer to come to Hyderabad and help her pack, then usher her onto the train and take her back to Madras. She thought of her final term at Rhodes, when Gayatri came to the house every morning to walk Vega to campus. How impossible it would have been to do it alone.

V ega told her parents that she withdrew from Hyderabad because she was homesick. It was a weak lie. Gopal's university connections ran deep, and Vega suspected they knew some version of the truth. But they never spoke of it directly, and for that, she was grateful.

"You need to return to your thesis," Rukmini had said one evening. They were walking along the beach. Vega was distracted by the sight of a young couple stepping into the waves, the woman laughing and jumping back when the water touched her feet. She found this type of thing intolerable. That female coyness. The pretense of surprise.

"I don't have a thesis, Amma."

"Then what have you been doing this past term?"

"It's only a thesis if you have an advisor. Otherwise it's nothing. It's a long essay."

"Then return to your long essay. If you don't work today, then you won't the next day. Or the day after that. Every year is only a culmination of days."

"I'm not interested in the subject any longer. That's why I've been spending so much time in the library. I'm rethinking my research."

It was true that she spent most afternoons at the library, either at Iyer Law College, where her father had faculty privileges, or at the British Council, which was beautifully appointed but strangely empty of any books she actually cared to read. "You can place a request, ma'am," the librarian said. "If the book is in our collection, it will arrive in four, five days maximum." But by the time the books arrived, Vega's interests had wandered again, and she'd place another request, knowing she would not bother to read those, either. She had gone to Hyderabad certain of her interest in maternal nutrition, but her repeated afternoons with Reddy had shifted the focus of her thesis. Now it was scattered, a series of arguments about colonialism and land rights that she was not even sure she believed. More immediately, she didn't know *where* she wanted to study. She had been back in Madras for a full month at that point and could neither imagine leaving nor staying another day.

"You had grand ambitions when you were a girl. Do you remember? You wanted to study at Oxford. Your appa was so proud. He would tell Naren, 'My daughter plans to become a solicitor.'"

"Children want all sorts of things, Amma. Ashwini wanted to be a marine biologist."

"And maybe she would have."

Vega didn't respond.

"It happens quickly, Vegavahini. You don't realize now. You'll see this only in retrospect. Just how quickly time passes."

The Gifford Fellowship closed the distance between Vega and her father. One day, she received a package from Gayatri with a worn brochure and a note included: *Two-year funded master's at Columbia University. Coordinated through the Department of State, so the visa won't be a problem.* The next day, her father lowered himself, shakily, onto the edge of her bed. When she was a girl, he would perch there in the same way as he read to her chapters from *Malgudi Days* and *The Hitchhiker's Guide to the Galaxy.* Once, when she and Gayatri were reading *Pygmalion* in class, he had helped them rehearse for their performance, playing the role of Pickering. Vega could still hear his voice, so much sturdier before the stroke: "Excuse the straight question, Higgins!"

"I perused this Columbia brochure. You left it in my study."

"I don't know anything about the program, Appa. Gayatri sent it."

"If you don't intend to return to Hyderabad, perhaps it is an opportunity to consider."

"I can't imagine going so far."

"Can't you? You've lived in the States before."

"That was different."

Gopal slid the brochure towards her. His hand was so frail, so bony. An old man's hand. After a few moments, he said, "I have one suggestion. You come with me to the bank right now. They can fax the application request. It's early morning in the States. If the office is efficient, as I suspect that it is, they will send you the forms in two, three hours."

She didn't expect her father's suggestion to work. It seemed impossible, almost supernatural, to hand her fax to the mustachioed man at the Bank of India and return the next morning to a stack of papers from Columbia University Graduate Admissions. At first glance, the application overwhelmed her. *Describe challenges you have faced. Identify a question in your field of study that you would like to further explore. How have the politics of your region influenced your academic interests?* She spent her days in her father's empty study, drafting pages that, in the evenings, she would tear from her notebook and toss into the garbage. She began taking long walks. She went, once, to Rhodes School. It was between terms, and the campus was empty except for a single groundskeeper in the distance. She remembered her earlier years at Rhodes, walking Ashwini to her primary school classroom. Every day it was the same routine: they would arrive late because Ashwini refused to wake up in the mornings and then ate her breakfast at a maddeningly slow pace. Still, when they arrived on campus, she would insist that Vega walk her to her classroom.

"I always fussed with her," she later told Gayatri. "She only asked for small things. Why couldn't I walk her to her bloody classroom?"

"You did walk her. Every day."

"Yes. But I always made it seem as though I didn't want to."

"Do you think at the end of her life, Vega, that she remembered any of that? Do you think she held this against you?"

That wasn't the point, Vega thought. The point was that she hadn't really understood what Ashwini's death would mean until she was gone. She had not anticipated that it would hit her over and over. That she would be haunted by small apologies, things she wanted to tell her sister and never would. But buried within that finality was a hard and unambiguous truth: there was nothing Vega could do, no amount of waiting and hoping that would bring Ashwini back. It made no difference whether she stayed in Madras or left.

She rewrote her essays. This time, her language felt looser, more honest. In the administrative office at Iyer Law College, she printed the full application, checked it over, and made a backup copy. As she waited for the admissions decision, she began a tutoring position at Madras School of Social Work that she had seen advertised at the British Council Library. The pay was negligible, barely enough to cover her rickshaw fare, but she came to love the students—young women from Salem and Erode and Pollachi, who had excelled in their small, government schools but were overwhelmed by the demands of university life. Vega loved how earnestly they followed her advice, read every article that she suggested, and meticulously revised their sentences. She worried that she would be short-tempered with them, or that she would find the job easy and dull. But the three-hour sessions passed quickly. Afterwards, the students would often linger in the tiny, windowless classroom and pry into the details of Vega's life: Was she married? Did she ever want to get married? Did she give her parents her earnings, or was she allowed to keep the money for herself? After the envelope arrived from Columbia, Vega waited a few days before telling them. There was something cruel and dismissive in sharing her news, she thought, as though they were merely an interlude on her way towards something bigger. On her final Saturday morning, a student named Sumitra slid a small package, wrapped in brown paper, across the desk. Inside was a thin notebook. "A gift from all of us," she said. "For your term papers."

Vega had been to the American consulate years earlier, with her parents and Ashwini, just before their move to Cleveland, but it hadn't registered to her as a significant event. They had been given a special early-morning appointment, and their visas were granted swiftly. But she later pieced together that it was the urgency of Ashwini's medical condition that made this possible. Now, the consulate was swarming with people.

The man in line before her was patting his neck with a handkerchief and muttering to himself. When she stepped closer, she could hear that it was a rehearsal of the interview ahead. *My name is Sendhil Kumar. I am studying for master's. I have been granted admission in Nebraska.* Just before they entered the building, the man bent over and rested his head against the doorway. Vega had an irrational hope that the door would close just before she could step inside. Instead, she walked behind him and stood at the taped line in front of the window. The officer, an American woman a few years older than Vega, pulled out the contents of the man's envelope without looking up.

"There's a spelling discrepancy in your name," she said.

"It's a typical thing, madam. Problem with alphabets, only. Names, they are sometimes spelled two different manners. Three different manners, sometimes."

"Don't tell me what's typical."

"Madam?"

"You need a new VFS Appointment letter. Make sure they spell your name just like it is on your birth certificate."

"That will take weeks, madam."

"Then I'll see you in weeks." She looked up before the man could walk away. "Next."

It seemed cruel to step forward, but Vega did anyway, holding her gaze as the officer scanned her admissions letter. After a long silence, she assumed that her application had been rejected. She felt relieved. She would return to the tight but familiar walls of her parents' house. But after a few minutes, the officer stamped the form and said, "You can arrive one week prior to the program, but the visa ends on the final day. One more day and you're in violation."

Though Vega was vaguely aware of this policy, the word *violation* was startling. "I don't intend to stay longer," she'd said. But the woman was already looking past her, nodding to the next applicant.

There was a flurry of packing and paperwork. Rukmini filled a notebook with the phone numbers of everybody she knew in New York and New Jersey. Naren sent a gauzy pashmina from Delhi and two crisp one-hundred-dollar bills. Gopal lectured Vega on the value of interdisciplinary coursework. "You must study philosophy," he'd said. "It undergirds all other scholarship." He looked happier than she had seen him in years, but there was something evangelical about his happiness. Something she didn't fully trust.

When Vega imagined her life in the States, she thought of her old house in Cleveland, the snap of cool air on the day they arrived, the driveway lined with smooth, oval rocks that Ashwini—eleven years old then—used to call dinosaur eggs. The house itself had an ethereal quality. There were carpeted floors that she and Ashwini loved to sink their toes into.

But outside the house, Vega had been miserable. She was fifteen years old, no longer cute but not yet pretty, and it seemed impossible to find one's way in suburban America without the currency of looks. She hated the cramped hallways of her school. She hated the cold. She hated the winter mornings when she waited alone for the school bus, the sky still pitch-black.

Ashwini, on the other hand, had loved Cleveland. She adopted American fashion and was adept at making friends. The house was littered with the detritus of those friendships: fortune tellers, plastic woven bracelets, cassette tapes. At the corner of her bedroom mirror, she had tucked a ticket stub from a roller-skating birthday party she'd attended. Vega often tried to rationalize their different experiences in the States. Was it because Ashwini was younger, or fairer skinned, that she was able to wedge her way into American life? But the reason, Vega had come to understand—a reason that was clearer after her withdrawal from Hyderabad—was more encompassing. Ashwini had a confidence that Vega never would. She forced the world to accommodate her. It seemed, now, like a cruel twist that Vega was the one going back to the States, that she was going anywhere at all, when it was Ashwini who, given this chance, was the one who would have thrived.

# 3

Rukmini had arranged for a former classmate's nephew and his wife to meet Vega at Newark International Airport. The couple was young, close to Vega's age. At the baggage claim, the husband shook Vega's hand as though it were a business deal. "Mohan," he said, with a formality that made her want to laugh. His wife, Shoba, wore a billowy pink kurta, a style that had been in fashion when Vega was in secondary school. One of the mirrorwork pieces at the neck was loose. As Mohan pulled the suitcase from the conveyor belt, Shoba held her hands protectively over her belly, and Vega saw that she was pregnant.

They lived in a tidy, single-level house, identical to all the houses surrounding it. Mohan dragged Vega's suitcase inside, and Shoba pointed her towards the guest bathroom where a spare towel had been folded and placed at the edge of the sink. Vega washed her hands and face. When she came out, Shoba was standing in the kitchen, pouring cups of mango juice. "The room is nice, Akka?"

The word *akka* was jarring. Aside from a few young cousins with whom she rarely spoke, nobody had called her that since Ashwini's death. "It's very nice. Thank you."

"You're studying to be a doctor?"

Vega laughed. "I'm not. Should I be?"

Shoba smiled shyly. "I'm asking, only. My sister wants to come to the States and study medicine."

There was a time when Vega thought she might become a doctor. She liked the idea of something so heroic. But she came to see that she had none of what it required—neither the heroism nor the acumen—to care for another person's body. Some years back, on a trip to Bangalore, a woman seated beside Vega struck up a conversation about her first months of motherhood. "I couldn't nurse," she said. "Inverted nipples." She had pulled down her sari and lifted a breast from her blouse. The woman's daughter had been sitting next to her, maybe seven or eight years old, reading a comic book and ignoring her mother, apparently having witnessed this very conversation before. It wasn't just that Vega found the interaction bizarre. She found it painfully depressing, and for years, the memory tugged at her—the little girl glued to the page, the woman seeking some comfort or solution for a problem that was no longer even relevant. Once, in Cleveland, she came upon one of Ashwini's CT scans on her parents' bedside table and she left the room quickly, closing the door behind her, feeling as though she had been punched in the chest.

After dinner, Shoba curled up on the bed next to Vega and showed her pictures of her old life, most taken outside her childhood home in Coimbatore—a small white villa with orange shingles on what looked like the outskirts of town. The album was endless and repetitive, grainy shots of the same building at different angles, all featuring Shoba, her two sisters, and her unsmiling parents. Midway through, Vega ran out of responses. "This one is of Marudhamalai Temple," Shoba whispered, and though Vega had never heard of the place, and could hardly see it in the hazy image, she'd said, "How lovely."

In the morning, Shoba made a pot of upma, three types of chutney, and mugs of sweet, milky coffee—the breakfast foods of Vega's childhood that she had long given up in favor of toast or a piece of fruit—packing the leftovers into a tiffin box for Mohan. After he left for the office, she rinsed and chopped the day's vegetables and soaked a pot of lentils for dinner. Then she led Vega into a small laundry room at the back of the house. "Separate washer and dryer," she said, opening a drawer at the top of one of the machines and turning a small knob to demonstrate the various settings. Vega had been awake since two o'clock that morning, and the rumble of the machine soothed her. She closed her eyes. She needed to be in New York in three days, and it had occurred to her only that morning that Mohan and Shoba were no more oriented in the States than she was. She had assumed they would transport her to campus. Now, that expectation seemed absurd.

"Perhaps I can ask Mohan about the train schedule," she said. "I can go easily from here. I only have one suitcase."

Shoba didn't respond. Instead, she filled a wicker basket with the clothes, walked to the living room and sat on the couch, watching a Tamil soap opera as she folded Mohan's slacks and smoothed the sleeves of his shirt. "We have Sun TV," she said. "We can get all the channels. You had Sun TV in Cleveland?"

"No." Vega didn't know how to continue the conversation. There seemed no kind way to explain that she didn't watch Tamil soap operas in India and would have no use for them in the States.

"That woman used to be very bad," Shoba said, nodding to the screen. "Now, she is good. But she is trying to advise her younger brother not to take a very dangerous job and he won't listen. He wants the money."

Vega fell asleep on the couch. When she woke, the laundry had been neatly stacked.

Mohan's return from the office set Shoba into motion. She changed into a sari, then warmed the dhal and vegetables. She poured small stainless steel cups of rasam and served it, ceremonially, on a tray. The food was ordinary, but Mohan's silence was heavy, so Vega complimented everything repeatedly. The most noteworthy addition to the table were the potato chips that Shoba and Mohan crumpled onto their rice. Vega did the same, then ate them by the handful until the bag was empty.

After dinner, Mohan took them to Marshall's. He sat on a bench outside, reading a newspaper as Shoba led Vega through the aisles of cosmetics, sampling hand lotions and examining bottles of nail polish. She wandered through clothing racks marked *Clearance!* and then to rows of shoes, studying the heels, once trying on a pair of loafers and staring at herself in the full-length mirror. With girlish secrecy, she led

Vega to the lingerie section, where they looked at lace-fringed bras and egg-shaped containers of pantyhose. In the end, Shoba bought only a jar of night cream. "I just love to look at everything," she said. "And to see all the people."

They stopped for ice cream on the way home, Shoba and Vega sharing a banana split, dividing it onto two separate plates, as Mohan quietly ate a bowl of vanilla. Shoba told the story of a cousin's wedding they had attended in Houston.

"Do you know her?" Shoba asked. "Her name is Malathi. She's from Madras, only."

"It's a big city," Vega said. "Likely not."

"Oh." Shoba looked briefly disappointed, then sliced into her banana with the side of her spoon.

"What do you read all the time?" Shoba asked. She had finished cooking and was settling on the couch with her laundry basket.

"Books related to my studies." Vega wondered how to bridge her world with Shoba's. In her three days at Shoba and Mohan's house, she had seen only two books: a copy of *The Bhagavad Gita* and *Hindu Names for Girls*. Shoba often sat with the latter in the evenings, running down the alphabetical list and reading names and meanings aloud to Mohan.

"Are they novels?" Shoba asked.

"Not novels, quite," Vega said. "They're books about ideas."

Though Vega often initiated their conversations in English, Shoba continued them in Tamil. English she seemed to reserve for words that were foreign or untranslatable: *car*, *mall*, *doctor*. In the mornings after Mohan left, and in the evenings just as he was about to return, she always mentioned his *office*, saying the word with a wide-eyed awe. He called the house once each afternoon, the only time the phone rang during the day, and Shoba jumped to answer, coiling the cord around her finger like a teenager, flush with an almost sexual excitement.

The morning Vega was to move to campus, Shoba came into her room with a stack of tinfoil packets tucked into a plastic grocery bag.

"You shouldn't go hungry," she said. "Who knows what they'll feed you there? Even Indian restaurants here, they don't serve our type of food. It's North Indian, only. Punjabi food."

Vega tied the bag's handles and rested it at the top of her closed suitcase. "This is all very kind, Shoba. Thank you."

"You can come on weekends, maybe? When you have no program? Or any classes?"

The English words made Vega smile. "Of course. And I'll call you from New York." But later, sitting beside Mohan as he wordlessly drove her to the train station, the promise felt hollow. She pictured Shoba in her empty home, watching Sun TV and waiting for the telephone to ring. "She'll be okay, you think?" she asked Mohan.

He nodded, as blankly as he had the previous evening when Shoba asked his opinion of the name Meghna, telling him that it meant *cloud*.

"Her mother is coming for the birth," he said. "They'll manage."

She sat through a week of orientation meetings with other international students—strangers who seemed somehow to already know each other, who huddled together speaking either their common language or their overlapping, accented English. The orientation topics were useful: how to open a checking account, where to purchase used textbooks, protocols for campus safety. But the air conditioner blasted, the students around her rustled and scraped their chairs and blew their noses, and Vega found it difficult to pay attention. She exhausted Shoba's leftovers on the first day and wandered the aisles of Key Food, staring at the multitude of yogurts and waxy apples and boxed cereals.

The Gifford Fellowship had provided her with two weeks of temporary housing in an undergraduate dormitory. "If you don't have access to funds," one of her orientation leaders said, "you want to look for a situation in which a couple of roommates are looking to fill an empty room. That way it will be furnished, and you can move right in." So,

Vega scoured listings in the Student Services building. Most of the available bedrooms she found were in Harlem, which she discovered was a quicker trip on foot than on subway, so she began walking the city, using a street map that had been included in the new student welcome folder.

By the end of the first week, the apartments were indistinguishable in her mind. The sinks were cluttered with dirty dishes. They were occupied only by white roommates, though the neighborhood itself was Black, and always, these roommates were polite and noncommittal. She often sensed that the room had already been rented to somebody else or—more plausibly—that they simply didn't like her. Sometimes, there was a detail that struck her as particularly odd or repulsive: a sticky mouse trap lying in plain sight next to the refrigerator; a toilet seat propped up, the rim splattered with shit; a pair of sneakers on top of a coffee table. Once, there was a plate of cookies on the kitchen counter, and Vega glanced at them as she walked past the entryway. She didn't expect to be offered one, but they caught her eye, and the woman—a brusque-sounding graduate student named Kate—asked her in a halting manner, "Would you *like* one?" Something about the interaction made Vega sad. Of course she'd wanted a cookie. Anybody would want a cookie. But the desire now seemed pitiful.

But Harlem itself thrilled her. On days she wasn't going to see an apartment, or sometimes after yet another failed visit, she would return to her room and change into something that made her feel edgy—one of the three tank tops she had brought with her (which she always handwashed afterwards in the bathroom sink); a wraparound skirt; or the denim shorts she had cut from one of Gayatri's old pairs of jeans—and wander the neighborhood, always via one of the more crowded throughfares. In suburban Cleveland, she had hated the conspicuousness of her skin color and clothing, how tainted she felt as a foreigner. On Frederick Douglass Boulevard or Lenox Avenue, surrounded by the commerce and accents and rush of urban life, she marveled over the realization that nobody seemed to notice her at all.

One afternoon, as she made her way from an apartment on 137th Street, she passed a cluster of Black men standing outside a corner store.

One was dressed in a tissue-thin, white sleeveless shirt—a style she associated with manual laborers in India. As she passed by, he lifted the edge of his shirt and wiped the sweat from his temple, and she felt something inside her lurch. It had never occurred to her to find this look attractive in India. Even with Gayatri, to whom she told everything, she could not imagine passing a construction site and commenting on a man's body. But here, taut arms and dark skin against white cotton seemed like the perfect masculine combination—not deliberate or attention-seeking, but simple and unabashedly sexual.

She went back to the corner store the next afternoon, and the next, but the man wasn't there. She considered following up on the apartment on 137th Street, though it had been impractical—small and overpriced, smelling faintly of urine. But at least if she lived there, she might run into him from time to time. She thought again about Sanjay, as she had on and off since leaving Hyderabad. Had she stayed, maybe they would eventually have gotten together. It still clawed at her, all those versions of her life that may or may not have been.

Sometimes in the evenings she'd wander the streets surrounding Columbia, trying to memorize the landmarks. Occasionally, she would see somebody she recognized from campus, and the fog would clear just a bit. She discovered a small deli run by a Bangladeshi family that sold sweet, milky tea for a dollar. One afternoon, as she slid her money across the counter, the young man—little older than a teenager—put up his hand. "You take. First day of Eid. Gift from us."

Vega stared at him, his uneven patches of facial hair, his T-shirt too big for his skinny frame. Maybe he assumed she was Muslim. Or maybe it was enough that they both came from the same general corner of the world. "Eid Mubarak," she'd said.

An acquaintance from Rhodes School, Aparna, was living in Chelsea, and she invited Vega for a cocktail party in her flat. "I leave for Bombay at the end of the month," she'd told Vega over the phone. "But we'll overlap until then, at least."

Vega agonized over what to wear, settling finally on a black V-neck dress that, in Madras and Hyderabad, made her feel so sexy and provocative that she'd only worn it twice, both times covered with a dupatta. In New York, she wondered if it was too simple. But the party turned out to be a relaxed affair. Aparna hugged Vega, then led her around the room, introducing her to a scattering of people, all standing in a circle so that Vega wasn't sure which name belonged specifically to whom.

"How are you finding it so far?" a man asked. He looked Middle Eastern. His arms were wrapped tightly around the woman next to him in what, to Vega, seemed to be a preemptive signal: *We are a couple. We are unavailable.*

"I'll like it as soon as I find a place to live," Vega said. "As of now, I've toured every available bedroom priced beneath eight hundred dollars a month, so my knowledge of the city is very niche."

"I've been on that tour," the man said. "Ask me later about my first apartment. It was next to the Brooklyn Navy Yard. The place was huge, though. I paid four hundred a month."

"Please *don't* ask him about it," the woman said. She was impossibly thin, with bangs that were cut so that they fell repeatedly in her eyes. Her appearance reminded Vega of the girls she knew from a distance when she lived in Cleveland. Girls with athletic bodies, and hair that seemed immune to tangles and knots. "I still have nightmares about that place."

There was some discussion of the old apartment, then the woman turned to Vega and asked, "Have you been to the States before?" It was a direct enough question, but Vega paused.

"Vega lived in Cleveland for two years," Aparna said.

Vega looked at her, surprised that she'd remembered this detail about her. Vega hadn't thought much about Aparna since they'd graduated from Rhodes. She had some vague memory that she had moved to New York to attend art school, but it wouldn't have occurred to her to get in touch had Gayatri not sent an email connecting them.

The woman looked up suddenly and tapped her fingers together.

"Oh! This is the friend you were telling me about. The future recipient of all your fabulous winter clothing."

"She is," Aparna said. "I was telling Sarah that I have a few things I don't want to take back with me to Bombay. I have to put the bag together, but I'll show you them soon. I'm still disorganized."

Vega wasn't sure how to respond to this. It bothered her to be a charity case, but she was thrilled by the prospect of something attractive to wear. The couple wandered off and Aparna led Vega to the table. "Come eat something," she said. "Then I'll show you the rest of the flat. By the way, the food in New York is lovely. There's a place in the village called Café Orlin where a small group of us like to meet on Thursday evenings. It's excellent, but not fussy. We'll go next week, maybe. I'd love to show you some of my favorite haunts."

Vega felt suddenly light-headed, a lag between Aparna's words and her own processing of them. She piled a paper plate with cubes of cheese and fruit, then followed Aparna into a tiny bedroom.

"You live alone?" Vega asked.

"I do. I lived in Gramercy until last year, with a few roommates. But it became a bit too much, just with our different schedules."

At Rhodes, Aparna had been one of the wealthier students. She wasn't showy like some others, like their classmate Jaganath with his bloated references to Dubai and London, to all the real estate holdings he would someday inherit. Aparna's wealth was more subdued. She wore edgy clothes—skinny black jeans, pointy flats, bright-colored tunics that she belted at the waist with mismatched fabric—and always shrugged away compliments. "It's old money versus new money," Gayatri once said. "Aparna knows she's rich. It's in her blood. Even if she lost all of her money, she would *still* be rich."

"It's nice to see someone from home," Aparna said. "Tell me what you're studying."

"I have a fellowship at Columbia. It's a two-year master's in sociology."

"I always knew you would do something impressive."

"Well. I hardly have yet."

"Nonsense. Just being admitted is impressive." In a quiet voice she said, "You know, we sent you a letter when you were in Cleveland. We wrote it together. We used different color pens, each of us, so you could tell our messages apart."

"I know. You did, and I'm sorry."

"I don't care that you didn't write back. I just want to know that you received it. We thought about you when you were gone."

Just thinking about Cleveland made Vega recoil. The other students terrified her. She couldn't understand their accents, the way they hugged and slapped hands in the hallway, their world of laughter and sports and sexual innuendo. They were all perfectly nice to her, in the charitable manner in which people cared for the dispossessed, in the way they would have been nice to an orphan or refugee. Teachers praised her penmanship and work ethic. They paused and glanced at her during class discussions, hoping she would speak and knowing that she wouldn't.

Meanwhile, Ashwini joined the school choir, begged Rukmini for trips to the mall, and acquired a best friend named Julia. "*Every*thing here is nice," she'd once told Vega. And in some ways, Vega's own experiences notwithstanding, Ashwini was right. They spent weekends in a nice hospital with a gleaming white waiting room where she and Ashwini discovered the bounty of American vending machines. They had nice doctors—Dr. Oakley and Dr. Glick—whose faces were seared in Vega's memory, who greeted Ashwini with beaming enthusiasm each time, and sent them back to India with an optimistic prognosis. "You can let yourselves plan for her future," Dr. Glick had told Vega's parents. "Start thinking about college and life beyond." But in the end, for all their niceness, they had also been wrong.

"I did read the letter," Vega said to Aparna. "I should have written back."

"No. That isn't what I mean. I want you to know that we were thinking of you. We wanted to see you as soon as you came back."

"I don't doubt that you tried, Aparna. Thank you."

"Enough of all this. Know that I'm here, at least for the time being. And if you need a place to stay while you're looking, my lease extends until the end of September. No cost, of course."

The offer was so generous, and it made practical sense. But when Vega thought about it, she could not imagine waking up in Aparna's apartment, waiting her turn for the toilet, going for dinner together to Café Orlin, and trying to revive an old friendship.

As Vega left that evening, Aparna said, "Come back in a week, tops, to take the clothes. They'll all fit you well. You've always had a nice waistline. And I would hate to give them away to someone with no fashion sense."

"I will," Vega said, though she knew she wouldn't.

She sent Aparna a brief note of thanks the next morning, telling her that she was busy with orientation, and promising to follow up at some point over the next few weeks. Some days later, there was a call for Vega on the dormitory phone, and she'd assumed that it was Aparna. But it was Sarah, the woman she had met at the party. "I hope it isn't weird that I'm calling," she said. "Aparna gave me your information. A friend of a friend is looking for a roommate. It's near Columbia. Super tiny converted two-bedroom. It's seven-fifty a month, and she hasn't listed it yet. I would call her in the next few minutes."

On a drizzling August afternoon, Vega walked along 121st Street, east of campus, until she reached Manhattan Avenue. The building was squat and gray, resembling what she imagined a Soviet housing block to look like. She was beginning to wonder if she would have to settle for one of the options she had already seen, if she would end up living in the Upper West Side apartment she had looked at the previous afternoon, where one of the roommates ended the tour by explaining to Vega the idiosyncrasies of the toilet. "You kind of have to jiggle the handle," she explained. "When that doesn't work, you just lift the lid to the tank and pull on this little flapper. It's not really an issue. You get used to it." Vega found herself thinking more and more about Aparna and resenting the ease of her life: her pristine Chelsea apartment, her unpaid gallery internship, and all her frivolous talk of textiles. "I've become particularly interested in vegetable dyes," she had told Vega. "Using native plants. I want to work with smaller batches and highly skilled artisans." Vega had nodded along, finding the conversation inoffensive and a little bit charming. Now, she wished she could go back and deflate some of Aparna's optimism. What would these small-batch textiles cost? Could the average Indian afford them?

She had no right to this resentment, she knew. Practically every day, during the dry months of October and November, she had watched their housekeeper, Vasanti, fill her jug with boiled water before leaving in the evenings, lugging it to the end of the road, from which she would take a rickshaw to the Adyar Depot, then the city bus to its final stop on the outskirts of Madras. Sometimes, Vasanti's son would come from his job as a driver for a family in Mylapore, hoisting the jug onto his shoulder. Vega had thought it was absurd, even implausible, that a man who worked by day as a driver could not simply borrow the car to transport his water jug. "They'd sack him on the spot if he even asked," Vega's father said.

"There must be an alternative," she'd said.

"What is this alternative, then?" Vega's father asked. "The public taps are dry as a bone."

Now, as Vega wandered down the dank hallway, looking for apartment 3L and staring at the takeout menus partly shoved under each door, she felt herself floating through a world that made no sense, a world of unnecessary suffering and arbitrary prices. The public tap water that should be free. The graduate students who couldn't bother cleaning the shit from their toilet seat, but who charged the entirety of the Gifford housing stipend to live among them: seven hundred dollars a month, which, if multiplied by twelve, was roughly one third of what her father earned per year in his position at Iyer Law College.

# 4

A woman with curly brown hair answered the door and introduced herself as Naomi. She was striking—not girlishly pretty, but with a lovely face and firm handshake and a style that Rukmini would have described as boyish. She wore cutoff shorts and a plaid button-down shirt rolled up to her elbows. "I'll show you the place," she said. "Sarah mentioned it's small?"

"She did. That's fine with me."

The apartment was sparse and, aside from an upturned table at the center of the living room, impeccably clean. "Don't mind this," Naomi said. "I'm trying to fix it up. One of our neighbors was unloading this coffee table, so I thought I'd put it together."

"I admire your acumen," Vega said. "I don't think I've ever put anything together in my life." She followed Naomi into the kitchen. It had the same look of the other apartments Vega had seen—cheap appliances, linoleum floor. But the sink was empty of crusted dishes. There was a rickety-looking table, on top of which was a bowl of oranges and bananas.

"So, what are you studying?" Naomi asked.

"I'm a sociologist. I'm interested in maternal health. Poverty, more broadly. You?"

"Anthropology."

"As in, archaeology? Digs and whatnot?"

"More the cultural side. My thesis is on Indigenous political identities and activism. I might be heading to Austin for a fellowship next fall."

They walked to the bedroom. It contained little more than a bed, a desk, a window, and a rod with wire hangers running along one wall. But it was quiet and brightly lit. Vega imagined herself sitting at the desk, her books splayed out, the glow of a tiny lamp like the one she had in Hyderabad.

When they made their way back to the living room, Naomi said, "If you're not in a rush, I want to put together this desk. I would love your help just holding it still so I can screw the leg in. Is that a weird thing to ask you to do?"

"I'm happy to," Vega said. "And I'm not in a rush." She had an optional orientation meeting that afternoon, a tour of the student health clinic that she had planned to attend because it seemed the responsible thing to do, in case of some eventual medical disaster. Now, she was happy with the thought of missing it. She wanted to run back to her dormitory, quickly pack her things, and move into Naomi's apartment. She wanted to wake up the next morning in that tiny bedroom.

Naomi brewed a pot of coffee and they sat on the floor. Naomi did most of the talking. She described the jobs she had held the past year—at a bar and as an intake coordinator at an animal shelter in Brooklyn—while she applied for graduate school. Vega held the table in place, occasionally handing Naomi a tool, aware of her own superfluousness.

"Is this your first time in the States?" Naomi asked.

"I lived in Cleveland for two years when I was fifteen and sixteen." She would have skipped that detail of her life if they were meeting in passing.

"Why Cleveland?"

"Family reasons. I don't remember it well." She rambled a bit, telling Naomi about the shock of winter, how she had hated waiting for the school bus in the cold, and Naomi nodded along, talking about her first winter in the States, how her mother had coated her cheeks with Vaseline. "I was only eight, though," Naomi said. "It's probably easier to move to a new country when you're a kid than a teenager."

Vega wondered how the conversation would be steered if she told Naomi about Ashwini. She had had this thought before, with Sanjay during her first term in Hyderabad, with the other Gifford students as they lounged on the couches in the International House dorms. But the words, when she practiced them, sounded at best like a non sequitur and at worst like a plea for attention.

"Where were you born?" Vega asked.

"Colombia. Outside Medellín."

"How was it for you, when you came here?"

"I don't know. I remember the details better than the big picture. We had more land and space in Colombia, and I remember missing that more than anything. And, of course, thinking we were going back and only realizing years later that we weren't." She turned her attention briefly to the table leg, then said, "We stayed with these people in Yonkers. The only thing I remember is that they had a pet rabbit. Their kids were in school, so I was bored during the day. They didn't have any books in Spanish, and my mother wouldn't let me watch TV. So, I just sat around and stared at the rabbit."

"Does this story have a tragic ending?" Vega asked. She imagined something terrible. Naomi playing with the rabbit despite repeated warnings not to, inadvertently killing it. The guilt she would have carried with her into adulthood.

Naomi laughed. "No. Why would it?"

"Every time someone tells a story about animals, I think it's going to end tragically."

"No. It was alive and well when we left. The point was just that the rabbit is really the only detail I remember. I can't tell you what those people's names were. In the afternoons, after their kids came home from school, we would put newspaper down and let it out of its cage. So maybe that's the tragedy. That I was eight years old, and the highlight of my day was watching a rabbit walking around a basement."

"When we lived in Cleveland, my mother wanted to plant a garden, but everybody told her that unless she planted traps, rabbits would eat all the vegetables. And she wasn't willing to set traps, so she never bothered with the garden. But then we never saw a single one." She drew her knees up and rested her chin on them. "And with that, I think we've exhausted the subject of rabbits."

Naomi laughed again. They were quiet as she finished the final leg and returned her screwdriver to the toolbox. Vega imagined sitting next to Naomi on that couch, their coffee mugs resting on the table, papers spread everywhere. She opened her mouth, trying to decide how to nudge the conversation forward, but Naomi spoke first. "Seven-fifty a month works for you?"

"Yes. That works perfectly for me."

"Great. I have two other people coming by today, but I'm happy just canceling those. If you want the place, it's yours."


Vega found one of the few on-campus jobs available to international students. For five hours each week, she worked at the university bookstore, unpacking shipments of textbooks and course readers and stocking the metal shelves. Her co-workers baffled her; they were mainly undergraduates who existed in a world of mopey grievance, arriving ten minutes late for their shifts, complaining about the dress code requirements and lack of sick days. "This place is owned by Barnes and Noble," James said. "That's why it has a corporate mentality." He was an earnest sophomore, a self-described Socialist who was often staring down and grunting at a marked-up copy of some political theory book—*Select Works of Edmund Burke*, John Stuart Mill's *On Liberty*. "Do you ever read non-European thinkers?" Vega once asked him.

"Sure," he said. "Like, Mao and shit. I've read all of it."

"I'll try again," Vega said. "Have you ever read a non-European thinker who is not Chairman Mao?"

"Sure," he said. "Gandhi? But he was a fucking sellout."

This was, Vega thought, essentially true. But it was one thing to come to this conclusion among her classmates in Hyderabad, another to do so with James. "If only India had morally upright leaders. Like Thomas Jefferson." If she had searched her memory, she could have come up with a more obscure example, but that was the best she could do in the moment.

"Jefferson was a pig."

"That was my point."

She may have found him more irritating if the job itself was not such a revelation. Aside from her paltry tutoring stipend from the Madras School of Social Work, she had never before earned a paycheck, and when she cashed it at the campus bank every two weeks, she was astonished by the thirty dollars and ninety cents she received in exchange—twenty of which she gave to Naomi for grocery money.

They ate dinner together most evenings, usually seated on the living room floor, foods that Vega would later remember with a nostalgia that almost ached: grilled cheese with tomato, stir fry with frozen broccoli, pots and pots of black beans. Eggs in every form: scrambled with onions and peppers, folded into a tortilla, fried alongside more black beans. One Sunday, Naomi made popcorn and Vega watched, mesmerized, as the kernels mutated and blossomed under the glass lid of the pot.

"Explain something to me," Naomi said. She was leaning against the wall, the bowl of popcorn on the table in front of her. It was cool outside for August, but the apartment was stifling, and they had cracked open the window. "How did you avoid learning how to cook?"

"Nobody ever taught me."

"Come on. Weren't people cooking around you? Didn't you see it happening?"

"I also watched you affix a leg to a table. But if another legless table appeared in my life, I wouldn't know how to begin."

Naomi gave her a funny smile. There was between them, Vega sometimes thought, a hint of flirtation—but it seemed more likely that she was imagining it. Naomi had once referenced an ex-girlfriend named Camille who lived in Boston, and though Vega was curious, she didn't know how to dig without sounding parochial. She had known of lesbianism as an abstract issue, a political matter. But in human form, that was something different. One afternoon, while thumbing through an anthropology textbook that Naomi had left on the coffee table, a photograph slipped from the pages. It was of a short-haired white woman, smiling comedically and pointing to a sign that read *Beware of Pickpockets and Loose Women.*

She stared at the photograph for a long time, taking in the details: the woman's olive-colored tank top, the small tattoo on her wrist, the thin bracelet that looked to be made of braided twine. So, this was the type of woman Naomi would want, the type of woman she would fuck in whatever way two women fucked. Briefly, she pictured the two women entangled, Naomi lying on top. Then, she moved herself into the image. Naomi undressing her, her finger between Vega's legs. She placed the picture back in the exact page and closed the book.

On Tuesdays, Naomi and Vega drank for free at a dingy bar called Connolly's, where Naomi's friend Monty worked. Vega wasn't accustomed to alcohol. She had grown up under the pendulum swing of Tamil Nadu's prohibition laws and she associated drinking with the long lines of bleary-eyed men outside of the TASMAC, waiting to buy state-sanctioned whiskey that was rumored to be laced with turpentine. But she quickly came to like the bitterness of beer, how loose and warm she felt after a pint. She liked the closeness she felt to Naomi the next morning as they made tea and toast, still dressed in the T-shirts they had worn the previous night.

"What's the story with Indian men?" Monty asked one night. He was taking a smoke break outside the bar. Vega didn't know what to make of Monty. Sometimes she found him endearing. At other times, his humor was overbearing—a bit too sexual and a bit too familiar. But he was the first openly gay man she had ever known ("A bit fuddy-duddy," Rukmini sometimes whispered of Naren Uncle), so her discomfort around him made her wonder if she was the problem, if she was the type of person to be at ease with Naomi's quiet lesbianism but put off by Monty's brand of pert gayness. And this pressure to like him, in turn, made her self-conscious.

"Well, there is an abundance of them. For starters."

"That *is* a good start." He blew out smoke dramatically. "I'm just making plans in case I run out of options here and have to take my chances abroad."

"I wouldn't take my chances in a country in which a sodomy ban is actually written into the penal code."

Naomi laughed. "She has a point. If you're going to fuck some hot Ugandan or Indian guy, I would do it here. Or in a neutral third country."

"Like Denmark," Vega said. "I've heard Denmark is very open."

"Well, aren't you funny," Monty said. Later, when Naomi was in the bathroom, he slid over to Vega's corner of the bar and batted his lashes.

"Is this supposed to mean something?" Vega asked. "This thing you're doing with your eyes?"

"You two are like a couple, you know that?"

Vega tried to look composed. She pulled her hair away from her neck and tied it in a bun. "We're roommates, Monty."

"I got roommates, too. You ever met them?" He elbowed her playfully. "You have not. So, you see my point. This thing the two of you are doing, it isn't a roommate thing."

# 5

ociology of Industrialized Nations was led by Professor Steven Seltz,
a man of heavy tweed and numerous publications on the German
welfare state. Most of Vega's classes were easy, a rhythm of short papers with tidy citations and animated discussions. But here, she felt like
a fool. She knew nothing about the European Central Bank, had no
opinion of Madeleine Albright or the Balkans. Oddly, Vega's father had
located one of Seltz's articles at the library at Iyer Law College and
had started following his career with an interest that, Vega sensed, Seltz
did not typically inspire. "He co-authored an excellent book about coal
plants," he wrote Vega. "You can find it in the collection at IIT. When
you next come, I will ask them to set it aside for you."

She was one of two international students in the class. The other
was an Afro Indian woman named Zemadi, who had been born and
raised in Kenya but had completed her undergraduate at Mount Holyoke, and, unlike Vega, was schooled in American politics. Weeks into
the semester, sitting on Zemadi's couch and sipping overly sweetened
chai, Vega realized that she didn't recall the last time she had made a
friend (she and Gayatri had known each other since primary school,
and with Naomi, she wondered if their relationship—at least on Naomi's end—was a function of proximity or obligation). In her early days
at Sri Vidya, and then later in Hyderabad, she had watched people
break into pairs and had regarded it with a sort of distance and inev-
itability. Of course, they would go off, and she would be left behind.
What worried her then—though she hadn't recognized it until this

moment—was the same thing that worried her now: people liked her on the surface. She was nice enough and sharp enough. But when they really got to know her, they would find her boring, and maybe a little bit depressing. Now, she listened to Zemadi talk about her family, the foods she missed from home, the one place in Harlem where you could find decent East African food, though it was overpriced and mostly Somali. Then Zemadi asked, "Do you have a boyfriend?"

The question made Vega laugh. It was so endearing and childish, the type of question that people posed in books or movies but never in actual conversation. "I don't. Why do you ask?"

"I don't know. It's a defining thing, isn't it? Having a boyfriend."

"Then I'm currently undefined. Do you?"

"Nope."

Vega glanced at Zemadi's bookshelf. "I read that during my first master's program," she said. "*Nervous Conditions.*"

"Did you like it?"

Vega paused. "I don't know. I liked the character. But I'm not entirely sure I understood it."

"It's hard to appreciate African literature if you aren't African. Maybe Indian literature is the same way. Europeans and Americans might pretend to like the books, but they don't really."

It was something Rukmini might say—the kind of overly simplistic comment to which Vega would vociferously disagree though she would suspect, deep inside, that Rukmini was right. "Maybe," she said.

They settled into an easy friendship, along with a Pakistani public health student named Halima. On Wednesdays and Fridays, when Naomi was working, Vega ate dinner in one of their apartments—egg curries and greasy frozen parathas, or sometimes leftovers sent by Halima's aunt and uncle in Queens. Vega welcomed these nights. With Naomi, she felt her life being propelled towards something uncertain and exciting. With Zemadi and Halima, there was an ease and a coziness, a freedom to fix herself a snack in their kitchens, to kick off her shoes and collapse on one of the couches. They watched terrible television together. She didn't feel the need to impress them.

Halima's fiancé, Adnan, was at the University of Massachusetts, earning his doctorate in English. There were artsy Polaroids of him scattered throughout her apartment—one in which he was leaning back in a chair and laughing, another in which he was blowing a ring of smoke.

"Do you think it's odd that Americans don't like to talk about poverty?" Vega asked one night. Their class that afternoon—a discussion of welfare reform policies—had been unusually stilted. Now they were at Zemadi's place, making mushroom curry. Normally, Zemadi and Halima did the cooking, and Vega washed the dishes, but Halima was running late, so Zemadi set Vega up with the cutting board and a bowl of tomatoes and Vega got to work clumsily. She had learned, in her two months in New York, that she was a terrible cook.

"How so?" Zemadi asked.

"In class, people will talk about economic stagnation in Europe or Soviet food shortages. But if somebody brings up social welfare programs in the States, nobody speaks."

"Well, they haven't experienced American poverty."

"Yes. But they haven't experienced a European poverty, either. Yet they're happy to talk about it."

Zemadi was quiet for a bit, concentrating as she measured water for the rice cooker, and Vega wondered if she had said something inane, though she knew it was unlikely. Zemadi wasn't inclined towards judgment and was, in that same spirit, impervious to embarrassment. A few days earlier, she had told Vega and Halima that, when she was in secondary school, she and one of her male friends had practiced oral sex on each other nearly every day for a full year.

"What do you mean you *practiced*?" Halima asked. "You practice *tennis*. Or *penmanship*. Not *sex* acts."

Vega and Zemadi both laughed. "Sex acts," Zemadi repeated, and Vega felt a new closeness to her.

"Like with anything," Zemadi said. "We wanted to understand how to do it. There were no feelings between us. He wasn't cute. He *knew* he wasn't cute. But he was a funny guy. And nobody else was interested in touching me. Also, we both improved. By the end I was quite masterful."

"What a waste, to bring such a skill to Mount Holyoke," Vega said.

Halima winced, but Zemadi found the comment hilarious, and it occurred to Vega how much she admired this quality in people: the ability to laugh at their own follies and weaknesses and desires. Briefly, she considered telling them about Sukumar Reddy, but she couldn't bring herself to.

"Americans are funny," Zemadi said. "They love talking about the Depression, and how poor their grandparents were, and then everybody found factory jobs and pulled themselves up. Or they're comfortable talking about third world poverty. But to talk about it here and now, it's beyond their imagination."

Vega still didn't know what to make of American poverty. In Madras, water shortages were simply a way of life, and she had become accustomed to the faucet shutting off every evening and remaining that way until late the next morning. In the States, it ran heavy and full at all hours. When they arrived in Cleveland, she and Ashwini had been shocked by the orderly flow of traffic, the availability of functional toilets everywhere they went. Before stepping into the cafeteria of their school, Vega had never before seen people pick at a tray of food, then unceremoniously dump the remains in the garbage. Even in New York, there was surprising excess: free napkins at every corner store, tampons in the library bathroom, an air conditioner that blasted her flat at all hours. None of these she particularly needed, but they were indicative of a larger generosity, a place where it would be impossible to starve.

Every Sunday, she and Naomi took the train to Stamford, Connecticut, where Naomi's mother and aunt cooked vats of beans and rice and a cheesy corn stew that Vega loved. Cousins piled in from their various corners—Hartford, Paterson, the Bronx. Years later, Vega would pass these names on the highway as she drove through the Northeast and would be reminded of the cream-colored linoleum floor, the smell of onion and baby powder, the unlabeled bottle of pink cleaning solution with which Naomi's mother was always wiping down the table. She would think of Naomi's collection of cousins: ten-year-old Daniel, curled up with a comic book. Eighteen-year-old Eddie, stomping across the living room in his paint-streaked work boots, coaxing Daniel to put down the book and play a video game. Eddie's twin sister, Alba, with her infant son, Gabriel, and her cosmetology aspirations.

"I want to have my own salon one day," Alba had told Vega one afternoon. She was sitting at the kitchen table, nursing Gabriel. "Naomi says you have to be good at math, and I always made As and Bs. I only left school for a year when Gabriel was born, then I came back and finished."

Alba had a gentle expression that reminded Vega of one of the deer from the Amar Chitra Katha comic books she read as a child—pretty and wide-eyed and bewildered. Talking to her always made Vega feel a little bit sad, and she wasn't sure if this was because Alba's hopes for herself were too small, or because they were too ambitious.

"Maybe Alba can move in with us," Vega said to Naomi one Sunday night. "We can take care of Gabriel while she takes her cosmetology courses." They had just returned from Stamford, and she was sitting on the couch, watching Naomi change the lightbulb on their floor lamp.

"She'd practice all her makeup skills on you. She thinks you're pretty. She told me she wishes she had your curls."

The compliment, even though it was only channeled through Naomi, made Vega suddenly disoriented. Earlier that afternoon, Eddie had asked Vega, "So, you like our girl?" He was playing a game called *Duck Hunt*, which Vega found disturbing, though she couldn't tear her eyes from the screen. Daniel, next to him, was wordlessly firing. Occasionally, he would yelp. Vega still hadn't figured out the limits of Daniel's English. She had only ever heard him speak in Spanish, aside from the shy greeting he always gave her. The only person he seemed to talk with of his own volition was Eddie.

"We've become close friends," Vega said.

Eddie shot some more ducks, then said, "She's a genius. You know she finished college in three and a half years? She went from Colombia to Columbia. You know many people who can do that?"

"I don't."

Eddie nodded, then reached over and tousled Daniel's hair. "I don't either. That's what I mean when I say genius. Maybe that's why you like her."

It may have been a meaningless comment, but it startled her, and she was relieved that Daniel didn't seem to pick up on the exchange. Now, she said to Naomi, "Nobody wishes they had curls. They only think they do."

Naomi set the old bulb on the ground. "I have curls."

"Yes, but yours are short. That doesn't count."

"I shaved my head when I was in undergrad. When I came home, I thought my mother would scream at me. But she actually laughed. She said I looked like a chihuahua."

"I'm sure it looked nice. In its own way."

"No. It didn't. Turns out, you don't really know how your scalp is shaped until you shave your head."

Vega collected the discarded bulb, the empty box, and the tattered plastic wrap. Then she pulled the last remaining beer from the fridge and poured it evenly into two glasses. When she came back to the living room, Naomi was sitting with her back against the wall, her arms wrapped around her knees.

"It's brighter in here," Vega said.

"That was the point."

Vega handed her a glass and sat next to her, the molding from the living room wall digging into her back. She thought, as she had on the evening she moved in with Naomi, that if she were given the chance, she would stay in that apartment forever. There would be no graduate program or student visa ticking towards its final days. There would be no reason to pack her bags, to ever move again.

One November morning, sitting at their rickety table over bowls of cereal, Naomi said, "Don't you have a birthday coming up?"

Vega's twenty-second birthday had passed the previous week, quietly and uneventfully, marked only by emails from her parents and Gayatri. *Promise that you'll do something nice for yourself!* Gayatri had written, and Vega assured her that she would. Instead, that night, she canceled her standing plans with Zemadi and Halima, ate cheese toast and a can of tomato soup for dinner, and went to bed early—relieved that Naomi was working, that the apartment was empty, that the day was finally over. Ashwini had died five years ago, in late October, and it wasn't just the anniversary of the loss that haunted Vega, but the fact of birthdays in general. For their entire shared lives, she and Ashwini had been three and a half years apart. Vega hated being reminded of the widening gap between them. Each year she arrived at another age Ashwini would never be.

"I don't really celebrate," she said. "I'm from a very poor country and we can't afford birth records. Let alone cake."

Naomi laughed. "This will be your first party, then. I'll cook. Or we can potluck. Monty can bring a cake. You can invite your other girls."

Naomi had only met Zemadi and Halima once, when they all ran into each other at the library, but the conversation hadn't gone much further than introductions, and Vega only realized, looking back, that she should have made more of an effort to merge her two social worlds. But the thought made her uncomfortable. She wasn't embarrassed by Zemadi or Halima, but theirs was a different type of friendship. Every few weeks they went shopping together at a Pakistani-run store called High Fashion next to Penn Station that sold sweaters and skinny jeans, all for under fifteen dollars, and offered a steeper discount if they bought in bulk. They talked about food and clothes and fluctuating waistlines. They were open about constitutional habits. A few weeks, earlier, Zemadi had announced, "I bought a sandwich from that Morningside Grocery and I've had loose motions all day. In the middle of class I had to excuse myself. But I walked all the way to the toilet on the third floor, because that is the only one where there is any privacy." Halima had nodded, knowingly. "Best toilet is in the financial aid office. It's always very empty. Of course, I go first thing in the morning before I leave for class. That's always my habit. But if I have an emergency, financial aid is the best option."

Monty was the first to arrive the next Friday, bringing a case of beer, a homemade carrot cake, and a boy who looked no older than sixteen. "It isn't what you might think," he whispered to Vega in the kitchen when the boy, Ezekiel, went off to use the bathroom.

Vega was horrified. "What did you think I thought?"

"I just mean, it's not anything like that. He's my roommate's nephew but he's staying with us, and I'm watching him for the night. The family kicked him out. Literally, they dropped him at the Amtrak station in New Hampshire with one change of clothes. They're religious nuts. He had gay porn in his room. Or so they said, but he won't talk about it. The point is, we're all taking turns keeping an eye."

"Is he okay?" Vega asked.

Monty shrugged. "For now. I mean, define okay."

Vega felt a new tenderness for Monty. A few weeks earlier, he had come to the apartment with a carton of coffee ice cream. Naomi was still in class when he arrived, and he put the ice cream in the freezer and set about scrambling eggs for their dinner. Somehow, over the course of their conversation, Vega told him the story of the woman on the train who had pulled out her breast.

"*Shit*," he said. "What did you *say*?"

"Nothing, really. It made me sad, though. Maybe that's why I still think about it."

"Well, *yes*, it made you sad. But it's also kind of beautiful. Like, here you have this woman breaking the silence around her body and her struggles. And she chose to open up to you."

"It's entirely possible that she opens up to everybody. She could be sitting on a Bangalore-bound train right now, revealing her nipple to a stranger."

"Well, maybe. But probably not. Maybe you gave off that vibe. Like, here I am. Confide in me."

Halima and Zemadi arrived, overdressed, with too much makeup on and a pot of biryani. "PST," Zemadi said, tilting her head toward Halima. "Pakistani Standard Time. I was ready one hour back."

The fanfare embarrassed Vega, but everyone else seemed at ease, making her wonder if there was something wrong with her. If she was incapable of revelry. The only person who appeared to share her discomfort was Ezekiel, who stood in the corner, turning the knob on one of the light switches until Monty gently pried his hand away.

Since their coffee table wasn't big enough, they all gathered with their plates on the floor. Monty told the story of one of his co-workers, who had broken a wineglass and sliced his hand open that afternoon. "And so we go to find the first aid kit, but there *isn't* a first aid kit. The shift manager can't find it. And I'm like, 'This is basic occupational safety shit. You are actually required by law.'"

"The difference between my home and this country," Halima said, "at least, in this respect, is that in Pakistan, there are no occupational safety standards or any such thing. Shops will not keep a first aid kit. But you can send somebody to fetch something if there is an emergency, and there is a pharmacy on every corner. Here, you will stand there and bleed. There is nobody to help you."

It was the kind of generalization that Halima was prone to, but the group nodded along anyway. Zemadi told the story of a woman named Liz, from Vega's Poverty and Mobility course, who had stopped Vega in the hallway after class and asked whether honor killings still took place in India. Zemadi hadn't been there for this conversation, but Vega mentioned it to her afterwards, not because she found it offensive—as Zemadi seemed to—but because she thought it was so earnest, so refreshingly honest.

"She had read an article," Zemadi said. "And she wanted Vega to speak on behalf of one billion people. If I had been there, I would have asked her, 'Do you hold yourself personally responsible for the Salem Witch Trials?'"

"It didn't particularly bother me," Vega said. "In some ways, I appreciated it. How many questions do any of us have, on a given day,

that we are too embarrassed to ask?" She stared across the table, where
Halima was spooning extra rice onto Ezekiel's plate like an overbearing aunt. He looked so small, so orphaned, so pathetically out of place
at a dinner party made up of twentysomethings. She felt a knot in her
stomach—rage, or sadness, or a combination of the two. What kind of
people abandoned a child in a train station? She had a memory of her
mother sitting next to Ashwini at night, stroking her hair until she fell
asleep. What was the point of all that love if Ashwini was just going to
die? It wasn't an investment in the future. Ashwini wouldn't pass any
of those memories down to her children. And yet.

"It's important to note that this wasn't some passenger on the subway," Zemadi said. "This was a graduate student. In *sociology*."

Vega tore her eyes from Ezekiel. If nothing else, he was eating.
Halima was seeing to that. "I think she was an undergraduate," she
said. "And honor killings do still happen. I've never *known* anybody
who has been a victim, of course, but it would be disingenuous to say
that the practice is obsolete."

"I worked at an animal shelter over the summer," Naomi said. "My
manager was really into narcoterrorism."

"I hate that type," Monty said. Vega had no idea what he meant
by this, so she couldn't pinpoint exactly why she found the comment
funny. She had long had a disproportionate reaction to this type of
humor—casual throwaway lines that other people seemed to scarcely
notice. She and Gayatri once had a chemistry teacher who, among
his malapropisms, frequently used the word "tit-bit." Vega had never
laughed at this directly—she found it particularly cruel to laugh at
teachers—but whenever Gayatri imitated him, she fell apart. Now, the
memory surfaced.

"Anyway," Naomi said, "I let it slip that I was born in Colombia,
and all he wanted to talk about was Pablo Escobar. He used to always
bring up Escobar's hippos. Did you know Escobar kept hippos?"

"Everybody knows that shit," Monty said. "He had a zoo of them."

Vega wished that he wouldn't curse so much in front of Ezekiel.
She tried to make eye contact with him, but he was concentrating on

his plate. Then Ezekiel said something quietly, and Vega couldn't tell if he was speaking to himself or the group.

A few seconds later, Ezekiel repeated himself, more audibly now, and Vega realized that he hadn't been speaking to himself as much as rehearsing his words. "What happened to the hippos? They shot them all?"

There was a pause, as they all processed the question. "No way," Naomi said, at the same time as Halima said, "Don't think such dark thoughts."

"Hell no," Monty said. "Big-ass animals like that? They'd trample any hunters who tried to get close enough. The government made them a sanctuary. They're living in the wild."

Ezekiel nodded. Halima spooned more biryani onto his plate.

After dinner, Monty and Vega took over the dishes and Naomi packed up leftovers. In the living room, Zemadi and Halima were setting up the Scrabble board and explaining the rules to Ezekiel. "I don't know why they're bothering," Monty said. "You girls are missing half the pieces. I tried playing last week. You have no vowels, basically."

Naomi laughed. "You say the craziest shit. You're telling me you came by last week when nobody else was here, set up the Scrabble board, and counted out the vowels."

"Except I didn't have to count them out. I could tell you were missing pieces. The bag is light."

"How did you know they were vowels? The tiles all weigh the same."

"I just knew."

Naomi closed the fridge door, still laughing, and Monty swatted her arm with a towel. Watching them, Vega felt a tug of yearning. She wanted to know somebody that well, to be adored in the way Monty and Naomi seemed to adore each other. She wondered if she and Ashwini might have become close as adults. Maybe Ashwini would have followed her to the States. They might eventually have lived together. More likely, they would have had separate lives, in separate cities. They would have traveled to visit each other. They would have met each other's friends.

Naomi drifted into the living room, and Monty turned to Vega. "You ever been homeless?" he asked.

The question surprised her. "No. I haven't."

She expected him to continue the conversation. Instead, he took the last bowl from her hands, dried it, and placed it in the cabinet. Later, he set the cake on the coffee table, sloppily frosted with a single candle in the middle, and insisted that they sing for her.

"It isn't even my birthday," Vega protested.

"I made this damn cake, girl. If I say we're gonna sing, we're gonna sing."

"Vega's not into birthdays, Monty," Naomi said. She was sitting on the floor, carefully sliding the Scrabble board to the corner of the room. Vega stared down at it. The game, it seemed, had been off to a slow start, a collection of small words with little value: *be*, *yelp*, *pig*.

Ezekiel spoke again, his only contribution since his question about the hippos. "I was born two days before Christmas. December twenty-third." He was sitting between Halima and Zemadi, looking like a little boy bolstered by his big sisters.

They were all quiet for a moment, and Zemadi spoke first. "I suppose the next birthday to come is yours, then."

They announced their birth dates and confirmed this, then Monty slid the plate in front of Ezekiel. "Go on, little man. Blow out your candle."

# 6

Vega had been looking forward to the holidays. Even in Cleveland, where little made her happy, she had loved the snow—the anticipation of it, staring at it through the window, the miracle of watching it disappear in her hand. But in New York, she quickly learned there was no snow, only endless cold. And by the middle of December, she was beginning to find the thought of Christmas depressing. Naomi was working longer shifts at the bar. And as the campus emptied, it all felt like a taunt—a national gathering to which she wasn't invited. She attended one holiday party, a sparsely attended event for Gifford fellows held at the International House, and spent the evening locked in conversation with two Polish chemists about the challenges of grant-writing. She kept wanting to extricate herself, less out of boredom than an anxiety that they were speaking English for her benefit. She left early in the evening with two unopened containers of pad Thai and the remains of a box of red wine. "You'd be doing us a favor if you took it," the coordinator said—a cheery French Canadian law student named Sylvie. "We'd expected a bigger turnout."

One morning, in the kitchen, Naomi said, "You're coming home with me for Christmas, right?"

"To Stamford?"

Naomi poured hot water into her thermos. "You got a better offer?"

Halima was going with Adnan to visit relatives of his in Rhode Island, and Zemadi to her college classmate's home in Boston. Both had invited her to join them. "These Boston people are rich," Zemadi said. "Big house in the suburbs. And they love Asians. They're always traveling to Agra or Angkor Wat or wherever. They'll be happy to have you." Vega said she would consider it, though she had no interest in spending the week in a house full of wealthy strangers. It sounded lonelier than being alone.

She and Naomi were the only ones in the train car on Christmas Eve. Naomi pulled off her woolen hat and shoved it into her coat pocket. Vega hugged herself and rubbed her hands together. She wore her down jacket, pulled from a stockpile of donations at the International House, but was still miserably cold.

"Monty was supposed to come too," Naomi said, "but he and his roommates are staying behind, so they're all spending the day together."

"First Christmas as a family," Vega said. According to Monty's frequent updates, Ezekiel's temporary arrangement was acquiring a permanence. When Monty talked about him, it was with the zeal of—if not a new father—a proud uncle. "The kid loves bell peppers!" he told Vega one night. "Have you ever known a kid who loved bell peppers?" A few weeks earlier, he'd taken Ezekiel to the theater to watch a movie called *Street Fighter.* Vega found this all baffling. How does a family just give up a child? How does a child just stumble upon a new family?

They talked a bit about Monty, how he had moved in with Naomi's family when he was sixteen and had lived there even after Naomi left for college.

"He told me once that he liked living with you," Vega said. "That he was happy."

"We both were. My ex, Camille, came from this wealthy New England family. They had a vacation home in Maine, and they would go to France over the summers. She used to talk about these magical memories from being a kid, and I would just think, is there something wrong with me? My happiest days were spent smoking weed behind the Shell station with Monty and renting movies from the Blockbuster." The train stopped at the Danbury station. Through the window, Vega watched a cluster of people outside: an elderly man, a couple in their forties, and two small children.

Naomi asked, "What about you? What were your happiest times?"

"I really enjoyed my vacation home in Maine."

"Shut up. For real."

"I did have some really nice childhood holidays. We would go to my grandparents' house in Mysore. It was a beautiful old house with a garden." Vega had been blissfully happy during those holidays. She loved being with her cousins, losing themselves in their world of imagined play, sleeping on the balcony and whispering to each other until they dozed off. But those memories seemed so distant, etched into a former version of herself.

Naomi was looking at her. Vega turned to face the window and stared at their blurred reflections. "I had a sister who died, five years ago. So, in some ways, my life was split into two parts."

"Vega."

She shook her head. "I haven't practiced talking about this."

"Well, you don't need to practice. You can just talk. I'm here."

"I mean it, earnestly. I don't know how to talk about this, so I don't want to. Not in any real depth. I just mean that, any good memories from when I was a child are irrelevant. Because when I think of them, I know that there is this terrible thing coming. And I want to scream and warn my former self. So, I don't know how to enjoy those memories."

"I'm just so sorry, Vega. I'm so damn sorry. If you want to talk, or not. I'm here."

"I don't think I do."

Naomi squeezed her hand. "What about right now? What makes you happy right now?"

"This," Vega said. "I think I'm happier now than I've ever been."

T hey were quiet for most of the walk. Outside the building, Naomi said, "We don't have to go inside just yet. Our neighbor's apartment is empty. That's where I was thinking we could spend the night if we don't want to get a ride back to the city. We could just sit for a bit."

The layout of the Martinezes' home—as it was labeled on a door-mat reading *Casa Martinez*—was exactly the same as Naomi's family's apartment, and similarly oriented towards Jesus-themed décor. There was a cross hanging over the door, and a painting of the Virgin Mary at the entrance to the kitchen. Naomi set their coats down and went to the linen closet, returning with a bundle of blankets and a pillow dec-orated with tiny fish, the ichthys that Vega recognized from her morn-ings in the Rhodes School chapel.

"I don't know why I'm getting blankets," Naomi said. "They're for later if you want to sleep here. I just felt like I needed to do something."

If they were in their own apartment, Vega would have busied her-self with a task. Maybe riffled through her backpack or walked into the kitchen and washed a dish. On the coffee table was a heavy book called *Spirit and Life: The Holy Sacraments of the Catholic Church*. She could not plausibly have thumbed through it.

"I'm so sorry about your sister, Vega. I understand if you don't want to talk."

"I do want to talk. I just don't know how."

Naomi put her hand on Vega's cheeks and looked at her with such intensity that she thought—despite the heaviness in the room—she might laugh. She'd always been one to do this. To laugh at the worst times.

"Are you smiling?" Naomi asked.

"I don't know why. I think I'm nervous." She started to fumble her way through another explanation, but Naomi was kissing her mouth, then her neck. Seconds later, they were in the Martinezes' sons' bed-room, lying on top of a Yankees comforter. Naomi's body was both fa-miliar and alien. The coarse hair, the sticky heat. She touched Naomi in the exact, narrow corridors where she wanted Naomi to touch her, embarrassed when Naomi adjusted her hand, and shocked when it worked, when Naomi gasped and writhed and fell apart underneath her. Rolling over, lying on her back, she slid her thermals down until they dug into the edge of her hips and let Naomi pull them the rest of the way. Her underwear came along with them, everything bunching at her knees, and she felt ridiculous. Like a child who needed help undressing. She wanted to say something. It seemed that too much time had passed without anyone saying anything. And then Vega felt it. The rush and rise she had let herself feel on so many nights, pretending her own hand was Naomi's.

Eddie greeted them at the door, slurring and effusive, wearing a green sweater and red apron. "Check you, cuz," he said to Naomi. "My genius cuz."

He hugged Vega and lifted her off her feet. It was a strange departure from their usual dynamic. Normally, he just waved at her from across the room. "Look at this beautiful girl. Are all the women in India as beautiful as you?"

"There are half a billion of us," Vega said. "There's some variation."

Naomi laughed a pitch higher than normal, and it surprised Vega to see that she was nervous. She slipped off her coat, then took Vega's and wandered to the closet to hang them up. Vega tried to follow, but Eddie trailed behind and cornered her next to the bookshelf. By then, Naomi had been pulled into the kitchen.

"You know where I actually want to go?" Eddie asked. "Brazil. I want to go to the beach and drink them caipirinhas and just *look* at the girls. If they ever deport my ass, I'm gonna take my dollars and cash out in Colombia. Then I'm gonna drive over to Brazil all the fucking time and drink caipirinhas. And I'm gonna eat a thousand fucking grilled shrimp. You believe me when I say that?"

"I think anything is possible," Vega said.

Eddie finally drifted towards a couch full of middle-aged men, and Vega went into the kitchen where somebody handed her a milky cinnamon drink. From what she could follow, there was much debate at the stove over the various pots, and some discussion of whatever was cooling on the counter. Alba, sitting at the table with a drowsy Gabriel on her lap, waved her over. "I bet you're sad that you're not with your family," she said.

Thinking of her parents snapped Vega out of her stupor. Even in the span of their brief phone conversations, she had run out of things to say to them. They told the same stories over and over again—errands her mother had run, her father's health news, the occasional update from his classes at Iyer Law College. For the past week, she had been thinking that she owed them a phone call, but she could never bring herself to dial the number.

"I made the chicken, so you have to try it," Alba said, ignoring, as she usually did, the perplexing fact that Vega didn't eat meat.

Vega stroked Gabriel's hand and was reminded that, in addition to her parents, she was overdue for a call to Shoba. She looked around the room again to try to find Naomi. She felt as though she were drifting, as though she might be imagining the entire evening.

It was after midnight when the party ended. Most of the uncles were sobering up with coffee and preparing to drive back home. One of the aunts said, in surprisingly clear English, "I not going with your drunk ass." Some of the women planned to stay behind, on the couch or the floor. Daniel was rubbing his eyes, and Alba and the baby were asleep in Naomi's bedroom.

Sometime later—maybe minutes, or maybe an hour, Naomi gestured for them to go. Vega had been deliriously tired moments before. She rarely lasted past midnight under normal circumstances, and in avoidance of a coconut cocktail that Eddie was passing around, she had drunk more beer than normal. But entering the Martinezes' home, she was wide awake.

On the couch, they stared at each other briefly, then Vega said, "So, tell me about your accelerated three-and-a-half-year course of under-graduate study."

Naomi smiled. "It's embarrassing. How impressed they are with me."

"It isn't. It's lovely, actually."

Naomi reached across the couch and ran her finger lightly along Vega's collarbone.

"I don't know what to make of any of this," Vega said.

"What if we don't have to figure out any of that right now? What if we just sleep next to each other? We can sort through it tomorrow."

The next few minutes were stilted. They took turns brushing their teeth in the small bathroom with its black and white tiles and glass bowl of potpourri. Then they changed, discreetly, in separate corners of the bedroom—Vega stripping down to the thermals she wore under her pants and sweater, and Naomi into athletic shorts and a T-shirt that read *Black Knights Basketball*. They fell asleep, Naomi's hand resting on Vega's stomach.

In the morning, Vega found Naomi at the kitchen table. She was sitting with a coffee mug in front of her, thumbing through the Martinezes' address book.

"A bit of light reading?" Vega asked.

"It's funny to look through this. There are so many families who've moved. All these people, they crossed out their old numbers and wrote in new ones." She stood up and poured Vega a cup of coffee, then held up a can with a triangular dent poked into the surface. "They only have evaporated milk."

"That's fine."

"It tastes like a camping trip."

"I've never been on a camping trip."

"If you had dated my ex, you would have been on many."

Vega didn't know what to say to that. She had, until that moment, found everything about Naomi to be thrilling and novel and magnetic. Now, she felt a desire to hurt her, to poke at her happiness and watch her deflate. "We need to clean the room," she said. "We should wash the sheets."

Naomi looked confused. "We'll get around to it."

"We should probably do it now." Looking around the bedroom that morning, Vega had been daunted by the mess. They would need to strip the bed, haul everything down to the basement. She was tired of laundry. Of basement units and staticky sheets and other people's lint. With fresh rage, she thought about Sukumar Reddy, smug and shirtless, drinking one of his insufferable green juices and leaving the unwashed blender in the sink.

"I don't think we have to worry about that now. I can take care of it later." Naomi sat back and chewed the corner of her lip. "I'm probably not going back into the city until tomorrow. We could go for a drive. I have Eddie's car. Nothing will be open, but we could go to Westport and see the coast."

"I should probably go back to the city today, if the trains are running." Vega regretted the line the moment she delivered it. She did not want to go back to the city. She wanted to stay in the Martinezes' apartment, fall back asleep next to Naomi on the unmade bed. Rationally, she knew that this was an option, that it was what Naomi also wanted, but it still felt out of reach. And that feeling made her angry. Specifically, it made her angry at Naomi.

Naomi nodded slowly. "I'll try again. I'm going to spend the morning with my family. Downstairs. You're welcome to come. Otherwise, I can drive you to the station. There is some train service today. It's sporadic, but I think there's an afternoon one."

"This isn't feasible, Naomi."

"*Feasible?* What the fuck is that supposed to mean? Who the fuck uses the word 'feasible' in conversation?"

"I only mean that it isn't practical."

"Thank you. I know what the word means."

Naomi stared at Vega for a few long seconds, then she left the kitchen. Vega could hear her in the bathroom, running the faucet, then the shower. A few minutes later, the apartment door opened and closed.

Vega brushed her teeth, got dressed, and sat on the rumpled bed, unsure what to do. She went back to the kitchen and washed the coffee mugs. Then she straightened out the couch cushions and wandered through the living room, looking at the framed pictures on the walls. Two boys at different stages. A toddler with a ball next to an infant in a stroller. Posed, with braces and collared shirts. In a graduation cap and gown. After some time, there was a knock on the door. Vega looked through the peephole. It was Naomi's mother. She came inside, holding a mug of coffee and a paper plate of sweet-looking rolls. Then she sat on the couch and patted the empty space next to her. "Merry Christmas," she said.

It was all so puzzling, and with the absence of any real common language, there was no point in even trying to sort through any of it. Vega took the plate and bit into the roll. There was a crust of sugar on top. The coffee was milky and sweet, reminiscent of Madras coffee. "No want you be sad," Naomi's mother said. "You're nice girl." She squeezed Vega's hand. They sat quietly until Vega had eaten the last roll and drained her mug.

"You finish here, come down," she said, before walking out. "Have breakfast."

It was such a sweet and illogical suggestion, delivered so carefully, and it was clear just how much planning and effort went into those few sentences. It was exhausting, Vega thought, to speak another language. To translate the individual words in your head, knowing that the composite would be barely coherent. She thought about Hyderabad, the hostel common room, the foil packets of takeout biryani. She thought about Sanjay. He had liked her so plainly, so publicly. He had offered himself to her. And what had she done? She had stopped talking to him. She had fucked Reddy, and then she had left.

"I will," Vega said. Instead, she walked down the steps, tiptoeing past Naomi's family's apartment, caught a taxi to the train station, waited for nearly an hour, and took the long, cold ride back to New York.

She spent the day cleaning the apartment and hoping that Naomi would walk through the door. That night she slept fitfully, waking up and dozing off again. Around ten a.m., she dragged herself out the door and down the stairs and walked to the first open store that she could find—an East Asian market she had passed countless times but never stepped inside. It was curiously packed with students. She filled her basket with whatever she could identify, though none of it provided much sustenance: a bag of lychee candies; rice crackers; Maggi noo-dles; cream-filled rolls flavored with green tea. Then she went back to 121st Street, tore through the food, and waited some more.

B y the end of the week, the apartment was unbearable. Most of the building's tenants had left for the winter, and the super had turned down the heat—slipping notices into their mailboxes in early December, to which Vega hadn't paid much attention. Now, the cold leached from the floor through her socks. Her nose ran constantly. She drank cup after cup of tea and was distracted by the steady pulsing of her bladder. Halima and Zemadi were out of town, or she would have retreated to one of their apartments. Once, she went into Naomi's room and sat at her desk, taking in the small changes since the last time she had been inside there. There was a copy of *The Oxford Handbook of Archaeology*, a Brooklyn College travel mug where she stored pens, a weekly planner filled with her tight, curled handwriting. *Fellowship app due*; *T.A. Notes*; *Alba cita con la doctora*. Vega hadn't known this about Naomi, that she used Spanish sometimes when speaking to herself. It was such a weightless thing to learn about someone. Still, she read the sentence over and over again, running her fingers over the letters.

Shoba called on New Year's Eve. They hadn't spoken since November, shortly before Thanksgiving. She was eight months pregnant now. Her voice was thinner. Vega imagined her vocal cords pressed against the weight of the baby.

"Best wishes!" she shouted, as though she were on the phone with Coimbatore. "We've been talking so much about you!" She updated Vega on her mother's travel plans, the new rice cooker that Mohan had bought, and she inquired—as she always did—about Vega's exams. Then she asked, "What do you think of Tara?"

"Tara?"

"For the baby. It means *star*."

"That's lovely, Shoba. It's a beautiful name."

On Sunday night, just over a week after Christmas, Vega returned from the library to find Naomi standing in the kitchen, slicing an apple, dressed in her bartending uniform: white shirt and black jeans. It had been enough time, Vega considered, for the anger to have dissolved but the desire to still be there. She imagined reaching out, touching Naomi's stomach, sliding her shirt upwards.

"I'll be out of your way in a minute," Naomi said.

"You aren't in my way."

"Do you have a minute, then?"

"Of course I do."

"There's a good chance I'll be in Austin by the summer. I think it might be best if I move out for the spring semester."

"The spring semester starts in three weeks. You're moving now?"

"You can find a roommate, or they can find new tenants. We're month-to-month, so if you decide to move out too, we should let the landlord know soon."

This was her opening, Vega realized. It was not too late to convince her to stay. Naomi stared down at her sliced apple as though she weren't sure of the mechanics of eating it, then she said, "The thing you told me on the train. Your sister. I want you to know how much I hurt for you when you told me. I don't know what I mean by this, except that you can't do much for people if you aren't in their lives. And I'm sorry I'm not in yours." She pulled a container from the cabinet, packed her apple, collected her backpack and boots, and walked through the front door.

Vega went into her room, lay on her bed, and cried so heavily that her chest hurt. She fell asleep, disrupted by a series of strange dreams, filled with remixed memories from her childhood: her mother holding her over the pit toilet on a train; peeling almonds at her kitchen table; Ashwini walking ahead on the street, then turning a corner. Vega running behind, trying to catch her. That was the dream that snapped her, frantically, from her sleep. When she stepped out of her bedroom in the morning, she saw that Naomi's things were gone.

# 7

Halima didn't ask any questions. She had been using her spare bedroom as a study, and by the time Vega arrived, had already moved her desk and bookshelf into the living room. "I was planning to rent it in the fall anyway," she said. "You're doing me a favor."

Vega filled her spring schedule as tightly as possible. In addition to her four sociology courses, she registered for introductory Arabic, because it was one of the few language classes in which there was available space. Halima patiently helped her with the script, praising her penmanship even when it was crooked, helping her pronounce the letter *gza*. "Very, very close," she said. "It's just a bit more guttural." Aside from the bits of Telegu that she tried to pick up when she lived in Hyderabad, Vega hadn't studied a language since her passive days learning Hindi at Rhodes School. She found it was satisfyingly mathematical, with none of the debate and friction of social sciences.

She woke up every morning thinking of Naomi but managed to put off her fantasies during the day—first an hour here and there, then the full duration of a class—the way she imagined smokers prepared for a long flight. But when she was alone in the apartment, she still touched herself, remembering the peculiar wonder of being with Naomi. Her two fingers sliding inside her, and then her tongue. She reminded herself that she was the one who had ended it. She had made a choice. Sometimes, this thought brought her comfort. Most of the time, it made her feel lost, utterly alien to herself, wanting both to fuck Naomi and to never see her again.

One February afternoon, at Morningside Grocery, she ran into Erick—a lanky white graduate student who had sat across from her in Sociology of Industrialized Nations. She had stepped in to escape the cold. He was buying a cup of coffee.

"Vega Gopalan, right?" he asked.

The use of her surname, and the sound of it in his accent, confused her for a moment. "That's right."

"So, what did you think of Industrialized Nations?"

"I love them," she said. "I vastly prefer them to poor ones."

He paused, then laughed. In class, she had found Erick grating. He had a way of sitting back professorially. When other people talked, his mouth was always slightly open, as though he were waiting for his chance to interject. But he also struck her as legitimately brilliant. Once, he had launched into an analysis of the Suez Canal so detailed and winding that she sensed that even their professor was a bit lost. Now she watched him as he tore open a packet of sugar and poured it into his coffee. She didn't find him attractive, but there was something appealing about exchanging easy banter with someone you once found intimidating.

That night, she ended up in his apartment, watching a documentary on the construction of the Panama Canal. "I've actually seen this one already," she said.

He looked at her sharply. "Really?"

"I'm joking."

They ordered Thai food, and as they set out the containers, she said, "You seem to have a keen interest in canals," she said.

"Why do you say that?"

"You talked about the Suez Canal in class, if I recall."

"Doesn't everybody?"

"Doesn't everybody like *canals*?"

"No. I mean, history and infrastructure. Having an idea and turning it into something that shapes the world economy."

She started to disagree with him, to explain that she was much more interested in the impact of grassroots initiatives than large-scale projects, but he had already turned his attention back to the documentary. After a few minutes, he pointed to the screen—a still image of Teddy Roosevelt saluting a crowd. "Now *that's* a progressive. Regulating big business. Strengthening the economy and pushing our interests abroad. Not being afraid of a fight."

The sex was the same as it had been with everyone except Naomi—exciting only in the moments leading up. He took too long fumbling with the condom—a brand she recognized from the free bowls in the library bathroom. Afterwards, they lay in his bed surrounded by his college hockey trophies and stacks of John le Carré novels. If she had been more drawn to him, she might have found those details endearing, an insight into another side of his character. But the room was dank. It smelled faintly of mildew. He politely asked if she wanted to spend the night, but seemed relieved when she declined.

Zemadi began dragging Vega along to a weekly lecture series in Knox Hall. The topics were esoteric, with long titles punctuated by colons that Vega thought could be expressed more succinctly. In Pursuit of Home: How Cross-Border Networks Affect Returnees' Migration Intentions; Emergent Boundaries and Identities: Asian and Hispanic Panethnicity Compared. She liked to tease Zemadi about these lecture topics. "On the Selecting of Outerwear," she said, watching Zemadi pull on her coat. "Weather-Related Decision-Making Among Contemporary African Graduate Students."

But she found the events strangely comforting. She was particularly drawn to the types of subjects Reddy had flippantly called "the soft social sciences"—issues not of life or death or disease, but of longing or statelessness. She listened to stories of Filipina migrant domestic workers, transnational adoptees born in Ethiopia and raised in the States. "We're supposed to recognize how lucky we are," one woman said. "We're supposed to realize that we were rescued from a life of hunger and poverty and unwantedness. But we have to acknowledge multiple truths; there is something missing when you're taken from

your country." Days before the enrollment deadline, she dropped her
Statistics course and instead registered for a class called Race and Making America. As usual, she had little to contribute to class discussions,
but the books drew her in. One afternoon, in a cramped corner table at
Max Caffé, she began reading *I Know Why the Caged Bird Sings*, going
back to her apartment only when the café closed and finishing the book
long after midnight, barely able to keep her eyes open, but unable to
put it down. She returned, over and over, to the author's description of
sex: *I had not considered how physical the act would be. I had anticipated
long kisses and gentle touches. But there was nothing romantic about the
knee which forced my legs open, nor in the rub of hairy skin on my chest.*
In the bathroom, she stared at her ashen face and red eyes, embarrassed
that this page, of all pages, of all she had read about war and migration
and health disparities, was the one that affected her the most.

I n India, she was one of the darker-skinned girls, a fact that she wore
proudly. In New York, she looked faded, her skin flaking and her lips
painfully dry. She was reminded of Cleveland, when she would study
the tips of her hair and find them brown and splitting, like a dying crop.

"It's the climate here," Halima said. "You need Vaseline. And when
was the last time you did an oil bath?"

"I didn't even bring any hair oil with me."

"All you need is coconut. How do you maintain curly hair without
using oil?"

They were seated on the couch, reading a copy of *Vogue*. The previous tenant received a wealth of subscriptions that still arrived each
month. *Cooking Light* and *Good Housekeeping*, they recycled immediately. *National Geographic* and *Newsweek* Vega skimmed out of obligation. But they poured over *Vogue* together. Halima's tastes had
evolved beyond High Fashion. On Sunday afternoons they walked to
Housing Works, where Halima looked through racks of strappy heels
and tank tops, trying to put together some approximation of what they
saw on the pages. Vega sorted through scuffed soles, examined shirts to

ensure they weren't missing buttons. She tried on dresses she knew she would never wear. They roamed the makeup counters of Macy's and came home with lipstick samples that Halima, with her pale skin and brown-tinted hair, was able to pull off. On Vega, they looked garish.

One afternoon at Macy's, she saw an Indian girl, maybe twelve or thirteen, following her mother around the appliance section. There were plenty of Indians in New York, but the ones Vega saw were either university students or professionals in their twenties or thirties, riding the subway dressed in medical scrubs or navy suits. This girl wore a long braid that dangled over her shoulder and a hooded sweatshirt. Vega watched her trail behind her mother, looking bored, studying anything of relative interest—a canister of rubber spatulas, baking sheets—idly running her fingers over the bar codes and nodding to whatever her mother was saying, in the manner of someone who knew she wasn't being spoken to, but spoken around. Vega left the cosmetics section and walked behind them. The mother was speaking Gujarati, and she could make out a few Hindi cognates.

She trailed behind as they rode the escalator to the third floor, watching as they sorted through racks of girls' sweaters. Sometimes, the daughter would pull something from the rack and carry it over for her mother's approval. She noted how the space between them expanded and shrunk as they walked, how the mother inspected seams and examined the quality of the fabric, how the daughter swung her arms—gangly, overgrown, still more a child than a teenager.

That night, she sat on the kitchen floor as Halima worked coconut oil into her scalp. Halima's fingers weren't nimble and rough like Rukmini's. Instead, she was slow and painstaking, separating Vega's hair into sections and gently brushing out the tangles. But Vega was reminded of those long afternoons, anyway, seated next to Ashwini, the room thick with the smell of neem oil, Rukmini's sharp, black comb scraping her ears.

"Your hair will be lovely in the morning," Halima said. "Nice, soft curls."

She slept with her hair wrapped in one of the thin Kerala towels

Rukmini had packed for her. The next morning in the shower, she rested her forehead on the tile as she let the water run down her back. She wanted to feel something, anything, good. In place of Naomi, she tried to imagine Erick's hand, then his tongue. She put her hand on her breast, then slipped her fingers between her legs. Through the closed door, she could hear the blare of the morning news, Halima talking back to the television and rummaging for something in the closet. The phone rang. The microwave beeped. She tried to orgasm, but nothing happened.

One Friday evening, Halima asked Vega to come to her fiancé's aunt and uncle's house in Queens. "You seem lonely," she said. "Maybe it will be a nice break."

"I'm not lonely."

"You have a multitude of social engagements?"

"I didn't say I was busy. I only said that I'm not lonely."

Halima waved off the distinction. On the subway, she told Vega the story about the library at the University of Massachusetts, where she had spent the previous weekend visiting Adnan. Vega hadn't done much that weekend. She had gone shopping at High Fashion with Zemadi, then—because Zemadi had plans with some friends from undergrad—spent the remaining day and a half working on a paper and eating the leftovers that Halima had left in the fridge. It wasn't terrible, but it wasn't enjoyable, either. Was that what loneliness felt like?

"The university wanted to build the tallest library in the state," Halima said. "Twenty-eight floors. But after one week, the bricks started crumbling. Do you know what was happening?"

"Ghosts."

"Idiot. Nothing of the sort. The architect hadn't accounted for the weight of the books. So they've had to cordon off the top floor. It can't be used because the architect did not have simple common sense. Americans are like this!"

Vega laughed. "This can't be the real reason." It was the sort of indulgent conversation Sukumar Reddy would want to engage in. If he were telling the story, though, he would add fictional layers that elevated his heroism. How he had seen the blueprints and tried to caution the architect—a pompous white man who refused Reddy's advice.

"It's one hundred percent true," Halima said. "Adnan has a clipping of an article. I'll have him send it." She changed the subject, describing an eyebrow-threading salon where she wanted to go after dinner. "The family is asleep by nine o'clock anyway."

The aunt, Nur Chachi, had been a Montessori teacher in Karachi. "You know Montessori?" she asked, in a slow, excruciatingly patient Urdu. "All mixed ages. They have them in India?"

"Yes, Aunty. They do."

"I was head teacher there," she said, switching to English. Here in Queens, she had worked briefly as an assistant in a Head Start program. "The children here, no good. Too much behavior problem." She took in tailoring now and showed Vega her most recent job—a child's dress, a sequined affair with a torn zipper that she had mended by hand.

The uncle, Faisal Chacha, drove a taxi, though he had been an accountant in Pakistan. "Six days each week," he said, pushing a plate of pakoras towards Vega. In English, he asked, "You're married?"

"No, Uncle."

"Get married. Be like this girl. She has a good future. You have a good husband, then you don't have so much work. Take care of the house, the children. Husband gives good support."

Vega wondered what support Faisal Chacha expected from Adnan, a man completing his doctorate in poetry. But she went along with it. "That's good advice, Uncle."

Over dinner, Nur Chachi proceeded with a list of questions: What work did Vega's parents do? Were they Hindu? Did she have brothers and sisters? At the last question, Vega steadied herself. "No, Aunty. I'm the only child."

Nur Chachi pointed to the wall, lined with framed photographs of what appeared to be the same boy: as a toddler being swung into the air;

at age seven or eight, holding a baseball bat; as a teenager on a podium, receiving some award. "Like our Javed," she said solemnly. "Only child. We had only him." For a terrible moment, Vega assumed that Javed was dead, until Faisal Chacha said, "He'll come soon. He has chess club."

As promised, Halima led Vega afterwards to a shop called Thread House, at the center of a strip mall, located next to a garish-looking boutique called Rahul Fashion Bazaar. Inside, a Punjabi woman named Komal waved Vega to a chair and tilted her head back.

"Not too thin," Vega said. "I like it to look natural."

Komal tucked one end of the thread between her teeth and begun winding it around Vega's eyebrows. In Hindi, she asked Halima about wedding plans.

"Coming along," Halima said.

"You'll do waxing here? Before the wedding."

"I have a lady in Karachi who does it."

Komal grunted. She finished the threading quickly, scattering bits of eyebrow hairs across Vega's face, then handed her a small mirror. "Better, no?"

Vega grudgingly accepted that it was an improvement. "Yes. Thank you."

"You need lip?"

"I usually do my lip on my own."

"On your own isn't working. You're South Indian?"

"Yes."

"That is why you have mustache."

"Do both," Halima said.

"I don't think I need both." But Komal wasn't listening. She ran the thread over her lip, then held up the offending hair as evidence.

The waxing took place in a back room, behind a curtain, where a woman, who looked Tibetan or Nepalese, slid Vega's underwear to the side and, using a tongue depressor, smeared one side of her vagina with a warm, honey-like substance. "You have too much hair," she said. "Your husband has no problem?"

"I don't have a husband."

The woman pressed a piece of paper against the matted hair and pulled it loose. Vega winced. "When you have husband," the woman said, "you come every week. Make him happy."

Halima was jittery after leaving the Thread House. Wedding talk seemed to be making her nervous, and she spent the walk complaining about Adnan's mother, a woman who was taking an abrupt turn towards religious adherence and was suddenly insistent that Halima wear a long-sleeved bridal lehenga. "And she used to be a *biology* teacher," Halima said. "Now she's lecturing everyone about virtue."

They climbed the steps to the subway station and settled on a wooden bench. "Whatever happened to your roommate? She had to move so abruptly?"

Neither Halima nor Zemadi had mentioned Naomi in the month since Vega moved into Halima's apartment and, though Vega was grateful for their silence, she sensed they must have suspected something. She could not guess *what* they suspected; what had transpired with Naomi must have been beyond the bounds of Halima's imagination.

"She has a fellowship in Austin."

"This semester?"

Vega wondered what would happen if she just confessed everything to Halima. She thought about Naomi so often that she was hardly aware she was even thinking of her, but there was always this faint presence in her mind, this reimagining of their lives together. Maybe it would be a disaster to tell Halima this. Or maybe it would be a comfort. "The fellowship starts in the fall. I think she needed to save money."

"Next question. Why isn't there a man in your life?"

Vega wasn't ready to move on from the subject of Naomi, but she wasn't sure she had a choice. "Because I don't want a mother-in-law dictating my sleeve length."

"Come on. You aren't lonely?"

"Aren't you? You've been to Massachusetts only three times in the past year."

Halima didn't say anything for a moment, and Vega assumed that she was quietly conceding the point. Then she said, "But I'm not *alone.* Loneliness is when you don't have anybody. Why don't you? There must be plenty of interested men."

"I don't quite know what to do with men." She felt drunk, though certainly there was no reason she would be. The last thing she had consumed was a cup of green tea at Nur Chachi and Faisal Chacha's table.

"Vega. Really. It isn't complicated."

"Not in that sense. I know what to do in bed. You climb on top. Or they climb on top. A few minutes, then everybody moves on."

Halima laughed. "I don't know about that."

"Perhaps you wouldn't. You, of the long-sleeved bridal wear."

"Enough," Halima said, still laughing. Then she tugged the end of Vega's braid. "You'll find somebody. Insha'Allah."


In February, Vega's advisor, Dr. Lipman, learned of a work-study opportunity at an alternative high school in Brooklyn called the Hope Center. "Any internship is coveted," Dr. Lipman said, in a tone that suggested that this particular one was not. "This is a way for you to contribute to the university's community engagement, while also developing the social context for your research interests."

Two mornings each week, Vega rode the subway one hour into East Williamsburg, where, standing in front of a windowless classroom, she taught from a prescribed curriculum called Workplace Communication. Most of her students fidgeted throughout class, but a few simply put their heads on their desks and slept. As she wrote on the blackboard to demonstrate the use of commas and the capitalization of proper nouns, she was reminded of the inane sentences she used to copy from her Wren and Martin composition book in primary school. *Horatio Nelson was a man of might. Thomas Edison invented the phonograph.* Once, she tried to jostle a sleeping student, and the girl swatted Vega's arm and said, "Leave me the fuck alone."

Over the phone, Rukmini said, "Such a noble pursuit. Being a teacher."

"It isn't quite what you're imagining," Vega said. "We aren't sitting under a banyan tree, discussing philosophy."

"Even grammar is noble. You remember those girls at the British Council? How much they loved you?"

"They loved me because I was an upper-caste girl and I spoke fluent English, so they felt they had to be deferential." Shamefully, she missed this deference. This was something she was learning about America: nobody seemed to defer to anybody.

"My belief has always been," Rukmini said, "that it is good to analyze. But when we analyze to the extent that we become unhappy, then we should force ourselves to think a little bit less."

In her fourth week at the Hope Center, Vega received a new assignment. She was given a small classroom of her own, composed of three teenagers, one from Haiti and the other two so inseparable that Vega assumed they were sisters, until she learned that one was from Mexico and the other Honduras. There, her childhood history with Wren and Martin composition books proved useful. Every morning, they diagramed new sentences, slowly making them longer and more elaborate. *I drink coffee. I drink hot coffee. I drink hot coffee with my mother.* One afternoon, the Haitian student, Angeline, uttered the group's first spontaneous English statement: "My mother no here."

"My mother is not here," Vega corrected, trying not to look too eager. It was astonishing. Like watching a child take its first steps.

"My mother is not here."

"Where is your mother?"

"My mother in Gonaives." The room went quiet, then Angeline said, "I drink coffee with my grandmother."

One March afternoon, Halima's fiancé called. "Adnan here," he said. "Halima isn't home," Vega said. "At the library, I think." She switched to Hindi—a language she stumbled through under any circumstances, made more clunky by the disconnect with Urdu. Still, with Adnan, the exchange made her nostalgic.

"Is the semester going well?" he asked.

"It is. You?"

"Well enough. Halima and I must be out of step. I just came from the library."

"Not the twenty-eighth floor, I hope."

He laughed. "Halima told you the story? These Americans. I tell you." He told her he was working at a coffee shop in Amherst. "Kuch bakhshish mil jati hai," he said. *Paid only in tips.* "When I go back to Karachi, I'll never be rude to another server again."

Vega hadn't thought much about Adnan until moving into Halima's apartment. The whole arrangement had seemed so typical—two people entering marriage with all the contractual obligations of religion and family. But she was surprised by Halima's tenderness whenever they spoke, her concern when he told her about the weather in New England or his literary rejections. "You're brilliant. Art takes time. The cold won't last forever." Listening to these conversations, Vega always felt as though she were intruding.

Now, Adnan said, "Please tell her I called. Tell her not to work so hard. To take breaks."

The apartment felt emptier after they hung up, and Vega was too distracted to return to her books. She grabbed her coat and walked outside. She assumed Naomi was still staying at her mother's place, but it seemed illogical that they hadn't yet run into each other on campus.

She walked up Amsterdam Avenue, ducking briefly into a falafel shop before deciding she wasn't hungry. She walked to Erick's apartment and then, in the vestibule, changed her mind. She bought a tea from the Bangladeshi corner store, then found a bench on 122nd Street, a block from the building she and Naomi had shared. She watched people pass until she drained her cup.

# 8

On a cold Tuesday in April, Vega received a call from the Financial Aid office. She was walking into the apartment just as the voice on the answering machine cut off. When she called back, a woman named Candace spoke to her slowly, in the tone of a medical professional delivering a grave prognosis. "You better come in," she said.

The next morning, she sat across from Candace, a glass bowl of peppermints between them. Candace took a deep breath. "I guess we should just get into it, then. We received an update from your university. You earned sixteen transferrable credits at University of Hyderabad." She pronounced the name slowly, with a dramatic roll of the r.

Vega had been expecting something far worse. An announcement that the scholarship was canceled, or that she had fallen short of some academic requirement. "Is that all? I attended university in Hyderabad for one semester."

"Here's the issue. The Gifford covers your tuition through forty-two credits. According to your transcript, you have a full semester already completed."

"I was told those weren't relevant to the scholarship, that only select universities qualified," Vega said.

Candace smiled grimly. "The only exceptions we make are for students from conflict zones. Which, unfortunately, your records indicate you are not."

Only later, when recounting the conversation to Halima and Zemadi, did Vega appreciate the absurdity of that line. Now, she sat across the table and stared at the stack of Post-its between them, where Candace was writing down numbers. "What exactly does this mean?"

"Well, the good news is you can finish a semester early. We had you on track for next spring or summer, but you can be finished by Christmas. At the close of the fall semester."

"My visa is valid as long as I'm enrolled as a full-time student."

"Precisely."

"This means I am effectively asked to leave after the fall. In six months."

"Well, your scholarship ends then. As with all of our graduate students, you can certainly exceed credits, but you will have to pay the tuition directly."

There was a flash of relief, until Candace showed her the numbers, divided into three columns. "We're looking at $10,700 for tuition," she said. "Then on top of that, the scholarship covers room and board, which would cost you $7,000. There's the health insurance fee, at $400. So, we should plan for $18,100."

Vega had never thought about the cost of schooling in such stark terms. She had grown up watching her mother haggle at markets, and occasionally would do so herself. Yet tuition at the Rhodes School, and later Sri Vidya and Hyderabad, was a set expense. Growing up, all of the families she knew sent their children to the same rotation of schools: Sishya, Bishop Cotton School for Boys, St. Agnes. There was only one person, a distant cousin, whose family had registered him for government school. "Tamil-medium school!" her mother had said. "They're crippling the boy."

It was a particularly jarring comment, given that the boy's father had survived polio as a child and walked with a limp. Nonetheless, nobody disagreed. Her mother had announced this at a family gathering, and another aunt, unrelated to the boy in question, said, "Might as well cut off his arms and legs."

Vega held the Post-it. "Where is this money supposed to come from?" She immediately regretted the question. That was not Candace's problem. Her job was only to deliver the news.

"Well, if you have an American guarantor, you might be eligible for private loans. And then we can offset with some work-study hours." Candace said something about borrowing money from family and friends, describing a Kuwaiti student who had contacted his former high school. "You won't believe the generosity of your family and social networks. People are *often* surprised." But Vega was only half listening. Candace had circled the number. Eighteen thousand dollars. In her head, Vega converted the figure to rupees. Then she folded the Post-it, tucked it into her pocket, and walked outside.

"Always, there is a solution," her father had said that night. "We'll find the money. You concentrate on your studies."

His voice was comforting. But it was her mother, who took the phone from him midsentence and shouted, "This is disastrous! You've lost your funds!" who seemed to be addressing the truth of the matter.

"You need a job," Halima said after Vega had hung up.

"I'm on a student visa. I can't have a job. Not a substantial one, at least."

"There are ways around that. I'll talk to some people I know."

She and Zemadi met for coffee the next day. "You might earn dollars here and there," Zemadi said. "But nothing to cover the entire cost. Not without private loans. The high-interest ones available to international students." A friend of hers had spent the previous summer working as a nanny for a family on the Upper West Side. "Forty hours a week, and they paid her well. Under the table and all. But still, it was enough only to cover her rent. Tuition, that's an entirely different matter."

They normally split the bill evenly. This time, Zemadi paid. "We'll find a solution. If nothing else, there are always people you can rely on."

She was supposed to visit Shoba the next morning and was happy when the rain gave her an excuse to cancel. She had wasted hours staring at Candace's Post-it, trying to make sense of the numbers, and couldn't imagine spending a full day in the stasis of Shoba's house. "I'll come next week," she said. "Hundred percent promise."

She had last been to New Jersey months earlier, shortly after Shoba had given birth, and had spent the day offering meaningless words of comfort as Shoba tried to coax her nipple into the baby's mouth. Shoba's mother hovered in the distance, a rail-thin, taciturn woman who occupied herself by grinding spices and boiling vats of kashayam that she claimed would help Shoba's milk supply. She intended to stay for the first six months, and her presence assuaged Vega's guilt over not visiting more often. At least Shoba wasn't alone.

"Maybe the weather will be nice next week," she said to Shoba. "We can take the baby for a walk." She wished she could explain her financial aid situation, but she knew Shoba would respond with the only solution she could ever think to offer: *Come to the house. We'll cook for you.* Months ago, Shoba and Mohan's spare room might have been an option—an inconvenient one, but an option nonetheless. Now, Shoba's mother was sleeping on the bed, and the rest of the room was occupied by a bassinet, a humidifier, and the rocking chair where Shoba spent most of her days, either lulling the baby to sleep or rousing her to eat.

"Amma says I shouldn't take her outside until June. Her immune system isn't strong yet."

"Then we'll stay inside," Vega said. "I don't mind." She hung up too abruptly, accidentally cutting off Shoba as she was saying, "I miss you, Akka."

A week after Vega's meeting with Candace from Financial Aid, her father came through with an offer: three thousand dollars that, with the help of ICICI Bank, he would deposit directly into her student account.

"That's too much," she said to him. To Halima, she told the truth. "It's a sixth of what I need."

"A sixth is better than nothing."

They were eating grilled cheese sandwiches slathered with chili pickle. Halima had arranged slices of pre-made cookie dough onto a baking sheet. The smells mingled—garlicky and sweet in the same inhalation.

"It will help with tuition," Vega said. "But then there's everything else."

The remaining challenge was housing. They both knew this, though neither had openly acknowledged it. Now, Halima broke the silence with an offer. "You can squat in my room," she said. "We'll bring in another roommate. She can pay half, and you and I can each pay a quarter."

Vega laughed. "You would really want to share a bedroom with me?"

"If it allows you to stay here."

"Something will work out," Vega said. They finished their sandwiches, then the cookies, and retreated to their separate rooms.

"How do you afford your apartment?" she asked Erick. It was a rare departure from their typical exchanges—brief, one-sided discussion of sports or foreign policy, followed quickly by sex.

"What do you mean, how do I afford it? We manage."

"*We?* But you live alone."

"Well, my parents help, as long as I'm in school. And by the way, that's a pretty typical arrangement."

"How generous of them." She hadn't meant to sound bitter, but it came out that way, and now she had no interest in making amends. Of all the Americans she had met, Naomi was the only one who talked openly about money, who was preoccupied by scholarships and teaching stipends and fellowships. She wished she could call her for advice. She disliked Erick for being unable to provide this, for being such a cheap substitute for Naomi.

"Look, I'm not apologizing for having some wealth. My parents are both lawyers. My mother made partner *before* my father did. And if you think it's easy for a woman to climb the ranks at a firm, you're crazy. They worked their asses off."

"I'm not asking you to apologize." She had said something similar to Zemadi once: "It isn't my choice, to be Brahmin. It's a thing you're given, that you can't give back. Even if you *want* to."

"Plus," Erick said, "I'm not sitting on generations of wealth here. My parents were working class. My grandparents survived the Depression. They pulled themselves up from nothing."

# 9

At the close of the summer, Vega's mother sent her an email, using an abundance of capital letters. *Call SUDHA. She Lives in NEW YORK. White Plains.*

Vega ignored the email. Rukmini called later that week.

"We saw Sudha's mother at Kalyani's wedding—you remember Kalyani? She was very upset that you haven't contacted them. Sudha's husband is a gastroenterologist. They have a large house just near Manhattan. You can stay beginning immediately."

Vega knew she had to accept the offer, but the thought of it was miserable. "I love living with you," she told Halima.

"You can love staying with me on the weekends," Halima said. "Free housing is free housing. This way, you can afford to finish the next two semesters. Go."

Sudha was one in a pair of sisters Vega had known growing up: Sudha and Ramya. They were distant family friends, notably pretty, about a decade older than Vega. She could not remember a single conversation she had ever had with either of them, but at the White Plains Amtrak train station, Sudha pulled her close. When she stepped back, she had a mournful expression—an attempt, Vega knew, to offer condolences without talking directly about Ashwini. "How is your family? You've all been so very much on my mind."

"We're all well," Vega said.

Sudha seemed content with Vega's answer, or eager to move on to an easier conversation. "You should have called on the first day. I was furious when I learned you were here. Living in some drab student housing. I called Ramya immediately when I heard."

She led Vega through the parking lot. "You'll find White Plains has a more cosmopolitan feel than most suburbs," she said. She was still pretty, Vega noted, but in a way that reflected some effort— henna-tinted hair, eyeliner, a gauzy kurta over black leggings. "There is a better quality of life. More of a small-town demographic, but an urban feel." She spoke with a hint of a British accent, though Vega was certain that Sudha, like she, had spent her childhood in Adyar.

Her Christmas Day taxi aside, Vega hadn't been in a car since rid-ing beside Mohan in New Jersey. Sudha's was plusher, with leather seats and a seat belt that extended itself with the push of a button. Mohan's car, she recalled, had only two doors, so that she would have to wait until Shoba got out and folded her seat forward, then climb out through the narrow space, as though exiting a cave. "Soon we have to sell it," Shoba had told her. "For a *minivan*." It was another English word that seemed to thrill her with its promise.

"Our girls will be so happy to meet you," Sudha said. "The young-est, especially. She loves guests."

"I look forward to it. I like children."

Sudha pulled into a gas station and opened her window. A tur-baned Sikh man took her credit card. When the window was again rolled up, she said, "Most of the Indians here are not gas station–types. Most are professionals. One of our friends, he is a gastroenterologist, and she is an OB." She lowered the window and took her credit card, signing her name without glancing up. As they drove away, she said, "They're *industrious*, these Punjabis. That much I will tell you. But they are here only to work. Send money to their villages. That's the mentality."

"I wish I could be so useful to my village," Vega said.

Sudha didn't respond. She navigated the roads instinctively, ca-reening past one turn and taking another identical one. To Vega, there was something disorienting about it all—this woman she had known since childhood, driving through this alien place as though it was the only one where she had ever lived.

"It's both good and bad," Sudha said suddenly. "Having these people."

"Meaning?"

"The girls will hear comments. Anjali is more attuned to it, of course. Maya is so small that it doesn't quite register. She's a *happier* child. Anything negative, she chooses not to notice. But their classmates only see brown faces when they go to buy gas, or to these 7-Eleven stores. It's hardly their fault, really, that they form certain assumptions."

Sudha's husband, Rakesh, had attended the Doon School, followed by the University of Pennsylvania and Johns Hopkins Medical School—facts emblazoned on the bumper of his car, a stack of alumni magazines, and one of the mugs upturned on the drying rack.

"You know Doon?" he asked. He was wearing an apron and slicing tomatoes.

"I've heard of it," Vega said.

"It's the kind of place that really builds you. Intellectually, in character, sport. Archery. Debate. You name it. But also, the qualities of sportsmanship. What it means to be part of a team."

"I play soccer," Maya said. "And gymnastics." When Vega and Sudha arrived, she had run to the door and hugged them both, then led Vega into her small bedroom where she showed her a purple pin with seven gold stars circling it. "I'm reader of the month," she said. "Two more books and I get a free pizza." Now, downstairs, she was drinking a glass of orange juice and arranging the tomatoes in overlapping circles.

"We only eat Indian food once or twice a week," Sudha said. "I hope you don't mind. Rakesh loves to experiment. He makes a lot of global food. Vegetarian, of course, although Maya eats chicken. I tell him sometimes he could have been a chef." She glanced toward the staircase and said in a low voice, "Anjali will come when she's ready." Vega would come to know the tone well—a practiced, contrived calm that Sudha often used when she talked about her elder daughter. "She likes to be uninterrupted when she's studying."

Rakesh squeezed a lemon into a bowl, then poured in olive oil. "When I arrived at Penn, I found I was far more prepared than half my classmates," he said. "I found my courses quite easy, in comparison."

"Well, in terms of *math*," Sudha said. "Of course, American schools can't compete with Indian schools in math instruction. Anyway, I often tell Rakesh how grateful I am that we didn't have a boy, or he would have packed him up and sent him to Doon. That's how much he loved it."

"I'm glad I'm not a boy," Maya said. "I don't want to go away. I want to stay here forever and ever and ever."

Anjali joined them just before dinner, mumbled an introduction, and began setting the plates as Maya followed behind with the utensils. The family ate their rice with a fork, compelling Vega to wipe her hands on a napkin and reach for hers.

"Vega is enrolled at Columbia," Rakesh said to Anjali.

Anjali raised her eyebrows. "I'm aware."

"These things matter," Rakesh said, looking at Vega, as though asking her to confirm his point. "You'll find out soon enough."

The food was surprisingly satisfying—a cumin-heavy rice pilaf, skewered chunks of eggplant and tofu, a spicy tomato chutney. But the conversation was too stilted, and the room too quiet, to enjoy the meal. In New York, she and Halima kept their windows propped open, often mistaking the noise from the street for each other's voices. Here she was aware of every sound—the scraping of the utensils, her own chewing, Maya sipping her juice.

"Anjali is a voracious reader," Sudha said. "She always has a book in hand."

"Both girls do," Rakesh said.

Because Maya seemed happily occupied, spearing a tomato, Vega turned to Anjali. "What sort of books are you reading in school?"

Anjali shrugged. "The usual. Dead white men, and then in February, they assign *Black Boy*." She took two bites in quick succession.

"Kanna," Sudha said. "Slow down."

Anjali reached across the table for more pilaf.

"I'm reading *Misty of Chincoteague*," Maya said.

"Everything is racismsexism," Rakesh said, blending them into a single word. "That is the theme of our lives these days."

Sudha put her hand on his wrist. "Vega is a sociologist," she said to Anjali. "She would be a good person to speak with about your interests."

Anjali looked briefly interested, then caught her mother's eye and looked down. "Maybe."

"Anjali bought me *The Lion, the Witch and the Wardrobe*," Maya said. "But I'm not going to read it until next year." The conversation moved from books to tennis lessons, to a chocolate pudding recipe Maya wanted to try, but Vega was stuck on the reference to *The Lion, the Witch and the Wardrobe*. Ashwini had discovered C. S. Lewis during their year in Cleveland. In the past, she had mostly read books that Vega passed down to her—R.K. Narayan and Jane Austen—less because she was interested in them, Vega realized now, and more to please her older sister. In Cleveland, she zipped through C. S. Lewis, then Tolkien and Richard Adams. She carted the books back to India and kept them in a stack by her bed. She had been rereading *Tales from Watership Down* when she died, a bookmark at its center, and Vega wondered if this had been a premonition. If Ashwini had been afraid of starting a story that she knew she would never finish.

After dinner, Vega packed the leftovers while Sudha loaded the dishwasher and Rakesh left the room to review the girls' homework. "She was a pleasant child when she was little. An *easy* child. I used to think it was jealousy, but really, she loves Maya. She's a wonderful sister." She closed the dishwasher and filled a kettle. "It's nice to have company. Rakesh goes to bed by nine. He likes to run in the morning and has to be at the office by seven o'clock."

The tea was herbal, served without milk or sugar, in a mug that read JHU Medical. Again, Vega missed Halima—her thick chai and platter of biscuits. The blare of *The X-Files*.

"Did you go to college in the States?" Vega asked. "I don't recall exactly when you left."

Sudha wrinkled her nose. "SUNY Oneonta," she said.

"Not a good experience?"

"It was fine, really. Coming from Madras, I didn't know better. They gave me a scholarship and I accepted it. Doon, being so prestigious, of course, Rakesh had people guiding him in the process. I didn't even know what an Ivy League university was. A vague sense, maybe, but I never would have applied." She blew on her tea. "Anjali has her eye on Smith. Rakesh, of course, is hoping for Penn. You know the college programs here are really geared towards making the children very competitive."

"Is it numerically possible for all the children to be competitive?" Vega asked. "Surely, if they're all competing with each other, some will make it and some won't."

Sudha opened a cabinet and began looking for something—sugar, Vega hoped—though it turned out to be a jar of multivitamins. "Well, the top ones work hard for their acceptances. I can say that for certain. Anjali's bedroom light is usually on long after we've gone to sleep." The phone rang, and she took the call in the sitting room next to the kitchen, mouthing *sorry* to Vega and holding up a finger to excuse herself.

Vega carried her mug into the living room where Maya was sprawled on the floor, eating apple slices and reading. "I'm stuck on a word," she said, sliding her book towards Vega.

"'Ephemeral.' It means 'temporary.'"

Maya gave her a wide smile that Vega realized, over the months, was easily won—in exchange for extracting a splinter, scrambling an egg, or reviewing rows of multiplication tables. "You're a really good teacher," she said.

On Tuesdays and Thursdays, Sudha dropped Vega at the train station before driving to her speech and hearing clinic in Tarrytown. "Rakesh and I just hate the thought of you wandering around the city for the full day without a place to go. It's not a safe area. If it were NYU, it would be one thing. But Columbia . . ."

It puzzled Vega, Rakesh and Sudha's fear of the city. Sudha had grown up in Madras, and Rakesh in the chaos of Delhi—a city Vega had only visited once on a family trip, Rukmini gripping her daughters' hands as they wove through Khan Market, Chandni Chowk, Humayun's Tomb. Her mother had refused to carry a purse, instead clipping a fold of rupees to the inside of her sari blouse. Years later, when Vega proposed applying for college in Delhi, Rukmini had shuddered. "Northerners are lawless," she had said.

"I'm in classes for most of the day," Vega said to Sudha. "And I have the library. Really, it's fine."

She had initially planned to spend those nights in the city, but Halima's roommate arrangement—a Japanese medical student—had fallen through. She was living with an architecture student named Caitlin who was sensitive to noise, allergic to dust, and explicitly requested that Halima not have overnight guests.

"I miss you," Halima said. "This idiot writes her name on her yogurt cups. As though I would eat flavored yogurt. We have designated refrigerator shelves."

She saw Erick once, while leaving the Low Library, and was relieved when he didn't suggest they get together. Instead, he updated her on his PhD applications. Acceptance letters were coming in. He had heard from three programs but, ironically, was still waiting on Columbia. "Political science is so cutthroat," he said. "There's really no point unless you attend a top program."

By winter, she was spending less time in the city. She had come to appreciate the ease of Sudha and Rakesh's home. There were fluffy hand towels and citrusy soaps in the bathroom. Bowls of fruit seemed to magically refill themselves, as did the fridge—with gallons of the 2 percent milk that Sudha favored, tubs of Stonyfield Farm yogurt, and packets of pre-sliced cheese. A woman named Rosario came in the mornings to wash and fold the laundry. Every evening, Vega's clothes were tightly stacked on her bed.

"We pay her very well," Sudha said. "This isn't like India, in that respect. And we never asked questions about papers or anything. My belief? Anyone who is willing to work deserves to make a living."

"She makes the best hot cocoa," Maya said. "She puts cinnamon in it."

"She's very good with Maya," Sudha said. "Very maternal and warm."

But it was this warmth that made Vega uncomfortable. In India, she was used to Vasanti's distant, scowling presence, her habit of working around Vega to avoid extended interactions. Rosario had her own set of keys and a pair of pink house slippers that she kept inside the closet. Maya hugged her when she came in, and Sudha always asked about her children.

"They're fine, Mrs. Ramkrishnan," Rosario always said. "Very good, very good."

"Rosario has the nicest boys," Sudha said. "Really, such polite children."

When bowls were chipped or clothes outgrown, Sudha set them aside to be given to Rosario so she could donate them to her church. "I always say, one man's trash is another's treasure."

"Unless it's broken, and it's actually trash," Anjali said. "Like, objectively trash."

# 10

The family planned to spend the first two weeks of June in Prague, an invitation from one of Rakesh's former classmates from Doon, who worked for the State Department. "Ten years ago, I wouldn't have said, let's go see Eastern Europe," Rakesh said. "You see, the world is really changing." He bought a Lonely Planet travel guide and tasked Anjali with developing a map, marking all the cathedrals they should visit. Afterwards, they would all travel to Denmark, where he would be attending a Bioethics Conference and the girls would continue sightseeing. Maya, in preparation, was reading *Number the Stars.*

"I so wish you could come," Sudha said. "The visa thing is just such a pain."

"I don't mind," Vega said. She had been relieved by the family's plans and was looking forward to a few quiet weeks, split between White Plains and Manhattan. Her graduate program ended in August, and she was due to fly back to Madras. She still hadn't accepted the finality of the move home, so she tried not to think about it. Instead, she focused on enjoying her summer. She was enrolled in one independent study course at Columbia and was also volunteering two mornings a week in Brooklyn, assisting with summer ESL classes. It was minimal work, overall, but enough to give her a sense of purpose. Halima's roommate would be away for most of June, and Vega imagined staying in the 123rd Street apartment until she had her fill, then returning to the tranquility of an empty house, studying here and there, then going back to the city when she was bored.

She had briefly considered staying in New York. Earlier that spring, she had been offered an unpaid research fellowship at CUNY Graduate Center, studying immigrant student enrollment in higher education. But sitting in the program information session, reading over the project abstract and timeline, it became clear that the fellowship simply didn't excite her. It sounded too easy—a bit of administrative work, some editing of grant applications, transcription of student interviews. She had loved the intensity of her two years at Columbia—how fatigued and dry-throated she was after a day of teaching ESL, how bleary eyed and triumphant after each paper she submitted. Recently, she came upon an essay she had written during her first fall semester, on the subject of government school-nutrition programs in India, and she was shocked to realize how imprecise her language was then, how lax and long-winded her sentences. She did not fully realize, until that moment, how much sharper she was now than when she first arrived.

But something else was tugging at her. She was homesick. She missed her parents, the smell of her childhood house. She wanted to walk to the beach. Sleep in the bedroom she used to share with Ashwini.

The day after she declined the offer, the professor in charge of the program, Margo Fink, called and asked Vega to coffee. They met at an Au Bon Pain next to the CUNY campus. Margo paid for the drinks, and they settled into a cramped, corner table. "I'm not here to convince you to accept the fellowship," Margo said. "I understand if it's a bit beneath your pay grade." She paused. "That was a joke, given that it is beneath anyone's pay grade."

Vega laughed. "International students don't have pay grades. We have visa considerations."

"Well, given your background, I think you probably made the right decision. But I was reading your writing sample, and I wanted you to know that you have real precision with your language and your thoughts. I hope that you consider further graduate work."

"I intend to," Vega said. She had been thinking about doctoral work in some loose, far-off way, but now she imagined it with more clarity. She described her work teaching ESL, her growing interest in researching the lives of migrant children. "I need more field experience in India before beginning a PhD," she told Margo. "I think there is value to working in one's home country for some time." Even as she said it, she wondered if she was just making an excuse, justifying her childish need to see her parents. As they parted ways, Margo said to Vega, "It sounds like you have a really solid plan." The phrase was comforting. Vega reminded herself over and over, as her final summer approached, that she would get a visa again, this time to return to the States and begin her doctorate. For now, she had a solid plan.

Sudha had made her a tray of lasagna before leaving, a gesture that Vega found slightly infantilizing. But she finished the entire thing within days, along with a carton of pistachio ice cream and two bottles of Merlot that Sudha had told her she should help herself to. She scoured the TV Guide in the late afternoons and curled up with movies she would have been too self-conscious to watch in anyone else's company—A League of Their Own, Waiting to Exhale—falling asleep on the couch and waking to the sound of Anjali's alarm, which Anjali had forgotten to turn off and Vega could not figure out how to permanently silence.

Without the family around, Vega quickly realized that the suburbs were unnavigable without a car. There was reportedly a town bus, but its route was elusive, and Sudha had cautioned Vega against it, saying the people who relied on it were "really, the most desperate, to the point where it's unsafe," adding, "Even Rosario doesn't ride it."

Partly for this reason, it was a relief to return to New York. Her timing was also good; Halima's roommate was packing when she arrived at the apartment.

"So, are you staying for like, the whole summer?" Caitlin asked. She was folding bedding and stuffing it into a duffel bag.

"I'm staying with a family in White Plains. I'll be here one night a week. Maybe two, maximum."

Caitlin looked up and stared at her. Then she picked up a bag and she shoved it on the top shelf of the bedroom closet. "Listen. I was thinking of subletting my room. But then, out of consideration for Halima, I figured I would just keep paying rent."

"Well, I'm glad you worked this out."

"What I mean is, if you're staying here, it wouldn't kill you to kick in some rent. To offset my costs for the time I'm not even here."

It was obvious now why Caitlin was packing her sheets. It wasn't for the purpose of deep storage, in the way Vega put her sweaters away during the summer months. She was worried Vega was going to use them. She wanted to offer to pay the full month of Caitlin's absence, but her financial reality tempered her pride. "If you'd prefer, I'll just stay on the couch."

Caitlin paused and stared at her. "You people are so fucking cheap." The duffel bag was obstructing the door, but she slammed it anyway, forcing it closed.

"It's a relief she's gone," Halima said later that night. "Do you know the idiot thinks I'm from Nepal?"

"I'm surprised she would even bother forming theories about where you're from." Vega told Halima the story of their exchange, embarrassed by her own limp reaction. Halima would have cursed at her in Urdu. Zemadi would have paid for the room, to spite her. Vega had stood there, watching the closet door bounce open again, unable to come up with a clever retort.

"The lady who does her nails is Nepali," Halima said. "Some place on the Upper West Side, and she asked if I knew her. Then she asked me, 'Isn't that where you're from? Nepal?'"

"Where is *she* from?" Vega asked.

Halima shrugged. "Ohio. Or Iowa. Who knows? Is there a bloody difference?"

She, Zemadi, and Halima quickly tumbled back into their old routines. In the evenings they cooked pots of channa masala or paratha and eggs and ate on the floor, plates balanced on their laps, with the windows open and the music always at a low, simmering volume. They studied together, too, reading each other passages from books that moved them. Halima was taking a class called Injury and Violence Prevention, and periodically interrupted to share a statistic that startled her on domestic abuse or American gun violence. "In Pakistan, when there is violence in the home, everybody says, *'Oh, Yeh aapke apne ghar ka maamla hai. Hamen is jhagde men nahin padna.'* It is a matter of your own house. We are not going to get involved in this issue. But imagine if there is a treatment for this sort of thing as a health matter? Then it becomes a public thing we have to talk about." Vega had noticed a shift in her over the two years, a quiet respect for what she used to call "American problems." Now, she was considering doctoral work in a discipline called Community Health and Behavioral Sciences. Vega liked this version of her. She was softer, less dogmatic.

One night, two of Zemadi's friends, a couple from Nairobi named Helen and Jimiyo, joined them. Helen was a medical student at NYU and Jimiyo was an investment banker specializing in proprietary trading.

"I know what those words mean, individually," Vega said. "Together, you may as well be speaking Turkish."

Jimiyo laughed, a wide and honest laugh that made Vega like him immediately. "It's not so complicated. It refers only to banks trading their own assets, rather than the depositors' money, so the profit margins are wider."

"Already I can tell you're bored," Helen said. She accepted a beer from Zemadi, then jabbed Jimiyo with her elbow. "I tell him always, don't talk about work, because people will have to pretend to be interested. But, you know, when he first accepted this job, he was trying to talk like an American. Do you know what he used to say?"

"I wasn't," Jimiyo said, smiling.

"Yes. You were. He referred to it as 'prop trading.' I imagined groups of grown men in their business suits exchanging stage props."

Zemadi said, "Helen and I were in theater together. We put on lovely plays, didn't we?"

"We did."

"African plays, mainly," Zemadi continued. "*The Lion and the Jewel. Sizwe Banzi Is Dead*." She turned to Jimiyo. "Why did you never join theater? It would have been fun, all of us."

"I'm too ugly," he said.

There was some laughter. Vega glanced at Jimiyo, taking in his smooth skin and feminine lashes and runner's body. This was the kind of line, she thought, that only a beautiful person could pull off. Helen smiled indulgently. "You could have been the lion," she said. "He wore a mask."

They rode the subway downtown to an Indo-Chinese restaurant on Lexington Avenue that Helen had read about. "This is Jimiyo's treat," she said. "He is the only non-student among us."

"Here's to prop trading," Zemadi said.

They ordered spring rolls, Gobi Manchurian, and chili-fried tofu. As they ate, Zemadi explained to Halima and Vega that she had been one of two Asian students in their class at Kenton College Preparatory School. "People used to tease me for my Swahili. They would say my pronunciation was wrong, then they would repeat the words I said exactly as I said them."

Helen touched her hand. "They were full of nonsense," she said in a soft voice, the mood deflating slightly. "Your Swahili is excellent. Better than mine, actually." Vega wondered if this was an unspoken tension between them over the years, if Zemadi had existed just a step outside of their tight social circle. Once, Halima had asked Zemadi if she had any boyfriends in secondary school, and Zemadi had put up her hands. "Kenyan boys and I don't mix well," she said. "Too much pampering at home."

"Indian boys?" Halima had asked.

"Indian boys don't date Black girls," Zemadi had said. Vega had wanted to push back, but she could not think of a single example to counter Zemadi's assessment.

They drifted towards discussion of where to live. Halima wanted to be home, in Lahore. Zemadi said she was still drifting. Helen wanted to stay in the States. "California," she said. "I've never been, but I want to visit."

"No way," Jimiyo said. "California is like this: either you have to live in the ghetto where there are no grocery stores, or in some white neighborhood where a loaf of bread costs seventeen dollars, every preschool is a feeder for Stanford, and everyone tells you about the safari vacations they took last summer."

"You haven't even been," Helen said, gently slapping his wrist. She turned to the rest of the group. "Jimiyo wants to go back to Nairobi. He's a mama's boy, this one. He wants to go back home so he never has to wash his own clothing again."

Jimiyo, smiling, rolled his eyes. "What do you think about all this, Vega?"

"California, specifically?" she asked. "Or the washing of one's own clothes?"

He laughed. "Either. Both."

"The first, I can't say. The second I think is generally good practice." They were all still looking at her, and she paused, then said, "Truthfully, I like the idea of an adventure. But the thought of going somewhere where I'm rootless, that seems very lonely."

Throughout the rest of the meal, Vega stole glances at Helen and Jimiyo. She imagined the two of them in Nairobi, their home surrounded by manicured gardens and brimming with staff. She imagined them drinking fresh juices, Jimiyo rubbing Helen's feet after work. With startling and bizarre clarity, she pictured Helen pregnant. She felt something akin to jealousy. It wasn't Jimiyo she wanted—though had she met him under other circumstances, had he been single, she would have been curious. It was the intimacy and ease between Helen and him that she envied, that made her want to have plans tethered to somebody else's.

Vega finally went back to White Plains at the end of the week. By then, the mail was jutting from the box. The newspapers were stacked on the front step, the blue plastic bags wet from the rain the previous night. She took a long shower, cleaned out the fridge, and called a taxi to the grocery store. Rosario had been to the house at some point in the past few days and had mercifully watered the plants and left a tray of tamales in the freezer. Still, some fruit and milk seemed the least Vega could do.

The driver was South Asian. From Bangladesh, he later told her. He turned down the music and adjusted the air conditioner. "This your house?" he asked.

"This? No. Not at all." It surprised her that she could look, to anybody, like the type of person to live in White Plains. As though she were settled enough in the States, or settled enough in her adult life, to own any type of home.

"This is good neighborhood," he said. "Many doctors."

"I see."

"I did two years medical college," he said. "In Dhaka." At a red light, he pulled a piece of paper from the briefcase on the passenger seat and held it to her. She assumed it was some confirmation of his medical studies. "See this?"

"Yes."

He seemed to be waiting for something more, so she said, "Maybe you can continue your studies here," she said. "Become a doctor in the States."

He snorted. "Easier for Indians. For Bangladeshis, it's impossible."

Vega didn't question his logic. They pulled into the A&P parking lot, and he opened her door for her. "I will wait," he said. Vega tried to assure him it wasn't necessary, but the man shook his head. "Not safe, this country. You can't always trust."

Sudha, Rakesh, and the girls arrived the next night. They had slept on the plane and wanted to stay up late and show her their pictures. "At least the Prague ones," Sudha said. "We had those developed in Denmark."

Even Anjali was talkative. She had met a group of backpackers, and now wanted to study abroad during her junior year. "I'm thinking Budapest," she said. "Or maybe some place *not* in Europe. Cuba. Or the Middle East." Sudha had bought an assortment of jams that she was lining up on the counter. Maya, though she was the groggiest of the group, wanted to show Vega the souvenirs she had brought her: a bar of marzipan chocolate and a Danish flag pencil case. "I bought one for myself," she said. "We'll match."

The girls went to bed and Rakesh retreated to the treadmill. "Back to real life," he said. "Though it wasn't a sedentary trip by any means. We walked miles each day. You know, the culture there is much more active."

Sudha put the kettle on, sat down at the kitchen table, and described a day trip they had taken to Odense, where Maya was enraptured by the Hans Christian Andersen Museum. "The whole trip really was lovely. Rejuvenating. So much time together with the girls." She chewed her lip and seemed to be searching for what to say. "Rakesh was gone quite a bit when we were in Denmark. But that was hardly a problem. We saw him in the evenings."

It occurred to Vega, then, what this was about. Rakesh was having an affair. It all seemed such a logical pattern: the vigilant treadmill routine. His constant conferences. The mornings he was off, ostensibly playing tennis. She wondered if she could leave the room before Sudha started to confide in her.

The kettle whistled and Sudha stood to pour the tea. When she came back, she said, "There were a few other kids at the conference. Mainly Maya's age, but even a few teenage boys. I thought Anjali might find them sort of charming."

"She seemed taken by somebody," Vega said, relieved by the change in topic. "Some group of backpackers."

"Ah, yes. The backpackers."

A few seconds later, Rakesh emerged from the basement, wearing his towel, as he always did, draped over his shoulders like a religious garment.

"Anyway," Sudha continued, after he had puttered around the kitchen for a few minutes then gone upstairs, "Anjali had no interest in these boys. Mind you, I don't want her to make poor choices, but the lack of interest was notable."

So, Rakesh wasn't having an affair. This was about something else entirely. "She's focused on her own plans right now," Vega said. "As she should be."

Sudha shook her head. "There is something to a mother's intuition. She's not oriented towards boys. And there was all the anger earlier."

Vega laughed, spilling some of her tea. "Not all angry girls are lesbians, Sudha Akka." She stood up to get the dishrag, and when she came back, was struck by Sudha's somber expression. They sat quietly for a few moments, then Vega asked, "This really worries you?"

"I don't want her life to be harder than it has to be. You know, you hear these stories. That boy in Wyoming. Awful things happen."

Vega was struck by the terrible possibility that Sudha's comment was not about Anjali at all, and that she, Vega, was the lesbian of concern. But Sudha brightened up seconds later, and Vega's worry passed. "She's lost a bit of weight, though," Sudha said. "Have you noticed?"

"She's always looked quite healthy to me." Anjali's appetite seemed fairly normal, not entirely dissimilar from the way she, herself, occasionally ate. But at the house, it was another source of tension. Sudha watched Anjali during meals, as though counting the bites. Anjali, either in oblivion or defiance, took seconds and sometimes thirds.

It was an unfamiliar dynamic to Vega, whose own mother had watched her throughout her childhood with the opposite concern, refilling portions of rice and vegetables, insisting she finish every meal with a bowl of yogurt, and once telling her she could never give birth if she remained so skinny. "Don't you want to be a mother one day?" Rukmini had asked Vega and Ashwini. Vega had been thirteen or fourteen at the time, only a few years into her period and said, "I don't think so." It was Ashwini, in a meek voice, who said, "*I* want to," and Rukmini had nodded, satisfied that at least one of her daughters could give her the right answer.

One Tuesday morning, as she was riding the subway to the Hope Center, Vega felt a tap on her wrist. She looked down. It was Alba.

Vega stared wordlessly. Then she looked at the child on her lap. "Gabriel," she said. "Look at him. He's such a big boy."

Alba nodded proudly, smoothing his curly hair. "He's talking and everything. He wants to grab everything. He's so smart."

"How is school?" she asked. "You're studying makeup?" There was an official term for this, and she was embarrassed that she couldn't remember it—that she came across as either too elitist, or too rattled by the run-in.

"Fine," Alba said. "I'm working right now, but I'm taking one night class. You've seen Naomi?"

"Not since she left for Austin." Vega smiled at Gabriel, in part to avoid looking at Alba. He had pulled a plastic car from Alba's purse and was running it along her lap.

"She comes back to New York in a few weeks," Alba said. "I don't know for how long. She's staying in Brooklyn."

The train pulled into Fourteenth Street, and Alba stood up, hoisting Gabriel with one arm and her bag with the other. She gave Vega a quick hug before walking out. "I'm gonna tell Naomi I saw you." The door closed behind her, and Vega hoped that it would bounce open, as it sometimes did, that she could chase after Alba and ask for Naomi's address or her new phone number. But it idled for a moment, then rattled towards the next station.

She emailed Naomi that night, sitting in the Low Library. *I saw Alba on the train. How are you? Maybe we can see each other when you come back to New York.* Next to her, an undergraduate sat with her chin in her palm, lazily playing Solitaire. Vega watched her, listening for the satisfying click of the cards sliding into place.

# 11

In June, Shoba and Mohan threw a belated birthday party for their daughter. Shoba had sent the invitation in December, when June, in Vega's mind, was still an abstraction. Now, as the date approached, Vega began to dread it. The loss of uninterrupted work hours, the transfer of trains.

But it also seemed a useful distraction; she and Naomi had been writing each other irregularly—a gap of one week, then three emails in one day. The messages were warm but not romantic; Naomi was starting a doctoral program at Penn in the fall, and she sent updates on her master's thesis, her dissertation proposal. But she would, as Alba said, be spending the summer in New York, and Vega sensed a reopening of possibility. She checked her email with a ferocity she associated with addiction, sitting at Rakesh's desk or at the Low Library and clicking refresh, setting arbitrary limits for herself. *I cannot check my email before noon. I have to wait fifteen more minutes. Twenty-six more minutes. I'm going to go into the shower and not think about it.* A day at Shoba's would, if nothing else, give her a day away from the computer.

Sudha offered to drive, bringing the girls along. "I wouldn't mind an afternoon in Edison. The girls have no Sunday activities. We can drop you off, do some shopping, then pick you up."

Vega thought Anjali would object to a day in New Jersey, but she was surprisingly agreeable when Sudha told her about the day trip. She braided Maya's hair, helped to buckle her seat belt, and easily gave in to her request for *The Sound of Music* for the car ride.

"You knew this family in India?" Sudha asked. They pulled onto the interstate. In the back seat, Maya was singing along to "The Lonely Goatherd."

"No. The husband is a distant relation. I stayed with them for a few days when I arrived. The wife is sweet. They took the baby to India for her first birthday, so this is some sort of belated gathering."

"We should have had them over," Sudha said. "It's a shame we didn't think of that."

The use of the past tense was jarring, though Vega had found herself using it as well in recent months. Throughout the fall semester, she often made loose plans with the assumption that they would eventually transpire—another evening in Jackson Heights with Halima, a weekend in Boston with Zemadi. She had two months remaining in the States and she knew, now, that those trips would not happen. She was beginning to think of her return to Madras not as a new chapter in her life, but the curtailing of a previous one. It hurt. She wasn't ready to go back. And what would happen with Naomi? Would they continue their correspondence long-distance, leaving open some future possibility? She wondered if this afternoon in New Jersey would be her last with Shoba.

"So many people took us in when we arrived," Sudha said. "And, of course, when Rakesh was in residency and we had absolutely no money, they were always generous. We lived with one of his aunts for some time. And then we shared an apartment with another couple and their baby. It must have been seven hundred square feet. You can't imagine."

"The first years must be the hardest," Vega said. "I wondered about this for Shoba. After the baby was born, especially. I wondered who she talked with. Even now, she must be lonely."

"Maybe," Sudha said. Vega glanced behind her. The girls had both dozed off, Anjali's head against the window and Maya's on her sister's shoulder. "Sixteen Going on Seventeen," played from the speakers. It was an awkward soundtrack to the drive, now that only she and Sudha were awake. Sudha didn't seem to notice, though. "The thing is," she said, "you rely on people because you *have* to in the beginning. So, it isn't quite lonely. When you *stop* needing people is when it becomes lonely. That's what I think." She finally turned off the music. "Do you think you'll want to come back?" she asked.

"I do," Vega said, and she told Sudha about her loose doctoral plans.

"Your parents must be proud."

"I haven't done much of anything yet."

"Nonsense. You have a purpose. What else is there?"

The drive was shorter than Vega expected. She navigated, using the directions Mohan had emailed the previous week from an account that, at the time, had made her laugh: mohan.engineer@aol.com. There was nobody with whom she could have shared the joke. Only Gayatri would have found it funny, but it was the middle of the night in Madras. She considered forwarding her the email, but it seemed an unkind thing to do, to make fun of a man who had opened his home to her upon her arrival.

Vega was wrong to assume that Shoba was lonely. The front door was open, and people spilled onto the lawn. A cluster of girls, Maya's age, played tag in the corner. Maya broke loose and joined them.

"Who are all these people?" Anjali asked.

Sudha hushed her. "Don't be rude," she said. But Vega had been wondering the same thing. Everybody was distinctly South Indian, almost all speaking Tamil. It was the reverse of watching a film with a familiar cast—strangers dressed as people she ought to recognize.

Shoba was standing beside the front steps, wearing a peacock-blue sari, surrounded by other sari-clad women. When she saw Vega, she broke away from the group and ran towards her, exclaiming over the gift. "It was enough of a present that you came!"

"It's nothing," Vega said. "Really." As always, Shoba's effusiveness made her feel guilty. Sudha was the one who had actually purchased the gift. She had stopped at the mall on her way from the office and returned with a pink dress and a three-pack of baby socks. "I bought size two," she had said. "You always want to go a size larger with children this small." Vega had nodded and thanked her, half listening to the advice, which she could not imagine would ever be relevant to her life.

Shoba spoke with Sudha as though they were old friends, thanking her for coming, and for taking such good care of Vega—prompting Vega to wonder if the two women knew each other, if there was some connection she may have missed between them. To Anjali, she said, "The older children are in the basement. We have a Ping-Pong table." She waved them inside to the dining room, where the table was crammed with pots of sambar and avial, and aluminum trays of lemon rice, chole, raita. "Aruna made the idlis. You've met Aruna? Please eat. There's too much food." She seemed happier, more vivacious than Vega had ever seen her. She ran quickly to the kitchen to check on the kesari—reportedly also being made by Aruna—then walked Vega and Sudha through the house, showing off the new curtains in the nursery, a series of family photographs hanging on the hallway wall, and a floral-patterned address book she kept next to the telephone. "I know so many people now. Just look." She opened it up to a page in the middle, the letter *L*, filled to the midpoint. "I meet somebody, and immediately I write their number." But it was the change in the baby that most surprised Vega. Tara was seated on Mohan's lap, dressed in a red pavadai and chewing her fist. When she saw Shoba, she smiled and raised her arms so eagerly that she nearly lifted herself into the air.

"She's lovely," Vega said. Though she found children sweet and interesting, she had little interest in babies, and her observations of Shoba's early months of motherhood only diminished their appeal. But Tara was radiant. When Vega last saw her, she had clung to Shoba with a primal desperation. Now she was playful, burrowing into Shoba's neck and smiling, then allowing herself to be lowered onto the floor. They had shaved her head for her first birthday (Shoba had mailed Vega pictures of Tara's annaprasana, in which she was starkly bald), but now her hair framed her face in soft, perfect curls.

"She's a good baby," Shoba said. They watched her take clumsy steps towards Mohan, then fall onto the carpet. "She's happy. Easy."

There was a man seated next to Mohan, dressed just as Mohan was, in brown slacks and a white shirt. He made clucking noises to Tara, then held his hand out and pulled her up. They watched her step forward once, tentatively, then steady herself and run to Mohan's lap.

Sudha and Anjali left to go shopping, but at the last minute, Maya asked to stay behind at the party. She had met some girls her age and they were tearing across the backyard with later plans for a Hula-Hoop competition. "I have to be there for it," Maya said. "I promised. And they need an even number."

"You don't mind keeping an eye on her?" Sudha asked.

"As long as I don't have to compete," Vega said. Now, she called Maya inside to eat, watched as she wolfed down her food, then made a plate for herself and found an available seat on the living room floor where the guests had formed a circle. When she'd first arrived and scanned the room, she thought that nobody at the party was her age, that she was at the midpoint between the teenagers huddled in the basement and the mothers crowded in the kitchen. Of course, Shoba was younger than she was, but Vega considered Shoba an anomaly— a child bride from a small town, who had become pregnant in the manner of child brides from small towns. Now she realized most of the women in the room were in their early twenties, mostly paired with one of the trouser-wearing men. In that crowd, Shoba and Mohan were indistinguishable. Vega, in her skirt and sleeveless kurta, was the one who stood out.

Two women beside her were discussing kitchen renovations, and she wondered if she should interrupt to introduce herself, when the man who had been seated next to Mohan sat next to her. "That's your daughter?" he asked.

Vega stared at him blankly.

"The girl with the dupatta. You were getting her food."

Vega considered pointing out that she would have had to have given birth at fifteen in order for nine-year-old Maya to be her daughter. Instead, she said, "I don't have any children."

"You're from Madras?"

"Yes."

The man switched to Tamil and introduced himself as Suresh. "Mohan and I were in school together. Their baby is like my own daughter."

It was a surprisingly tender comment. "She's really a lovely baby," Vega said.

"We've met before, I think. We studied together at IIT, maybe?"

Vega laughed. "You're most certainly confusing me for somebody else. Though I did visit the campus often. My friend Gayatri studied there." She always enjoyed her weekends at IIT, in part because she liked Gayatri's friends. But Suresh struck her as the dullest type of IIT graduate—a man who had spent his childhood singularly focused on gaining admission and had nothing to show for himself beyond that achievement.

"Which hostel did she stay?"

It had been three years since Vega set foot on the IIT campus, and it surprised her how quickly the name came back to her. "Sarayu."

"That's where we've met, then. I was in Narmada. We held events together, the two hostels. We had a Holi party every year. Perhaps you were there."

To Vega's relief, Mohan and another man bounded into the room, and Suresh was dragged into a conversation. She stood to clear her plate. In the dining room, Aruna was setting out bowls of kesari.

Sudha and Anjali arrived in time for cake, and in time to see Maya and the tangle of girls perform a play called "Dragon Princess," which they insisted they had spent the afternoon rehearsing, though it all seemed impromptu. Afterwards, Vega went into the kitchen where Shoba was packing leftovers into ziplock bags. "You want channa? We have too much. Even cake we have."

Vega shook her head. "It was all lovely, though. I ate too much."

"You met Suresh. He's almost a brother to Mohan." Shoba told a winding story about an apartment they had all shared in New Brunswick. Despite Vega's protests, she pressed a bag of lemon rice into her hand. "I'll invite him next time you come," she said.

In the car, Sudha glanced in the rearview mirror and whispered to Vega, "Anjali looks nice, doesn't she?"

Vega turned around. The nose ring was so small it was barely detectable, but Anjali seemed so placid, so content, that she did, in fact, look nice.

"You saw somebody you know?" she asked. "The man you were talking to?"

"He recognized me from Madras, but I don't recall him."

"That's how New Jersey is. Everybody is connected from back home." Sudha looked in the mirror again. "Rakesh is going to scream when he sees the nose ring. But who cares?"

# 12

Naomi was a shade tanner and had put on the slightest amount of weight. They hugged for a long time, Naomi swaying side to side. "Holy shit," she said when she pulled away. "It's really you." She looked lovely. Vega wanted to hug her again. To sink into her.

"Did you think I would send my understudy?"

"I had my fears. I don't know."

They had originally planned to meet the following weekend. Naomi was housesitting in Flatbush for the summer and was back and forth between there and Stamford until her program started at Penn. She had sent Vega the Flatbush address, and they had confirmed the time. But on Sunday, two days earlier, Vega mapped the distance between Stamford and White Plains and sent Naomi a message. *What if we meet over the next few days? I'm only twenty minutes away.* She sent the email quickly, before she could talk herself out of it, worried she was being too eager. But Naomi wrote back a few minutes later. *Sure thing.*

They took the rear exit out of the Stamford train station and walked towards the parking lot. "If you have time, I was thinking we could go for a drive," Naomi said. She unlocked the door of a worn-looking maroon car.

"Is this yours?"

"I had to buy a car when I was in Austin. I should have offered to pick you up. I was so distracted this morning that it didn't even occur to me."

"Are you busy with classes?"

"No. I'm actually just adjuncting this summer." She turned at a stop sign, then said, "Oh. You mean, is that the reason I was distracted?"

"I don't know what I meant. I'm just saying anything that comes to mind because I'm nervous."

"I've been nervous since we got in touch."

Vega stared at her as she drove. "Do I look different to you?"

Naomi laughed. "A little bit. I don't think you wore your hair loose when we lived together. It was always in a braid. Maybe there are other things. I don't know. Why do you ask?"

"Because you look a little bit different. I was just wondering if you were having the same experience I was."

Naomi pulled onto the highway. It was strange watching her drive in the same way, Vega imagined, it would be strange to see her jump rope or turn a cartwheel. An ordinary skill suddenly announcing itself.

"I think that was our issue last year, right?" Naomi asked.

"What was our issue?"

"You and I not having the same experience."

Vega didn't answer. The highway split into a two-lane road marked by signs that held no meaning to her, for landmarks she had never heard of: Downtown Norwalk, the Goddard School of Westport. Sometimes, she liked being in a place that was foreign to her. Other times, like in this moment, it unsettled her. In her first months in Cleveland, she had been gripped by the peculiar fear that her parents would kick her out of the car as they wound through the gray maze of streets that surrounded the hospital, and she would never be able to find her way back. She had forgotten that fear until now.

"Would you say that's accurate?" Naomi asked. "You felt one way and I felt another?"

"I would not say that's accurate. No."

They turned onto a narrower road, and then into a gravelly lot. Naomi parked the car and turned to Vega. "Then what would you say happened?"

"Do you realize we've spent the duration of the time we've known each other doing things that are familiar to you?"

Naomi looked puzzled. "You mean because I used to bring you home?"

"No. Not just that. I moved into your apartment. And then, everything from there. You had been living in New York for years. You knew how to fix coffee tables and cook. Every time we took the train, I was following you. I was always going someplace you had been countless times. Even now. Do you know I don't even know how to drive a car?"

"I trust you're going somewhere with this, but I really don't know where."

"You have ex-girlfriends, Naomi. If I wanted to acquire an ex-girlfriend, I wouldn't know how to begin."

"You date a woman. And then you end things."

"It isn't a joke. There's an imbalance between us. I could not have brought a girlfriend home to my parents. They have no frame of reference. I would have had an easier time explaining to them that I'd become a gold prospector. Or an aerobics instructor." Even as she spoke, Vega was aware that none of what she was saying was true. Her parents didn't care about frames of reference. They had always loved her simply and without condition. Vega was the problem. She could not imagine surrendering herself to a relationship, allowing herself to be happy, when she knew the likelihood—the real and mathematical likelihood—that the relationship would end. She couldn't bear another loss.

The beach was rocky and gray, beautiful but cold-looking. There was a group of mothers with their young children, and an elderly couple walking a dog, but it was otherwise empty. She and Naomi made their way to a small, sandy inlet and sat down. Vega slipped off her sandals.

"I should have brought something to eat," Naomi said.

"You don't always have to feed me."

"I did think about this, after I left. How you managed to eat."

"I moved in with Halima. She did most of the cooking."

"I'm glad you found your way. I mean, in general. That you weren't alone."

"I wasn't alone. But I missed you. I thought about you constantly."

"That makes me feel like I wasn't crazy. Like I wasn't imagining things."

"No. You weren't." Vega wrapped her arms around her knees.

"You cold?"

"A little bit."

Naomi slid closer so their legs touched. She slipped her hand into Vega's skirt—a red wrap that Vega had worn constantly in Hyderabad, and that still reminded her of Hyderabad—and put her hand on Vega's bare knee. Vega felt herself softening. She could have this. She always forgot, until the moment she was touched, just how much she loved being touched.

"Could you tell me something?" Naomi asked. "And be really direct?"

"I think so."

"Could you give this a real chance? Be with me? Have a relationship?"

"I don't know how I'm supposed to answer."

Naomi's right hand moved upwards, her finger sliding slowly just inside Vega's underwear. "Is this what you want? Just to fuck?"

It wasn't a fair question, Vega thought. What she wanted was so detailed and far-fetched that it would have embarrassed her to say it aloud: an apartment with Naomi in Philadelphia. The two of them in graduate school. Evenings on the couch, reading each other's dissertation chapters. In this fantasy, she was a sexier, bolder, less fearful version of herself. She and Naomi kissed in public. They went to wine bars. They had a small and perfect circle of friends.

Naomi was behind her now, her left hand inching up Vega's shirt, her thumb grazing Vega's nipple. She thought again of Sukumar Reddy. *Do you want to fuck me outside?* But she did want to fuck Naomi outside. She wanted to fuck her loudly, on that cold sand, not caring who walked by. The woman and her children. The couple and their dog.

She said Naomi's name, over and over, the final time nearly shouting it into her ear.

Naomi played music on the way back—a loud, dissonant, male voice, all the songs sounding exactly the same. They didn't talk until they reached the White Plains train station.

"You didn't need to bring me all the way here," Vega said. It was an inane comment. Naomi had offered, over and over, to drive Vega all the way to Sudha's house. And Vega had insisted that she was fine, that she could easily call a taxi.

"I don't mind. It doesn't make a difference."

"Will we see each other again? I can still come to Brooklyn."

"Is that what you want?"

"Of course it is. I wouldn't have asked otherwise."

Naomi touched Vega's lower lip, then dropped her hand. "I really like you, Vega. I don't know if there's a more artful way of saying it, but it's the truth. I just like you. I've liked you from the minute I met you."

"I know that," Vega said, realizing only later, on the train, what a small and incomplete response that was.

She and Naomi planned to meet on the second Friday of July. That morning, when the family was out of the house for Maya's soccer game, Vega stood in front of Sudha's full-length mirror wearing a black-and-white cotton dress she had bought in Hyderabad—at the time, with Sukumar Reddy in mind. It cut low and clung to her breasts. Later, walking the ten blocks from the Atlantic Avenue station to Naomi's Brooklyn apartment, she felt something rising in her, akin to the feeling she used to have when her period approached, a light cramping, a feverish awareness of all the parts of her body she wanted somebody to touch. Over the past few days, her fragmented thoughts of Naomi had developed into a clear plan: she would go back to Madras, find a job, then begin her doctoral applications to Penn, Temple, and Columbia. She could picture this life in perfect detail. The apartment she and Naomi would find together. Their shared bookshelf. The glow of their lamp in the evenings. The different version of herself—the sexy, bold, fearless version—that would love and be loved by Naomi, without the constant fear of impending loss.

She passed the landmarks Naomi had given her: a restaurant called Puerto Viejo, a laundromat, and a tiny red church. Naomi lived on the first floor of a brownstone, and Vega pressed the buzzer and waited. Moments later, she pressed it again, then knocked on the door and listened for any sound of movement from the other side. When Naomi still didn't answer, she circled the block, catching a glimpse of herself in the window of the laundromat, her shoulders hunched under the weight of her weekend bag. She came back and knocked, then buzzed again. But there was nothing.

She took the train back to Manhattan and settled at the library to check her email. There was nothing from Naomi. *I went to your apartment*, Vega wrote. *Did I have the wrong address?* A few minutes later, she followed with another message. *I need to see you before I go back home.* Next to her, a woman was bent over her course reader, applying her highlighter with so much force it squeaked. Vega sat numbly, determined to wait just an hour. But an hour passed, and she waited another.

At six o'clock, she made her way to Halima's apartment. "She isn't home," Caitlin said. "She's staying in Queens or whatever for the night." Vega slept on the couch, trying to ignore the angry clamor of Caitlin unpacking her suitcases. The room was unbearably hot. When Caitlin finally closed the door and turned off her lights, Vega kicked off the sheets. She punched the cushion until her knuckles were raw.

Her summer classes were winding down, and there was no practical reason to stay in the city. She spent her days in White Plains, mindlessly boxing her clothes for her return home, then realizing a particular bra or T-shirt had been packed and upending the entire thing. She checked her email obsessively, sometimes waking up in the middle of the night and tiptoeing into Rakesh's study. In her last message to

Naomi, she had written, *I'm terrified I will never see you again.* Naomi had ignored Vega's previous apologies, but this was so desperate that she was certain Naomi would respond, though she never did.

In the evenings, Anjali was withdrawn and moody, but Maya clung to Vega, wanting to play endless rounds of Memory and perform the song she was rehearsing at camp. It was a production of *Fiddler on the Roof.* "I can't believe you won't be there to see it," Maya said, laying out the cards. On the couch, Anjali rolled her eyes for no apparent reason.

"She's pulling away because she's going to miss you," Sudha said. "We all are. I cannot imagine how the house is going to feel next week."

"She should come to Madras," Vega said. "I'll show her the city." But she knew the plan was unlikely. She had seen American families on their visits to India—the novelty of the rickshaws and cows quickly giving way to boredom, dull visits with one distant relative after another, and occasionally a trip to a jewelry shop. She had no foreign cousins of her own, but she recalled a set of Gayatri's who would come every few years and spend afternoons lying on the floor, listening to their Walkmans, responding to every question with a grunt or single-word answer.

"That's a lovely idea," Sudha said.

The family took her out for a farewell dinner at a Thai restaurant in a strip mall, and she tried to push thoughts of Naomi to the corner of her mind. She had emailed her so many times that the messages felt free of meaning or consequence, like a letter bottled and tossed into the ocean. It would never get anywhere.

"What's the plan when you return to India?" Sudha asked.

"I'll apply for doctoral programs in the fall. In the meantime, I'd like to gain some NGO experience." She held on to the fading hope that Naomi had meant to meet her at the apartment, but that some emergency had arisen, so she hadn't wavered from her earlier plan. She would apply to schools in Philadelphia and New York. She and

Naomi would see each other back in the States. The NGO plan was something she had been loosely considering, but now, saying it aloud, it sounded concrete and steady. "I worked at an orphanage for a bit, sometime back. I could volunteer temporarily while I find something longer term."

"Like in *Annie*," Maya said.

"After that?" Rakesh asked.

"Eventually, I'd like to work with an NGO that is engaged in structural change. Something that is performing charitable work, but also influencing policy."

"That's all well and good," Rakesh said, "but I have friends in these sectors. Corporate social responsibility and whatnot. They will be the first to tell you that when NGOs rely on foreign donors, there is a certain financial precarity."

Sudha put her hand on Rakesh's wrist to hush him. Even Anjali was listening. Vega watched Maya work her chopsticks, held together with a green, plastic band.

"Well, there is a growing investment in women's health. In the past, we considered economic empowerment and health to be separate areas of focus. But now, there are microcredit programs." This wasn't fresh information. It was the type of thing people talked about even during her undergraduate years at Sri Vidya. But she was surprised by how easy it was to inject the conversation with language from her classrooms at Columbia and make her plans sound radical, a worthy culmination of two years of graduate study. "Many of these programs, in preparing women to be the breadwinners of their family, are tackling both women's rights and poverty."

"So multifaceted," Sudha said. Even Rakesh nodded. Anjali asked, "Like how?"

"When women are able to earn, they can have a voice in their families and communities. But they can also contribute to the well-being of the NGO. Making it self-sufficient."

"That's what I like to see," Rakesh said. "Private-public partnerships."

Maya picked up a clump of pad Thai with her chopsticks and shouted, "Ta-da!"

She went back to New York two days before her flight, to see Zemadi, who was flying back to Nairobi that night. They had planned on lunch, but Zemadi's day was hectic, and they met instead at the CVS near campus, where Zemadi was making a last round of purchases: lipstick for her cousins and copies of *People* and *Essence*. She had applied for doctoral programs in the UK and was still waiting to hear about program funding. Vega pictured her in a dim hostel room, maybe at the London School of Economics, working her way through leather-bound sociology journals, the rain falling outside. Standing on the curb with Zemadi as she waited for a taxi, Vega said, "This is only going to sink in after a few days. When I dial your number, and nobody answers."

Zemadi hugged her tightly. "Do you remember when Halima was telling us about the Brown Muslim Student Association? But you didn't know she was referring to the university, so you said, 'They don't allow Black Muslims?'"

"I do remember that." It had been a fairly inconsequential joke at the time, but thinking of it now made Vega's throat tighten and her eyes burn.

Her plans with Halima didn't materialize either. They talked briefly on the phone that evening when Vega was back in White Plains.

"It all happened so quickly," Halima said. "I thought two years would *last* longer." Her voice shook. There was the sound of running water in the background, then the flick of the stove. She was making tea. It seemed impossible that they would never again have one of their evenings together, lying on the floor and eating parathas. Watching *The X-Files*. Vega already missed the smell of their apartment.

"We'll have a reunion before you know it," Vega said. "All of us." She assured Halima that she would see her at the wedding, though they both knew this would be impossible. Vega would never get a visa to visit Pakistan, just as Halima would never get one to come to India.

# Part 2

# 13

After the joy of home faded, Vega realized she was as annoyed by her parents' old habits as she was by their new ones. Her father still circled articles in the day's *Hindu* he wanted her to read—dry, economics pieces on demonetization, or grisly accounts of drought and farmer suicide. There was a new homeopathic doctor in their lives, a specialist on poststroke health, who called every other morning. Her mother spoke to him with a hushed reverence, scribbling notes. Vasanti's meals, once the high points of Vega's day, were now soft and flavorless: millet, yogurt, and a single vegetable.

"It's healthy for all of us," Rukmini said. "For our prevention and for his healing."

Vega pretended to be engrossed in the articles as they ate. Her father chewed slowly and audibly, and her mother sat beside him, refilling his water glass and wiping the specks of food he spat onto the table.

She made a list of twelve NGOs and called the numbers listed on their websites. None answered. She began to send emails, several of which bounced back. She began to look forward to the quiet moment in the afternoon when the power shut off. She would lie on her bed, in her hot room, and feel the pressure of her job search temporarily lifted. But it was then, when she was no longer gripped by existential questions—where she was supposed to live, what she was supposed to do with her life—that she was most aware of the low, simmering sadness of losing Naomi. It seemed futile to imagine a future with her, but she had nothing to replace that fantasy with. Nothing else she was looking forward to.

"Nobody finds a job by emailing," Gayatri said. "You need to network."

Aside from her parents, Gayatri was the only person she had wanted to talk with during her time away, but their schedules now proved hard to coordinate. Gayatri had taken a job in petrochemicals and was working long hours. The thought was depressing. Gayatri, a girl who had once read everything she could find about Vandana Shiva and Jane Goodall, was now involved in something called mud drilling.

"Jaganath's having a party," Gayatri said. "He isn't the most interesting of characters, I realize. But everyone will be there."

"Not *everyone* will be there," Vega said. She had been curious to see Guru, another Rhodes classmate who had, according to Gayatri, asked about Vega over the years. But he had apparently moved to Calcutta and was engaged to a Bengali girl. "She's also a chemical engineer," Gayatri said.


Jaganath held court in the middle of the circle, dressed in a tight black T-shirt and black jeans. It was a look that Vega's teenage self would have found attractive, and she was grateful those moments hadn't lined up in their lives—her then and his now.

"If you do go abroad, you can't do it the way the previous generation did it. Going to work for somebody else, saying, *Oh, thank you, boss sahib, for your paycheck.* You should go on your own terms, or not go at all."

Vega had never liked Jaganath. He was what her father would call *thutchan*, calculating. Now, she found herself nodding with the same reflexive loyalty he had always generated among her classmates. He had been the first in the group to travel abroad, and throughout their childhood brought back meaningless tokens from Switzerland that they rushed upon—francs in their smallest denominations, blurry Alpine photographs, train ticket stubs.

"I have no interest in going abroad," their friend Aarti said, stretching her legs out on the grass. "Moving to New York or Los Angeles. Living with ten other flatmates." She was wearing high-waisted jeans and a black tank top. Vega had been the one to teach Aarti how to thread her upper lip, buff the calluses from her feet, and paint her nails. Now the sight of the jeans irritated her, as though Aarti had taken Vega's guidance and outpaced her.

"Those are details," Jaganath said. "I'm talking about bigger things. This is the time to enter the capital markets. Evaluations are inflated everywhere."

A man named Murthy shook his head. "It's bullshit. This dot-com nonsense, that any fool can show up in the States and attract investors." Vega recalled that Jaganath would sit behind Murthy in Hindi class and knock his pen to the floor repeatedly, a strange and mundane cruelty none of them had thought to question. Now they sat next to each other, drinking imported beer as though the intervening years had absolved Jaganath and smoothed all the creases and tensions of childhood.

"It isn't bullshit," Jaganath said. "And half of these venture capitalist types are Indians. Looking for some fellow from home to give money to. Go to San Francisco. Seattle. They're all there. Deep pockets, man."

Vega wandered off to find the bathroom. The main house was locked, and Jaganath had pointed them towards a small building beside the garden. "The annex," he had called it. When Vega came out, Murthy was standing by the door.

"Toilet is in here," she said.

"I know. Just escaping the crowd for a bit."

He was thin, with an uneven stubble and a vaguely Gandhian look—khadi kurta, jeans, brown sandals. Vega wasn't attracted to him, but he looked like pleasant-enough company. In the distance, Jaganath had changed the music from Nirvana to something more buoyant. Hindi club music. She could see the others starting to dance. She sat down on the bench and Murthy joined her.

"You just came back from the States?"

"Two-year master's program."

"I'm thinking of applying for something similar."

"You did something in the sciences, no? I remember it wasn't engineering. I filed you under non-engineers."

"Geologist. There's a doctoral program in Berkeley I'm considering. Did you ever visit California?"

"No, but I hear there is an abundance of venture capitalist types."

He laughed. "Just looking for a place to put their money."

"Precisely."

After a few quiet moments, he said, "I suppose we should make our way back to the group."

Only a few people were dancing. Jaganath was still holding court. He raised his eyebrows when Vega and Murthy approached. "Gone for a while." To Murthy, he said, "I didn't think you were man enough." There it was. The adult cruelty. Vega picked up a Carlsberg and retreated to the edge of the circle.

In the rickshaw, Gayatri said, "That was a bore. I feel badly for dragging you."

"It was fine. More importantly, I didn't sneak off with Murthy. I hardly know him. He had some questions about the States. We talked. Nothing more."

"I wouldn't care in the least if you did. But you remember him, no? Murthy?"

"Of course. Vaguely, I mean. We were all at Rhodes together."

"His father was killed in the scooter crash. It happened just here. In Adyar. His brother was thrown from it too. You must remember that. The brother is paralyzed from the waist down."

"I remember the accident. I didn't make the connection with Murthy, though." There had been some mournful whispers for a while, and some cautionary lectures from parents about scooter riding. Eventually, everybody stopped discussing it. The way, she assumed, they no longer discussed Ashwini's death.

"He has a good job here. He also has a boyfriend. Australian fellow. Met him while traveling."

It would be such a relief, Vega thought, to tell Gayatri about Naomi. There would be no judgment. Gayatri would squeeze her hand, help her sort through all of it. Instead, she asked, "How do you know all of this?"

Gayatri shrugged. "We've talked a few times. The point is, he has a professional future here, and loads of family obligations, but no real future in any other way. It just seems worth pointing out. You may not be happy here. And you may not even be happy in the States. But at least you have the option of either place."

The Mukti Foundation operated out of a rental flat, housed in a building between a Shiva Temple and an Indian Overseas Bank. The director, Gowri, had been a Rhodes graduate. She wore a stiff-looking cotton sari, and tucked a pen behind her ear.

"Our number one priority is nutritional assistance for under-privileged mothers." She showed Vega a brochure. On the cover, a circle of women sat around a lectern, leaning forward attentively. Some had children on their laps. "Our efforts are three-pronged." Gowri set down the brochure and held up three fingers. Vega looked past her, through the window that overlooked the building's courtyard. There was a group of interns—two German women, and an Indian American girl named Sandhya. Vega imagined Gowri sitting with them in the weeks prior, delivering the same lecture.

"One is direct assistance. We build trust through distribution of foods. Two is women's education. We deliver guidance on nutritional practices through lectures and pamphlets. And three is community education. We organize street theater performances in our target slums to show people the importance of nutritional access. You'll work with my niece, Charanya, who is in charge of all field visits. She isn't in the office today." She nodded toward the window. "The interns are here through a Microsoft grant. They provide computer training three days each week to local children. The other days, they accompany you and Charanya to the slums."

She showed Vega the open document on her computer. "We are currently updating to a new spreadsheet. Microsoft has also given us a new computer, but it is not compatible with our previous program. For today, you can update our donor information and our expenses." She stood up. "I'm meeting today with our donors. In the morning, I will introduce you to Charanya. There are two toilets. Eastern commode next to the entrance. Western commode down the hall, across from the grant office."

Charanya appeared the next morning. She wore a large gold-hoop nose ring and handloom sari, and carried a jute bag with the word *Mukti* emblazoned across it. "Have you engaged in fieldwork before?" she asked. Vega had been sitting at her desk when Charanya came in. There was another chair, but Charanya instead sat cross-legged on the floor, as though making a point.

"I haven't," Vega said, looking down at her.

"Tomorrow we'll make our first visit. We have a clear protocol for our interactions with our target population. We explain our mission, that we are not a Christian organization, and we are not an orphanage. We offer our nutrition information, and for women who accept it, we provide them with a small bag of dhal. For those who are not interested, we flag them for being disinterested, and we follow up on a previous visit. As you are new to fieldwork, you will shadow me for the first few months. You can introduce yourself, of course. But beyond that, I will lead the conversation. You're a Columbia graduate?"

"For my master's. I did my undergraduate here. At Sri Vidya."

The conversation drifted back to the topic of fieldwork, but minutes later, on her way out, Charanya said, "I was admitted to Barnard, for undergraduate. I declined the offer. I don't believe you need to go abroad for a good opportunity."

The comment tugged at her for the rest of the day. Privately, she seethed over Charanya's impression of her. Publicly, she tried to correct it. She took her lunch break with the rest of the staff, addressed them in Tamil, and nodded attentively when Kumari, the office grant writer, discussed her son's preparation for the Joint Entry Exam. She even made a point of using the Eastern commode. By afternoon, though, she learned this last effort was pointless. Only the German girls seemed willing to squat over a pit toilet. The others lined up outside Kumari's office, waiting for the Western commode.

The next morning there was a black car parked outside the gate. The interns were already waiting in the back seat, with the windows rolled down. The driver was leaning against the door. He nodded to Charanya and Vega.

"Ganga is our most valuable staff member," Charanya said in Tamil, as Ganga opened the door for them. "He knows every street in Madras."

If there was a form of condescension that Vega found most curdling, it was this, the type that masqueraded as respect. She squeezed into the back—four across, without seat belts. "Namaskar," she said to Ganga.

"Good morning, madam," Ganga said.

In the car, Vega learned that the German girls, Annie and Katrin, were from Stuttgart and taking a gap year before beginning university. They had chosen to come to South India after reading *The God of Small Things*. She learned that Sandhya had grown up in Houston and graduated from Rice and planned to spend a year at Mukti before attending law school. She also learned that Ganga's daughter had graduated with a bachelor's in commerce from Sri Meenakshi Government College for Women. Though Vega hadn't heard of the university, and knew nothing of commerce, she said, "Excellent."

"She's *very* bright," Charanya said. "So hardworking." She turned to Ganga. "*Ille*, Ganga?"

Ganga kept his eyes on the road. "Yes, madam," he said.

Olcott Kuppam was no more than ten kilometers from Vega's childhood house, just blocks from a juice shop where she and Gayatri used to stop after school, but she had only ever seen it from a distance.

"This is one of our neediest slums," Charanya said somberly, leading them through a maze of narrow streets. "It has an eighty-seven percent malnutrition rate." Two women sat on the roof of a house, patching a hole. Another was wringing wet clothes into a plastic bucket. A few children stood in their doorways and stared, but scattered when Vega, Charanya, and the interns approached. "We're combating nearly impossible statistics," Charanya continued. "Forty-seven percent of children under age three are malnourished. Fifty percent of our target mothers are anemic."

Charanya did most of the talking. She greeted the mothers in their doorways, explained the importance of protein-rich diets, took notes on their food intake, and presented them with a bag of dhal and a single onion in exchange for their time. The women's responses were mostly indistinguishable—flat and disinterested. "Persistence is key," Charanya said. "And follow-up. Our follow-up initiatives are written into the grant. We have to remember that seventy percent of women here have only basic literacy. There is significant distrust in education."

At their seventh or eighth house, a woman came to the door, holding an infant daughter. The baby was naked, except for a frayed *kodi* tied around her waist.

"You should put a cloth on her," Charanya advised the mother. "For sanitation." Behind them, Sandhya whispered her translation to the Germans.

The woman nodded, took in the lecture on nutrition, and timidly responded to Charanya's questions. Yes, she still nursed the baby. Yes, she boiled her water before drinking it. For lunch, typically she ate tamarind rice.

"You need some dhal or yogurt along with it," Charanya said. "And some vegetable at least once each day."

"Yes, ma."

"Physical stimulation is also important. You must talk and play with her."

Sandhya translated. The woman nodded pliantly. She was younger than Vega. Maybe the age of the German interns. Before they walked away, she turned the baby around to reveal a rash spreading across her back. "What do you think, *Akka*?" she asked. "My mother-in-law says she needs medicine."

Charanya glanced briefly at her notebook. "It could be heat."

"How much will the medicine cost?"

Vega looked past the mother, into her dark, narrow house. She wanted to say something comforting. The rash looked mild enough, and whatever medicine it required was likely cheap. But before she could speak, Charanya tucked her notebook into her tote and took a step back. "We aren't doctors, ma. We are nutrition specialists." She gave her the dhal and onion, and they walked to the next house.

By the afternoon, Vega was tired of Mukti. She was tired of the eagerness of the interns, of Sandhya's halting Tamil, the way they all murmured *hmm* in agreement when anybody spoke. More than anything, she was tired of Charanya—of her excessive use of the word "slum," of her barrage of statistics. She hated that, though she had to use the bathroom, she had bristled at Charanya's suggestion that they find a public toilet. "It won't be so bad," Charanya said. "What do you think the people in the slum use? Only some five percent have indoor plumbing."

"I'll wait," Vega said.


Gayatri thought Vega was overreacting. "I don't understand why everything is so theoretical with you," she said. "It may be condescending, but if you're giving dhal to people, and they need dhal, who gives a damn what the tone is?"

"It's not the work I want to do with my life," Vega said. "These smug women, all the lecturing about tamarind rice. There are people in the world engaging in radical, important work. *That* is the experience I want."

"And where are these people?"

"I don't know. But they are not at Mukti."

They were eating at a new restaurant in Besant Nagar called "Salaam, Bombay," named after a film Vega had seen in the theater with her parents some years back, a gripping portrait of slum life after which she had cried and entered several weeks of purposeless self-flagellation, thanking Vasanti to excessive levels, and volunteering at an orphanage called Banyan Tree, where she spent her shifts inventorying donations of rice and enriched wheat biscuits. Vega had been horrified when Gayatri told her the name of the restaurant and suggested they meet there. "Who names a restaurant after a film about human suffering?" she asked.

Now, Gayatri speared a cube of paneer tikka and said, "What about the Microsoft initiative? That must be somewhat useful."

Vega had visited the computer center only once. It was a dimly lit room a few blocks from the Mukti office, on the other side of the Indian Overseas Bank. The German interns floated between two boys in government school uniforms who were idly manipulating cells on an Excel spreadsheet. But she didn't have the energy to argue with Gayatri.

She avoided field visits for the next several weeks, occupying herself with administrative tasks, grateful for the thick folder of donations and expenses that had yet to be updated. She offered to help Kumari draft a Soros Foundation grant and began carrying a pair of headphones to the office, taken from her Lufthansa flight, ignoring the din of Charanya and the interns in the background. They held debriefing meetings following each field visit, but as she had not accompanied them to the field, there was no point in attending. "Vega works on the programmatic side of things," she once overheard Charanya explain.

One Saturday, she ran into Sandhya at the Biotique in T. Nagar, holding a jar of saffron dew cream. "I love this shop," she said. "It's all so natural."

She and Sandhya had only spoken a few times, and the conversation was always stilted. Still, she had no plans until evening, so when Sandhya asked if she wanted to join her for a coffee, there was no reason to decline. They found a table at a Coffee Day. She and Sandhya ordered mango juices that arrived swirled with pink syrup and topped with a maraschino cherry. After the first few sips, it was sickeningly sweet.

"Is most of your family in Chennai?" Sandhya said.

Vega paused. The city had announced the name change when she was still in the States, and *Chennai* still sounded foreign to her. "My parents are." She recalled the phrase she had used when talking with Nur Chachi. *Only child.* But she couldn't bring herself to say it again. "How are your law school applications coming along?" she asked.

"I'm thinking of deferring for a year, even if I get into my top choice. I think I can do better work in India than in the States. Like, the fieldwork here is meaningful. Programs in India don't have these crippling overhead costs. Everything can be direct and impactful. You get a twenty-thousand-dollar grant, and you can get basic nutritional access for an entire village. You can fund direct aid *and* capacity building. What would twenty thousand give you in the States? You have corporations and law firms blowing that on a single weekend retreat. Money is nothing there. Nobody cares about affecting change."

"But there is meaningful work to be done in the States. I'm not an expert on America, but my impression is that not all of its issues have been resolved."

"Possibly." Sandhya paused, then took a long sip. "But here people care about addressing poverty. Charanya is always collecting books and money for Ganga's kids. It's part of the culture."

Vega laughed. "I think if anybody had a choice between an adequate salary, and the occasional act of charity, they would choose the former."

"It isn't charity, exactly. Anyway, one issue in the States is the white savior culture of the nonprofit field."

"But there is a Brahmin savior culture here, no? Most of us have Brahmin names. We attended English-medium schools. And now we walk through villages, lecturing poor women on nutrition."

"But it's different. We're all Indian. There's a shared foundation." Sandhya fidgeted with her straw. "I had this argument with this roommate of mine before I came here. She's super Texan. White girl. Republican. The kind of person who says things like, 'I don't dislike immigrants. I just think they need to come here legally.' In any case, she pierced her nose over the summer. She has this big, gold hoop. And I asked her, point-blank, 'When have you ever had an interest in the East? Or, frankly, brown people at all?'"

"There's nothing sacred about a nose ring, is there? I feel full license to wear pants whenever I want, without worrying that I'm offending Westerners by dressing in their traditional garb."

"But that's like saying, 'If there's a Black student association, why can't there be a white student association?' It's not the same thing."

"I suppose the difference is this: Some fifteen percent of India's population can't afford dhal. Ganga's family is in Madurai, and he lives apart from them so he can work at Mukti and send his daughter to Sri Meenakshi Government College. Nose ring arguments seem trivial in comparison."

Sandhya stared at her. "Have you traveled much in the States? Outside of New York?"

"A bit."

"Come south. Come to Texas. Then tell me what you think."

Vega was tempted to argue but changed her mind. They finished their juices and made idle conversation about Sandhya's upcoming trip to Kerala. She asked for the check, insisted on paying, and took a long route home, past the turnoff for Olcott Kuppam.

# 14

She ran into Murthy at Higginbothams bookstore days later. They lingered in the literature section, browsing novels by Bapsi Sidhwa and Rohinton Mistry that they both deemed too depressing to bother with. Child brides shipped off to remote villages. Young men forcibly sterilized. "When did Indians become so Dickensian?" Murthy asked.

"It's the dilemma of the postcolonial novel, no? Do we show the tragedy of daily life, or are we supposed to portray ourselves as healed and ready for self-governance?"

"So, either way, the writing is for a Western audience? We have to show ourselves as we want them to see us? Not tell the stories we want to tell?"

"I suppose so." Vega picked up *The God of Small Things*. "I feel a cultural pressure to read this," she said. "But I really have no desire to."

"How did you avoid it? It was splashed all over the papers when it came out. She won the Booker."

Vega shrugged. "I was in the States when it was published. Catching up on my James Baldwin." She hadn't mentioned Baldwin as a nod to Murthy's sexuality, but she regretted the slip a moment later. She could have chosen any number of writers. Why Baldwin? But Murthy seemed not to notice.

"I wouldn't recommend the book, if you're tired of tragedy," he said.

Vega imagined making a life with somebody like Murthy. She hadn't allowed herself to feel any real attraction to him. She was not one to enjoy far-fetched fantasies—actors, cricket players, and other impossibilities. But it was nice to think about someone besides Naomi. And she pictured meeting a man with Murthy's gentle intellectualism, his Gandhian look. A man so aloof his affection was surprising.

She left empty-handed, and he with a book of crossword puzzles for his mother. "She has an obsession with these," he said. "She'll spend hours on them." Vega hoped he would keep talking, maybe suggest they go for a coffee or a juice. But he nodded to her, then walked in the opposite direction.

She began sending her résumé to other NGOs, mostly in Madras, but one in Bangalore and two others in Bombay. All advertised similar work to Mukti. *Through our rural toilet project, funded by UNICEF, we teach basic sanitation to villagers. Using theatre as a medium, we teach reproductive health to underprivileged girls.* Still, she told herself that any interest from another organization would give her permission to quit her job at Mukti and start something fresh. A few friends from Rhodes School had moved to Bombay after college, and she knew of others in Bangalore. Maybe a new city, some new roommates, would provide a welcome change.

She had drafted multiple emails to Naomi, none of which she ever sent. Still, she felt a touch of anticipation, days later, when she saw she had a new message. But it was only from Shoba, written with the formality of a turn-of-the-century telegram.

> Dearest Vega: I wonder if you remember our friend
> Suresh. He is a very good and nice man. He will come
> to Madras at August end to visit his parents. If you give
> consent, I will send some items from the States.

The email had been sent from mohan.engineer@aol.com.

Weeks later, when she returned from work, her mother said, "A man came to see you. He said he would try tomorrow morning." For a moment, she hoped it had been Murthy. But Rukmini kept looking at her, then said, "He is somebody you met in the States, apparently."

Suresh came to her house on a Sunday afternoon. He was more pleasant-looking than Vega remembered. Even a bit attractive. They took a walk towards the beach, then ended up in a tea shop where, he said, he used to come during his IIT days. He had studied engineering, he said, but his best memories of college came from his time in the theater. "We performed Beckett," he said. "You've seen *Waiting for Godot*?"

"I haven't. I read some of his poems in undergrad."

"*Godot* is a lovely play."

He walked her back to her porch and, before leaving, said, "I would be very happy to see you again."

"What was it he dropped off?" Rukmini asked, later that evening.

"Just miscellaneous stuff."

"Don't say *stuff*."

"Items, then. Miscellaneous items." Suresh had brought a ShopRite tote carrying a few things Vega had left behind at Shoba's house and wouldn't have missed: an unopened jar of night cream that Shoba had coaxed her into buying, a hair clip, the cardigan she had worn on her flight from Frankfurt to Newark when she'd first arrived. Had Shoba asked, she would have told her simply to throw it all away.

"Give the things to Vasanti," her mother said. "She's very resourceful."

Suresh's version of the States was different from anything Vega had ever known. It was sequestered and suburban. He had been living in New Jersey for the past seven years, working for the same software company. He loved his colleagues—men from Kentucky and Queens and China. Once a month, they went out to eat together, usually for Szechuan food. He loved Newark Airport and spent weekend afternoons at the windows overlooking the tarmac. He loved playing tennis, something he had never done during his years in India, where all the tennis courts were attached to private clubs. In the States, in New Jersey specifically, they were open to everybody. There was one close to his flat. He went often and would spend hours there. Mohan was his doubles partner.

They were at the beach at Theosophical Society, a place Vega chose because it was walled off from the rest of the city and she was confident they wouldn't run into anybody. Suresh had arrived, looking tense, carrying a bottle of lime soda and two stainless steel cups. In the hour since, he had relaxed. He had slipped his sandals off, asked her questions about Mukti, and listened as she recounted a sanitized version of her years in New York. He confessed he had noticed her at the party. "Shoba said that you were so smart. The smartest person that she knows."

Vega laughed. Her reputation with Shoba hadn't been earned through any demonstration of academic talent, but because Vega could navigate the New York City subway system. At the party, Shoba had taken her from room to room, introducing her to a series of indistinguishable, sari-clad women, saying, "Vega is like a big sister to me. She knows to take the train!"

"She said you want to earn a PhD." He looked reflective. Vega noticed, for the first time, how long his fingers were. His thin frame, that of a man who liked to play tennis. He had Murthy's gentleness. That air of decency.

Normally, Vega wasn't drawn to people like Suresh—people who led lives of innate, doglike happiness. But in the time between their visits, she found herself thinking about him. She didn't fantasize about *him* specifically—certainly not in a sexual way. But she fantasized about stepping into his life. She wanted to live in a cozy apartment. She wanted a perch from which to start her PhD. She wanted to never again worry about a student visa or mercurial financial aid package. She still fantasized about Naomi—about the two of them living together in Philadelphia, their lives pulsing with friends and lectures and dinner parties and sex—but the fantasy was tinged with bitterness, a delusion that left Vega even more desperate and lonely.

Marriage had not crossed her mind until Suresh proposed in late October. They had known each other a little over a month and she still considered him to be Shoba and Mohan's friend, which made him— despite the affection she felt—parochial by association. She laughed, then said, "Are you mad?" She had had a similar reaction, early in the summer, when Rukmini had said to her, "Perhaps it's time to meet a nice boy." She had spoken so gently, but despite her tone—or maybe because of it—the line had stung.

A few days later, Suresh tried again. "We can make each other happy," he said.

They were walking to the IIT campus to meet Gayatri. Gayatri and Suresh, it turned out, had known each other briefly at IIT, and had worked together in something called the Process Systems Engineering Unit. There were no shared interests connecting the three of them, but Vega liked that Suresh and Gayatri liked each other. And she liked the feeling, once again, of being part of a circle of friends.

He stopped on the sidewalk and scratched his head. The gesture made him look like a little boy. "Think about it," he said. "That is all I'm asking of you." Looking at him, Vega's life shifted into focus. A green card. A PhD. A man who was kind, and who asked so little of her, who had no power to hurt her. She didn't answer him that afternoon, but a few days later, she met him in the empty flat of one of his former classmates. She didn't feel any desire when he kissed her, but a deep, almost familial sense of comfort. He undressed her nervously, handled the condom as though it might break, and came quickly and apologetically. "It's okay," she told him. "It really is okay, Suresh." He confessed that he'd only ever been with one other woman; he'd had a Christian girlfriend in college, but he'd always known that she wouldn't marry him—that her family wouldn't allow it—and for a while, after they parted ways, he'd assumed he would never marry anyone. Hearing this, Vega hurt for him. All the happiness the world can seize from you. Those awful fates determined at birth.

# Part 3

# 15

Shoba was the next person to learn about the pregnancy. This wasn't intentional. Days after her meeting with Margo, Vega gagged in Shoba's kitchen while eating a banana. She spit the mess into a napkin. Shoba gasped, then clapped her hand over her mouth in delight.

"Are your nipples sore?" she asked, after Vega tossed out the napkin and washed her hands. Her earnestness made Vega laugh in spite of the nausea.

"My nipples are fine. Thank you."

"You should be tested. See your doctor. He will tell you for certain."

Shoba had just given Tara a bath and the child was sitting in the next room, assembling a set of wooden train tracks and singing to herself. In some ways, Shoba and Mohan's house was so Indian, its interior was indistinguishable from any middle-class home in South India. But Shoba had acquired a love for American toys over the past few years, as Tara entered her toddler stage, and Vega found it both surprising and endearing: the boxes of LEGOs, the animal-themed puzzles, a plastic bowling set.

She and Shoba stared at Tara for a bit, then Shoba said, "I have a very good book. She walked to her bookshelf and pulled out a copy of *Ayurvedic Garbha Sanskar: The Art and Science of Pregnancy.*

"I don't think pregnancy is something I need to study for," Vega said. But when Shoba walked to the stove to warm Tara's milk, stopping en route to the kitchen to kiss the child's head, Vega leafed through the pages anyway. They were yellow with age, and had the sweet, mildewy smell of the books she used to buy at the Murugan Old Book Stall. She felt an aching desire to be back home in Chennai. She missed the Rhodes School canteen. The dingy music studio next to the Hotel Saravana Bhavan where she used to walk Ashwini to veena lessons. She had even woken up one morning thinking of the kitchen at Mukti, remembering the smell of cigarette smoke and sweat and cooking oil. These had been flashes in her life, meaningless at the time. Why on earth would she miss the Murugan Old Book Stall? For all she knew, it no longer existed. On her last trip home, she hadn't even gone.

Shoba returned, holding a stainless steel, child-sized cup. "It was my mother's copy." She gestured to Tara, who joined them at the table and slid onto Shoba's lap. "I don't think she read it fully. Women are supposed to go to their mother's house for the delivery. That's the custom. We only need the books because we don't have our mothers."

It was surprisingly profound. Vega sat and watched them—Shoba smoothing Tara's hair behind her ear, Tara tilting her head back and draining her cup, a drizzle of milk running down the side of her mouth. She was nearly four years old, but still loved to curl into a slim fetal-like crescent when her mother held her. Vega watched as Tara slipped her hand into the opening of Shoba's kurta. Then she felt it: the tug at her nipple, the ghost of a finger on her breast.

When she returned to the apartment, Suresh was on the couch, watching a documentary. He had just come from an evening tennis match with Mohan and was wearing his baby-blue shorts. Most of Suresh's clothes were equally unmemorable. He owned Dockers in three colors and paired them with plaid shirts that hung too loosely around his frame, always with a white T-shirt underneath. She looked down at his thighs, where the shorts cut off. They were matted with hair. He had a slim build, but when he sat down a hint of flab hung over his waistline. She wondered if the child would look like him, if it would have his personality and habits. If it would speak with his flat affect, watch wildlife documentaries and true crime stories, read *Forbes India*. She wondered if she could manage to love it, nonetheless. She went to the bathroom, where she drew a warm bath and sank into the water.

A few days after Suresh had proposed marriage, they stood in his childhood home in Egmore, surrounded by both sets of parents. His mother, Kamala, trembled with emotion. She showed Vega a series of photographs from Suresh's childhood and an athletics award he had received in secondary school, stamped with the signature of the Tamil Nadu Chief Minister. After they ate, she took Vega aside and showed her a gold bangle she had been saving, all these years, for Suresh's wife. It was too tight. Kamala smeared Vaseline onto Vega's hand. Even then, it scraped her knuckles as Kamala slid it on.

In the weeks following the wedding—a dismal and quiet affair in the Mylapore Gymkhana—Vega took comfort in the reminder that marriage wasn't death. She could undo things if necessary. And she wasn't even sure she would need to. She still liked Suresh's company. He was more reserved in the States than he was in India, but he occasionally offered a detail that endeared her to him—a childhood bout of malaria from which it took a full year to recover, his love for the film *Chariots of Fire*, a Polish roommate during the summer he lived in Birmingham, who liked Indian food and for whom Suresh used to make dhal makhani. Vega imagined those details coloring her rough sketch of him, bringing him to life, making her love him over time.

CUNY's offer letter in the spring of 1998 came with a fellowship, along with a handwritten note from Margo Fink. Thanks to Vega's marriage and consequent green card, there was no need to apply for a student visa. On top of her fellowship, she was eligible for a teaching stipend. She knew she was beholden to Suresh—at the very least, for her new immigration status—but for the first time in her life, she felt independent.

The next challenge was the substance of her PhD. She started her doctoral work with the intention of researching something in the field of reproductive rights. But within the first semester, her coursework began to feel lifeless. She agreed with most of the journal articles she read—articles about postnatal health access, breastfeeding rates, birth control—but with every paper she wrote, she found she had fewer original ideas to offer. She began attending lectures and readings, not only at CUNY but at NYU, Columbia, Hunter. Once, sitting in a lecture hall at NYU, she listened to a legal scholar discuss the American foster care system and she found herself wanting to raise her hand, to jump into the conversation; it wasn't that she had never thought about the subject of foster care, but she had never considered that she was entitled to an opinion.

Weeks later, she met with one of Margo's former advisees who had completed her doctoral work on the topic of Kindertransport, and she spent the following days reading both this woman's dissertation and every footnoted article she could locate. She audited a course at Hunter College called Race, Immigration, and Motherhood. She returned to the Hope Center as a volunteer and, over the course of the semester, pulled together a group of students, three from Central America, one from Yemen, and another from Somalia, who wanted to take part in a year-long interview project. She lined up translators. She tossed aside her old notes and began her research from scratch. It was like discovering a new room in a house she had lived in forever.

For a blissful semester, she immersed herself in her new research topic. She loved every component of her doctoral work—teaching, coursework, her weekly sessions at the Hope Center. Suresh was fine, mainly because he was peripheral. Vega felt sturdy. She thought occasionally of Naomi, but was no longer drawn into elaborate fantasies that, when they passed, left her flattened and wanting. Sometimes, she wished she could run into Naomi, only so that Naomi could see how well Vega was doing, how impervious to heartbreak. How she could make and remake her life in any way she wanted.

The pregnancy set things into quick and dizzying motion. Suresh wanted new furniture. He wanted to save for a larger house, with room for their parents to visit. He purchased life insurance and opened a college fund. Vega had never before been troubled when they received bills made out to Mr. and Mrs. Suresh Narayan. Now, those envelopes enraged her. She couldn't recognize herself in this new life. One afternoon at Shoba and Mohan's house, a little girl handed her a container of chutney and said, "Here, Aruna Aunty. My mom said to give this to you." Confused, Vega opened the lid, trying to make sense of the exchange. It took a few moments to dawn on her. The child had mistaken her for Aruna, the woman who made the idlis.

V ega was long overdue for a trip to White Plains. She hadn't seen the family since she first returned to the States almost two years earlier. Now Anjali was home from Smith for spring break, and Sudha asked Vega to come to the house so that they could, in her words, "fete the mom-to-be."

"We could have hosted a proper valaikuppu for you!" Sudha had added. "It isn't too late. Send me a guest list. Maya can help me plan!" But Vega had no interest in a party, or any of the ritual celebrations of pregnancy. She had actually hoped to go to White Plains alone, to savor the quiet of a solitary car ride, but in the end that proved impossible. Suresh never had weekend obligations, beyond his Saturday singles matches with Mohan. That morning he came home from the tennis court, wearing his baby-blue shorts, showered quickly while whistling "Chariots of Fire," and came out smelling, as he always did, of Irish Spring soap.

While Suresh dressed, Vega collected the gifts she had bought for the girls—a set of glow-in-the-dark bracelets for Maya, whose literary tastes she still could not follow, and for Anjali, Zadie Smith's *White Teeth*, along with a sleek black Moleskine journal. She spent money differently than she had during her graduate years at Columbia. This was a change ushered in by her marriage to Suresh. Though he was frugal and disciplined, balancing his checkbook and scrutinizing the water and electric bills at the close of every month, he spent casually whenever he felt like it. Shortly after Vega arrived, he had bought himself a Wilson tennis racket, then a rice cooker, and a subscription to

*National Geographic.* "I'm setting aside savings, of course," he told her, "but we can manage a few things here and there." Her first purchases felt reckless: a tube of plum-colored lipstick and a new pair of shoes. When Suresh didn't comment, she allowed herself a winter coat. She bought the books Margo recommended, rather than waiting for them to arrive by inter-library loan. Once a week, she stopped for a cup of coffee and a bagel on her way from Penn Station. She no longer agonized over each purchase at the grocery store, trading in an item she liked for a slightly cheaper one that she liked slightly less.

In the car, Suresh said, "The Monte Carlo semifinals are playing right now. Alami and Pioline."

"I don't mind," Vega said. "If you want to listen." Was this really the man she was going to have a child with? What had she done to her life? She closed her eyes, grateful for the white noise, and was asleep before they reached the highway.

"Look at you!" Sudha said. "You're positively glowing." She kissed Vega's cheek and pulled them both inside. "Rakesh is making masala dosa. The girls just ran to the store for a few things." She nodded to the tote bag in Vega's hand. "You know, with one child out of the house, I've finally found the time to read. Every Sunday, I go to the Barnes and Noble, order a latte, and choose a book. I finally read *The God of Small Things.*"

Rakesh was at the counter, chopping cilantro. He wiped his hands on his apron, shook Suresh's hand, and said, "Waning days of freedom!"

"He's teasing, of course," Sudha said. "It's the most wonderful journey."

Rakesh pointed to the window. Suresh's blue Toyota was parked on the street, just visible. "That isn't a two-door, is it?"

"Four-door, of course," Suresh said.

"Are you leasing or buying?"

"Buying. We will likely buy a second car as well when the baby comes."

Vega was the one who had prompted the decision to buy a second car. She had learned how to drive the fall she arrived in New Jersey and had come to love the freedom of it. Still, the topic of discussion struck her as bizarre—both too personal and too mundane to talk about so openly.

"You might want to consider something bigger," Rakesh said. "Not necessarily a station wagon, but something that gives you more back room."

"Now there isn't anything wrong with a station wagon," Sudha said. "Audi makes a very sleek one. A good price."

It was a ridiculous turn in the conversation, and Vega assumed Suresh was as confused by it as she was. But he said, "I've been thinking the same thing, actually."

The girls returned, holding a greasy white bakery box and a bouquet of tulips. Maya was fascinated by Vega's belly. She wanted to touch it, put her ear to it, and feel the baby kick. "They can hear already," she said. "And they have nerve endings." Anjali was warm and affectionate. Still, Vega caught her looking at her a few times, a curiosity tinged with disgust, before turning away quickly.

They arranged themselves around the table, and Suresh ladled the sambar. There was a brief discussion of travel. The family had just returned from a trip to British Columbia, and Rakesh couldn't recommend it highly enough. "There's more to the Americas than we realize. Don't make the mistake most new immigrants do. Traveling only to go back home."

Vega knew Suresh was just this type of new immigrant, hoarding his vacation days with a squirrel-like vigilance, determined to spend a month in India every two years. But he seemed happy enough to listen, inquiring about the quality of the hiking outside of Vancouver, and asking Maya questions about whale watching.

After lunch, Anjali wanted to show Vega her course materials. They dried the last of the pots, and Vega followed Anjali to her bedroom. It was unchanged since the year she spent in White Plains, still decorated with a frilly white bedspread and matching throw pillows. A framed

print of a daisy hung over her desk. Vega imagined Sudha painstakingly selecting these for her daughter, delivering them with such hope
of pleasing her. The thought was depressing.

Anjali held out a bound reader, titled "Anthropology of War and
Peace," and Vega flipped through it. "You're reading Partha Chatter-
jee," she said. "I read him as an undergraduate. *Nationalist Thought
and the Colonial World*. Everybody was talking about the book when
it came out. He taught at Columbia, but he arrived just when I left."
She felt a tug of jealousy, but wasn't sure what brought it on—Anjali,
her professors, or even the course readers themselves. She wanted her
articles to be bound and widely taught. Or she wanted to be where
Anjali was, just beginning her life, everything wondrous and radical
and new.

In the living room, Rakesh was holding up a signed photograph of
Al Gore. "We hosted a fundraiser at the house. Just a small thing, but
we managed to raise over five thousand dollars. I'm a Clinton guy, so
I'm feeling very good about Gore."

Anjali and Vega slid in and sat beside each other on the couch like
schoolgirls, Vega observed, briefly forced to sit with the adults. She
glanced around the room. Suresh was nodding intently. Maya was arranging scones on a plate.

"Of course, in a town like White Plains, we have so many like-
minded people," Sudha said. "A very large Jewish community here,
very educated. So they gave generously. We host a number of fundraisers in the area. People take turns hosting."

"The Clinton years were good for all of us," Rakesh said. He had
passed around the photograph. Even Sudha and Anjali took a turn
with it, though they had presumably seen it before. Rakesh returned it
to the mantel.

"If you hate women, they were great," Anjali said.

Sudha ignored her. She offered Suresh milk and sugar for his tea,
then poured for everyone else.

"People thought highly of Clinton, no?" Suresh asked.

He seemed genuinely curious. It was the extent of the political engagement Vega had heard from her husband. Recently, she had to gently explain that he shouldn't use the term "Red-Indian." "Native people?" he had asked, to which she had said, "Fine. That should do."

"You see, Suresh, what happened over the years is simple." Rakesh leaned over and blew into his mug. "You had benefits that were so generous that women had babies for the financial support. Clinton implemented work programs. He created incentives to get jobs. It was highly successful."

Suresh's nodding was maddening. Vega felt as though she were watching one of his wildlife documentaries, the prey dumbly prancing around, unaware that the predator was lurking. She always wanted to shake the screen, shout "Run!" Now she wanted to shake Suresh, tell him, "Think! Speak!" She saw the way Anjali's eyes narrowed, assessing Suresh's blandness, his simplicity. Had they only been with Sudha and Rakesh, Vega probably wouldn't have registered this feeling, but in Anjali's presence, she felt painfully embarrassed.

"Boys used to make jokes about cigars and kneepads when I was in high school," Anjali said.

"Be appropriate," Sudha said.

Anjali shrugged, spilling a drop of tea on the floor. She wiped it with her sock. "Well, that's your Clinton. Good for all of us."

They were quiet for a few moments, then Maya picked up the plate of scones and began passing it around.

After tea, Rakesh offered to let Suresh test-drive his car. "It's not a station wagon," he said. "We're past those days. But it's an Audi, so it will give you a sense of the make of the car. If that's what you're in the market for."

Vega wasn't sure if Suresh was being polite when he accepted, or if the offer actually appealed to him. Nonetheless, it was a relief to watch them leave.

"Maybe we girls can take a walk," Sudha said. "You aren't too tired?"

"Not at all." Back when she was a master's student, living in Sudha and Rakesh's home, this would have been the moment when she invented an excuse to slip back to Manhattan. But her apartment with

Suresh offered no more stimulation than the house in White Plains, so she was in no rush to go anywhere. "I'd love a walk," she said.

Anjali and Maya joined them for the first round, then went back to the house, Anjali with a bland excuse that she needed to check her email, and Maya to watch an episode of something called *That's So Raven*.

"Only one episode," Sudha said to her sternly. They watched the girls run ahead, then she turned to Vega. "You must be feeling quite anxious."

"Do I seem anxious?"

"Not at all. But it would be impossible not to be."

They walked slowly, past the many Al Gore signs, and the sole George W. Bush sign. "Another thing," Sudha said. "Many people complain about high property taxes, but the way I see it, those are the taxes that fund schools. So, you *want* a district where you are paying quite a bit. Make sure Suresh is aware."

Vega had spent entire class sessions at Columbia debating the role of property taxes in school funding. But now, there seemed no point to a theoretical argument. They slowed their pace as they turned the corner onto Sudha and Rakesh's street. "You know," Sudha said. "Rakesh and I didn't know each other very well before we were married. We met a few times, and he seemed nice enough. But we only came to really *know* each other after we were married. I couldn't have known his opinions, his tastes. How steady he would be, but also how interesting."

They approached the house. Suresh and Rakesh stood in the driveway, inspecting the interior of the Audi. Rakesh was explaining some feature of the seat belt, and Suresh stood with his arms crossed, nodding his endless nod. Vega could see their steadiness—husbands who cooked and cleaned, who concerned themselves with car seat installations. But interesting was another matter.

# 16

Rukmini arrived when Vega was eight months pregnant, and she immediately began rearranging the furniture. Suresh had finally replaced the lawn chairs with a couch and had purchased a bookshelf so that Vega's textbooks and novels were no longer stacked against the walls. But to Rukmini, it was all wrong.

"I believe in the principals of Vastu Shastra," she explained to Suresh. "Everything needs to be organized to facilitate light and wisdom. A proper home life."

Rukmini had never expressed any interest in home decoration during Vega's childhood, but perhaps Vastu Shastra was an extension of her new homeopathic lifestyle, like the elimination of rice and milk from her diet. Years back, it would all have aggravated Vega. She would have moved everything to its original place and laughed at Rukmini's pseudo-spiritualism. As it was, she was so relieved to see her mother that she wanted to cling to her, to cry. When Vega told Gayatri about the pregnancy, Gayatri's response was as tender as it was impractical. "Come home," she had said. "If you want this baby, come home and let us all help you." Now this was all Vega wanted. She wanted Rukmini to take her back home.

Suresh, as always, seemed nonplussed by the redecorating. "Thank you, Amma," he said, and went into the kitchen to warm dinner.

Vega hadn't taken any summer courses. With Margo's urging, she was exploring coursework options closer to home for the upcoming semester. "You can knock a few classes out at a local university while remaining enrolled in CUNY," Margo said. "It won't affect the trajectory of your doctorate, and it'll make your life a hell of a lot easier in the fall."

Rukmini believed school could wait. "Enroll in the spring. You need to take a semester. You won't be healed by August."

"I'll be fine, Amma." But by July, the last month of her pregnancy, Vega was beginning to suspect that her mother was right.

"You don't know how difficult it can be," Rukmini said. "How much work there is. And who will be with the baby after I leave? How do you trust a stranger to care for a newborn?"

At the grocery store, the dairy products expired days after her due date. On the television, there were trailers for films that would be released when the baby was one month, two months old. *Coming soon!* Still, the mechanics of giving birth seemed impossible. She stared occasionally at a small ship encased in a glass bottle, resting on their living room mantel. Suresh had bought it before she arrived, on a beach trip with Shoba and Mohan. She had paid only scant attention to it in the past. Now, it terrorized her. The wide mast of the ship. The thin neck of the bottle. She had fantasies of cracking it open, of somehow pulling the ship loose.

Suresh was at the office when Vega's contractions started, and even in the throes of her pain, she was grateful for his absence. What would he have done? Nodded excessively. Perhaps paced the room, practicing his backhand.

Rukmini was a task master. She boiled a pot of kashayam to speed up the labor. She rolled a tennis ball against Vega's lower back, kneading out the pain. "One at a time," she said. "Like you're moving up a mountain." She called Suresh at the office and told him to be on notice, then left a message with Vega's obstetrician. Vega had no idea where she found these phone numbers. Were they posted on the fridge? Had Rukmini and Suresh planned these details without her notice?

Suresh came home in the early evening, said something she couldn't follow, then went into the kitchen to rinse his Tupperware. It seemed such a mundane thing. She couldn't imagine doing anything mundane ever again. She watched Rukmini on the couch, the laundry basket at her knees, pairing socks. The obstetrician called. Suresh answered, spoke with her briefly, then tried to give the phone to Vega. She shook her head, walked into the bathroom, and vomited.

Rukmini brought a glass of ginger ale and tucked Vega in as though she were a child. She dozed off for indeterminate lengths of time. Minutes, possibly, or maybe even an hour or two. Then the pain shot through her and she sat up, jolting Suresh awake. She wanted him to do something, anything, to move the process forward. Instead, he sat up and stared, looking small and confused. Finally, Rukmini opened the door, tennis ball in hand and said, "I think it's time we go."

On account of her scoliosis, a childhood condition she thought she had outgrown, Vega's obstetrician had advised against an epidural. But her obstetrician wasn't there when they arrived at the hospital. Instead, there was a petite nurse who strapped her to a bed and called for the anesthesiologist. Rukmini and Suresh were in the waiting room. Vega couldn't speak through the pain, but she tried to shake her head. The nurse gave her a bowl of ice. She was wearing pink lipstick. Candy-colored. When she bent over to adjust the IV, she left a smudge of it on Vega's gown.

Somehow, though, the shot never materialized. Another obstetrician—a woman Vega didn't recognize—arrived in a wordless flurry. She crouched between Vega's knees and said, "You can push now!" But the command was unnecessary. Vega could already feel the baby tearing through her. She put her hand between her legs and felt its head. There was the strange sensation of touching what should have been her body, but was, in fact, not hers. She pushed again, and the baby came out, fast and slick. There was a round of applause, as though she had safely landed a plane. She closed her eyes. Someone placed the baby on her chest. Seconds ago, the being had been inside of her. Now it was soft and sentient. It was breathing. And there was Rukmini, standing over Vega, her voice shaking. "She looks just like our Ashwini. You've brought her back to us."

Suresh's affection for Asha was startling. He swaddled and held her whenever she wasn't nursing. He sang her old Tamil film songs, and occasionally American ones in which he bungled the words: *Twinkle, twinkle, little stars.*

Rukmini said, "At least he's a natural father. Your appa was the same way, from day one. With both of you." The comment was meant to soothe Vega, but instead it made her anxious. When she looked at Suresh, she saw the endless stretch of shared life ahead. In twenty years, in fifty years, this child would still be theirs. She would still bind them. Shoba visited, carrying Tara with one hand and a bag of aloo parathas with the other. Sudha sent a set of pink onesies, and a card on which she had written, *Sending all our love! Gift receipt enclosed!* Rukmini brought a green blanket, crocheted by Gayatri, using impossibly soft yarn. Vega's father called every morning and night, his voice shaking with emotion. "Don't forget to eat. Make sure she's warm. Go for daily walks."

"Of course, Appa." Vega was eating well enough, thanks to Shoba and Rukmini, and Asha was certainly warm, having been cocooned in a blanket since her birth. But walking was another matter. Vega's body was still torn, and the stitches felt inflamed. "It's all perfectly normal," the nurse said. "You're healing just fine." Vega doubted that, but she thanked her anyway. It was a different nurse now, with orange-hued lipstick, a powdery-looking woman who smelled appropriately like talc.

"Mine are teenagers," the nurse said. "But I tell all our patients, I remember it like it was yesterday. You never forget it. Especially the first one."

Vega winced as the nurse pulled up her mesh underwear. She watched her refill the ice bucket and supply of sanitary napkins, then, as an afterthought, refold the fleece blanket at the foot of Vega's bed. She was so petite, it seemed impossible that she could ever have pushed out a child. Now she walked quickly, her sneakers squeaking on the linoleum floor. "Remember," she told Vega. "Fluids and rest. Fluids and rest."

But at night, when it was quiet and Asha lay, half dozing on Vega's chest, all of these people—their advice, their gifts, their noise—were utterly inconsequential, running through her mind like meaningless song lyrics: *gift receipt daily walks perfectly normal*. She examined Asha's palms and the perfect curl of her ear, kissed her mouth, wrapped her hands around the entirety of her back. She marveled over her breath, the impossible fact of her breath. She touched the scab around her belly, the remnants of umbilical cord. For the first time, the arc of her life seemed to be shaped by a peculiar and perfect logic: This was the reason behind every loss, every wayward step. This was why she had been born to begin with. So that she could make Asha. So that Asha could exist.

One month after they brought Asha home, Rukmini instructed Suresh to drive her to the mall. "You stay here!" she told Vega. "I'll shop for you. You need more practical clothes. You can't breastfeed in these idiot kurtas."

Were Vega planning to go with them, she would have found the outing unbearable. As a child, she and her mother spent hours in Naidu Hall, where Rukmini pointed to every sari that caught her eye and the salesmen unfurled them for her, one by one. Rukmini would examine the fabric and haggle over the prices. In the end, she would buy nothing. They were all too plain, she would say. Or too busy. Too synthetic. Then there was the frenzied set change, the men refolding the saris and preparing for the next customer. It all made Vega cringe—the obsequiousness of the salesmen, the pile of clothes left behind in her mother's wake. But Rukmini would be oblivious to the damage, sighing loudly, complaining that it was impossible to find good quality anymore. Even Ashwini, a devoted shopper, avoided these trips.

"You really don't mind?" Vega asked Suresh at breakfast. He was standing next to the stove, eating his toast. The counter was scattered with crumbs. Normally, the sight would have irritated her, but now her reaction was mellowed by sympathy. She imagined Rukmini, sorting through the aisles of Macy's and JCPenney, examining the sturdiness of each button, asking to see every sweater in a different size, accepting every sample of perfume. Then there would be Suresh, waiting on the bench in the middle of the mall, working his way through *The 125 Best Brain Teasers of All Time*, maybe pausing to buy a cookie from Mrs. Fields.

Suresh opened his mouth, but Rukmini spoke first.

"Of course he doesn't," she said. "How else will I get there? You need clothes and an afternoon alone with the baby."

The offer of clothing didn't much appeal to Vega. She had worn a small rotation of leggings and T-shirts over the past month. The most reliable item in her wardrobe was the old cardigan she had left behind at Shoba's house years back that had made its way to Chennai, via Suresh. But the prospect of an afternoon alone, with only Asha, was wonderful.

Asha fell asleep shortly after Rukmini and Suresh left. Vega sat in the kitchen for a few minutes, taking in the small noises of an empty apartment—the buzz of the window unit, a neighbor opening and closing a door, a passing car. She made a messy sandwich—a fried egg with chili pickle, rolled up in an aloo paratha—and settled in front of the television. *Sleepless in Seattle* was just starting. Vega thought she might watch for a few minutes, long enough to finish her sandwich, but it drew her in. She had seen the movie before, with Halima, but it seemed sweeter this time, the characters more charming and the love story more plausible.

She made a cup of tea and went to her computer. There was a list of emails she needed to respond to: old notes of congratulations from her cohort, another from a professor offering her a gently used Pack 'N Play, and PDFs of articles sent by Margo. Instead, she looked up

Naomi's photograph once again on the UPenn graduate student page. She was looking to the side, her curly hair cut shorter. Vega clicked on her school email address and let her mouse hover over the name. Then she shut the computer down.

It was starting to drizzle just as Asha woke, and Vega picked her up and held her next to the window, staring at the gray of New Jersey. Then she carried her to the bed and lay beside her. The milk from one breast dripped onto Asha's cheek as she nursed from the other, and Vega wiped it away, then ran her finger along the baby's chin. After some time, Asha fell asleep again, the nipple still in her mouth. Vega kissed her forehead and stroked her belly. She dozed off beside her, waking only to the sound of Suresh and Rukmini coming home.

"Everything made in China," Rukmini said, when Vega came into the living room. "But I bought you some decent wrap-dresses. That will be easy enough to use for nursing."

Suresh had dropped onto the couch. As predicted, he was holding a wax paper bag from Mrs. Fields with half a cookie remaining. When they left the room—he to check on Asha and Rukmini to hang the clothes—Vega broke off a piece. It was macadamia nut. She let it fall apart on her tongue.

Margo visited on a Tuesday in October, carrying a box of galleys from Columbia University Press, and a copy of *The Lorax* for Asha. Suresh was at the office and Rukmini out for a walk when Margo arrived. Rukmini had made something of a friend, a retired gallery owner who lived on the next block, who had visited India twice, and who Rukmini described as "very cultured." The fact of this woman was hard to believe. Vega hadn't met any of her neighbors, beyond a passing hello. It hadn't occurred to her that she would live in New Jersey long enough to make the effort worthwhile.

"So, this is home?" Margo asked. She set the box down and bent over Asha, who was stirring on Vega's lap.

"For now, at least."

She expected Margo to ask a follow-up question, but she just said, "Let's trade. I'll hold the baby, and you go through the books." She went to the bathroom and washed her hands, then joined Vega on the couch and eased Asha onto her lap.

Margo had a son, but she rarely talked about him except to say that he had moved to Colorado for college and stayed after graduating. There was a small photograph of him on her desk, dressed for a hike and staring past the camera. "He has his own life," Margo once said. "We talk once a month or so." It was a passing comment Vega hadn't thought much of at the time. Now, looking at Asha, it was unimaginable that she would ever grow up, wander off to another corner of the world, need nothing more from Vega than an occasional phone call. She had wondered, since those hazy nights after Asha's birth, if it was normal to love one's child so much. To crave her skin, the folds of her palm. It couldn't be normal, she reasoned. If it were, how did Rukmini seem to be so blithely surviving? Why didn't she choose to die after Ashwini died?

There was an odd assortment of books. *Legal Pluralism in Ethiopia*; *The Subculture of Skateboarding*; *Perspectives on Death and Dying*. "Nothing on your specific research questions," Margo said. "But some of these are younger researchers, and their writing is engaging. I'm supposed to bring them to the department next week, but I thought you should take a look first."

Vega picked up *Legal Pluralism in Ethiopia*. "I know this author's name," she said.

"Mengistu," Margo said. "She's from Berkeley. She's been publishing some non-academic papers too. She had a piece in the *Atlantic* last month. Without putting too much pressure on you, this is where I see you in a few years. Once you really sharpen your research questions."

Vega ran her finger along the binding of *Legal Pluralism in Ethiopia* and opened to the table of contents. She felt the same mix of excitement and envy that had surfaced a few months earlier, sitting in Anjali's bedroom and leafing through her course reader. Only this feeling was infused with an arrogance she had never before experienced. She could do this, too. She could write a book.

Rukmini came home, greeted Margo effusively, and went into the kitchen to set out lunch. "It must be hard for them, to have you so far away," Margo said.

"I think it is, in some ways." Asha was making small, fussy noises in Margo's arms. It had been two hours since she'd nursed, and Vega's breasts were starting to fill. "But I don't know how I could have moved forward in academia if I had stayed in Chennai."

Rukmini stepped out of the kitchen, holding a dish towel. "Of course you have to *do* something here. Something you couldn't have done at home. Then, only, is the sacrifice worthwhile. That's my opinion."

Vega went into her bedroom to nurse Asha. When she came back to the living room, Margo and Rukmini were seated at the table over plates of idlis and chutney.

"The intellectual minds tend to stay put," Rukmini was saying. "The doers come to the States. The engineers and the doctors. Not the scientists, the artists, the poets. So it isn't a brain drain, really. We keep our best."

Rukmini had delivered a similar speech, weeks ago, at Shoba and Mohan's house, when she discovered one of the guests had never read Jane Austen. "Is that typical of people in your field?" she had asked. "To not read books?" The woman, a pulmonologist living in Chester, hadn't said much in response, had simply stood up and refilled her plate. Later, in the car, Rukmini said, "These people really are of a different intellectual class entirely. Good riddance to them, I say."

"I think I've cautioned you about this before, Amma. If the Communist Party ever rose to power in India, you wouldn't fare well. You'd be hanged on the spot."

"At least I wouldn't die an idiot," Rukmini said.

It may have been the delirium of new motherhood, or Rukmini's characteristic lack of self-awareness—Vega imagined that Suresh, who was driving the car and well within earshot, was not well-versed in Jane Austen—but the comment had made her laugh, quietly at first, then uncontrollably. A few days later, as though he had been mulling over this conversation the entire time, Suresh said to Rukmini, "I read *Sense and Sensibility* during my B. Tech."

"Is the baby asleep?" Margo asked Vega.

"She always falls asleep when she nurses. It's her only pattern of behavior that I seem to have cracked."

"Well, they change, of course. The moment you figure something out, it goes away."

After lunch, as Rukmini was clearing the plates, Margo said, "Listen, I wanted to add one more thing. I want you to keep your eye on every conference you can get to. There's the annual social science conference in Chicago, but that might be a bit ambitious this year, in terms of the baby. There's a smaller working group that convenes at NYU, and another hosted by the UPenn Press."

Vega paused, feigning interest in the skateboarding book. "Tell me about the ones at NYU and Penn."

"There's nothing much to tell. Just register with your CUNY code and it will be free."

"The UPenn Press conference is at Penn itself?"

"I'd imagine. I can't think why it wouldn't be."

She and Naomi hadn't seen each other in three years. Had Vega known, at the time, that three years would pass without any contact between them, she would have found it unbearable. But, looking back, it was the perfect window of time—brief enough that Naomi might still feel something, but distant enough that they wouldn't have to untangle all that went wrong. "I'll plan to attend both," she said.

"Good." Margo nodded towards the pile on the floor. "Now tell me which books you want to keep."

R ukmini left just before Christmas. "When next I see the baby, she'll be walking," she said. "It hurts my heart."

"It won't be long, Amma." They were standing at the gate at Newark Airport. Vega was holding Asha in a carrier—another gift from

Sudha and Rakesh. With her hands free, she was arranging Rukmini's boarding passes in her wallet. In the distance, Suresh was standing at the window, staring at the planes.

"Come to India in the summer. Appa needs to meet his grandchild. You can manage the flight on your own. I know you can."

"I know."

"Keep her safe. Manage your studies and keep her safe." Rukmini pressed her cheek against Vega's, kissed Asha's head, and boarded her flight.

In the weeks after Rukmini's departure, Vega ping-ponged between thrilling freedom and desperate loneliness. She delighted in her ability to snack again without her mother constantly prodding her to eat properly, and to doze off while nursing Asha without the sounds of footsteps and banging cabinets in the background. She was relieved to no longer facilitate conversation between Rukmini and Suresh, who—once they departed the comfortable terrain of food and Asha—seemed to have no common interests.

But she missed waking up to the smell of frying onions. She missed the small observations Rukmini made of Asha, full of grandmotherly wonder. *Look how strong her grip is. She loves when you sing for her.* She had cooked Asha her first solid food, dhal and rice pounded with ghee, and coached Vega as she eased the spoon towards Asha's mouth. One afternoon, Rukmini accidentally called Vega "Ashwini." This happened so often when Ashwini was alive that they mechanically responded to each other's names. But now it caught Vega by surprise. She and Rukmini moved through the rest of the day in a stunned silence. As she was packing to return home, Rukmini said, "I have some of her things. Jewelry and whatnot that I planned to leave for her. The coral necklace. You remember."

Vega remembered, but vaguely. Her mother's jewelry box had been a thing of fascination when she and Ashwini were younger. There was a time when she would have known exactly which pieces were going to go to her and which would go to Ashwini. It hadn't crossed her mind in years.

"They'll all go to Asha, of course. It will mean something to her, eventually."

She had been shaken by this realization, after Ashwini's death, that all the private memories they shared no longer held any meaning to anyone besides her. Who else knew how much Ashwini had cried over those damn kittens? Who else had been there when they ogled the contents of the Cleveland Hospital vending machines? When Vega first had her period, Ashwini—gripped by the news—had asked, over and over, "What *kind* of hurt is it? Does it hurt like a cut?" Had she lived, this may have become a joke between them. But the memory was worthless now. Vega felt something akin to that loss as she watched Rukmini fold her clothes—the kurtas she had worn over and over during the last six months, the saris she hadn't touched because they had barely left the house. There was nobody in the States who shared Vega's loss. Aside from Suresh and Sudha, with whom she never talked about her sister, and Naomi, with whom she no longer talked at all, nobody knew that Ashwini had existed.

February came. She tucked her breast pump into her backpack and boarded the train to Philadelphia. She felt so certain that Naomi would be there, that Vega would breeze into a lecture hall and find her seated near the end of a row with an empty chair beside her. Sometimes she imagined they would meet in the elevator or stairwell, or perhaps walking across campus.

But the conference itself was sparsely attended. She had to ask for directions twice. Nobody, it seemed, had heard of UPenn Press. When she finally found the building, the first session was already underway. A pert undergraduate pointed her to a table covered in blank name tags and black markers, and another with platters of melon and tiny water bottles. The presentation topics were equally uninteresting: *Polishing Your Abstract*; *Copyright Infringement*; *Finding Your Voice in Science Writing*. She sat through a session on women in publishing and listened as the presenter droned on about the problem of gender bias in peer-reviewed articles. A series of graphs was projected onto the wall. The attendees, mainly undergraduates, were bent studiously over their notebooks. Vega's breasts hurt. She slipped out, found the bathroom, and pumped in a stall. That night, back in New Jersey, she drafted an email to Naomi: *I went to Penn, hoping to see you. Maybe I should have written first. Maybe it wouldn't have mattered. I miss you.* But she deleted the message before she could allow herself to send it. Then she slid into bed next to Suresh.

# Part 4

# 17

V ega met Winston Kinney at his Thursday afternoon seminar at Montclair State, called Epidemiology of Aging. He wore a wedding band, though he never talked about his wife, and after mentioning Asha once in passing, Vega never said anything about her life beyond the university. There were weeks of flirting, office hour sessions held with the door closed, during which she pulled her chair next to his and they pretended to pore over her papers. At night, she let Suresh touch her, imagining Winston's hands moving down her breasts and stomach and opening her legs. Throughout the day she replayed the Anglicized lilt of Winston's Jamaican accent, the way he pronounced the *u* in *ecumenical* as a double *o*, and said "full stop," to emphasize a point. Physically, she found him thrilling and electrifying and new. But there was also something familiar about him. He had grown up reading P. G. Wodehouse and Sherlock Holmes, spent rural summers with his grandparents in a town called Portmore. When he told Vega about those summers, she imagined him tearing through a house identical to her own grandparents' home in Mysore. She was curious about him in a way she never had been with Suresh. She wondered what Winston had been like as a little boy.

One afternoon she said to him, "You need a TA. It isn't possible to teach three courses, including a seventy-person lecture, without a TA."

"I have a third world work ethic," he said.

"I don't know about that," Vega said. "But you do have third world enrollment numbers."

He raised his eyebrows. "If you can think of anyone who might be qualified."

It was a thrilling proposition. It was also feasible. Vega had spent the past semester at home with Asha, then enrolled at Montclair State for the spring—on leave from CUNY until the following fall. In the mornings, she dropped Asha, now six months old, at the campus childcare center. Though she remained a constant force in Vega's day—missing her, running over to nurse her in the afternoons—this arrangement gave her a freedom she hadn't felt since Asha's birth. On top of this, her coursework was effortless. There was Economic Sociology, led by a professor named Dr. Cowen, a man on the very brink of retirement and consumed by material she had covered during her early graduate school days: Adam Smith, Malthus, Amartya Sen. Her seminar, Race and Ethnicity—led by a professor close to her age—was effortless for a different reason. She read through the course packet in a single week and ordered the full texts of the excerpted chapters. She fell asleep while reading Dorothy Roberts's *Killing the Black Body*, and when Asha woke up to nurse, she reopened the book. She had taken similar courses at CUNY. But there, she had felt a tenuousness, as though she were merely auditing, as though her job were to be quiet and listen. "It's the in-between," one of her CUNY classmates, Kavita, had said. Kavita was one of the few other Indian students she had met, and though they had little in common, occasionally she made a point that lingered with Vega. "Indians are neither here nor there. We're not white, but for the most part we exist within a white America. So it's hard to know when we have the right to speak."

This had been true at CUNY. But at Montclair, the students were younger, largely white suburbanites, and Vega quickly noticed that she was the sharpest person in the room. She was also the darkest skinned. When she made a reference to the third world, the class quieted with a respectful acquiescence. For the first time in her academic life, she didn't have to work particularly hard to impress her professors. Even with Asha's relentless demands, she had time on her hands.

She stayed in Winston's office later than usual, reading student papers. She didn't know enough about public health to offer any substantive feedback, so she focused on small edits, corrections to grammar and margins and footnotes. Once, she let her eyes linger on him, his lips slightly parted as he stared down at the page. She knew that she could have him. And it felt, from that moment, just a matter of time.

Suresh was in the bedroom when Vega and Asha walked through the door, and Vega could hear his voice as she moved through the apartment. He was talking with Vikas, a college friend who lived in Houston. It was a weekly phone call that he always recounted to her later, less to share Vikas's side of the conversation, it seemed, than to replay it for himself.

He joined them a few minutes later in the kitchen. Asha was sitting in her highchair and Suresh pulled gently on her toes, then leaned over and kissed her forehead. Vega expected him to comment on their late arrival. Instead, he said, "Vikas has a new doubles partner. Punjabi guy." He took the bowl of rice and dhal from Vega, mashed it further, blew on it, and extended the spoon to Asha.

Vega had never met Vikas, nor been remotely curious about him, but he animated Suresh in a way she had never seen, so she felt a sort of distant gratitude.

"We discussed a visit," he now told Vega. "Sometime in the spring. With Mohan and Shoba, too. We can bring the girls. Make it a proper reunion."

Vega thought about all the reunions she wished she could have: a trip to Nairobi with Zemadi and Halima. A week in Paris or Rome with Gayatri, walking the length of the city, lingering in cafés. "That would be nice," she said. Asha lifted her hand and swatted the spoon. It disappeared under a cabinet.

Vega and Winston first went to his flat together under the pretext of finding a paper, an early piece he had written on the care of patients with dementia in four Jamaican parishes. "It was well regarded at the time, actually. Rather a breakthrough study in the use of qualitative data."

There was no need to find the paper, which Vega had already read. She knew, also, that Winston had not amassed enough publications to misplace one; all of his articles were compiled in a thin binder on his bookshelf. But she played along as he riffled through the files in his office. "If you don't mind," he said, "I must have them back at my place."

He lived in a tidy, sparse studio, on a commercial strip of Bloomfield Avenue. His sports coat hung on the back of a chair. A single pair of running shoes was lined up next to the door. There were no photographs, no women's clothes. The wedding band should have been evidence enough, but it struck her—thrilled her a bit—that there were no signs of a shared life.

"You live alone?" she asked.

He gave her a small smile. "You really want to get into all of that right now?"

She didn't. There was a bed in the far corner of the apartment, and she followed him there. He sat down, pulled her between his knees and looked up. The angle made him seem boyish, almost pleading. He slid his hands to her waist. She was wearing one of the wrap-dresses Rukmini had bought for her for the purposes of breastfeeding, and he looped the strings around his fingers.

"I want to see you," he said.

She touched his chin with her thumb. "You are seeing me."

"No. I want to see all of you."

He untied her dress, unhooked her bra, and slid her underwear down her legs. She had never before known that desire could hurt, that there was a small knot inside her that could wind itself so tightly that it ached. He ran his tongue over her nipples, and she worried she would leak into his mouth, but she didn't, or if she did, he didn't notice.

When he lay her on the bed, she had an impulse to apologize for her stretch marks, for the excess flesh around her stomach, but she couldn't find the words. They worked together to undo his clothes. His body was taut, almost sinewy, his skin a shade darker than hers. He opened her legs and played with her so softly she was afraid to move, afraid of knocking his hand away, and when he slid inside her it was easy, not the coarse and rutted entry she had come to know with Suresh. She said his name, and he said hers, his voice muffled by her hair.

Later that week, he lay next to her, tracing on her arm the circular mark of her childhood smallpox vaccine. They had hardly spoken over the previous two days. In class, they barely acknowledged each other. Afterwards, she had graded his students' papers and left them in his mailbox, neatly clipped together, and he followed with a quick email, indistinguishable from so many others he had sent her that semester. But that morning, when she arrived on campus, he was waiting for her outside the social sciences building. It was cold and drizzling. His hands were stuffed in his pockets. She followed him back to his apartment, and seconds after he opened the door, they were on his bed.

Now, it was nearly noon. The drizzle had turned to rain, and through the small window in his living room, the world looked gray and punishing. For a moment, Vega indulged in a fantasy: she and Winston were married, and Asha was their child. In a few minutes, Winston would make some tea, and they would spend the afternoon working from home, their books and papers spread across the kitchen table. Later that evening, they would set Asha in her highchair while they cooked dinner. They would play music and have a glass of wine. Winston would lie next to her at night while she nursed.

"We match." He turned to his side and showed her the mark on his arm. "I don't recall the last time I was with a woman who had this."

The line snapped her out of her fantasy. "What are you saying? Your wife is susceptible to smallpox?"

He kissed her nose. "You're funny."

"And you're married." She had looked through Winston's apartment once when he was in the shower, hoping for a photograph of his wife, but had found only a single trace of their marriage—a tube of lip balm, the surface stained pink.

"And you aren't?"

That was different, she thought. Her life with Suresh was something, though it wasn't exactly a marriage. But she couldn't explain that to Winston, in part because she didn't fully understand it herself. Sometimes she thought that Suresh's view of their marriage was similar to hers: a plank that steadied the foundation of a happy immigrant life. Other times, she considered the awful possibility that he loved her. "Is this part of your master plan? Your unvaccinated wife will die of smallpox, and you'll be a free man?"

He laughed. "My wife's English. She was born immune to our third world diseases."

"English?" Vega turned to him. She had assumed Winston's wife was Jamaican, maybe a childhood sweetheart for whom his affection had faded over time, an arrangement to which he had resigned himself. There was no reason this revised impression of his life should hurt her, but it did.

"I've told you this, I thought."

"You didn't. I assumed she was somebody from home. I don't know why."

"She's a professor of anthropology. At Bryn Mawr."

"You met in graduate school?"

"Does it matter?"

"She must be a smart woman."

"You're a smart woman too." He put his hand on her bare hip and she plucked it off and set it on the sheets.

"Whoa," he said.

"This is idiotic, Winston."

"What do you mean by idiotic?"

"What does anybody mean by idiotic? The word has one meaning."

He stood up and pulled on his underwear, and she thought he was about to walk away angrily. But he went into the bathroom. A few seconds later, the toilet flushed, and he came back. "Okay. You want my thoughts?"

"I don't know. Do I?"

"The way I see it, we can spend our time discussing our marriages and the mistakes we made in our lives. Or we can give ourselves one, maybe two days out of the week when we make each other happy." He put his hand back on her hip. "Look. Mine wasn't a green card marriage, but it wasn't far from it. I was working as an adjunct at three universities. That was where I met Ellie. She was an assistant professor at Temple, and I watched her career from the ground up. I saw how she and her friends waltzed into the job market with their degrees from Cornell and Michigan. They had choices at every step of the way. They *chose* their disciplines, and they *chose* their doctoral programs. And on the other end of that, they had three or four offers. Each rung led to another rung. And I was sitting there with my piece of paper from Rutgers."

"People have all sorts of paths, Winston. I did my undergraduate at Sri Vidya. Have you heard of it?"

"No."

"Precisely."

"I'm going to tell you something about me, Vega. When I was a kid, I wanted to live in a neighborhood called Norbrook. I wanted a two-story cement bungalow with a long driveway and a swimming pool in the back. I liked the idea of people bringing me shit. You know why I wanted that?"

"Because of the neocolonial condition." She meant it as a joke, but he seemed to consider the possibility.

"Sure. Yeah. But also, I was a child. My values were off. And I didn't know how big the world was."

"I think it's too big sometimes."

"What do you mean by that?"

Vega closed her eyes. "I don't know. We can't get back to things. We seize the best opportunity, but it happens to be on the other side of the world, and we can't get back."

"You're saying you want to go back to India?"

"I don't know what I want."

He smoothed her hair. Nobody had ever touched her hair, not romantically at least, and she didn't know, until Winston, how good it felt. "We're allowed to change, is all I'm saying. We're allowed to want different things at different times. We're allowed to be happy, even if it's not what we thought happiness would look like."

This became their routine. She met Winston at his apartment on Friday mornings, dropping Asha at the day care center just when it opened, and rushing to be with him by eight o'clock. They spent hours in his bed. Afterwards, they would stop at a coffee shop on Bloomfield Avenue. They browsed in Chatham Booksellers, where he bought her copies of magazines—the *Atlantic*, the *Nation*, and once a slim volume of poetry by Claudia Rankine.

"You're aware Friday is not technically a weekend, no?" she asked. "You can get away with this in India. Possibly Jamaica. But I think in the States, they are fairly attached to the concept of a five-day workweek."

He laughed. "I'll make up for it tomorrow."

Sometimes, they ate lunch at an Ethiopian restaurant in South Orange. At first it seemed brazen to be in public together, but Winston was unconcerned. "They know me here," he said. "The owner's married to a Jamaican girl." He was playful with the servers—young men who looked, to Vega, to be newly arrived and bewildered, touched when Winston addressed them by name and inquired about their weekends, the health of their mothers and grandmothers, their visa applications.

He slipped into a gentler, musical style of speaking on those afternoons. She, in turn, taught him Tamil phrases he tried earnestly to repeat, mangling them delightfully. "What language do you speak to your daughter in?" he asked.

They rarely spoke about Asha in specifics. The question both charmed Vega and made her uneasy. "I suppose a bit of both."

"Well, when she gets older and starts responding only in English, then what? You'll insist she speak Tamil, or you'll let it go?"

"That seems so far away. She's just a baby." In reality, Vega spoke mainly English at home, just as she had growing up, and Suresh spoke mainly Tamil. If Suresh had his way, Asha would grow up like Tara, who understood English but prattled in Tamil. For whom Tamil would always be her home language, her native tongue.

"Well, yes," Winston said. "But babies grow up."

One afternoon, over bottles of Habesha, he told her the story of the Rutgers professor he had met when working as a tour guide at Port Royal. Though Vega had heard a skeletal version, she examined this new one for details, trying, as she always did, to piece together the fuller story of Winston's life.

"The shit I made up as a tour guide," Winston said. "You wouldn't believe. All sorts of shit about Jamaican naval history." He shook his head. "Anyway, when I told him I wanted to study medicine and become an American doctor, he told me the truth about things. He told me no hospital in the States hires from Caribbean medical schools. He said they're something of a joke. Told me of a grant to study aging, that it was an emerging field nobody wanted to enter, because when old people die don't nobody care. It's not interesting or political. There's no right or wrong to it. It's just the way of life."

Vega, warm from her Habesha, reached across the table. Their hands were sticky and streaked with stew. With Suresh, she would have found this revolting.

"I owe the man," Winston said. "If not for him I would be here emptying bedpans. But sometimes I see these big scholars who didn't need a grant, whose families paid their way. And people like me have to work twice as hard in our research, and still don't nobody care about aging."

He told her other stories, too, and each time, she sat entranced, like a child being read to. "My first flat was in Crown Heights, the summer before I started at Columbia. I shared it with five men. All Jamaican guys. It was a word-of-mouth thing. Two to a bedroom, and one on the couch. The Huxtable residence, it was not."

"It sounds like it had a certain charm."

"Maybe. What made it interesting is that our paths wouldn't have crossed back home. Two guys were taking classes at Kingsborough Community College, working at a grocery store around the clock. I was a middle-class mama's boy from Kingston. One guy was from this neighborhood in Kingston, Arnett Gardens. When I was a kid, my mother told me I was not allowed to go there, under any circumstances. I couldn't even walk through it. And there he was, living in the next room, drinking from the same carton of milk, pooling money for beer and calling cards." He put his hand on her knee and slid in closer.

"Where are they now, these men?"

"I could probably find out, but I didn't have enough of a connection with any one of them to stay in touch. Thing is, I miss the whole collective of it. Coming home so damn tired at the end of the day. Watching sports. Listening to these boys complain about their bosses or their girls or whatever. Just being."

Vega didn't know what to say. Sometimes she ached so much for Ashwini that there was no room for any other longing. Other times, the feeling was compounded by other losses: Naomi; evenings with Halima and Zemadi; her girlhood with Gayatri before Ashwini was sick, when their lives were airy and free of consequence. Even beneath the weight of this sadness, the acquaintances still tugged at her. People she had passing conversations with. Friends of friends she'd likely never see again.

Winston wiped his hands and reached for the check. "It's the things that aren't all that special at the time that you end up missing."

One night, Shoba called as Vega was washing dishes. Asha was asleep. Suresh had just finished his call with Vikas and was in the television room, watching the news, practicing his backhand in the air.

"I've missed you," Shoba said. "You and the baby."

They had seen each other only once since the semester started, a dinner at Chand Palace with the men sitting across from each other, locked in their own conversations, while Vega and Shoba tended to the girls. Tara ate pliantly, but Asha rejected her food and reached for Vega's shirt. Vega and Shoba spent nearly an hour in the parking lot, pushing Asha in her stroller, hoping she would doze off. It had been such a waste of a night. "I'm sorry," Vega said. "It's been hard to find time these days."

"Don't be sorry. You're so busy with school." Shoba paused, as though planning her next words, and Vega wondered if she had somehow found out about Winston. Maybe this was why she called. Maybe she had driven past them in Montclair or South Orange. But that didn't seem possible. Vega and Winston weren't discreet in public, but they weren't terribly obvious, either. And Shoba didn't have a driver's license. She had failed her test on the first try and had since been putting it off.

"Can you come on Saturday?" Shoba asked. "Come for coffee, when the men are playing tennis."

Shoba still made plans around the men's schedules, as though Vega, too, didn't know how to drive. But Vega always played along. "I'd love that," she said. "I'll have Suresh drop me."


Winston had to leave town on Friday and asked if they could push things back to Monday. "Meet me straight at the apartment," he had said. "We can go to campus from there."

Normally, on weekends, she was so consumed by Asha that she didn't think much about Winston. She spent days with her at the park, or reading to her in the brightly lit children's room of the Parsippany Public Library. There were always small moments, when Asha dozed off next to her, or when she smiled spontaneously, that Vega wondered if she wouldn't need any love besides this. If she could be happy in a world tightly enclosed around the two of them.

That weekend, though, the anticipation distracted her. She only remembered, as Suresh was leaving for tennis on Saturday morning, that she had promised Shoba she would visit. They took separate cars, Suresh to the tennis courts, and she towards Edison.

Tara opened the door, painstakingly. If she stood on her toes, she was now tall enough to reach the lock. "Big girl!" Vega said, bending down to kiss her. On the kitchen table, Shoba had set out a pot of upma, sliced fruit, and homemade yogurt.

"You didn't have to do so much, Shoba."

"I wanted to. There's so much I want to talk about."

*Shit*, Vega thought. She knows. But her anxiety gave way to a feeling of relief. She could sit in Shoba's kitchen and calmly explain the whole thing. How much easier would it be to walk away now than in five years, ten years? Asha would have no memory of any of this. Suresh was a man of logistics. He would plan. He would manage.

"I'm expecting," Shoba said. "Ten weeks." She smiled coyly, almost embarrassed to be sharing the news. For reasons she couldn't understand, Vega sometimes tried to imagine Mohan and Shoba having sex. Tara slept in their bedroom most nights. Where had it even happened? On the couch?

"I'm so happy for you." Vega nodded to Tara, who was sitting on the floor, dangling a pair of plastic keys in Asha's face. "She'll make a wonderful sister."

"My sister is coming to stay for a bit," Shoba said, spooning the upma. "She'll come before the baby is due, then she'll stay to help."

Vega wandered over to check on the girls. They seemed fine, but she was feeling restless. If it didn't require so much effort to get them all out the door, she would have proposed a walk. She fixed a loose barrette in Tara's hair and wiped some drool from Asha's chin. When she came back to the table she said to Shoba, "You know, if you need another driving lesson, I'm happy to show you. Really. It's the easiest thing. And you'll need to get yourself back and forth."

Shoba shook her head, her hands resting on her belly though there was no visible bump to protect. "There's really no need, Akka. I'm happy as is."

# 18

On Monday morning, she and Winston arrived at his apartment at the same time. He was unshaven and dressed in a T-shirt and jogging pants. He kissed her as soon as they closed the door. "I left as early as I could," he said. His wife's friends were visiting from London, he explained. There was much drivel about wine. They had spent the days talking about films he had never seen.

She walked to his bed, hoping he would stop talking. It was one thing that he had a wife. It was another that this wife was an actual person with opinions, with friends who flew across an ocean to see her.

He undid the top button of her blouse and then the second. Two Saturdays back, Vega had maneuvered Asha's stroller around the racks of the lingerie section of Macy's. In the dressing room a woman who appeared to be Vega's age, but nonetheless addressed her as *mom*, wrapped a measuring tape around her chest and rib cage. She had leaned towards Vega and, with a sisterly intimacy, advised her not to be disappointed if her breasts seemed deflated from nursing. "You're doing the right thing, mom," she said. "Treating yourself to something nice. Men notice these things." The dressing room suddenly seemed so cramped, the lights artificially bright, and the task so provincial. She bought two lace bras, both overpriced, and in the car she felt an impulse to apologize to Asha.

"It's nice to be here," Winston said. "Without all the white people and all the pretentions."

"Perhaps you've never considered this. But if you have children, they'll be half-white. The half-English type, specifically."

"Fortunately for me," he said, "my wife doesn't want children."

"Never?" Vega asked.

"That's the idea."

"Do you want them?" she asked. She had known childlessness to be a circumstance but never a choice. She found it at once both enviable and desperately sad.

Winston ran his hands over her shoulders. "I suppose it isn't really my decision, is it?"

Vega was newly conscious of his eyes on her. She put a hand on her stomach, stretched in ways his wife's would never be.

One cold Saturday Vega agreed to accompany Suresh to Newark Airport to watch the airplanes. They bundled Asha and she squirmed, fat and padded in Suresh's arms as he tapped her fingers against the glass. "There it is," he said. "Lufthansa. The 747. You see?" To Vega he said, "You can spot the 747 from its hump. Like a whale hump." His proclivities, Vega sometimes thought, would be endearing if he were eight years old.

He bought a bag of miniature donuts, and they sat in the waiting area of one of the gates, breaking off bits of sugary crust and plying Asha as she played at their feet. "There is talk that eventually they'll discontinue the three-engine planes," he said. "They aren't fuel-efficient. They'll use them for cargo only."

"Is that so?" Vega asked. On a few occasions, back when Suresh was more of a mystery to her, she had been touched by his affection for planes, as though it might give way to other interests and concerns, revealing a man she could spend her life with.

"Takeoff is when the engine matters," Suresh said.

"You've told me," Vega said.

Suresh continued anyway. "Landing is a different matter. That depends on the skill of the pilot. It isn't so automatic." They sat for another twenty minutes or so. "That was the part I most looked forward to, when I went to England. The flight."

He had told her a little about the summer he had spent in Birmingham, but always in small bursts, and at unexpected times. Shortly after they married, he had poured a bottle of beer into two glasses and after draining his half, sat back on the lawn chair in their living room. "It was so cold there," he had said. "Everybody was so angry with us. All the time." One evening, in a convenience store, a security guard had accused him of stealing a pack of cigarettes and upturned his briefcase. He had stepped on Suresh's pen, breaking the tip and smearing ink onto the floor. "They call the stores Pakis," Suresh had said. "They call people Pakis too. Sri Lankans, Indians, doesn't matter. They call everybody Pakis." Most of her conversations with Suresh, until that moment, had revolved around logistical matters and cultural observations, and she had been embarrassed by his willingness to bare himself, this husband she hardly knew.

In the car, he removed Asha's coat and buckled her into her seat, kissing her cheeks noisily, then joining Vega at the front. "We should take her back to India before her second birthday," Suresh said. "While it won't cost for her ticket."

"We should."

"Not India, only. I want to visit Houston. See Vikas. Get all the guys together."

"Suresh," Vega said. His name sounded strange, too pointed, given that she could not have been speaking to anybody else. She turned around and distracted herself with the rim of Asha's car seat.

He asked if she wanted to stop at Chand Palace for dosa, but Asha snored softly from the back seat. "No need to wake her," Vega said, and they drove home.

I n bed, Winston said her name, rhythmically and desperately and sometimes, towards the end, as though it were a question. Afterwards he asked if she was cold, if he needed to adjust the heat or bring her another blanket. Once, her stomach growled as they lay beside each other, and he walked quickly into the kitchen, returning with a plate of cheese and sliced apples. He stared at her as she ate. She was not as self-conscious of her stretch marks, her body less slack and dimpled when she was lying down.

"What's next for you?" he asked.

"In what sense?"

"I mean, after you finish your doctorate. You have to go somewhere from there. Don't make the same mistake I did. Being so grateful that you forget to fight for the next thing. As though these institutions are doing you some favor."

"I don't feel they're doing me a favor. I'll find a position close to here, eventually." What she considered telling him, because maybe he would understand, was how often she looked up academic jobs in impossible, far-flung towns and cities, places that were exotic to her simply because she had never before considered them: Auckland, Toronto, San Diego. Sometimes, she imagined life in Chennai. A job at Presidency or Sri Vidya. A house close to her parents.

"Why here?" he asked. "You could go elsewhere. Start over."

"My husband's work is here. What do you expect me to do?"

"I expect you to think bigger than your husband," Winston said. "Bigger than your life right now."

"We can't all be free to think big," she said. "At least, not in a geographic sense." It was too narrow a response, she knew, but it was also the fullest and most encompassing truth she could manage. She didn't want to grow old with Suresh. She didn't want to wipe bits of his chewed dinner from the table. She didn't want to spend her life in the confines of her marriage, but it was one thing to imagine a different future, and another to begin the process—the awful, mechanical process—of remaking it.

I n the spring, Winston was invited to present at a panel discussion at Princeton, as a replacement for a reproductive health specialist who had canceled at the last minute. For two weeks he corresponded with the event's organizer, Paul Eastman, asking Vega to review each of his messages before sending them, to ensure they contained the right balance: measured, and not too eager. He wanted her to join him for his preliminary meeting with Eastman, if only for her company on the drive to Princeton and back. "It really is our research," he said. "It would be absurd for you not to join."

In the car he rested his hand on her leg. He removed his jacket at a red light, pulling his left sleeve free, then extending his right arm towards Vega, a move so breezy and expectant that she knew he had done it before. She held the jacket on her lap.

She spent the early part of the morning in the library during Winston's meeting, reading first in a dimly lit nook and later, when her eyes were strained, at a desk set among the stacks. She walked outside shortly before she was supposed to meet him and followed a circular path around the campus, sitting eventually on a bench across from the building he had entered earlier. Once she saw a man and woman who appeared to be colleagues, but as they approached, Vega noticed the intimacy with which they leaned towards each other, their shoulders grazing as they walked. She saw only one other brown face—a man in a green uniform squatting beside a rosebush and spreading mulch onto the bed.

Winston arrived thirty minutes later than expected. "No longer tentative," he said. "Officially confirmed."

She touched his hand, but he pulled it away and suggested they walk a bit. They found a coffee shop on a narrow street across from campus, marked by a chalkboard and single sidewalk table. Vega sat outside and watched him through the door, speaking with another customer, smiling as he placed the order and pulled a bill from his wallet for the tip jar. He returned with two paper cups. The table teetered from the unevenness of the sidewalk, and he steadied it, then folded a napkin and tucked it under one leg.

"You talk so easily with people," she said.

"People like speaking with me," he said. "I think it's the accent. They find it nonthreatening."

Vega realized a moment too late that she was supposed to have laughed. She considered sharing one of the milder observations she had made of Princeton: How unhurried the students were. How quiet and pristine it was, compared to Montclair State, even CUNY, where the sound of construction cut through classrooms. But for the first time his buoyancy annoyed her. She told him about the gardener, the only other dark-skinned man she had seen on campus. "It feels rather skewed, doesn't it? In terms of demographics. I mean, this is what I would have expected of a university like this twenty years ago. But not today."

"Work is work," he said.

"You don't actually believe that. Not fully."

"So, what should a Black man do?" he asked. "Turn down blue-collar work because it makes white people sad? Wait until nighttime so nobody can see him?"

"I'm not white, Winston."

"You're not Black, either."

"What does this have to do with your meeting? Why are you starting a fight with me?"

"I get tired of being jovial. You ever get tired of things?"

She laughed. "Yes. I do. On occasion, I get tired of things." In her mind, she went over the things she was tired of. She was tired from the relentlessness of milk—pumping it, storing it, providing it. She was tired of Suresh's chewing, the way he hummed softly when he read. Tired, too, of the times she was happy to see him, grateful when he drew Asha's bath or made dinner or wordlessly folded the basket of laundry. And there were other offenses she might have talked about, if there was anyone with whom she could talk about them. At the hospital, she had come so close to an epidural. Later, the lactation consultant had shown her pictures of white infants latched to their mother's nipples, and said, "Now, we *encourage* breastfeeding. Is that something you plan to do?"

"How else will she eat?" Vega had asked, to which the woman had responded: "Now, now. We ask all the new moms their preference."

These moments had upset her, but she wasn't sure which were

prompted by skin color, and which were simply American practices. And in Chennai, when she had stomped around with the women from Mukti, she may as well have been white. She was a Brahmin woman with a clipboard, going from house to house with unsolicited advice. She had wondered, over the past months, how she would have responded had she been in the position of any of those women. Had somebody appeared at her door, handed her a bag of dhal, and questioned Asha's protein intake.

Winston was quiet for a moment. Then he said, "People from the developing world will always be accused of being too simple and sentimental. No hard numbers to back up our research. Of course, if we are too clinical, they will call us dry and unfeeling. I need to strike a balance."

"That's quite a generalization, Winston. The developing world is large. I don't imagine anybody makes the same assumptions of me as they would a villager from Bihar."

Winston seemed to be barely listening. "Eastman never showed. He sent his researcher and another assistant professor. A guy junior to me who has to approve my talking points."

"Did he offer any explanation?"

"You know what you said earlier? That point about nobody comparing you to a villager."

"Yes. I stand by it. Nobody would make the same assumptions about me as they would a villager from Bihar."

"That's the difference. When someone follows me around a store or walks past me to shake hands with one of my white colleagues, it doesn't matter if I'm from Kingston or Addis or Newark. Or if I grew up in a nice little bungalow or a shanty town. They don't see a difference. When somebody does that to you, you can have an opinion on this shit."

"I'm not from the first world, Winston."

"That is unrelated to my point."

"Don't confuse me with your wife. I didn't grow up with her socialized medicine. Do you know where good doctors in India go? They go to the States." She was rambling now, and it felt good. She was tired of Winston. Tired of his self-importance, of his false camaraderie with the servers at Café Abyssinia, of his false claim to suffering. What had Winston ever really lost? Battles of ideas. Opportunities, maybe. But what had he ever held and loved and actually lost?

They took a different route home than they had that morning, driving along the street that, had they continued for an additional block, would have passed Asha's childcare center. Vega turned around to see the edge of the building. "That's where my daughter is," she said.

Winston nodded, distracted.

"Winston. I'm sorry."

"You're good. You didn't do anything wrong."

Vega thought of asking if he wanted to stop at the center and meet Asha. She imagined the moment so clearly it felt inevitable—Winston admiring the baby, all of her fingers gripping one of his. But Winston turned and the street disappeared.


Asha refused her dinner that night and clung instead to Vega's nipple. She woke in the middle of the night with a cry that gave, after a few minutes, a hopeful sign of dissipating before rising in volume. By the time Vega was standing over Asha's crib, Asha's face and shirt were crusted with regurgitated milk. Her cheeks and palms were hot and her back slick with diarrhea. Vega rinsed her in the bathroom sink, then returned to the nursery and, with Asha in her arms, slowly sank onto the floor. When she woke, Asha's open mouth gaped around her nipple. Suresh must have slept through all of this. He was in the shower. Through the closed bathroom door Vega could hear him humming, an old Tamil film song her mother used to play. She realized, as she listened, that she still knew the words.

For the following two days, Vega worked as Asha napped on her chest, then alone in the evening in the dim light of the living room. She researched comparative rates of hypertension and dementia, then returned to an old publication of Winston's, exploring the impact of multigenerational living on adolescent health. She compiled concise tables, sourcing each figure, and fell asleep on the couch.

On the third night, Suresh slipped behind her as she was washing dishes and put his finger on her arm, a gesture that felt warm and familiar. She thought, for a moment, of pulling his body to hers, until she realized he was not Winston. Still, she let her back rest against his shoulder.

"Let me finish this," he said softly. "You should go and get some sleep."

She finished Winston's talking points the day Asha's fever subsided, then drove to his apartment the following morning. He answered the door, shirtless and wearing only basketball shorts.

"Strong, virile talking points," she said. "Nothing qualitative about them. Pure numbers."

He waved her inside. "You're funny."

"Well. Thank you."

"We haven't spoken in some days."

"I, too, noticed." She had been awake since five o'clock, and it irritated her that Winston was still not dressed.

She sat on the couch and closed her eyes as he reviewed the data, listening to the scratch of his pen on the page. Eventually he tapped her leg.

"Am I waking you?" he asked.

"No," she said, her eyes still closed.

"Ellie is coming to Princeton for the talk, then staying through Wednesday. I'm always grateful for your help with the course. But if you need to use your time in other ways, I understand."

She opened her eyes.

"Vega." He looked so small and pathetic. For a moment, she felt sorry for him.

"What do you think?" she asked. "Do you want me there?"

"I think it would be for the best if I attend on my own."

The afternoon was bleak and meaningless. She sat briefly at the library but couldn't focus on anything but the sounds of the other students—the shuffling and whispering and nose blowing. She searched her thoughts for a distraction, a single thing to look forward to, but nothing came to mind.

# 19

By the end of the semester, the thought of returning to CUNY was a relief. Vega still woke up every day gripped by sadness and boredom. Asha was a delight, but she was no salve for this particular loss. Vega missed the thrill of Winston. She missed the feeling of wanting and being wanted. Sometimes, she fell asleep thinking of him and dreamed of Naomi, waking up in a tangle of grief.

But she couldn't go back to CUNY until she solved the problem of childcare. As Vega would no longer be a student at Montclair State, she wasn't eligible for day care services at the university. She found two options for Asha: a dimly lit center in Denville, next to a Dairy Queen, and a bright building in Morristown that cost more than her graduate stipend, and where they boasted their use of the Singapore Math curriculum.

"Maths?" Suresh asked later. "For babies?"

"That's what she said. And she said they have a very diverse population. She made it a point of telling me there were lots of Indians."

"Either way will be fine," Suresh said. "She's a happy, healthy baby. She will adapt quickly." He stood up, washed his plate and fork, and set them in the drying rack. It surprised her, still, how fastidious he was. He had grown up like every other Brahmin man she knew, fully removed from the labor of cooking and cleaning. Even her father, who considered himself a feminist, who devoured books by Sarojini Naidu and Ismat Chughtai, had never, in Vega's memory, washed a single dish.

"It's a forty-five-minute drive to either center. She hates the car.

It'll be too much for her." She wasn't soliciting Suresh's advice, she realized, as much as trying to extract some sort of miraculous third option. She had known from the moment she stepped into each of the centers that neither would work. One was too grim and the other too cheery, both too far from their apartment and the CUNY campus. "You barely left the house in your first year," Rukmini had told her, a few months after Asha was born. "I stayed with you all the time, and of course, we had the house girl. Kumari. Do you remember her?" At the time, Vega had been able to ignore her mother's input. Now she wanted to call her, to scream into the phone, though it was the middle of the night in India. *There is nothing like that here! We don't have house girls in the States! Of course I don't remember Kumari!* She could feel the rage forming inside her. What did Americans do for the first five years of their children's lives? There had to be some reasonable solution, something in between a building staffed by strangers and the drudgery of spending her entire day with her child.

The answer came in the form of Shoba, now six months pregnant. "You'll bring her here," she said. "We'll watch her at the house. End of story."

"That's nonsense, Shoba. You can't take care of her, and Tara, plus the new baby."

"As it is, Tara has morning kindergarten," Shoba said. "The house is too quiet. And my sister is coming to help. I won't hear of anything else."

"It won't be for long. Maybe just a few weeks, until I can find a permanent solution." That wasn't entirely honest. Vega was aware that a permanent solution wouldn't materialize, and she would have less time to look once the semester began. Still, it felt better to say that. It assuaged some of her guilt.

Shoba smiled. She was knitting a green blanket, identical to the ones she had made for Tara and Asha. "It makes me happy to have her. She's like a daughter to me. Like my own flesh and blood."

Vega was offered the chance to teach an additional section of Introduction to Sociology, and accepted it readily, less for the additional
funding than the chance to spend both Tuesdays and Thursdays in
New York. When Margo suggested Friday afternoon for their standing
meeting, Vega agreed to that, too. On those days, Suresh went directly
from his office to Shoba and Mohan's to pick up Asha. Asha no longer
nursed ravenously, so Vega was able to feed her in the mornings and
at night, and no longer had to pump during the day. Shoba sent her
cheery emails, still from Mohan's account: *Baby is fine! Nice day so we
played in yard!* It wasn't happiness, exactly, but it was a kind of freedom.

One Thursday, her office hours ended early and she went for a long
walk to the Housing Works where she and Halima used to occasionally
shop. It was late August, but already getting cool in the evenings. She
had spent the previous fall trapped inside her Parsippany apartment
with Asha, building her days around an afternoon stroll that rarely materialized, usually thwarted by naps or nursing or her own laziness.
Now, she was looking forward to the coming months. She bought new
boots, slim black jeans, and two cowl-neck sweaters. She had her hair
cut on Spring Street by a stylist who convinced her to try a new shade
of lipstick and a product called *Be Curly*. "Hair like yours, you need to
embrace it." He stood over her shoulder, staring at her reflection. "One
more thing. Don't blot your lips. It washes away the color."

Rupa, Shoba's sister, was the first to comment on her hair. "It's very
dramatic, you know. Like an artist."

Vega laughed. "You have clearly never seen me draw." She liked
Rupa. She was a bolder, more inquisitive version of Shoba, charged
with optimism about her prospects in the States. She had begun her
undergraduate coursework in Coimbatore and had moved to New Jersey both to help Shoba with the children and complete her degree at
William Paterson. When they first met, she told Vega—without a hint
of self-consciousness—that she had only visited Chennai twice in her
life: the first time was for her appointment at the consular office, and

the second was to board her flight to Newark. She seemed to admire Vega, always seeking her out and asking about her classes, but the admiration made Vega feel uneasy. Between the two of them, Rupa was the more dogged one, the one more certain of her path forward.

Now, Rupa led her into the living room where Asha was pushing a small, wooden ladybug across the floor. "She's a happy baby," she said. "The happiest baby. All day she smiles and plays."

Lately, this did seem to be true. Asha was beginning to walk and to happily prattle in some fusion of English and Tamil. She could spend hours moving from one side of the floor to the other and was so tired by the end of the adventure that she napped for hours, then slept through the night. Suresh, too, seemed even more at ease. On the evenings he picked up Asha, he lingered in Shoba and Mohan's kitchen. By the time Vega came home, he and Asha had finished their dinner—usually at Shoba and Mohan's—and she made herself a sandwich after Asha had gone to sleep, enjoying it in the quiet of her empty kitchen with the hum of Suresh's nightly news in the background.

At CUNY, the courses she taught were loud and energizing. She had a cluster of students who reliably reported for office hours, never to discuss anything specific, but to generally share their ideas and questions and grievances: The faculty wasn't diverse enough. The writing center was understaffed. Was she going to the poetry slam the multicultural center was organizing?

"I wish I could," Vega told them. "I have to get home to the baby."

In her New Jersey life, parallel to Shoba's, motherhood made Vega feel small and domestic. With her students, it gave her an aura of sophistication, as though she had crossed the threshold into adulthood. The way, she imagined, her PhD would make her feel. They called her Dr. Gopalan, and she never bothered to correct them.

In early September, she learned that an early chapter of her dissertation had been accepted for publication by *The Journal of Women and Society*.

"Is it possible this is a mistake?" Vega asked Margo. She had emailed back and forth with the editor for the past week, but she still was hesitant to trust it. She kept expecting them to solicit her for a donation or ask for her credit card information, and for the entire thing to be revealed as a hoax.

"Don't be an idiot, Vega. You're published. And it's the first of many."

Zemadi emailed, saying she would be in town at the end of the month for a few job interviews. *Would love to meet!* Vega wrote. *It's been too long.* She didn't mention Suresh or Asha in her response. She suggested to Zemadi that they meet for dinner downtown. During her Columbia years, she rarely ventured below Fourteenth Street. These days, her New York seemed larger. Sometimes, she fantasized about moving to the city with Asha, settling into a two-bedroom apartment lined with books, and a large window overlooking a busy street.

O n Monday evening Margo called her, just as she arrived home. "They sent a copy of the journal," she said. "I think they meant to send it to your campus mail, but it was routed here."

Vega paused. She could hear Suresh through the open nursery door, reading *Harold and the Purple Crayon*. Vega had brought home a stack of books on a recent walk to the Strand, but it was Suresh who sat with them each night, holding Asha on his lap as she squirmed and reached for the pages. "A physical copy?"

"A physical copy."

She knew the publication date had passed, but even then, the fact of it was dizzying. Margo's voice blended with Suresh's. *He drew a whole picnic of pies.* In her daze, she pictured the journal as she did the book. Small. Thin. Purple.

"What does it look like?"

"What does it look like?" Margo laughed. "It's beige. It looks like a journal. Come straight to my office when you get to campus and I'll give it to you. Reach out to the other authors, too. Start your networking."

In the morning, Suresh said, "You're awake early."

She had mentioned the journal to him, but he had responded with

no more enthusiasm than she imagined she revealed when he updated
her on his doubles matches. Now, she tried to sound casual. "My article
came out yesterday. There's a copy at the department."

Suresh busied himself making toast. She assumed the conversation
had passed, but a few minutes later, he said, "I can take her this morning. To Shoba and Mohan's."

She waited for him to step away from the counter, then slid her
toast into the oven. She had told Margo, recently, that she and Suresh
were better roommates than they were spouses. They took turns with
appliances, reviewed the water bills together, and divided household
tasks. She took care of their weekly grocery trips to ShopRite, and he
the ones to Patel Brothers. It was efficient and tidy. They never fought.
They both wiped down the bathroom sink after brushing their teeth.
To this, Margo had said, "Even the best roommates get annoying after
a while."

"You don't have to," she told him. "You pick her up in the evenings."

"It's no problem," Suresh said. "I like the extra time with her." He
wiped his crumbs into the sink. "And it's a big day for you."

Without the detour of Shoba and Mohan's house, she took an
earlier train than usual, and it was still crowded with morning
commuters. Normally, she was able to find an empty row. Now, she
took a seat next to a woman who seemed to be rehearsing lines for
a play. She wore headphones, but the cord dangled, unattached, over
her shoulder. She had blond hair worn in dreadlocks, and the edges
brushed against Vega's shoulder. They felt like jute, like the produce
bags her mother used to carry. Vega tried to read but was distracted
by the woman's lines. *I usually have fillet steak and mushrooms. I like
mushrooms. I like smoked salmon very much. I like having a salad on the
side. Green salad. I don't like tomatoes.* She was still rehearsing when the
train screeched into the station, talking to herself as she stood up and
inched her way to the exit.

Penn Station was thick with people who all seemed to be standing still. Only as Vega approached the exit did she realize the cause of the density. People were coming into the station, but nobody seemed to be leaving. She squeezed through a crowd and pushed open the door. The air was wonderful. Both warm and cool. But outside, under the scaffolding, another group was swarming. Everywhere she looked, people were looking up at the sky, like they were waiting for something to fall.

She walked quickly across town, then up the stairs of the sociology building. Margo was standing in the department lounge. That, too, was crowded, but nobody was speaking. "What on earth are you doing here?" Margo asked.

Vega stared at her. "My journal," she said. "This is our scheduled time." She could see it was the wrong response, but she couldn't imagine why.

Margo came closer and put her arm around her. "We need to get you home. In fact, we need to all do that. We need to all just get home."

Everything was a rumor. Nothing was verified. There had been a plane crash. In one row of the train, a woman was crying and rocking in her seat, the man next to her ignoring her. Vega tried to do the same. She thought about the woman she had sat next to that morning. Why would a white actress wear her hair in dreadlocks? Her lines pulsed, inanely, in Vega's mind: *Green salad. I don't like tomatoes. Green salad. I don't like tomatoes.*

She drove directly from the train station to Shoba and Mohan's. Their front door was open, and only the screen door closed. Inside, Vega saw two pairs of men's shoes. Mohan's and Suresh's. She walked into the kitchen. They were all seated on the floor, Tara on Shoba's lap and Asha on Suresh's. When she saw Vega, Asha raised her arms. Vega lifted her up and wandered to the kitchen. Shoba had cooked that morning. The stove was cluttered with pans. There was an untouched pot of rice on the counter.

"People were jumping from windows," Shoba said. "I saw it on the news."

"Enough," Mohan said, nodding to Tara. "She understands every-thing you say."

Suresh's words were equally useless, but his tone gentler. "You can't let yourself dwell on these things. Try not to think about them."

Vega only then noticed Rupa, seated on the floor in the corner of the living room, watching Sun TV. The news covered the crash on re-peat, the same video clip over and over. The newscaster was talking about the *Tvin Tovers*. It struck Vega how amusing this would have been in another time, another context. She set Asha down and walked over to Rupa.

"It's madness," Rupa said.

"We don't know the full story, Rupa. It may have been an accident. That would be tragic, but it wouldn't be madness."

Rupa looked at her with the same trusting expression she had worn when Vega explained the process of securing student visas. "You don't think they'll send soldiers? Make a war?"

Who was *they*? Make a war? Across the room, Tara was building a wall of blocks and Asha was watching, rapt, with that same innocent trust. The same unearned admiration. "Nobody is going to attack," Vega said. "Nobody is sending soldiers anywhere."

Mohan wanted Shoba to dress differently, to look unmistakably Hindu. He advised Vega to do the same, using more words in a single conversation than Vega had heard from him since they first met. "You should wear a sari and pottu. You need to make clear you aren't Muslim. Make sure nobody looks at you and thinks, 'Oh. That woman. She must be a sympathizer.' I am telling Suresh also, buy a U.S. flag for the mailbox. Even a small one is enough."

Vega wanted to point out that anyone they needed to worry about likely could not discern between Hindu and Muslim dress, that the nuance would be lost on them. But she didn't have the energy. The next morning, when she came to the house, Shoba answered the door wearing a pottu, along with her normal kurta and leggings. The saris were too uncomfortable during pregnancy, she said. This was the compromise she and Mohan had struck. But her appearance still bothered Vega. The pottu made Shoba look old.

Vega had planned little for her Tuesday class beyond a moment of silence and a somber transition to the scheduled discussion of Betty Friedan. But she quickly realized that she had misjudged the mood in the room. Her students had spent the past week mired in public grief and were too fatigued from all of it to care about second-wave feminism, about the plight of bored housewives. The air felt thick, and the respect contrived. She ended the moment of silence early, shuffled her papers as she gathered her thoughts, then asked, "How is everyone feeling?"

There were three other immigrant students in her class—all women—from China, Poland, and Bangladesh. Initially, Vega had imagined some level of kinship with them, particularly the Bangladeshi woman, but they had been quiet during discussions so far, and none had attended her office hours. She noticed they were part of a small cluster of students looking down at their desks, all engaging in the same meaningless shuffling she had been doing moments before.

"Honestly, I just want to fucking kill them all."

That same *them*. Who were *they*? The student speaking was normally mild-mannered and hid under a baseball cap. Now he sat back, arms folded, as though waiting for someone to challenge him. Nobody did.

And then there was Lily, a graduate student in social work, who wore a thin, gold cross around her neck. She gave the impression of a person who had all the heart of a social scientist, but none of the intellect. "There are a lot of these stories coming out of all these narrow escapes. And I've been thinking about them a lot. Like, my roommate's uncle was supposed to be working in the mail room, but he had a doctor's appointment. So, it feels like, you know, divine intervention."

There was more quiet. Then Gabe, one of Vega's favorites, a Puerto Rican man from Queens and a regular office hours attendee, said, "That's some bullshit. Everyone else deserved it because they didn't *pray* hard enough?"

Somebody made a comment about the heroism of first respond-

ers, and Vega kept stealing glances at Gabe and Lily. He seemed to
have moved on, but she was visibly wounded, almost cowering in her
seat. Vega wanted to reach out to her. She imagined asking her to stay
after class, assuring her, "We all stay stupid things sometimes." But
Lily left before Vega could catch her.

Rukmini called every evening, fluctuating between hysteria and
gloom. The hysteria, Vega found, was easier to manage. Her mother's
conspiracies she could at least refute.

"It was Pakistan," Rukmini said. "There's evidence."

"There is no evidence it was Pakistan, Amma."

"It was reported in the *New Indian Express*."

"That paper is garbage, Amma. Why are you reading it?"

"In any case, so many Indians died."

"It was an attack on an international city. The victims were from
everywhere."

"I'm hearing horror stories," Rukmini said. She had learned from a
neighbor that a boy from Chennai was among the dead. He had written his parents an email after the first plane hit, telling them how much
he loved them, how grateful he was and how sorry. Initially, Vega pictured a small boy, sitting on his knees to reach his computer. Then she
realized what Rukmini meant when she said "boy." A man, maybe in
his twenties or thirties, but a boy still, depending on who told the story.

"His name was Sekar," Rukmini said, as though his name would
matter. As though Vega might have personally known him. Later, she
searched for his name online, but the only thing that came up was
a mention of a missing investment banker named C. V. Sekaran, age
thirty-four. She wondered if that could have been him, if one half of his
family was searching while the others knew the truth. That night, she
cried in the shower. In bed, she pulled Suresh towards her. She never
initiated sex, and when she did acquiesce to it, she had to escape into a
fantasy, imagining Naomi's or Winston's body in Suresh's place. Now,
she wrapped her legs around him, trying to draw him in closer.

Rupa had lost weight. The hat she had been crocheting for Sho-ba's baby lay unfinished on the bookshelf, next to the copy of *Hindu Names for Girls*. In place of breakfast, she had started drinking something called Amrit Nectar Paste mixed with hot water. The entire house smelled like ointment.

"She thinks she won't be granted a student visa now," Shoba said. "She thinks the U.S. is going to close all their consulates."

Vega felt pressure to respond with something factually grounded, to offer some measured prediction about Rupa's future. Because Suresh was a citizen when they married, her own green card application had been little more than an administrative hassle, guaranteed the moment she dropped it in the mail. She made useless comments, as vacuous as Shoba's. *You must have confidence. It's too early to know anything.* In the mornings, when Rupa stared numbly at the news, Vega alternated between maternal warmth and irritation, the same she felt when she passed the man who huddled outside of the Fifth Avenue Au Bon Pain with his blanket and paper cup. In some moments, she wanted to take him home and feed him, and in others she wanted to scream at him to stand up and pull his life together.

Suresh, surprisingly, was both compassionate and task oriented. "It's a lonely situation," he said. "She has nobody, aside from Shoba and Mohan." It was an odd comment, given that Shoba and Mohan had long been enough company for him. If Vega disappeared from his life, she suspected he would manage. If Shoba and Mohan were to disappear, he would fall apart. Or, he would have to move to Houston, to live near Vikas. Vega reasoned that his concern for Rupa was an extension of his affection for her sister and brother-in-law. Or maybe it was what Rukmini had pointed out on the day of Asha's birth. He had a fatherly quality. He was a natural caretaker. He offered to give Rupa tennis lessons on Monday evenings. With some coaxing, she accepted.

"You don't mind?" he asked Vega. "As it is, you're home with Asha on those days. You won't have to rush home from the city."

"Not at all." It was a relief, in fact. For the past month, she had felt she owed both Rupa and Shoba some token of gratitude for the time they spent with Asha, and she had held on to a vague intention of taking them out to dinner, or maybe for a day of shopping. But she had made no concrete plans, and now she had no desire to be anywhere but on campus or in her home. Anything aside from work or Asha felt like a waste of time.

"I'm so tired all the time," she told Margo during their Friday meeting.

"We all are," Margo said. "Grief is an exhausting thing."

She opened her mouth to object. It wasn't grief, per se. Who could she have been grieving for? People whose names she didn't know? C. V. Sekaran? The department secretary, Vicky, had passed around a photograph of her brother-in-law who had been working in the restaurant of the World Trade Center. He was standing on a boat, smiling, wearing a safari hat. And then there were the smaller losses inside the larger tragedy. Zemadi had canceled her trip to New York. Halima had written some weeks back: *Adnan is applying for academic jobs abroad, but we don't have much hope for a visa under the circumstances.* "I suppose it is," she said.

# 20

One week, Asha started saying words. The following week, she began connecting them, like scattered puzzle pieces coming together to form parts of a picture. Vega assumed she favored English, but one evening, she listened as Asha and Suresh read their nightly stories. "Anda nai veynum," Asha said. *I want that dog.*

Vega wasn't charmed in the way she normally was when she heard Asha talk. Instead, she felt a creeping sense of loss, a realization that her daughter could split herself neatly in half, giving one part to Vega and the other to Suresh. As though Asha already knew her parents occupied different spheres.

Shoba's baby came in November. They named her Veena. Suresh fulfilled the role Shoba had after Asha's birth, making pots of sambar and kitchdi, pouring them into empty yogurt containers and delivering them on his way to work. "I know Rupa is there to help with the cooking," he explained to Vega. "But this way, she can focus on the girls, and Shoba can rest."

"You're a good friend to them," Vega said.

Shoba and Mohan threw a small Christmas celebration, and Vega was surprised to see the railing streamed with holly and a small, plastic tree at the center of the living room. "Rupa wanted to decorate," Shoba said, greeting her at the door. She had torn during labor, and walked uneasily, almost limping. Combined with her pregnancy weight, and the *pottu* she still wore, she looked as though she had aged twenty years.

Next to Veena, the girls also looked shockingly grown. Tara was sitting on the floor, between Rupa's legs, and Asha dashed over and slid in beside her. They bent over the baby, like two sisters glowing over their new addition. Vega assumed that she had once held Ashwini this way, and the sight of the girls sparked something in her, some combination of sadness and aching love. Rupa looked up and smiled. She had dressed up for the occasion. Red lipstick, a black and gold sari, and, endearingly, a snowman pin clipped to her blouse.

"You look like a proud chiti," Vega said, hugging Rupa. She touched the baby's cheek.

"The proudest," Rupa said.

In addition to decorating the house, Rupa had made rice, korma, and three vegetables. Vega placed their meager contribution—another sambar, cooked by Suresh—on the stove. "I'm so sorry I didn't do more," she said to Shoba. "The end of the semester is so busy."

Shoba nodded knowingly. "Exams."

There hadn't actually been exams. Vega never issued them in her own class, and students' final papers had been submitted weeks earlier. She had her own dissertation chapters to submit, but that was no more demanding than any other time of the year. She nodded anyway. "Yes. Exams."

It was smaller than the regular crowd. Shoba and Mohan had invited only one other couple, Aruna and her husband Vijay, who arrived with their usual idlis and their two sons. The boys were dressed in slacks and sweater vests, with their hair combed sternly to the side. Vijay was also carrying a brown paper bag with what looked like bottles of wine.

The women retreated into the living room and crowded around the baby. Vega followed Vijay into the kitchen, hoping she could find a task to occupy her. She had found Aruna boring from the moment she met her, but she was usually able to mine Vijay for something interesting. He had moved to the States in his final year of high school, earlier than anybody else in the group, and lived briefly on Staten Island before attending Syracuse. He had the same job as all the other men, something in software design, but he had an American affect and often made references nobody else in the room seemed to catch—references Vega believed were designed for her response only, and that she sometimes worried were an attempt at flirtation. A disparaging comment about popular culture. A reference to editorials from the previous week's *New York Times*. It was usually a bit too staged and deliberate, but a welcome alternative to the conversations that took place among the women.

Vijay opened the bag. "We stopped at Bottle King. Following our president's advice to go shopping. We will save the country through consumerism."

"I don't think Shoba and Mohan drink," Vega said. "But I'll have a glass."

He poured two plastic cups, a bit too generously, and handed one to Vega. "So, how is New York these days?" he asked. "Still reeling, I imagine."

"Difficult to say. I don't leave the area around campus too often." She tried to think of a way to change the subject. She hated talking about September 11. In her classes, students were divided and intransigent, one side hurling facts about the Taliban and the CIA—as though they had studied the subjects for years—and the other shouting stale arguments about retribution. "Every asshole is a foreign policy analyst or a national security expert," Margo observed.

She and Vijay wandered into the dining room, where the group seemed to be migrating. In the corner, Aruna was saying to Rupa, "I don't let the boys play with just anybody. Especially in these times. You must know the families first."

Vega felt an urge to shift to the corner and rescue Rupa from whatever unfounded advice Aruna was providing. But Vijay was still talking, asking if Vega had read the Nicholas Kristof column on Pakistan.

"I've been saying this since the day of the attacks," he said. "The United States has to choose between its alliance with India and its backing of Pakistan. Pakistan has been harboring terrorists since the 1950s. But now they're a strategic ally to the Bush administration. So, we're backed into a corner."

Vega was nodding along. She was sure if she worked hard enough, if she blocked out all distractions, she could form an opinion. But Asha was standing at the table, reaching for a plate. Suresh was nowhere to be found. And she could hear Aruna, still in the corner with Rupa, saying something about Plainfield Public Schools. "We looked at a house there, and I said to Vijay, 'nothing doing.' The white families there are even worse than the Blacks."

Vega excused herself and walked to the table, where Asha was holding a plate and reaching for one of the pots. Vega spooned some of the rice and korma and found a quiet place in the living room to feed her. It was an old habit, left over from Asha's year of ravenous nursing, when Vega was constantly seeking out private corners every time the baby fussed. She found herself missing the quiet time now that Asha no longer needed it.

She looked around the room as Asha ate, trying to match the cluttered space with the house where she had arrived six years ago. At the time, New Jersey had seemed so barren and desolate, and she had thought of Shoba and Mohan in the way she did the explorers she used to read about in school: Vasco da Gama landing on the shores of Calicut, Moksadeva crossing over into the Hindu Kush. It seemed an adventure without reward. She had found Shoba's daily routine depressing—waking up early, dressing in a freshly ironed kurta, waiting all day for Mohan to come home. She once told Vega that the grocery store made her nervous. "There are too many types of jam. It's very stressful to choose." She was no more independent these days. If anything, she was weighed down further by two children. Still, she seemed to delight in it. Theories that Vega and her students built around Betty Friedan, the drudgery of domesticity, didn't seem to apply to Shoba's life. Sometimes, Vega pitied her. Other times, she envied her.

Asha finished her food and was chewing on the plate, spitting out wads of red paper. Vega collected the mess in her hands and picked her up, hoping to pass her off to Shoba or Rupa so she could use the bathroom. She walked into the dining room. They weren't there, nor were they in the kitchen. She paused by the glass door, overlooking the patio, and then saw them sitting at the table. Rupa was bent towards Suresh, and for a moment, Vega wondered if she was consulting him about something technical. Her visa application, graduate programs, her tennis backhand. But that wasn't the expression on her face. She looked enamored. Like a woman falling cautiously in love.

In the car, Vega said, "She looks so happy, Rupa. So much better than before."

"Yes."

"You remember how nervous she was? After the attack? I think the time with you helped. Your tennis lessons and whatnot."

Suresh fidgeted with his seat belt. In the back seat, Asha was saying, "Appa. Amma appa amma appa."

Even looking back, Vega wasn't sure where her anxiety ended and her relief began. She imagined freedom. Contacting Naomi again, or maybe seeing Winston. Moving with Asha to an apartment in the city. But then, of course, there was the thought of Asha split in half. Speaking Tamil in one home and English in the other. Asha, who couldn't possibly understand what was happening. Who was in the back seat saying, "moon moon moon," at the same time as Vega said, "Suresh."

Suresh looked at Asha in the rearview mirror. He swallowed audibly.

"Suresh. If you need something." She didn't fully know what she meant by the offer except that, whatever he wanted, she wanted him to have it.

"Appa!" Asha shouted. "Moon."

Suresh stopped at a red light. He reached his arm back and stroked Asha's hair. "I know, kannama. It's following us."

For weeks, they spoke of little besides logistics. It was a plan Vega had silently committed to shortly after the Christmas party, but it quickly became clear this new arrangement wasn't a departure from the old one. The start of the semester was busy. She and Suresh talked of sending Asha to the nursery school Tara used to attend, but for now, Vega still dropped her with Shoba and Rupa on her way to New York, and Suresh picked her up every evening except for Mondays, when he continued his tennis lessons with Rupa. He took over the grocery shopping, buying the usual rotation of foods, along with the occasional item he found on sale. One week, there was Breyer's strawberry ice cream in the freezer. The next, she found a twelve pack of Lever 2000 soap bars in the bathroom cabinet. Vega had only known Suresh to use Irish Spring and was surprised, each morning, by this new smell when he came out of the shower. This was the extent of the change in their lives.

At CUNY, Vega flirted with another graduate student, a statistician named Edwin she had met while studying at the Law Library. She didn't expect it to go anywhere, but she returned every afternoon to the quiet stacks, hoping to see him and usually succeeding. They drank burnt coffee from the thermoses on the first floor and took breaks together over the large jigsaw puzzle—*Paris, City of Lights*. An impossible mess. The entire border was blue, and all of the buildings the same shimmering gold. They made little progress on the puzzle, mainly staring down and shifting the pieces as they talked. To her relief, he asked little about her life but was happy to talk about his. His parents had divorced when he was seven. He had attended an Episcopalian School in Connecticut called St. Albans. "You know what our school motto was?"

"Tell me."

"*Every Boy, Every Day.*"

"This is not possible."

"Oh, it is. It was painted across our hallways. There was a huge sign outside the school. Really makes you wonder the composition of these advisory boards."

She told him about the Rhodes motto. *Fabricating Excellence.* When she was in school, nobody besides Gayatri saw the humor in this. When she once laughed about it in front of her mother, Rukmini had said, "Well, that is the point of school, is it not? Would you prefer they fabricate mediocrity?"

"Did it work?" Edwin asked. "Did they make you excellent?"

"When your tuition is ten times the per capita GDP, you see some results."

Occasionally, their hands brushed or their feet knocked into each other underneath the puzzle table, and they casually pulled back. If Edwin had been more direct, complimented her looks, or even lingered for a bit longer when they touched, maybe the spell would have been broken. But the pretense of nothingness made it exciting. She had a series of fantasies about him—in the library stacks, in an apartment she constructed in her mind, a replica of Erick's but with better furniture. One afternoon, after a two-day gap, he said, "My girlfriend is coming to town. She's flying in from Iowa."

Vega fidgeted with the puzzle pieces. "I always confuse Iowa and the other one. Idaho."

This wasn't true. She had aced geography as a primary school student, and for some unknown reason, they were forced to learn the map of the United States. But it was the first thing that came to mind. Edwin held two gold pieces together. "Yeah," he said. "Everybody does."

One Saturday in February, Vega drove Shoba to Randolph, where she and Mohan had made an offer on a house. "It has a bigger yard," Shoba said in the car. "And a swing set for the girls. It's almost like a dream."

The real estate agent, a middle-aged woman named Dierdre, arrived with damp hair and a cardboard tray of hot chocolates. "My goodness, you look just like sisters," she said. "You must get that all the time." She was inexplicably breathless, having only walked from the car.

Vega considered correcting Dierdre, gently explaining that nobody had ever told Shoba and her that they looked alike, because it simply wasn't true. Instead, she pried a cup loose. "Thank you," she said, at the same time as Shoba said, "She's *like* another sister to me."

"That's a wonderful thing about your culture," Dierdre said. "I was telling Shoba this. I so admire your closeness. That sense of community."

"Yes," Vega said. She looked at Shoba, who was opening and closing the gate, seemingly amazed by the mechanics of it.

"We can start with the back," Dierdre said. "Because that was the part you were most excited about. I *know* how it is with young kids. That private space is a wonderful thing."

"This is why I wanted Vega to see it," Shoba said. "Her daughter is like my own daughter. She will also be spending time here."

The backyard was large, divided by a gate from the equally large backyards surrounding it. Also identical to the other yards was a playground set, dropped into the center, the focal point of the entire thing. "Like a private park," Shoba said, taking Vega's hand and squeezing it as though they were the couple purchasing the home.

"It's very nice, Shoba. Really." But the sight of it made Vega uneasy. She imagined Asha spending her afternoons in this yard, alongside Shoba's girls. Already, Asha treated Shoba and Mohan's house as though it were her own. She knew where Shoba kept their tin of digestive biscuits, the cups and plates, where Tara stored her box of crayons. She liked to sit beside their kitchen window and watch the birds. Shoba found this all endearing, but something about it gnawed at Vega. She had always been puzzled by Shoba's contentment, wondering how anybody could be happy with a life so small. Now, she wondered, if this was how it started. A swing set. A gate around one's yard. If Asha grew up here, even in part, would she come to want little more than this? She remembered talking to Gayatri once, observing this quality in Kavita, one of their friends from primary school—at the time, the three of them had been a tight circle. "She's the type of person who thinks three-hundred-and-sixty-five happy days is the same thing as a happy year," she had said, thinking that Gayatri would understand the difference. But Gayatri just looked at Vega, perplexed, and said, "Vega, that *is* a happy year." Vicariously, at least, Vega had come to agree. She liked the idea of Shoba settling into this home, occupying this pleasant life. But for Vega, there would be a pounding restlessness. What would come next? And after that?

Inside, the house was pretty and unremarkable. Dierdre chatted about the kitchen appliances, the island at the center, the separate dining room. She took them to the basement, an unfinished cave of gray cement, and told them to imagine it as a playroom for the girls. She walked them up the stairs, commented on the maple flooring, floated through a series of small bedrooms, and made repeated references to something called a stackable unit. Vega had the feeling these details were lost on Shoba. But when they walked into the main bedroom, Shoba clapped her hands like a child awaiting cake.

"Imagine waking up to all this sunlight," Dierdre said. To Vega, she continued, "Her husband is such a sweetheart. He said, 'If she's happy, I'm happy.' And just look how happy she is."

"She's a very good real estate agent," Shoba said later in the car. "She likes Indians very much. Indian food, Indian movies. And she won't take advantage. She won't say, 'Oh, they don't know this system, so I'll simply charge extra fees.'"

It puzzled Vega how, after nearly seven years in the States, Shoba still did not notice when people talked down to her. "That's good. I'm happy you can trust her."

"You've been to the park here, no? Where the tennis courts are, where Mohan and Suresh practice?"

Vega had no idea where the tennis courts were. She had never been even remotely curious. But Shoba insisted they visit the park. It was too cold to stay long, but she wanted to show Vega the walking path and the small lake that it wrapped around. "We can go for walks on Saturdays," she said. "When the men are playing."

They stopped at a bagel shop for lunch, then drove back to the turnpike and followed signs to Brundage Park, Shoba pointing out every landmark of note: a mini-golf course, a Dairy Queen, a farm that advertised cider donuts and fresh eggs. "It's a very commercial area," Shoba said as they pulled into the parking lot. "Many businesses."

It was colder than it had been just hours before, and they were walking so briskly that Vega wouldn't have noticed the courts, had

Shoba not pointed them out. The gate was locked. A sign hung over the edge, reading, *Closed for Winter. Reopening in April.*

"See?" Shoba asked. "What did I tell you? So close, we can even walk from the new house."

At home, Asha had just woken from a nap. She was sitting at the kitchen table, rubbing her eyes, sleepily working her way through a pile of steamed apples. Suresh was making tea. Without asking, he poured Vega a cup, added some milk, and placed it in front of her. "House was nice?"

In the car, she had rehearsed her conversation with Suresh, each version gentler than the previous. More conciliatory, more plan oriented. Now, she couldn't remember any of it. "It was. Shoba seems happy." She mixed her tea, then reached for the sugar. "You haven't been playing tennis on Saturdays."

"Mohan is too busy with the baby. We'll start in the summer."

"But you still go on Mondays."

"Rupa needs some time away from housework."

"I saw the tennis courts, Suresh. They're closed. Until spring."

He looked stricken.

"You don't have to tell me any details, Suresh. It's okay."

"We talk, Vega. Nothing more."

She wondered, briefly, if it would be useful to tell him about Edwin. Winston she would never mention, but Edwin was a more manageable story, just enough of a betrayal to relieve Suresh of his guilt. But she had a feeling it would cause more harm. Even without love, a betrayal still hurt.

# 21

Margo proposed dinner the following week, telling Vega she had some news she wanted to discuss. They met at an Italian place in the West Village and squeezed into a corner table. Margo ordered a bottle of house red. "You don't mind?" she asked. "We could get something better."

"I can never tell the difference," Vega said.

They ordered plates of mushroom ravioli, and on their second glass of wine, Margo said, "I saw that posting you mentioned. The one at Seton Hall."

Over the past few months, Vega had been building a list of job openings within range of New Jersey, all lecture and adjunct positions, and though she often sat at her computer with the specific intention of submitting her résumé, something always stopped her. It wasn't just that the positions were menial—she knew it wasn't uncommon to work as an adjunct for a few years after graduate school—but these jobs seemed so static, so dismally local. She imagined them holding her in place, year after year.

"I haven't applied yet," Vega said. "But it seems like the best option. At least locally. I'll be teaching four courses each semester. Two introductory sections."

"I'm not saying it's terrible, but here's another path to consider. I have a former classmate. We did our PhDs together at Wisconsin. She's the head of the sociology department at Louisiana State University. They're hiring an assistant professor, ideally with a Global South focus, but they really want someone who works in the realm of feminist theory and sociology of family. They haven't even posted the job yet, but she gave me permission to mention it to you in advance."

For a moment, Vega wondered if this was some sort of administrative request. If she could spread the word, post the job on an announcement board. But Margo was nodding, wide-eyed, as though expecting an answer.

"You want me to apply?"

"Why wouldn't you?"

"I won't be defending my dissertation until May. I didn't think I'd be a contender for a tenure-track position."

"I think you'd be surprised."

"I worry I don't have enough to distinguish my research. A lot of people study sociology of family." She knew she was pulling an old trick from her childhood—wooing the encouragement she needed, the same as when she stood in front of Gayatri's mirror during their Rhodes School days, complaining about her weight or her hair. She wanted Margo to say, "You're exceptional! You're the best candidate I've seen in years!"

"Every space is crowded with ideas," Margo said. "What distinguishes anyone? How many political scientists study the Cold War? How many historians are sitting in their offices, whacking off to more documents about Jefferson?"

"Countless," Vega said. "No doubt."

Margo laughed. "My point is, your teaching reviews are stellar. And you're an excellent writer and researcher."

Vega took this in. They ordered tiramisu and coffee. Finally, she said, "The logistics seem impossible."

"I'm sure the logistics seemed impossible when you moved to the States. But here you are."

"That was a different situation entirely. I was twenty-one. I have a child now."

"Fine. I get that. But here's what I recommend. As your advisor, but also as a friend. Apply. Get an interview. Talk up your research and your student reviews. And once you have an offer in hand, then you make the decision. But don't think about logistics yet. Stay focused on getting the offer."

Suresh and Vega's interactions were as pleasant and mechanical as ever. One Saturday, as they were driving to the dentist, she found a bobby pin in the cup holder of his car. She didn't bother mentioning it. She was coming to enjoy their time together, the quiet meditativeness. The sudden lifting of pressure.

Her only source of anxiety was the Louisiana State interview, arranged to take place by phone during the first week of April. In the days leading up to it, she assured herself that it was simply a screening, nothing more, that she was unlikely to advance. The call was scheduled with an associate professor, a scholar of family and criminology, and Vega managed to find a copy of her book—*Birth Behind Bars* at the Low Library. She told Suresh she had a late meeting, rode the subway to 116th Street, and spent the evening on the same couch where she used to study during her Columbia days. She practiced her talking points obsessively—on the train, on her way to and from campus, as she moved from one household task to another. But in the end, the conversation moved so quickly she couldn't remember any of the lines she had rehearsed. And then, two weeks later, the call came from the department.

It had seemed needlessly cruel to tell Suresh about the interview in advance. But the offer was a different matter. That night, she lay next to him in bed. He was reading a novel. Vikram Seth's *An Equal Music*, borrowed from Mohan. The entire exchange puzzled her—Mohan possessing a novel to begin with, Suresh having any interest in literature. She would have assumed he wasn't actually reading, using the book to avoid conversation, but occasionally he grunted, seemingly surprised by the events on the page.

"I have some news."

He looked up. Asha was asleep, and the room felt large and quiet without her presence to distract them. Vega breathed deeply. She had spent so many hours preparing for her interview, but this was the hard conversation, the one she should have rehearsed.

"I have an offer. It's an assistant professor position."

"That's wonderful news. CUNY itself?"

"Suresh, these positions are incredibly rare. Nobody is hired from their own doctoral program."

He put the book down and Vega stared at the cover. A soothing, aquatic blue. A man's torso. What in hell was he reading?

"Where, then?" he asked.

"Louisiana. Baton Rouge."

"How can we do that? My work is here." He picked at the side of his thumb. He had stopped chewing on his cuticles, but this—the finger picking—seemed to be the last vestige of the habit. In a moment, Vega knew, he would clench his fists to stop himself, the way he always did.

"Suresh. You deserve to be happy. Fully happy." Her throat was tight, and it hurt to get the words out.

"There are couples who live together," Suresh said. "They stay in the same house, just to raise their children. It's possible."

"Suresh." She felt as though she were holding the last two years of her life in her palm, finally able to see them with clarity. Of course, he had loved her. Of course, she couldn't have loved him back—not as his wife, at least. But she had never before cared for him as much as she did in that moment.

He was quiet for an unbearably long time. Then he said, "She needs to go to the doctor regularly."

"Of course she does, Suresh. Why would we not take her to the doctor?"

"I'm with you when you take her. Each time."

"Maybe we can arrange to take her together, still. We can discuss that."

"You never talk about your sister. Everything I know about her, your mother told me. Heart conditions are genetic."

"Ashwini's condition was different, Suresh."

"I know. Tetralogy of Fallot."

She steadied herself. "It's entirely treatable in infancy. Any American hospital, nowadays, will detect it early. The problem was that we didn't. Unless you catch it in the beginning, it's hopeless."

She had never been able to say this aloud, or even admit it to herself. If somebody had looked at Ashwini at birth, had examined her hands and noticed the telltale clubbed fingers, she would have needed nothing more than a surgical heart procedure. A shunt operation, it was called. When Asha was born, Vega had pressed her hands flat and examined her fingers. "There's no reason to think anything is wrong," the pediatrician had said. He talked to her slowly, with a rehearsed patience, as though Vega were a hysterical mother, pumped full of hormones and old-world superstition. But even when the echocardiogram revealed nothing, when the chest X-rays were perfectly normal, Vega asked him over and over: *What if there's something you're not seeing?*

Now, Suresh asked the same question. "How do you know she's healthy?"

"I specifically asked. She's healthy. I'll continue taking care of her. And so will you."

He didn't respond. She put her hand on his arm. "I want you to begin your life. That may be easier, at the beginning at least, if you have some distance."

"There's distance, and then there is too much distance."

"I'm thankful for it all, Suresh. And I'm so glad we have her."

He was crying now, quietly, staring at the ceiling. She relaxed her grip on his arm, but let it rest there. They fell asleep with the light on.

# 22

They spent the second half of the summer in Chennai, Suresh staying with his parents and Vega with hers. They had planned for Asha to divide the time between sets of grandparents, but she was too unsettled and jet-lagged to be moved from home to home. In New Jersey, she had breastfed occasionally, more from habit than hunger. In India, she chewed on Vega's nipple throughout the day and held on to her breast at night. Vega saw Gayatri only twice. The first was a stilted visit at Vega's home, Rukmini hovering over them with more tea and biscuits as Asha sat on the floor, scratching at a heat rash spreading across her neck. The second time, Vega left Asha with Rukmini. Suresh and his parents planned on coming later, and it seemed easier to leave than to explain the condition of their marriage.

"What do I say to P.N. and Kamala?" Rukmini whispered, following Vega onto the steps. "How do I explain why you aren't here?" Vega's own parents had been surprised when she told them about the divorce, less by the fact of it than the timing. "I rather assumed you would wait until Asha was older," her mother had said. But P.N. and Kamala, Vega knew, were a different matter. They were old-fashioned. Divorce, in their minds, was something that existed in faraway tabloids. Bollywood actors. Charles and Diana.

"Suresh has told them, Amma. They understand."

"Yes. But what do *I* say to them?"

"Just be normal, please." She paused. "And kind. Just be kind to them."

Vega met Gayatri on the beach. They had planned on getting lunch, but instead, dropped onto the sand and slid off their shoes. "We can eat here," Gayatri said. "I can get us a pizza or some pakoras or whatever." They stared at the restaurants in the distance, simple shacks with over-priced food, usually crowded with Europeans. "That's fine with me," Vega said. But neither of them moved.

"How are you?" Gayatri asked. "Tell me honestly."

"I don't know. Fine, I think." After a pause, she said, "Asha isn't usually so fussy. She was just overwhelmed."

"That is what you think I'm worried about?"

"I know that isn't what you were talking about. I just want you to know she's a happy baby."

"I have no doubt she is. And that you're a happy mother. At least, with respect to her."

"That's true. I am happy." She hadn't fully realized, until saying it aloud, how true that was. Being with Asha made her happy. Being Asha's mother made her happy.

"Well then? What's the plan? And don't bullshit me. I'm not Rukmini."

"Suresh is going to stay in Chennai a few extra weeks. He has the vacation time saved up. I want to go to Baton Rouge and get settled. He'll follow with the things we left in New Jersey and spend a few days with us."

"And then he goes back to New Jersey?"

"For the time being."

"Is there any plausible way, really, he could end up in Baton Rouge? Long-term."

"Houston is a possibility. We've discussed it. He would be closer, at least."

"In that case, why pretend? Make your arrangements. Every two weeks, every month, whatever it is. People divorce. Even here, it's becoming more and more common." She dug her feet deeper into the sand. "And Asha will adjust to whatever it is."

"People always say that about children," Vega said. "I don't actually think it's true."

"Then that will be her challenge," Gayatri said. "God knows we all have something. But if you stayed unhappily married, then *that* would be her challenge."

"Fair point."

"My only advice? Be honest. Decide what you and Suresh want. Be direct with each other, and with everyone else."

Despite Vega's efforts to linger at the beach with Gayatri, Suresh and his parents were still at the house when she returned. They seemed on the verge of leaving, but Vega soon realized it was a prolonged departure that, by the pace of things, could have started hours earlier. Kamala was crying in a silent, shaking manner that made Vega want to apologize, to take it all back, to return to New Jersey and undo the entire separation. It was such a sad display that Vega expected the entire house to be mired in sympathy. But Rukmini was refilling a bowl of pistachios. Asha was napping on the floor. The men were standing next to the bookshelf, discussing steel exports.

Kamala hugged her. The men didn't look up. Vega heard P.N. say, "Make no mistake! China is still our top buyer."

"Seeing you is like a dream," Kamala said. They walked outside and sat on the steps. Vega gripped her mother-in-law's hands. She had known women like Kamala her entire life—women so desperate to please, so blindingly happy with the happiness of others—and she had always found them vapid. In her mother-in-law, though, those qualities had been endearing. Now, they were the qualities that broke Vega's heart.

"You're a good mother," Kamala said. "I know you'll take good care of Asha, always."

Vega fingered her bangle. She had meant to remove it earlier and set it aside to be returned to Kamala. She couldn't possibly do that now. It would require procuring some Vaseline, and the process would seem uncomfortably ceremonial. Maybe she would send it to Rupa, if Rupa and Suresh eventually married. It would be her way of giving them

her blessing, telling them she was happy for them, that everything had
turned out for the best.


R ukmini sobbed on the drive to the airport, but Vega was too nau-
seated by the traffic and diesel to feel any emotion.

"It's the stop-and-go," her father said. "It's terrible these days."

The traffic hadn't, in fact, changed considerably in the four years
since Vega had been home, and she knew her father was talking just to
distract them. Still, the sound of his voice was comforting. At the gate,
Rukmini was still too emotional for coherence, but her father pulled
Vega to him. It was the first time they had hugged since her childhood.
Even when she left India for the first time, he had simply shaken her
hand, checked that the envelope from ICICI Bank was tucked securely
in her purse, and delivered some parting wisdom on the dangers of
credit card theft. But now he squeezed her so tightly, she was afraid
she would hurt him. She could feel his ribs. She could lift him off the
ground if she wanted to.

On the plane, Asha nursed ravenously, biting down when Vega's
supply was depleted. In her delirium, Vega was reminded of the tube
squeezer her father affixed to the end of his toothpaste. Somewhere
over Northern Europe, they both dozed off. Vega woke, even more
delirious. She tried—propelled by the habits of marriage—to pass a
sleeping Asha to the man next to her. But the man wasn't Suresh. He
was a stranger, whose thick arms spilled over onto her seat. He was
watching an action movie. A car chase, followed by a shoot-out in a
parking lot. Vega tried to go back to sleep, but the images pulsed on the
screen, even with her eyes closed.

She had a three-hour layover in Newark. As the plane descended
and Asha stirred from sleep, Vega considered calling Shoba. They had
last seen each other towards the end of the semester, an uneventful
Thursday night, when Vega picked Asha up from the house. Vega didn't
have the courage to tell her in person about the separation, or about her
move to Louisiana. Instead, she wrote her a long letter thanking her

for everything, assuring her that they would see each other often, and that she would always be a second mother to Asha. They spoke on the phone later, but it was Shoba—in tears—who sounded hesitant to get together. Vega had nearly called her so many times since that conversation, hoping they could meet for a walk, or a tea, or take the girls to the park, but it always seemed too complicated. Mohan would insist on driving her. Rupa might choose to come. They would stand awkwardly, all the sadness of saying goodbye and none of the closure.

Once in the airport, Asha's needs wiped away any traces of Vega's guilt. Strapped into the stroller, she arched her back and screamed. Vega pried open the tin of chapatis Rukmini had packed, and Asha tore one apart and tossed it onto the floor. She had used the toilet on the plane, but now her underwear and dress were soaked with urine. When she finally quieted, Vega stared at the damage surrounding them. The two pieces of carry-on luggage, the rickety stroller, the carpet strewn with crumbs. A shoe Asha had kicked off lay on the floor, next to the towerlike ashtray.

She managed to drag the stroller and bags into the bathroom and change Asha on a large, gray table that, had Rukmini been with her, Vega would have felt compelled to disinfect. As it was, she gave Asha a packet of saltines left over from the flight, plunked her down, then pulled off her wet clothes and shoved them into the side compartment of her carry-on. Back in the cavernous hallway of the airport, she stared at the rush of families all around them. A mother fussing with her daughter's hair. Siblings walking wordlessly beside each other, their parents trailing behind. Spouses sharing the load of bags and small children. Holding Asha in one arm and everything else in the other, she felt shrunken by the enormity of these strangers' presence. In a country of three hundred million people, she knew maybe twenty. And she had given them all up, but one.

# Part 5

# 23

Ameya was a distant niece of Rakesh. The connection had felt so tenuous months ago, when Sudha called to make the introduction, that Vega had written the number down, folded the paper in her wallet, and promptly forgotten about it.

"She's a doctoral candidate at LSU," Sudha had said. "An environmental scientist. You can always stay with her. We don't want you to be alone with a child and untethered."

Vega assured Sudha she would be fine. The department had arranged temporary housing, a one-bedroom apartment tucked into a suburban street that was tranquil enough on the evening Vega and Asha arrived. The secretary had emailed her weeks back to let her know they would also stock her fridge and cabinets. The gesture seemed wonderfully generous at the time but was quickly revealed to be the work of an undergraduate intern. There were bottles of ketchup and mustard, Domino sugar, and a tin of instant coffee on the counter. Inside the fridge was a loaf of white bread and a tub of margarine. She found, also, two boxes of macaroni and cheese and a six-pack of applesauce.

It was just past nine o'clock at night, and Asha was rubbing her eyes and squealing, on the thin border between sleepiness and rage. Vega held her in one arm, and with the other hand she assembled the best meal she could manage—macaroni, lubricated by margarine—then watched, disgusted, as Asha devoured the entire thing along with two cups of applesauce. She bathed her quickly. Then, unable to find any bedsheets, upended her suitcase and pulled out the two towels buried at the bottom. Asha finally fell asleep, lying on a towel on the unmade bed, Vega's nipple in her mouth, her arms splayed out on the bare mattress.

If Vega hadn't been so hungry, she might have fallen asleep next to Asha. Instead, she stood up and pushed the suitcase into the corner to be sorted through later. In the kitchen, she washed the pot and leafed through a stack of delivery menus. One looked passable: *Mexicali Grill: South of the Border in Central Louisiana*. She scanned their offerings of quesadillas and burritos, then came to the list of "hard sell tacos," a misprint that made her laugh so hard she was afraid she would wake Asha. She had always delighted in this sort of thing: muddled metaphors, the wrong words blurted out. But now, her laughter was excessive, amplified by the bare walls.

At two o'clock the following afternoon, Vega stood on Ameya's porch, clutching a Grand Sweets bag filled with cashews and ribbon pakora that Rukmini had shoved into her suitcase the day before she left Madras. "You didn't have to bring anything!" Ameya said, waving them in. "You're coming direct from India, no? You must be jetlagged. The baby, too."

Ameya led them into the kitchen, a small and tidy room that was brightly lit from the windows along the back wall. "I'm sorry I don't have any proper toys for her to play with." She rummaged through her cabinet and pulled out a colander and wooden spoon. "Does she like banging things around?"

"If you don't mind the noise."

"Not in the least." She filled a pitcher of water and they settled at the kitchen table. "Sudha said you're from Adyar. Where did you go to school?"

"Rhodes for secondary. Then Sri Vidya for undergraduate."

"I'm from Nungambakkam," Ameya said. "I studied at St. Agnes. I did my undergrad in Kolkata, though."

Her manner of speaking made Vega nostalgic. Later, she knew, the

conversation would slip into a search for common acquaintances—
people who had receded into Vega's distant memories. The thought of
it soothed something in her that she hadn't realized was hurting.

"So, you're staying on Lakeshore for the time being?"

"It's just a temporary thing. The department arranged it. I'll find
something permanent in the next week or so."

"That's the fraternity row. It'll be madness when the semester
starts. You'll want to get out of there as soon as you can. Before the
students arrive."

"I gathered," Vega said. Already, there had been unsettling signs.
She had woken in the middle of the night to a thud and a series of
shrieks mixed with laughter. Standing on the porch that morning, the
air smelled of piss. A container of Chinese food had been tossed by
the garbage can on the sidewalk, noodles strewn on the cement. She
hadn't really intended to call Ameya at all, certainly not on her first
day in Baton Rouge, but she found the number in her wallet and was
relieved when Ameya answered on the second ring.

"She really is sweet, your daughter. How old?"

"She just turned two." They looked over at Asha, still fully occupied by her spoon and colander. The gestures had been so simple. A bit
of space on the floor. Some things to bang together. But Asha seemed
happy for the first time since they left New Jersey. Vega's throat tight-
ened. She turned away and wiped her eyes on her sleeve.

To her relief, Ameya ignored the tears. "I'm not sure if Sudha mentioned, but I leave at the end of next summer for a research position
in Minneapolis. If you're comfortable squeezing in for a year, we can
manage. Then you and the baby could each have your own room."

When she first accepted the position at LSU, the quiet and ano-
nymity of a new place had appealed to her. Now, she didn't want to
live alone. She would have followed Ameya to Minneapolis if that were
possible. It seemed reckless to form a new friendship, to bring someone
into Asha's life who would be gone in a year. The tears came faster, and
Ameya couldn't pretend not to notice.

"Listen," Ameya said quietly. "Take your time with the decision.

It's no pressure." She walked into the bathroom and returned carrying a stream of toilet paper.

"I'll have to arrange things with her father. He plans to come one weekend a month. And one weekend a month I'll be in New Jersey."

"That's fine, of course."

"I'm separated," Vega said. "Getting divorced." She blew her nose so loudly she should have been embarrassed. Instead, she felt enormous relief. She had never said the words so directly before.

"I can always leave for the weekend when your ex comes. We can make arrangements. Don't worry about any of that."

"I'm not worried, now that I say it. It's just a lot of small things." She had developed an elaborate task list, even typed and formatted it with bullet points so it looked, at a glance, like a meeting agenda. But now, when she ran through it in her mind, she realized how much minutiae was buried inside each item. Securing day care. Finalizing her syllabus and course reader. Buying a car. In New Jersey, she and Suresh had gone to the dealership and DMV together. How did one buy a car without a car? And in the middle of this, Asha would need to eat. She would outgrow her clothes. She would need other people in her life besides Vega. She wished she could tuck Asha back inside her body and deliver her when things were settled. When she had a car.

Ameya put on the kettle for tea. "Will she eat fruit?" she asked. "I have bananas. And oranges in the fridge." She sliced a banana onto a plate. They watched as Asha pulled up the pieces and smashed them in the general area of her mouth.

"The rent is four hundred a month." Ameya walked to the fridge for an orange and split it in two, then gave half to Vega. "You can take your time and think it over. But I can tell you it would be good to have you both. It would make this place feel like a home."

Suresh visited in August, carrying a stack of parathas, a suitcase full of Asha's clothes, and a check for the value of Vega's old car. He was staying in some distant suburb, with a friend of a college classmate.

The man had dropped him off at Vega and Ameya's house, offered a perfunctory invitation for Vega to visit his house anytime, and warned her about the crime in East Baton Rouge. "Very unsafe area," he said. "Even during the day, it's all the time drug problems." Even Suresh looked relieved when the man drove away.

The first hour was rocky. Asha was disoriented and she cried when Suresh held her. Ameya, with whom they overlapped in the kitchen, mistakenly addressed Suresh as Sampath, then overcompensated by asking him repeated questions about the world of software engineering.

"Would you say your work is very coding oriented?"

"Well, no," Suresh said. "That is a different thing."

Ameya eventually left for the library and Asha amused herself with a puzzle—one of the items Suresh had brought in the suitcase, made new in the months since Asha had seen her toys. Vega poured tea and she and Suresh settled into the familiar terrain of logistics. "You were able to sell the car so quickly?" she asked.

"Yes."

"They paid cash?"

"Not quite. But that's the value of it." He sipped his tea and chewed a piece of paratha. This was what it looked like when he was hiding something. With Suresh, a lover of details, who could expound on the difference between Agassi's and Sampras's backhand, or the value of premium versus regular gasoline, vagueness was a telltale sign.

"But you sold it?"

"Hmm."

There was no point in probing further. She was grateful for the money. Given that he had purchased the car for her in the first place, it was more than she expected.

"Your classes are going well?"

She nodded. "Two introductory sections, all large lecture formats, plus one seminar. I haven't had as much time for research, but I'm sure I will. The teaching is enjoyable."

They made dinner together, the familiar choreography of cooking suddenly clumsy in the dimensions of this alien kitchen to which Vega herself hadn't fully adjusted. Bathing Asha, too, was like this. The old routines made new. Suresh bent over the tub, talking in a voice that was both sad and too animated, sounding like an estranged uncle. Afterwards, he tried to read *Harold and the Purple Crayon*, but Asha squirmed and pulled the book from his hands.

"She's been more restless in the evenings," Vega said, when they had managed to settle Asha into her crib. "She won't even let me read to her, sometimes."

This was partially true. Asha, at two years, was difficult to predict. Blueberries, once her favorite snack, she now chewed and spit on the floor.

"It's okay," Suresh said. "She was tired, I think."

"We can show you the lake tomorrow. And there's the zoo. We can pack a picnic." They hadn't yet discussed the arrangement of the weekend—whether Suresh wanted to be alone with Asha, or whether he wanted Vega to go along with them, either for the purpose of helping or maintaining the illusion of a family. But she kept talking anyway, listing more activities than they could possibly fit during Suresh's forty-eight hours on the ground. The university campus. The Arts and Science Museum. "And, of course, we'll come to New Jersey in two weeks. We can fly in on Thursday night, itself. We'll have three days."

"Vega," he said, cutting her off gently, in the way she had done to him so many times. "Long-term, I wonder if it is easier for me to come here than for you to come to New Jersey."

She felt the first hints of relief. She had put off thinking about the New Jersey trip until she and Suresh survived this weekend in Baton Rouge. But when it crossed her mind, even briefly, she was gripped by anxiety. All the pretense of connection, of normalcy. She and Shoba spoke at least once a week—Vega put it in her calendar to call on Friday mornings, and Shoba sometimes called during a lull in her afternoons—and it was always a comfort to hear her voice, to talk about food and children, and for Vega to know that she had, for the most part, been forgiven. But it was one thing to speak with someone, and another to see them. And she couldn't bear the thought of Asha settling into the New Jersey apartment, letting her reacquaint herself with the habits of her old life, then prying her away.

"For one thing," Suresh said. "It will cost more for you to go there than for me to come to Baton Rouge. Partly, it's just a matter of cost."

"That's a lot of travel for you," Vega said.

"I don't mind." He looked away, pretending to be interested in something on the bookshelf.

"Suresh. Tell me one thing. You didn't sell the car, did you?"

"There was no need, really. We would need the second one."

"You and Rupa."

He fidgeted with the edge of a placemat. "She wants to learn how to drive. It was easier this way. Fewer transaction costs."

Vega imagined Rupa in her old car, pushing Carnatic music tapes into the stereo, fidgeting with the heat in the winter. She pictured her in the apartment, using the pots and pans, adjusting the settings on the toaster. Most of those items Suresh had bought before Vega arrived, so it made sense that Rupa would use them. Sentiment aside, there was no reason for them to buy anything new.

"Ameya leaves in the spring?" Suresh asked.

"In July."

"You'll be alright when she's gone?"

Vega felt the same prickling of tears she had felt when she first stood in Ameya's hallway. "I have Asha," she said. "We'll be fine."

# 24

Summer in Louisiana was disorienting, stretching well into October. Nowhere else, outside of India, had Vega felt the salty sting of sweat in her eyes or slapped so constantly and feebly at mosquitoes. She covered Asha in citronella repellent every morning, but by afternoon, the child was covered in red welts. And then there were the sweeter reminders of home. The occasional smell of jasmine. The okra and eggplant she and Ameya bought at the farmers' market. Despite Vega's conversion to the use of sunscreen ("It's a myth that only white people need it," her pediatrician had said), Asha's arms and legs had turned a beautiful rust color. One morning, Vega noticed her sitting on the stoop, mesmerized by the sight of a lizard fanning its red throat. Vega had never seen one outside of India.

"Palli," Vega said. "Adha oru palli. Do you remember when we saw them at paati and thatha's house?" She rarely spoke to Asha in Tamil—something even Ameya had noted—but now the words tumbled out, easy and unplanned.

In the evenings, she and Ameya took Asha to the lake near campus. It was Vega's favorite place in Baton Rouge, a grassy area surrounded by sprawling live oaks that reminded her of the banyan trees in Chennai. Sometimes they were joined by two of Ameya's friends—Priya and Vishal, who brought along their three-year-old son and newborn daughter. They were Indian American, both coastal engineers, and had met while serving in the Peace Corps in Bolivia. They spoke to their children in Spanish, which Vega found, depending on her mood, either puzzling or impressive.

"Our priority at the moment is river diversion," Vishal explained to Vega. "Priya and I are involved in a large-scale project to redirect the Mississippi River so it can spread the sediment we need for marsh creation." Their son, Amin, toddled over to show them a rock he had found. "Que bella," Vishal said. "Enseñale a mami. Anyway, the project is really just to keep the problem at bay. It's no task for what we're up against."

"Not with the rising sea levels," Priya said, examining the rock. "We can only fight it for so long."

Though Amin was only a year older than Asha, Priya and Vishal were already in the process of researching kindergarten programs. "I mean, Priya is," Vishal said. "She's the queen of the spreadsheets."

"Hardly," Priya said. "Anyway. We're looking into the Waldorf School. I have mixed feelings because Vishal and I were products of public schools. But we're scientists, and the data on small class size is hard to argue against."

Vishal rolled his eyes. "Not that the data makes a difference. Generally, I believe in data, of course. But my feeling is, kids don't need much."

"Stop your bullshit," Ameya said. "You were the one who wanted the Waldorf School. Sending Priya to every corner of the city for social emotional tests and IQ tests."

Vishal shrugged, ignoring the point. "I'm happy with whatever Priya's happy with. She tells me what forms to fill out and I fill them out." He leaned back on the blanket and propped his head up, as though they were on a beach. Vega found his manner even more irritating than she found Priya's—a man who wanted the outcomes, but not the optics of pursuing them. That work, he left to his wife.

In New Jersey, there had been subtle reminders of racial difference— salespeople who spoke too brightly and too slowly, or the turbaned gas station attendants who addressed her quietly in Hindi, like India was a shameful secret they shared. But in Baton Rouge, the divide was stark and unapologetic. Yard signs reading *Save St. Marks*, flanked her neighboring houses. Vega had assumed it was something innocuous, maybe a nursing home or library program facing budget cuts, until a flier appeared in her mailbox. *The Save St. Marks neighborhood association believes in creating a community and independent school district within East Baton Rouge, made up of like-minded and law-abiding citizens.* Daphne, a neighbor whose son attended Asha's day care, offered her analysis one morning in the parking lot. "We have to clean up our schools here. People who earn more are paying more in property taxes. But families from other parts of East Baton Rouge are able to enroll their kids in our schools, because of the way districts are drawn." She lowered her voice, though there was nobody else within earshot. "You've seen the local elementary school. Do you really think you'd send Asha there?"

Vega had liked Daphne. She seemed straightforward—a woman who worked in human resources, who wore sensible shoes, who seemed always to be carting one of her older children to soccer or ballet. During Vega's first carless weeks in Baton Rouge, Daphne had driven her back and forth from campus. Now, Vega stared at her blankly. "Do you mean because it's predominantly Black?" She had passed the school countless times, but after years in New York, where Black and white children seemed to rarely overlap, the racial demographics hadn't surprised her. And who was she to question any of it? She had spent her life in parochial schools, where she could count on one hand the number of her classmates who weren't Brahmin.

"Not at all. I'm talking about the *quality* of the schools. I don't care if people are red or purple or green."

"But people aren't red or purple or green. They're brown and Black and white. Somebody could plausibly say this about Asha. They could drive past a playground where she is playing and say, 'I don't want to send my children to school with brown children.'"

Daphne put her hand on Vega's arm. "Honey, nobody would ever say that about you. And certainly not about your little girl. She's so well-mannered."

A few weeks earlier, Vega had been walking to her car on the north side of campus. It was a Friday, late afternoon on a beautiful day. Two men were standing near her car. "You want us to move?" one asked. From a distance, they had looked to be undergraduates. Now, she saw they were older, around their mid-twenties.

"Yes. Please."

"Then make us move. Mexican bitch."

Vega couldn't recall much of what happened next, except that she managed to get into her car, collect Asha from day care, and drive home. She hadn't yet told anyone. In part, the incident was too embarrassing to talk about. But she also suspected that, if she did mention it, she would be forced to file a complaint with campus police and begin a tedious and ultimately fruitless investigation. Now she recounted it to Daphne. "You'd be surprised. What people are willing to say aloud," she said.

"Well, that's horrible. Of course, wherever you go, you get some people who are trash." Daphne was quiet for a bit, and Vega expected her to offer something conciliatory. Instead, she said, "I certainly hope you told them you aren't Mexican."

H er colleagues were all affable, all white, with the exception of Charles—a Black linguist in his mid-sixties who seemed indifferent to the members of the department but was revered in the sort of distant way one might admire Gandhi or Mandela. There was a large photograph of him on the department website, and everyone seemed to nod a bit too earnestly on the rare occasions he spoke. Shortly after she arrived, she learned he was a finalist for a position at Tulane. Once, during a department meeting, she saw he was completing a crossword puzzle under his desk.

The women were all childless, the men with kids and wives who they mentioned in passing, making Vega's identity as a mother as novel as Charles's Blackness. Of the seven, three were criminologists. "I study *urban* criminology," her colleague Bert said, when he'd first introduced himself to Vega. "Debra's work is different. She studies delinquency. Mark's work focuses on the school-to-prison pipeline."

"So, you're all criminologists?" Vega had asked.

"Well, different aspects."

She immersed herself in their research in her first weeks. Despite her interest in quantitative research, she found Bert's and Debra's work dry—his, an analysis of the population changes in Atlanta public housing, and hers, a discussion of juvenile recidivism in Chicago. Mark's work, in contrast, was a painfully bleak portrait of out-of-school youth. The blurb on the cover, written by his former advisor, read: *A stirring portrayal of innocence lost, and the rage that swells within our forgotten children.*

She was revising her dissertation into a book, while also researching a new paper on reproductive health access among immigrant women in Louisiana. She had been proud of both projects at first, thrilled by their magnitude and importance, but she was beginning to doubt herself. In the mornings, when she reread the pages she'd written the previous day, the language sounded so sentimental, so bloated with false authority. "You have an outsider's insight into American healthcare," Margo had told her. "*Emphasize* that. Talk about the small ways in which the system narrows our choices. Nobody is willing to compare the controls placed on American women to, say, Indian women. You understand both systems."

But Vega wasn't sure this was true. She had visited the redesigned Mukti website and had clicked through photographs of adolescent girls holding framed awards or seated in circles with their hands raised. None of it moved her. An updated slogan read *Be the Change SHE Wants to See!* The German interns were featured, as was Charanya, who had been promoted to something called "chief entrepreneurship officer."

At CUNY, teaching had been the highlight of her week. At LSU, her lectures called to mind a failing stand-up routine. She rewrote and rewrote her seminar notes, convinced with each new draft that she had found the hook to energize her students. She placed controversial questions on the board to prompt discussion when they walked in: *Should women's reproductive choices ever be governed by the state? Is marriage inherently patriarchal?* Always there was a heavy and bored silence, after which the same rotation of three or four students would speak up, their points drawing only from personal experience and never from the assigned readings. *I've known a lot of women who had abortions just because it was more convenient; Me, personally, I wouldn't want to get married unless I found someone who really respected me.* At CUNY, she would have known how to unpack this statement. "Why do we object to women making choices of convenience?" she might have asked. "Let us define respect!" But at LSU, the conversational thread was so fragile she was always afraid of breaking it, of the class descending into more painful silence.

She had a star student in her first semester, a Vietnamese American undergraduate named Sydney who wrote crisp and eloquent essays about women, labor, multigenerational families. "You really should consider doctoral work in this field," Vega had told her during office hours. "You're good enough to be admitted to a fully funded program." Sydney had taken this all in, offering noncommittal responses. But one December afternoon, she'd lingered after class. "I should have mentioned. I'm actually applying to dental hygienist programs. I'm the oldest in my family. I really need something stable."

I n the spring, Vega was invited to present at a conference at Emory University. Ameya offered to watch Asha, and it would be the first time in two years Vega traveled anywhere alone. It was also her first formal invitation, the first event in which her name would appear on the agenda, in which she would be required to submit an abstract in advance. A woman named Lorraine booked her flight and hotel room, asked her to keep her receipts for reimbursement purposes, and corresponded with crisp formality (*Dr. Gopalan: We are so pleased that you will be joining us.*). The title of "Doctor" still thrilled her, and Vega threw herself into her research until her talk—a discussion of contraception

access for South Asian immigrant women—felt meticulous and polished. But two weeks before the conference, as she practiced in front
of her bedroom mirror, it all sounded stale and rehearsed. She could
imagine the tepid clapping, the polite questions, the canned responses
she would offer.

Lately, she had felt less of a teacher than a performer. She traded
in her standard black pants and button-down shirt for long Indian
skirts and kurtas, batik scarves, large gold hoops. In the classroom, her
arguments became increasingly dogmatic. The more she made wild
claims, stripped of all nuance, the more her students seemed to listen.
"Women's bodies are policed by the state," she argued. "Immigrant
women are doubly controlled, by gender and country of origin." In
reality, she found certain aspects of her life at LSU shockingly easy.
A childcare center located on campus. A pink-and-blue-hued obstetrician's office where they ran a battery of free screenings Vega would
otherwise never have thought to ask for: cervical cancer, HPV, HIV,
urinary incontinence. More and more, she tormented herself with the
useless thought that, had Ashwini been born in the States, she would
still be alive.

"The problem is," she told Margo over the phone, "it sounds good,
but it isn't actually true. Wealthy South Asian immigrants have similar
contraception access as wealthy white American women. It's inaccu-
rate to reduce it all to race."

"Well, you need to account for culture. Different cultures face different pressures."

"Yes, but there isn't some singular third world culture. And if I'm
speaking to a predominantly white audience, nobody is going to question anything I say. At least, not publicly." She had a creeping sense,
during department meetings, that her colleagues were on edge when
she talked, gingerly agreeing just to end the conversation. Recently, she
had raised the example of Sydney Nguyen. "I worry sociology is losing
excellent students because they don't see themselves reflected in our
faculty." There had been a heavy silence, and Vega felt, as she often did,

that they had all arrived at a collective response and were silently deciding who among them would deliver it. "That's certainly a valuable point to consider," Mark said, before moving to the next agenda item.

Margo had wanted to fly down to hear Vega's presentation, but her son and his girlfriend were in New York for a wedding, and she wanted as much time with them as she could manage. "Fingers crossed," she said, and Vega wasn't sure if she was referring to the conference or to her son's visit. It stung her, again, to imagine Asha as a grown woman, passing in and out of Vega's life, calling her only when she happened to be in town.

# 25

She was in the lobby of the lecture hall at Emory when she saw Naomi. They stared stiffly at each other for a few moments, Vega frozen and Naomi fidgeting with an empty water bottle. Naomi spoke first. "My god. Vega."

They retreated to an empty corner of the room and leaned against a small, circular table.

"You look just the same," Vega said. She had often wondered if she would ever be attracted to another woman. She had tried, once, to force some interest in one of her classmates at CUNY, a gender studies scholar named Olivia. They had gone out for lunch during Vega's first semester, but she had found Olivia to be too much. Too aware of her femaleness, her queerness, too open about topics Vega didn't care to discuss over a meal: the politics of sex work and sex toys and sexual repression. By the end, they had talked so much about sex that Vega had lost any desire to have it.

But with Naomi, she remembered the feeling of wanting to sink into another body, to lose herself in her. She remembered touching herself at night, too cautiously to really enjoy it, always afraid Naomi would hear her through the wall.

"I don't know why I'm pretending I'm surprised to see you," Naomi said. "I was at your presentation."

"I'm glad I didn't know you were there. I would have been too nervous."

"I know. I was thinking of finding you earlier, but I don't think I would have been able to give a presentation if I knew you were in the room."

"How is your family?"

"Good enough. Daniel's still living with them. Eddie's still floating around. He has a good job, actually. He finished his electrician's course. Alba has a second kid, but she's steady. You know."

"And you? How are you?"

"I'm at George Mason, in Virginia. It's not the best fit, but it's okay for now."

She talked about the department, university politics, the size of her lectures, and the quality of her students. As she listened, Vega felt the fluttering of possibility. She imagined pulling Naomi from the drudgery of her life, driving to some midway point weekend after weekend. Eventually, they would find jobs in some small and perfect town. Naomi would be a good stepmother. Rukmini, in time, would make sense of it.

"You're happy at LSU?"

"I don't know what to think of it yet. I like teaching, in general. But I don't know if I've found my stride. It's either too easy or too hard. I can't quite tell."

"I know. It can be lonely sometimes, in a strange way. Anyway, it's been, what, six years? Tell me about your life."

"God. Six years." It would be the right time to tell her about Asha, the last moment before the omission took the form of a lie. Instead, she said, "I went to a conference at Penn, once. Years ago. I was hoping I would run into you. That's pathetic, isn't it?"

"No, it isn't. But why didn't you let me know? I would have planned to meet you. It's a big campus to hope for an accidental run-in."

"An accidental run-in would have been more exciting."

Naomi laughed. "Only because it would have been so unlikely." She looked suddenly pensive. "You're here through Sunday?"

"I am. And you?"

"Tomorrow afternoon. I'd suggest dinner, but I have this obligation tonight. A friend of mine from Austin, who lives here, is hosting a film screening at his place. It's just a small gathering. I would skip, but I already committed." She paused, expectantly. "Maybe join me. And then, afterwards we'll see."

The two final words compelled Vega. She had no interest in a film screening, or a small gathering of Naomi's friends. But the thought of what could come after was thrilling.

For the rest of the afternoon, Vega moved through the motions of the conference, going from lecture to coffee reception to panel discussion. When people spoke to her, she nodded and tried to appear interested in the conversation, but she was always scanning the room, always aware of Naomi's presence.

In the evening, Naomi approached her and touched her arm. They walked across the parking lot, almost wordlessly, to Naomi's rental car, then pulled out of campus, towards what Vega assumed to be downtown Atlanta. "So, where are we going, precisely?"

"My friend Tony's screening his film. He's actually doing his doctoral work here. This is his first film, and it received some acclaim. It's kind of a deviation from what he originally set out to do. He used to be obsessed with German cinema. When we were in Austin, he used to come over and make me watch Fassbinder films with him. Do you know Fassbinder?"

"I don't."

"You're not missing much. Anyway, Tony's decent. And I think fairly talented."

Twenty minutes or so later, they parked on a street that blended blight and opulence, in the manner Vega could never get used to about American cities. There was a gas station on the corner that appeared to have been gutted, though people still milled about, a few relaxing on the cement floor as though it were a public park. They continued past a sushi bar, a dank-looking pizza place, and a bodega that sold lush flowers and copies of the *New York Times*.

"You seem to know your way," Vega said.

"I actually interviewed for a job at Emory. I was a finalist, so I spent a few days at Tony's place. I like the city."

Tony was born and raised in Rio de Janeiro. His girlfriend, Luisa, was of Mexican descent, raised in Chicago. She had coppery hair and a warm smile and wore a white dress made out of T-shirt material that hung off one shoulder. On the drive, Vega had learned she was studying clinical psychology at Georgia Tech. Later, Vega overheard her ask Naomi about Daniel in a tone of genuine interest, and the fact of her concern made Vega like her.

There was Adrian, another filmmaker, who was also Brazilian. His boyfriend, Trenton, a trim Black man with a dancer's posture who taught English and theater in Atlanta public schools. A cluster of anthropologists, all of whom seemed perfectly pleasant, contributed something to the spread on the table, and showered Tony with more congratulations.

"The Pulitzer Center did a write-up," one of the anthropologists said. "They said he's part of a new wave of human rights cinema."

Tony wove his hands through his curly hair. "Look. This is the only thing I want to convey in my work. For centuries, we've been letting other people tell our stories. It's our turn. The art we produce has to tell *our* stories."

There was a murmur of agreement. Vega was still on her first sips of wine but was suddenly tired and disoriented. Most of the people in the room appeared to be around her age, in their late twenties or early thirties, but for some reason she felt old.

The film, *Os Perdidos*, was set in a favela, a two-hour stream of brutality. Within minutes, a young woman was killed by her jealous husband. Later, a small child was killed by a stray bullet, and a teenager by a targeted one. Occasionally, the violence was interrupted by an artistic, panoramic shot: clothes swaying on a line in the breeze, a dog sniffing through trash. In the end, the bright protagonist, who had managed to avoid the allure of gang life, kills the local ringleader, then boards a train to Rio de Janeiro towards an uncertain future.

Somebody snapped off the television and turned on the lights. Tony was biting his lip, looking nervous and proud, like a child who knew he had nailed an audition. Seated on the couch, his arm around Adrian, Trenton said, "Tony, you motherfucker. You are a once-in-a-generation talent."

Everybody returned to mingling and wine drinking and congratulations, but Vega could barely move or speak. She had winced through much of the film, closing her eyes any time a child was the focal point because she kept expecting the crack of a bullet. The group spread out, some drifting towards the table. Luisa was setting out tiny chocolate cupcakes. Adrian was leaning forward and asking Tony questions about his next play. Vega misunderstood the question and for a strange moment, pictured *Os Perdidos* onstage, all those fallen bodies lying there as the curtain drew to a close. But Tony said, "There's a whole world of amateur student film festivals like LA Student or CineYouth. But we want to play in a bigger pond."

Adrian was nodding. "Right," he kept saying. "Right."

Luisa returned from the table, licking frosting from her finger. "Tell them where you're submitting, Tony."

Tony tilted his head back, looking exhausted by the question. Vega was struck by the strange possibility that he visited a tanning salon, that he was of European descent—white by Brazilian standards—and in the States wanted to seem darker-skinned than he actually was. "Sundance and South by Southwest, obviously. Montreal and Nashville. Calgary. And then a few smaller ones." He went on for a bit about notification dates, how to ensure he had heard from the more prestigious festivals before accepting any smaller awards. "That can happen, you know. You accept the Krieger, then Sundance gets back to you, but you're already committed."

"So, these were all local actors?" Naomi asked.

"Residents of the favela. And I paid them according to the FIA-LA scale."

"That's the Latin American arm of the International Federation of Actors," Luisa explained.

"That's no joke, man," Adrian said. "That's legit."

Vega had been aware Naomi was watching her with a nervous expression. On the way back to her car, she said to Vega, "You're quiet suddenly."

"Does Tony always talk like he's being interviewed by the BBC?"

She snorted. "Kind of, I guess. You didn't like him?"

"I thought Luisa seemed nice."

"I guess not, then."

"He was fine. I just grew up with so many people like that. People who live privileged lives in India, but the moment they travel abroad or talk to foreigners, they want to establish themselves as experts on poverty."

"And nobody would ever say that about you?"

Vega looked at her, surprised. "I don't claim to know things that I don't." She knew if she stopped there, she could skirt an argument, but she felt a sudden anger that she didn't want to quiet. "Tony has all the markers of a middle-class childhood. An upper-class one, I would guess. And if that were a film about white children in America or Europe, nobody would watch it. It would turn people's stomachs."

"I don't disagree. But if you've grown up in a corner of the world nobody has given a damn about, there's value to telling your story. Or having your story told."

"Fine. But would anyone make a film about white children slaughtering each other?"

"Maybe not." Naomi unlocked the car doors, then sat with the keys on her lap. In the silence between them, Vega was reminded of her father, the plodding way he spoke after his stroke, as though he was given a daily allotment of words and was always measuring them out. She rarely missed her parents, but when she did, it was with a force so strong she could hardly breathe.

"Can I tell you something petty?" Naomi asked.

"I'm sure I won't find it petty."

"No, you will. Because it was. The background to the story is that I never really wanted to study Mesoamerica. I always wanted to study these small tribes in Colombia: the Tayronas and the Muiscas. That was always my dream. But I can't travel abroad, for citizenship reasons, so my advisor at Columbia pushed me to focus on Mesoamerica. It wasn't ideal, but it all worked out. But when I was in Austin, one of the students in my cohort, she was a Cuban girl from Florida, she was going to Colombia on a dig to begin her doctoral research. And the more I thought about it, the more it bothered me. I would lie in bed at night and think about how fucking unfair it was, and how *I* should have been going on that trip. So I started talking about her. It was just childish academic shit, saying her work was unoriginal, and she wasn't a great writer. But it got back to her, and one day she came up to me and she said, 'I've always respected you. And I thought we were friends. If you have some feedback on my writing, I would be happy to hear it directly.' She was speaking in Spanish, too, which was a good touch on her part. It made me feel worse."

Vega smiled. "I think you can forgive yourself. People have committed more egregious acts out of jealousy."

"Fair enough. But I realized I had spent so many years thinking about who had it easier than I did, and resenting them because they had the one, single thing I wanted at the time."

"You never seemed to be a particularly aggrieved person."

"Not on the outside." She turned to Vega. "I liked having the last word, though. Maybe that's what I thought I was doing when I didn't show up that day."

"In New York, you mean?"

"The day we planned to meet."

"It was a long time ago," Vega said, though it didn't feel like a long time ago. They stared at each other for a few seconds. Even in the dark, she could see that Naomi's lips were open slightly. Vega ran her finger along the side of Naomi's face and tucked a strand of hair behind her ear. She expected Naomi to lean in. Instead, she pulled back.

"I need to tell you something," Naomi said. "I'm in a relationship. I have a girlfriend."

Vega dropped her hand. The car felt small and hot. "When did you plan to tell me this?"

"I don't know. I got caught up in the conversation. It was good to be with you. I'm sorry."

Vega didn't respond. She wanted to say something sharp and defiant, to somehow accuse Naomi of misleading her without revealing that she was naïve enough to be misled. Finally, she said, "If you had told me, we still would have spent the evening together. But it would have been a more honest evening. I don't understand you." She wished she had never come to the conference. She wanted to be at home. She thought of Asha, her wet mouth and sticky hands, her cottony voice. She missed the smell of her daughter's shampoo, the weight of her body on her lap. What the hell was she doing here? Why had she wasted her night in that apartment? The film came back to her in wrenching flashes: the dead woman. The emaciated dog.

"We've both misfired, Vega. Over the years, I mean. We've both hurt each other without meaning to."

"I didn't know what I was doing. Surely you can understand that. I was twenty-two-years old."

"I was too," Naomi said.

"It's different, Naomi. I was struggling then. I was grieving."

Naomi had just started the car. Now she turned it off, pulled the key from the ignition, and set it on her lap. She looked at Vega. "I know. I understand that."

Six years ago, after Naomi left, Vega spent three days alone in their 121st Street apartment feeling utterly aimless. Eventually, Monty had knocked on the door. He helped Vega haul out the recycling and clean out the kitchen, then carry the sheets and towels to the basement laundry room where they sat on the bench, facing the machines. He told Vega that Naomi had found new subletters who would take the place furnished. If Vega wanted, she could just pack her things, then leave two weeks of rent and a cleaning fee. He told her how sorry he was, how much he would miss her, but how firmly he believed that things happened for a reason.

"I know," she said. "Like famine."

Monty flicked her shoulder. "You and Naomi could have been something, you know."

He offered to spend the night, but she told him she would rather be alone. Over the next few days, she packed her suitcase, wandered the aisles of the East Asian market, and waited for Halima and Zemadi to return to the city. She still missed Naomi viscerally; she missed the rhythm of anticipating her, the sound of her key in the door, the charge of being in the same room. But she felt, alongside her loneliness, a new and cutting self-awareness. Even if Naomi had been madly in love with her, and if Vega had found the language to explain that love to her parents, she could not have fully returned it. There was something broken in her. She knew how to desire a person, but not how to care for them. Her relationships over the years since had confirmed this understanding of herself. But there was one protected source of joy. Sometimes, when she watched Asha grip a crayon or pull on her socks, her expression so focused and so breathtakingly sweet, Vega wondered if this was the one great love in her life. If she might fail at everything else except motherhood.

Naomi suggested dinner, but Vega declined, saying she needed to catch up on work. She had consumed nothing that evening except for two glasses of syrupy red wine and some pretzels, and she was hungry, but the prospect of sitting across a table from Naomi, talking blithely about their lives, depressed her. They parted ways in the hotel elevator, and Vega went to her room. She considered calling her parents. It was nine a.m. in India, and they would just be returning from their morning walk. Instead, she ordered room service and turned on Al Jazeera. It was soothing. The weather reports were all in Celsius, the news anchors all Arab, African, or South Asian, and all with a hint of a British parochial school accent. She ate dinner in bed, watching a documentary about cacao farming in Ghana. The following afternoon, she took a taxi to the airport and flew back to Baton Rouge.

# 26

Ameya's departure loomed, always in the distance, until suddenly it wasn't. "What am I going to do when you leave?" Vega asked the night before Ameya's flight. They were sitting on the kitchen floor, wrapping her glassware set in T-shirts and stuffing each piece into padded corners of her suitcase.

With Ameya's help, Vega had managed to juggle her schedule over the previous year. Ameya picked Asha up from day care two evenings a week, allowing Vega to work in the undisturbed calm of her office until she raced home to make dinner. They packed each other's lunches and took turns folding laundry. But it wasn't just the logistical ease. Ameya knew Asha's favorite foods, knew she liked cucumbers sliced into spears, that she called the bits of core in her apple slices "plastic." She brought home gifts that had come to clutter the front lawn: a red scooter she found on a campus giveaway website, boxes upon boxes of sidewalk chalk, an inflatable pool. She referred to herself in the third person when talking to Asha. *Give Aunty Ameya a hug. Let Aunty Ameya help you with your shoes. Give Aunty your apple, kanna, and I'll cut off the plastic.*

The previous December, on Suresh's insistence, Ameya had flown with Vega and Asha to New Jersey for the holidays. A few days before the trip, a pipe had burst in Shoba and Mohan's basement, and Vega assumed that the plans would be canceled, but Suresh was adamant. He had taken the week off from work. "There is room in the apartment for everybody," he said. "It will be a wonderful time."

He was right. The apartment was cramped that week, but lively. Shoba came over every day with the girls, Suresh took over most of the childcare, and Vega and Ameya spent their days reading, playing cards, or chauffeuring Shoba, who delighted in frivolous errands, but still didn't know how to drive, to Dunkin' Donuts. In the evenings, Rupa and Mohan joined—she from class and he from work—and, after the girls were sleeping, the adults gathered in the living room to watch Sun TV dramas or old Masterpiece mysteries. One night, as they settled into the guest bed, Vega told Ameya the room had once been her study. Ameya was astonished. "You *lived* here?"

"Where else do you think I lived?" Vega asked, which made Ameya laugh until Vega, too, was laughing. Some weeks later, Rupa sent a framed photograph of Ameya from Christmas morning; she was sitting cross-legged on the floor, Veena and Asha crawling on her lap. Vega had set it on the bookshelf. Now, she imagined explaining this photograph to Asha when she was older, when Asha no longer had any memory of Ameya.

"You'll make friends," Ameya said. "You'll be busy with work and with Asha. And you'll manage." She was leaving behind a few appliances that were too large to travel with and easy enough to replace when she arrived in Minneapolis: a blender, an idli steamer, a rice cooker. "This way, you can cook. Get into a routine. Take care of yourself. And call Priya and Vishal. It would be nice for Asha to have a playmate." This last point was true, but Vega knew she would never call them. She liked them enough to know she would feel their absence, but not enough to chase a friendship.

"Just promise me you'll keep in touch," Vega said. "Even if I have all the friends in the world, I'll still miss *you*."

They dropped Asha at day care and drove to the airport, where she and Ameya bought coffees and lingered near security until the last possible moment. Afterwards, in the short-term parking lot, Vega leaned her seat back and cried. She moved through her afternoon classes in a daze and left campus early, planning to take Asha for ice cream, or maybe to the lake. But when she arrived at day care, Asha was fussy. "Children pick up on things," Asha's old day care teacher used to say. Vega generally thought this was nonsense, at least when applied to babies and toddlers. Now, she wondered if there was some truth to it. They went home to their empty house, where Vega drew Asha's bath and set the rice cooker.

# 27

That winter, Vega hired a babysitter, a cheery undergraduate named Emily who reliably picked Asha up from school, made her a snack, and sent Vega misspelled updates and reminders: *Letting you know your out of milk! On r way home! We should be their in ten minutes!*

"Do you have a boyfriend?" Emily asked one evening as she was pulling on her boots.

"What?"

"You know? A boyfriend?"

Vega glanced at Asha, who was seated at the kitchen table, coloring, within earshot. She wanted to whisk her away, draw her evening bath, and close the door between them and Emily. She did not want her three-and-a-half-year-old daughter to know what a boyfriend was.

"I don't. Why do you ask?"

"It just crossed my mind, you know. I mean, you're pretty."

"Thank you," Vega said. It was such a careless and instinctive response, and she tried to retract it a moment later. But Emily was already out the door.

"She asked if I had a boyfriend," she told Ameya over Skype, a few nights later. "This babysitter of mine." It was beginning to occur to her how much she complained and fretted when she and Ameya spoke. On their last conversation, the subject had been McDonald's. She and Asha had stopped to use the bathroom and Vega had been puzzled when Asha asked if she could order chicken nuggets. "When have you had chicken nuggets before?" she asked.

"Birthday parties," Asha said. "And Emily sometimes." As far as Vega knew, her daughter was a vegetarian. And there she was, sitting on her knees so she could reach the table, strangely dexterous with the small packets of dipping sauces.

"What is so terrible about dating?" Ameya asked. She had been equally unfazed by the McDonald's story.

"It isn't terrible. But I would never think to ask anybody that question."

She looked past Ameya, into her sparse and tidy apartment. "It's good enough for now," Ameya had told her, when she arrived in Minneapolis. "Some of my colleagues are interesting. The stipend is better than at LSU." She had a lead on a few academic positions for the coming year—one in Toronto and another in Stuttgart—and would be equally content with either, and she was seeing a Norwegian man who studied something related to hydroelectricity. It depressed Vega, sometimes, to hear about evenings Ameya spent with people she would only know for another year. She was afraid that her own life was beginning to look like that.

"No need to meet somebody just for the sake of dating," Ameya said. "But it would be good to be open to it."

"Maybe when Asha is older," Vega said, less because she believed it, and more to end the conversation. She had slept with two men over the past year. Both were LSU professors, one a chemist and the other a geographer. They were pleasant, in a boring way, and attractive enough. But afterwards, she couldn't recall any of the desire that had led her to the men's apartments to begin with. She imagined improbable scenarios in which Asha walked in and saw her mother—her cutter of apples, her nighttime consoler—in bed with a stranger. Late at night, when she was too restless to sleep, she looked up Naomi's name online, zooming in on every blurry photograph, reading and rereading her student reviews. Occasionally, she searched for Winston, as well. She learned he had moved to Rutgers. The previous semester, he had published a series of articles that Vega had read in their entirety, down to the footnotes, hoping to find some piece of him tucked somewhere inside. But the language was so distant, so academic. The articles could have been written by anyone.

"You deny yourself experiences you *know* you deserve. If some other woman told you, 'Oh, I shouldn't be sleeping with men because I'm a mother,' you would call them sad and repressed. But in your actual life, you don't see it. You're too distracted by the theoretical."

Vega laughed, though there was a needle of truth in Ameya's assessment. It wasn't just sex she was theoretical about. She thought back, guiltily, to the playdates Asha often asked for and Vega always made excuses to avoid. She was happy with Asha's friendships at school. When people asked, she praised the economic and racial diversity of Grant Elementary. She liked that Asha's friends were a mix of Black and white children along with a scattering of Central American or Vietnamese, that they seemed happily untouched by the racial division beyond their playground. But she was irritated, too, by the celebrations of mediocrity. The misspelled student work posted in the hallways, the easy math worksheets Asha brought home stamped with suns and stars, the nonsensical guided reading books, every title ending with an exclamation point. *My Lost Dog! Bring on Spring!* If one of her colleagues had written a paper on the subject of inclusive educational models, she would eagerly have embraced the theories. But in practice, in her own child's public school, it all grated on her.

One night, in early August, Suresh called. For the past three years, he had steadily and predictably flown to Baton Rouge on the last weekend of the month. His visits were pleasant enough. Asha neither anticipated them eagerly nor cried when he left, and Vega was relieved to spend the two days quietly working. The previous summer, when he announced that he and Rupa were getting married, Vega let Asha give in to the excitement. She had flown to New Jersey with Asha and handed her off to Suresh at the airport and spent the weekend in Margo's apartment, eating takeout and wandering the city. She called Suresh in the mornings, ostensibly to check on Asha, but the familiar voices in the background tugged at her. Shoba's. Her ex-mother-in-law's. Even the sound of Mohan drew her back to her old life. Her Christmas trip, three years earlier, hadn't stirred any emotions in her, but the wedding made her unexpectedly lonely. Each time Vega called the house, Asha was too excited to talk. She was sharing a bedroom with Tara and Veena for the weekend, and answered the phone breathlessly, eager to get back to the girls, who were now officially her cousins.

Asha was sullen on the return flight. For weeks after, the only thing that seemed to console her was television. In the evenings, Vega let her stare numbly at the screen, rewatching episodes of *Curious George*. Everything about their lives seemed blanched. They ate a small rotation of easy, boring meals every night: dhal and rice. Frozen broccoli zapped in the microwave and topped with grated cheese. Pasta with jarred sauce. She could hear Charanya's voice: *That isn't sufficient. Physical stimulation is also important. You must talk and play with her.*

"I'm so sorry to call late at night," Suresh said, sounding tired. He was washing dishes in the background.

"Is everything okay?" she asked, switching to Tamil. She had been grading papers at the kitchen table, but now settled down on the living room couch, farther from Asha's open bedroom door.

"Rupa had a bit of a loss. I have to postpone my trip."

"What kind of loss? Are you both alright?"

"She was some eight, nine weeks along. The doctor says these are normal occurrences. Even among healthy women, such things are frequent."

"You're saying she had a miscarriage?"

"Yes. That is the situation."

"Oh, Suresh. I'm sorry. For you both. How is she?"

"Okay. She won't take leave from school."

"I thought she had a clinical clerkship this summer. Surely she can miss a week."

"The work is too demanding, she says. If she takes time to rest, she won't be able to make up all that she missed."

True to her original plan, Rupa had completed her undergraduate degree at William Paterson and begun medical school at Rutgers the previous year. Vega wanted to offer the sort of maternal suggestions Rukmini might have voiced: *You must take rest. Your body must heal.* But she suspected Rupa was right. She could not afford to take time off. Clinical clerkships moved forward. There were no consolation points awarded to women recovering from a miscarriage.

"She has a good doctor?"

"Yes."

"I'm sure she's following good advice, then. And she knows her limits."

Suresh turned off the water. Vega pictured him drying the dishes, sliding them into place on the shelf of their old apartment. Then she remembered that he and Rupa had bought a new house in Randolph, close to Shoba and Mohan. What she was picturing of his life was all wrong.

"She's missing her mother," he said. "But Shoba has been very helpful." He paused. "I feel badly for Asha. To cancel seeing her."

"I'll explain it to Asha. I don't want you to worry about all of that." They had said all they needed to, but he was lingering. "Suresh," she said again.

"Hmm."

"Please send her my love. I know you'll take good care of her."


Asha said little the next morning when Vega told her that Suresh had postponed his trip. "He isn't coming?" She was drawing, and looked up, still clutching her crayon.

"Not right now." Vega knelt next to her, kissed her cheek, and tucked her hair behind her ear. Asha hadn't inherited Vega's curly hair. It was thick and straight, as Ashwini's had been, with little whisps that Vega clipped back every morning. More than any other ritual of motherhood, this was when Vega was most viscerally reminded of her sister: when she was separating Asha's hair into sections, brushing it, sliding the barrette into place.

"Why not?"

"Rupamma isn't feeling well. He needs to be with her."

Asha returned to her drawing, seemingly untroubled by the news. But late that night, she was sullen and pouty, pushing her dinner around on her plate and refusing to take a bath.

"The tub's dirty."

"It isn't dirty, kanna. It looks like it is because it's a white tub. But it's perfectly clean."

"It has pink stuff all around it."

"That's just from the soap. I'll sit with you. I'll put in bubbles. Okay?"

Vega sat on the edge of the tub and poured from an apple-scented bottle of bubble bath that Emily, for some unknown reason, had given her months back. Asha lay down, the foam pillowing around her, then asked, "Why don't I have a grandmother?"

"What do you mean? You have two paatis and two thatthas."

"I want to see them."

"You saw your Kamala Paati and P.N. Thatha last summer. At Appa and Rupamma's wedding."

"I want to see the other ones."

"We see them on the computer." It was a Saturday ritual, sitting at Vega's desk with Asha on her lap as her parents shouted the same questions on repeat: *How is the weather! How are your studies!*

"I want to drive there."

"We can't drive there. Remember I showed you on the map? There are oceans we have to cross. We have to fly to get there. And flying is a special thing you can't do every day."

"Alice's grandma picks her up from school."

"We'll see your paatis and thatthas soon."

"Tomorrow?"

"No, kanna. But soon."

One afternoon, sitting in her office, she saw an email from Gayatri sent earlier that morning. *I imagine you've heard the news by now. Difficult thing, no? Can Skype later if you want to talk, my morning your night.*

Vega wrote back immediately. *What news?* It was past midnight in India by then, and useless to expect a response. Still, she checked her email obsessively throughout the day. She tucked Asha in hurriedly that night and called Gayatri at nine o'clock—seven thirty in the morning India time—just as the long-distance rates dropped. Gayatri would be drinking her coffee by now, on her way to the office.

"Hey da," Gayatri said. "Ugly news, no?"

"*What* news, Gayatri? Why would you send me such a vague message? Did somebody die?"

"You're joking, Vega. You must have heard." Gayatri paused and sipped, then came a long and maddening silence.

"Heard *what?*"

"Reddy. It's all over the news. There was a big article in the *Deccan Chronicle.*"

"It's a bit difficult to find the *Deccan Chronicle* in Louisiana, Gayatri. What in hell happened?"

"I'll scan the article when I'm at the office. Seems he was carrying on with a student. Her family brought some complaint, and the university canned him. They found him last week. Hanged himself."

"Gayatri." Vega rested her forehead against her hand and breathed slowly, picturing Reddy swaying from his verandah. It was likely not where it had happened, but once the image appeared in her mind, she couldn't erase it. She had received small updates on him over the years—mainly from Gayatri, whose college classmate was on the faculty at Hyderabad University. But occasionally his name would come up in a search for articles, and she would think back to *Decolonizing Classrooms*, a book she had misplaced somewhere between Chennai and Baton Rouge. The arguments now seemed so bloated, so detached from reality. *The English language contains no nuance. Dravidian languages are the most sophisticated on earth, rivaled only by the languages of our African brothers, the Bantu people.* Some months back, Gayatri had mentioned that Reddy's daughter, Ambika, was an undergraduate at Cal Poly, studying architecture. "I believe she will be constructing land-based buildings," Gayatri said, and Vega had laughed harder than the joke really invited, touched that Gayatri would remember such an obscure reference from such a long time ago. Now she thought of Ambika, alone with her blueprints in some dank student housing. Or maybe flying home for the funeral rites.

"The article wasn't one-sided," Gayatri said. "Some students spoke highly of him, saying he was the only professor who didn't teach through rote methods. He embraced Socratic discussion and debate. That sort of thing."

"That was true of him," Vega said. "Students really did love his class. He just had a strange way of loving them back." They were both quiet. Vega glanced at the clock, aware that Gayatri was probably running late for work. But she wasn't ready to hang up the phone. "What do you know about the girl who came forward?"

"They haven't released her name. She was an undergraduate. Eighteen, maybe nineteen years. His daughter's age, for fuck's sake."

For weeks she was in a fog, reading every bit of information she could dig up. The obituary was scant. *Educated in Oak Ridge International School, and later the Universities of California at Berkeley and Michigan. Died in his home. Survived by his mother, sister, daughter, and two nephews.* The *Deccan Chronicle* called him a "brilliant and troubled social scientist." Gayatri sent her everything that came her way: gossip from the faculty, a feminist rebuttal from the university's student weekly, quotes from the unnamed girl's lawyer.

But it was Ambika Reddy she couldn't stop thinking about. Ambika Reddy whose name she searched online, finding a thumbnail picture—pretty, smiling—receiving the Cal Poly Global Undergraduate Award. She remembered her scattered items throughout the house: red bicycle, Cadbury wafers in the fridge, school uniform hanging on the clothesline. The way he used to talk about her. *She's my artist, Ambika. An absolute creative.*

Ashwini came back to her in short, vivid bursts. Banging on the bathroom door. One hand on the railing while she slipped on her shoe. Her childhood birthday parties in Mysore, always wearing a new dress. At the cafeteria in the Cleveland hospital where their parents always let them order enormous wedges of chocolate pie that Vega found delicious for the first few bites, but nauseating by the end. Ashwini scraping the plate clean. Her friend, Julia, lying on her belly on Ashwini's bed. Julia, who had introduced Ashwini to French braids, Cat's Cradle, Tolkien. Where was Julia now? Had anybody even contacted her after Ashwini died? Vega told herself she would look her up, that she would find a way of getting in touch. Instead, she lost hours each day clicking through the Crime section of the *Advocate*, and later at night sitting frozen before the local news. A seven-year-old girl shot on her way to a dance recital. A teenage boy leaving a basketball court. *Such a goof. Such a good boy. Always looking out for his brothers and sister.* Stray bullets and stray bullets and stray bullets. She attended a series of lunchtime lectures, delivered by a visiting criminology professor named Cassie. "We have to ask ourselves *why* our young boys are so pained that they resort to violence. We have to understand that trauma begets trauma." She sat next to Debra and Mark and Bert and nodded and murmured in constant agreement, though the arguments felt distant and incomplete. She began leaving work the moment her office hours ended, so she and Asha could arrive to the safety of home before dark. She pulled the kitchen table away from the window, leaving deep gashes on the wooden floor, and moved Asha into her bed to sleep.

# 28

For weeks, she moved through the motions of her day, delivering stale lectures and paying scant attention during department meetings. But there was also a feeling of restlessness. Her research bored her. Her statements on feminism and immigration were dull and repetitive. She had been so proud of her publications as they trickled out over the past year. Now, going back to them, she had the same reaction as when she read Winston's papers months back. They could have been written by anyone.

She began keeping a journal, waking up at five each morning and writing for an hour before Asha woke up. She polished a few pieces and sent them off, never expecting a response. But one April morning, there was an email from an editor at the *Nation*.

> Dear Professor Gopalan: We have received your submission, "On Brahminism," and would love to run it in our May issue. Many thanks for sending us such fine work.

"If Reddy were alive, he would boast about you," Gayatri said.

"I don't think Reddy was particularly interested in me as a scholar."

"He would be now. He would tell everybody you're his protégée. He'd invite you to be a visiting professor and he would take credit for your research."

This was likely true, Vega thought. She found the comment both funny and unbearably sad.

On the afternoon her copy of the *Nation* arrived, she lay the magazine flat on her coffee table. She had sent the final draft to the editor a month earlier and hadn't read it since. Now she was worried that she would find the sentences slack or the arguments weak. But the language surprised her. It was sharper than she remembered. That night, Asha said, "Read it to me."

"You may not find it very interesting, kanna."

"I like the part where it says your name."

Vega pulled Asha onto her lap. "I can just read my name, then." But she read it all, settling Asha into the crook of her arm, and marveling over the sound of her own words.

> *The first recorded Brahmin to strive for American citizenship was Bhagat Singh Thind. In 1913, he arrived in the United States from his native village in the Indian state of Punjab, part of a small wave of Indian immigrants in the early twentieth century. But, unlike many of his fellow countrymen who arrived in California to fill a desperate need for agricultural workers, Singh did not seek the life of a migrant farmer. He sought an education. And he sought to stay. Over the following years, Singh financed his degree from the University of California, Berkeley, through summer labor in Oregon's lumber mills. He enlisted in the United States Army during World War I, and after returning to his adopted home, petitioned the U.S. government for the right to become an American.*

Midway through, she felt self-conscious. It was ridiculous to subject a child to the history of the Chinese Inclusion Act, the Asiatic Barred Zone, *Ozawa v. the United States.* But when she paused, Asha said, "Keep going. It's funny."

"It's *funny*?"

Asha shrugged. "I like it. I like when you read."

She wondered if she should give Asha some context to help her make sense of the article. In an attempt to talk about caste, she had recently ordered from India a children's biography of Ambedkar called *The Boy Who Asked Why*. But, just as when Vega tried to bring up the subject of race, the conversation led to the same meek conclusion about fairness and kindness. Vega was not sure—she never was sure—whether or not this was enough. If she was having the right conversations. She kissed Asha on the head and smoothed her hair behind her ear.

> *In 1923, when his application for citizenship was denied, Thind devised a unique play. Replicating the brutal caste hierarchies of his native India, he categorized himself as a high-caste Aryan of North Indian descent who met the official definition of a Caucasian. His lawyers argued he was ethnically connected not to those excluded by the Asiatic Barred Zone, but to the white settlers moving west in droves, staking their claim to American land.*

Her colleague, Mark, assigned Vega's article in his Race and Ethnicity course. The following week, one of their sociology majors, Seema, a bubbly Indian American sophomore who frequently invited Vega to meetings of the South Asian Student Alliance, sent her an email.

> Do you mind if I post your piece on Campus Talks?
> We're trying to get more professors to contribute. Also,
> I really loved this paragraph: "Bhagat Singh Thind has
> given caste-privileged Indian Americans strange shoul-
> ders to stand on. But when we examine his history, his
> racialized claim that he deserved a place in America,
> I am not sure who is to be blamed. A brown man who
> claimed to be white, or a white country that demanded
> whiteness as a requirement for citizenship."

Vega wrote back: *I don't mind at all. Though I'm not sure anyone would read it.*

Vega was right. The article elicited only one response on the first day. Still, it surprised her.

> *My parents run a corner store in Shreveport. I was happy to read this. I get tired of the Brahmin doctor stereotype.*

She began posting each week, tepid one-line messages linked to various articles related to immigration. Slowly, she began writing more. There was a strange vulnerability to it that reminded her of standing in front of Reddy, she naked and he fully clothed. She included her name, but students were often anonymous, with absurd handles: spaghettieddie; gaysian1990; therealsouthernbelle. She assumed therealsouthernbelle to be white, but one morning, she woke up to this message:

> *I'm a dark-skinned Sri Lankan girl. I was reminded, reading your post, of how my mom didn't want me to spend too long in the sun when I was growing up. I don't want to be too critical of her because I know she always meant well. But it's like she was trying to make sure that I would never be mistaken for a Black woman. Thoughts?—TRSB*

There were mundane matters in her life, too. She had a leaky faucet that had been worsening so gradually she wouldn't have noticed had Emily not pointed it out. Emily's uncle Bert was a plumber, she said, and the next morning at seven o'clock, Bert stood on Vega's doorstep holding a box of tools and looking precisely as she expected a plumber named Bert to look: sunburnt and middle-aged, wearing navy Dickies pants, a white T-shirt, and an LSU baseball cap. "This is an easy fix," he said. "Just a damaged O-ring. I'll see if I have a spare one in my truck that's the right size. If I do, I could get this finished up by the time you head out." He took apart the pipe and poked the inside with various contents of the toolbox. "You're from India?"

"I am."

"I got a customer from Turkey."

"I've never been."

"Me neither. Furthest I've gone is Mexico. My wife doesn't like airplanes and that was as far as I could convince her to go. But I watch a lot of those travel documentaries. You can really see how people live. Anyway, Emily tells me all about your little girl. She really enjoys her."

"Asha really enjoys her too. I couldn't manage without her." Only now, saying it aloud, did she realize how true it was.

"Emily's the responsible type. She was always like that. Even when she was a kid, her parents never had to get on her about homework or chores or anything, you know?" He went outside, propping the front door open with the latch, and came back a few minutes later. "No luck. But I'll tell you what. I can get one for you as soon as the store opens. Leave me that key, if you're okay with that, and I should have it done by the time you get home." Before leaving, he poked his head into the kitchen. "Mind if I ask you something?" In the bathroom, he had pulled back the curtains around the tub. "Listen, this is outside the work I do. But you have this ring of mold around here. Your kid doesn't use this bath, does she?"

"No," Vega said, though it wasn't true. Asha bathed in that tub every night.

"You want to get rid of that as soon as you can. It just takes some bleach. Do you have any at the house?"

She froze. "I don't believe so." Her house had been falling into gradual disarray since Ameya left. Other people's suggestions just made her feel more lost and overwhelmed. Her neighbor Daphne: *You need systems. Everything in its place.* Rukmini: *Hire a house girl! There must be some Mexicans, no?* Ameya, whose attempt at consolation stung most painfully: *You're doing your best.* And then, here was Bert, middle-aged plumber, watcher of travel documentaries, his words so comforting she thought she might cry: "How about I grab some for you when I pick up that O-ring. Bleach is cheap. I know it's hard to find time for these things when your kids are little. You have an old sponge?"

"That I do have."

"Just give it a quick scrub and let it sit overnight. Throw out the sponge. But anyways, I'll get that bleach for you. One thing I can take off your hands."

There was so much she wanted taken off her hands. Her fridge was a minefield of expired foods. And she was tired of the clutter, tired of kitchen cabinets stuffed with items she never used. Tired of Asha's drawers she could barely close because they were filled with clothing long outgrown.

She wasted hours researching ways to occupy Asha during the week so she could get more done: soccer clinics, basketball clinics, swim lessons, some sort of Waldorf Saturday program, but all required Vega to be on-site. What she really wanted were the typical arrangements the women around her seemed to rely on: Daphne, whose husband took the kids on Saturday morning. Her office assistant, Monica, who always seemed to be ferrying her three children to or from her mother-in-law's house.

She took a day off from work and enlisted Daphne's housekeeper, a Filipina woman named Rosie, who helped Vega toss half the contents of her fridge, haul away boxes of kitchen appliances and Asha's old clothes, and talked, in a steady and calibrated voice, about her two teenage children in Manila. "I'll send for them next year. Maybe year after. My girl, she says, 'I want come.' My boy, he want stay because friends. But they go good school there. Private school. So, what to do? Here, school is no good." On her way out, she pocketed Vega's twenty-five-dollar tip. "You're a nice girl," she said. "Just like Ms. Daphne."

---

**Professor Gopalan:** *I knew a woman once who was unable to fly because, though she had spent her life in the States, she was not a U.S. citizen. Those of us who acquired our visas and green cards easily, who have never been forced to live apart from our children, who have been able to replicate and grow* *the wealth with which we arrived in this country, who have been able to depend on wealthy and well-established relatives who shared in our luck, we are just that: lucky. We are no better or smarter or more lawful than anybody else. We're just lucky.*

---

**latinachemist:** *I feel invisible in this country, but also too visible. There were times when I was a teenager when I couldn't eat. I spent years being afraid my family would be deported. I transferred here from junior college because my family has to pay international student tuition for me to attend, even though I was raised in Louisiana. I'm going to leave with so much debt that my classmates, who are citizens, won't have.*

**mattfrommonroe:** *no one forcing you to stay here.*

**Taylor1989:** *is she a dyke?*

**rachelbeth:** *As a white woman, I really appreciate hearing stories like these. Latinachemist, I'm with you. I've got your back. If I ever have a million dollars (or half a million or a quarter million), I'm going to help you pay off your debts. Because that will be like paying mine off too, if you know what I mean.*

**mattfrommonroe:** *pretty sure she's a dyke*

One afternoon, she ran into the geographer Seth, at the campus coffee shop. He was more charming than she remembered, funnier and more attentive. Some days later, they ended up in his bed. Afterwards, he lay next to her, staring at the ceiling and talking about his sons—ages thirteen and fifteen—who were becoming strangers to him.

"They're just so close to their mom," Seth told her. "And I don't resent her for that. But it's so transactional between them and me.

Everything is: Can you take me here? Can you buy me this? They used to get *excited* when I came home. Used to run to me."

He was sweet and bookish, passionate about concepts she had never before considered—climate data, sediment transport—but also sturdy in that uniquely American way, with rough hands and a wood-working studio in his backyard where he had built the kitchen table, his sons' bookshelves, the desk in his study.

He sent her emails throughout the weeks—articles or political cartoons she might like, or short messages telling her he couldn't wait to see her. She imagined the two of them in a real relationship, super-imposing Asha onto her picture of what their lives would be. Asha meeting his children, the five of them strolling through farmers' markets or carrying picnics to the lake. In her mind, it was all beautiful and uncomplicated; Asha was always well-behaved, everyone got along, it was always a Saturday.

One evening, he invited Vega for dinner. They ate eggplant parmesan, washed the dishes together, then had sex where they always did—in a nautical-themed guest bedroom, wallpaper lined with tiny blue boats and anchors, presumably decorated by his ex-wife. His actual bedroom, the one he and his wife had shared, Vega had never set foot inside. Afterwards, he sat on the bed, looking tired and resigned, his chest hair matted, his stomach spilling over his boxer shorts. "I don't know if I can do this. I'm sorry. I know what you must think of me."

"Do what?" Vega asked, regretting the question the moment she asked it. She maintained her composure, but once in the car, she cried until she was exhausted, driving in circles around her block. Then she went into the house, sent Emily home, deleted every email she had ever received from him, and curled up next to Asha's sleeping body.

---

*Dear Professor Gopalan,*

  *I am responding to your recent message by email, as it is the format I prefer to these public discussion boards. I would like to share a small observation I have made over*

*my twelve-year tenure at the university. Each semester,*
*in my end of course reviews, a minimum of two or three*
*students will say that I am inaccessible or unwilling to help*
*them with academic struggles. At least one will complain*
*that my accent is difficult to understand.*

*I am puzzled by this. I have strong friendships with*
*many Americans (as well as people of other nationalities)*
*who seem to understand my words quite easily. I also make*
*myself available through office hours, though students*
*rarely take advantage.*

*I wonder, often, if there is an element of bias in their as-*
*sessment. Of course, one must be cautious about such quick*
*judgments of others. But your messages have prompted such*
*thoughts.*

*Sincerely,*
*Dr. Ranjan Vyas*
*Department of Biology*

One spring Saturday, she ran into Priya and her children at the lake. Priya called Amin over. "Ven aqui! Tu recuerdes Asha?"

Vega settled in the grass, watching the children run off. Priya's daughter, no longer a baby, was kicking a ball in the distance. "She's so big," she said.

"She just turned three," Priya said. "And your little girl. Look at her."

Priya had called and emailed a few times over the years, extending invitations to picnics and birthday parties, but Vega had always been noncommittal in her response, knowing every time that she had no intention of going. This information must have made its way to Ameya, who, across the distance, had become increasingly concerned that Vega was anti-social.

"Make friends!" she had shouted to her once, over Skype. It was such a hollow and useless piece of advice, like telling somebody to fall in love. Vega had tried to explain to Ameya, never with much success, that she found the veneer of friendship lonelier than being alone. The previous semester, when Suresh was in town, she had joined her department for their monthly happy hour at a dim sports bar off the interstate. It was pleasant enough, with a few funny exchanges and some banter about teaching, but there was nobody there she particularly wanted to talk to, and the experience left her feeling both vapid and indulgent. When she returned to the house, Suresh and Asha were building an elaborate construction out of magnetic tiles. There were remains of Nutella toast on the counter. Vega wished she had stayed home with them.

The three children were quickly engrossed in a game—some fusion of kickball and hide-and-seek. Asha was laughing, the deep belly laugh she had inherited from Vega's father. Amin kicked the ball and they all scrambled for it.

"I'm not sure if Ameya mentioned," Priya said, "but we're moving back to Houston."

"She didn't mention it." Vega felt a tug of something—not quite disappointment, but akin to it. She didn't like Priya enough to respond to her invitations, but she liked the thought of periodically seeing her. The promise of future friendship. "Is it job-related?"

"Yes and no. I got a decent offer from a consulting group. It's a lateral move, but good enough. Mainly, it's because my parents are there, and my sister and her family just moved back."

"That sounds nice, then." Vega looked away, trying to seem interested in what the kids were doing. She had mostly broken the habit of imagining what Ashwini's life would have been, but sometimes a phrase struck her, and she played it over and over in her mind. *My sister and her family.* Ashwini would never have children. Vega had not thought to grieve this loss until Asha was born. She would never be an aunt.

"Vishal's staying here. For the time being."

Vega looked at her. "Will he join you in Houston eventually?"

"Unclear. We're taking some time apart." Priya paused. "Meaning, we're separating."

Vega tried to remember what she wanted people to say to her when she told them about her divorce. But that was a different situation. Priya, sitting with her chin on her knees, looked like she was about to cry. "That must be difficult," she finally said. "I'm sorry."

Priya shrugged, not very convincing in her show of indifference. Her eyes were glassy. "You managed it, didn't you? People do this all the time, right?"

"That doesn't make it easy." Vega tried to sound soothing. In reality, she was stunned. Priya and Vishal seemed such an intact unit, with their shared Peace Corps days, their weekend camping trips, their constant use of "we" and "our." *We'd love to have you over to our place! We just got back from Oaxaca! It's our favorite city.* Did couples like that actually divorce?

They sat for over an hour, Priya talking about the logistics of the separation, their plans to put the house on the market, how the children were processing the news. "If you're up for a drink or something," she said, "Vishal has the kids tomorrow night. If you can find a sitter, I could stand to get out."

But the next evening, just before Emily was expected, Priya called to cancel. "I'm so sorry. I'm just so tired. We were at the zoo the whole day, and it took the energy out of me. Can we take a rain check?"

Vega had a fleeting thought that she should set Priya up with Seth, then realized the absurdity of the idea. "Are you sure?" she asked. "I would be happy to just bring you dinner. I could leave it at your door."

"Positive. I'm just beat. I might skip dinner and go to bed."

If they had been close friends, Vega would have pushed harder. Instead, she read Asha a story, *Caps for Sale*, while she waited for Emily to arrive. Then she splashed water on her face, drove aimlessly for a bit, and had dinner at a Greek restaurant where she and Ameya had once eaten. She walked along Baton Rouge's tiny strip of downtown and stopped at the Cinemark where, limited by screening times, she watched *Munich* in an empty row. This was freedom. If she were in New Jersey, she could leave Asha with Suresh and do this sort of thing. But the movie was devastating. She cried through most of it. Afterwards, she sat outside on an empty bench and watched a woman shutter the Urban Outfitters across the street. Why did she watch violent films? Scenes that seemed to hardly bother other people stayed lodged in her memory for years. She thought about *Os Perdidos*. All those people at the party who were probably still friends, the two couples that were probably still together. *When we were in grad school, he used to come over and make me watch Fassbinder films with him. Do you know Fassbinder? You're not missing much.* She felt as though she were missing everything.

**brownandredallover:** *Bobby Jindal for governor!*

**mattfrommonroe:** *Bobby Jindal is a f\*\*\*ing brown monkey*

**Taylor1989:** *Yeah but you still gotta vote for him*

# 29

In late June, one month to the day before Asha's sixth birthday, Rupa gave birth to a baby boy. They named him Vikram. Vega and Asha cooed over him on Skype. The fridge was covered with Asha's skeletal drawings: *This is me taking Vikram for a walk. This is me feeding him. This is us if we get a dog.*

"I don't think Appa and Rupamma want a dog," Vega said, laughing. "I think one child is enough." She caught herself too late, the unintentional cruelty of forgetting that Asha was also Suresh's daughter. "Two children will be enough to keep them busy," she said gently.

But Asha didn't seem to catch the mistake. "When we go up to see them, Rupamma says I can hold him as long as I'm sitting down."

They flew to New Jersey on the weekend of July Fourth. Suresh picked them up at the airport and they drove directly to Shoba and Mohan's house. It was the first time Vega had seen the house since she and Shoba visited it together. Vega recalled the smell of paint and cement, the real estate agent leading them from one empty room to another, explaining the concept of open floor plans and the importance of exterior lighting. Now, it was covered in bright Jaipur rugs. The closet was crammed with shoes, winter coats, tennis rackets, a hanging mesh organizer containing puffy hats and gloves—the girls' in pink and purple. A small puja room had been constructed in the alcove beneath the stairs, and Vega stared at it briefly as she slipped off her shoes, taking in the incense, the garlanded statue of Ganesha, framed images of other gods she couldn't identify.

Asha had initially been disappointed that they weren't going directly to see the baby, but she was cheered by the sight of Tara and Veena. Shoba kissed her twice before setting her loose and the three girls ran into the backyard. Vega watched them through the window, their thin brown limbs, strangely muscular, bounding towards the swing set.

"Look at you," Vega said, hugging Shoba. "You're a periamma, now."

Shoba laughed and waved Vega into the kitchen to eat. "He's so beautiful, that boy. The biggest eyes. I tell you, he cries only when he's hungry. Otherwise, like a *sadhu*, he just sits there. So calm. Like his sister."

Asha had not, in fact, been a calm baby, but Vega accepted the comment for its intended purpose—an acknowledgment that they all still saw Asha as Suresh's child. "How is Rupa managing with sleep?" she asked.

"Very well. He wakes up once at night, only."

"Rupa offered to let Asha stay with them, but I don't want them to feel any pressure." Vega looked through the window again at the girls. Asha had been fixated on Vikram, insistent upon sleeping in Suresh and Rupa's house so she could see him first thing in the morning, but Vega wondered if her preference had shifted in the past ten minutes. She, Tara, and Veena seemed entirely lost in their private world.

"There's no pressure," Shoba said. She adjusted the flame beneath a pan and set to work rolling out balls of chapati dough. "She should sleep where she is comfortable. It's like one big house, between the two. There's no difference."

Vega went to the bathroom to wash up. When she came back, Suresh and Mohan had wandered in from the garage and were standing in the living room, locked in conversation about floor insulation. Vega last saw Mohan nearly four years ago, during Christmas. Since then, he had shaved his mustache and lost a bit of weight. Had they passed each other on the street, Vega might not have recognized him. Now, he gave her a stiff handshake, then patted her on the arm as though she were a grown nephew, home for a visit. "Everybody looks well," he said.

"We are well. The girls seem so happy to be together."

He nodded and gave a small, measured laugh. "This is all they've talked about this week. Every morning they ask, 'When does Asha come?'"

They joined Shoba in the kitchen. Suresh chopped cilantro. Mohan took over the chapatis while Shoba called the girls in for lunch. Vega, whose reputation for culinary incompetence seemed to have clung to her, was tasked with setting the table. Afterwards, she joined Suresh at the cutting board. Mohan was within earshot, but he seemed, as always, not to be paying attention.

"You must be tired," she said. "The first month is so difficult."

He smiled. He had finished with the cilantro but was still staring down at it, almost dreamily. "It's wonderful. But also, you worry about every small thing. Is he eating? Is she recovering?"

Vega had a memory of him in the days after Asha was born, tucking her swaddling blanket around her, rocking her to sleep. She recalled the way he struggled with the car seat ("the Octopus!" Rukmini used to call it. "So many bloody straps!"), always jostling the baby awake in the process of buckling her. Vega had been so battered by labor, so physically swollen and emotionally lost, so tired of his clumsiness and her mother's commentary. It had never occurred to her to ask what he was feeling.

The girls tumbled in, then followed Shoba's instructions to wash their hands. When they were all seated at the table, Vega took them in for the first time. Tara, now ten years old, with a wide smile and glasses that kept slipping adorably down her nose. Veena with two braids and a pink headband, reaching for the chapatis.

"We played 'running bases,'" Tara announced in English.

"You taught your cousin all the rules?" Shoba asked in Tamil. To Vega, she said, "This is a game they love, but they are always complaining that you can't play with only two people." She passed the pot of avial to Mohan, who scooped a helping onto each child's plate. Vega was relieved to see Asha eating with the same enthusiasm and familiarity as Tara and Veena. She didn't seem to share Vega's trepidation, her feeling that she was a guest in a life that had, at one point, been hers.

There were some logistical uncertainties to the afternoon. Asha wanted to see the baby, but she also wanted to keep playing with Tara and Veena. In the end, it was decided that Suresh would bring both Asha and Vega to the house for an hour, then drive them back as soon as Vikram had gone down for his next nap. "We'll have a big sleepover tonight," Shoba promised. This seemed to settle Asha's concerns.

"This is a lot of driving for you," Vega said, when she and Suresh were in the car. In the back seat, Asha was dozing off. She looked soft and babylike, the way she always did when she slept.

"I don't mind. As long as she has a nice time." After a few quiet moments, he said, "Shoba is always reminding the girls to speak to her in Tamil. They start school and they forget. Most of their friends are Americans. A few Indian girls, but those are mainly Gujaratis."

"In all fairness, I'm not sure how to say 'running bases' in Tamil."

He glanced at Asha in the rearview mirror. "She understands well, it seems. When we speak to her, she always follows."

It was a reprimand dressed as a compliment, and Vega wasn't sure how to respond. Of course Asha understood Tamil well. But she had not initiated a conversation in anything besides English since their first months in Baton Rouge, when she was a toddler, using what turned out to be the last reserves of Tamil that Suresh had given her.

"I'm trying my best, Suresh," Vega said. It was a child's trick, trying to sound mournful enough to elicit sympathy she didn't necessarily deserve. She remembered Winston, sitting across from her at the cramped corner table at Café Abyssinia. "When she gets older, and starts responding only in English, then what?"

Vikram had enormous eyes and a catlike yawn. He settled easily onto Asha's lap and Rupa held them both, guiding Asha's hand to support his neck. Vega had expected her to look swollen and matronly, similar to Shoba, whose body had taken on a permanent softness after Veena's birth. But she was trim, almost muscular. Earlier, Vega had noted the new addition of a treadmill in the basement, and next to it a Discman and odd assortment of CDs: Phil Collins, *Bollywood Dream Themes*, *The Phantom of the Opera*.

Later, when Suresh was giving Asha a bath, getting her ready for her sleepover with her cousins, Vega and Rupa sat in the living room—Vega holding the baby—on the same couch she and Suresh had owned in their Parsippany apartment.

"Suresh is so impressed with your writing," Rupa said. "He has been telling everybody."

"That's kind of you, Rupa. Thank you." Suresh had been surprisingly enthusiastic about Vega's article, subscribing to the *Nation*, calling Vega the morning it was published and emailing her often to share articles about the original Supreme Court case. "The detail that puzzles me," he said, "is that the judge who wrote the opinion was *himself* foreign born. An Englishman. It's rather fascinating." He had run off multiple copies and sent them to both her parents and his, through one of his cousins who was flying to Chennai. "You're quite famous!" Rukmini shouted into the computer. "News has reached us all the way from New Jersey!" Her father's response was crisp. "I have checked all of your citations. Very thorough research."

Vega stretched out on the couch. She had forgotten how contagious an infant's drowsiness was. She wished she could place him on her chest and fall asleep, the way she used to with Asha. "Your mother is coming soon, no?"

"July end. She has a three-month visa."

"And Suresh says you're returning to work in August."

Rupa smiled. "When I first told him this plan, he was upset. He was worried it was too early."

It surprised Vega, this sliver of insight into their marriage. She did not think of Suresh as a protective husband, or even a particularly opinionated person, nor did she think of Rupa as someone so resolute. Now, she listened as Rupa talked about her commute and her upcoming clinical rotations, her interest in emergency medicine, and Vega was struck by the solidity of it all: Rupa's plans. The life she and Suresh were building.

Later in the hallway, as they waited for Asha to get dressed, Suresh said to Vega, "I wish we had arranged for her to spend some more time here. I could have flown to Louisiana with her at the end of the summer. Even a few weeks would have been nice."

"It would have been too much for you this summer, Suresh. You can't be responsible for her right now, in addition to a baby."

"Shoba would have helped. It would have been no extra work, really."

Vega tried to think of a new explanation, but nothing came to mind. There was no reason she couldn't have arranged her summer so she and Asha could be in New Jersey. Her own teaching load was light—a single graduate seminar. Asha spent most of July and August at the same LSU science camp she had attended for the previous two years, a pleasant but unremarkable place from which she returned every afternoon, clutching ziplock bags of homemade slime or the contents of dissected owl pellets. But every year Vega treated the start date as sacrosanct, a deadline by which they needed to be back home.

Asha came out from the bedroom, dressed in her pajamas, smelling like baby soap. Suresh directed her to the bedroom, where Rupa was nursing Vikram. "Say good night to your brother and Rupamma," he told her. Vega watched her bend over to kiss the baby, her wet hair falling in his face.

Vega spent the next day in a satisfying flurry of errand-running. Rupa's car was low on gas and due for an oil change, she had run out of nursing pads and a particular type of fenugreek tea that could only be found at the Indian grocery store, and she needed to fax a copy of her green card to the student records office. "It will require some

driving," Suresh said. "There are limits to what Shoba can provide." In
Vega's memory, it was the closest he had come to a joke.

Vega adjusted the seats and mirror in her old car. She avoided the
highway, taking the long route to Patel Brothers Grocery. Along with
the tea, she bought a box of mangos for the three girls and a bag of the
spiced cashews Suresh liked. She initiated the conversation in Hindi at
the cash register, and later at the gas station where a man named Yash-
dev tended to Rupa's car, explained the importance of engine mainte-
nance, and told her about his son who had received a full scholarship
to study accounting at the College of New Jersey.

There was a line at the Office Depot, and she stared at the photograph on Rupa's green card as she waited in line to fax the forms. Rupa
had a steady, determined gaze. She was wearing a white blouse. The
green band at the top of the card read *United States of America Permanent Resident.*

"We get a lot of these," the man operating the fax machine said.

"I imagine," Vega said. "There are a lot of us."

She was in no rush to return to either house. Rupa and the baby
would be sleeping, and Suresh and the girls had set off for a day at
a petting zoo. She drove towards Montclair. There was no reason to
think she would run into Winston, certainly not on a Saturday in the
summer. But she was in the mood for a drive, and once she exited the
highway the roads became achingly familiar. She drove through downtown, past Mediterranean grills and Latin American grocery stores and
brick buildings with red awnings. She found Café Abyssinia and went
inside. She remembered it as a dimly lit place, an enormous portrait
of Haile Selassie at the entrance, and aside from herself and Winston,
occupied only by middle-aged Ethiopian men. The portrait was still
there, but now the area was brighter and more spacious. She sat at a
table next to the window and ordered a plate of sambusa. There was
an East Asian couple next to her, and across from them two women
in hijabs. A table of white, professor-looking types. A thin Black man
in a white T-shirt who, from a distance, could plausibly have been

Winston. She remembered the small jolts she would feel in her first years at Sri Vidya when she was still reeling from Ashwini's death, still convinced that every person who bore some resemblance to her sister could actually *be* her sister. Still allowing herself to be crushed, every time, when the girl came closer and revealed herself to be just another stranger.

# 30

Halima was living in a suburb of Pittsburgh. It was ostensibly a college town, though the college itself, Rampart University, seemed to exist more in signage than in actual campus. A billboard on the highway boasted *The Number Five Clinical Electrophysiology Program in the Nation!* Gray clusters of apartment buildings offered nine-month leases.

Vega and Asha had flown to Pittsburgh on their way back to Baton Rouge. Initially, Vega worried the trip would be strained. She and Halima had barely spoken in years. But at the airport Halima pulled her close, then wrapped her arms around Asha. "Look at you," she said, her eyes suddenly wet. "We let too much time pass."

Halima had lost weight. Her skin was paler, and the subtle makeup she wore in New York had been replaced by a thick foundation and dark kohl that made her look older than her thirty-two years. But she was still beautiful, still regal in the way Vega had found so intimidating years back.

They clutched the children's hands as they walked across the parking lot, then drove to the small downtown for ice cream—a two-block stretch flanked by maroon university flags. Halima and Vega leaned against the wall, watching the children seated on a bench. Halima's son and daughter, Karim and Safia, were six and four. Asha sat between them, with a cousin-like familiarity, nodding along to a long and convoluted story Safia was telling about their neighbor's birthday party. "There was a trampoline," she said. "You had to take off your shoes. I had lemonade and one cupcake, but I didn't like the frosting."

"It wasn't a trampoline," Karim corrected. "It was a bounce house."

Vega squeezed Halima's hand. "You're happy here?" she asked. "Cold weather aside?"

Halima tilted her head from side to side. "It's a good start for Adnan. Next year, insha'Allah, he can find something in a bigger town." He had spent three years teaching at Faisalbad University in Lahore, but had barely made enough money, according to Halima, to cover the cost of petrol. "We would have stayed if it were possible," she said, sounding almost apologetic. From Lahore, Adnan had received three tenure-track offers in the States, but his visa application had delayed his arrival for one year. Only Rampart had been willing to hold the job for him. He was now teaching three sections of introductory composition and one poetry course. He had published a slim volume of poetry in both Urdu and English. Later, Vega thumbed through the copy on their bookshelf, struck not only by the lovely sparseness of the language, but by the dedication on the opening page: *For Halima, Karim, and Safia. The stars in my sky.* Halima's visa didn't allow her to work, but she was volunteering at a health clinic three days a week, analyzing data on something called Vivitrol injections. Vega stared at her blankly.

"You've never heard of Vivitrol?" Halima asked.

"No."

"It's an experimental treatment for drug addiction. Mainly opiates. We use it to prevent relapse." She said the cases had initially been startling. People in their twenties and thirties, many of whom came for treatment with small children in tow. The clinic had opened a babysitting room, also staffed by volunteers, so patients could drop their children for a bit and quickly receive their shot. "So many who've come from good homes," Halima said. "Then they start to use drugs and it's all over. *Bas.* How quickly people can undo everything good in their lives."

That night they sat on the couch, drinking mint tea. The children had fallen asleep while watching a movie and now lay on the floor in their pajamas, covered in thin, woolen throws. Adnan was washing the dishes. He had cooked dinner—lentil soup, rice, and vegetable kofta—and refused Vega's offer of help. "You go catch up," he said. "Halima has been looking forward to your visit for months." It touched Vega to see how loving he was, how giving of his labor. The kind of husband she imagined Suresh was to Rupa.

"Is it difficult for you?" Halima asked. "Seeing Suresh with another child?"

"It isn't. I like that Asha has a brother." She paused. "And it makes me happy to see Suresh and Rupa. They're well suited. It was difficult to leave. For Asha, in particular." This was an understatement. On the morning they left New Jersey, Vega had woken up with an ache in her chest, a grief she hadn't anticipated. Asha was in tears. The stop to Pittsburgh had made it possible to coax her onto the plane. Before taking off, Vega sent a message to Suresh: "My love to Rupa and the baby, and everybody else. Missing you all already." She stared at it for a few seconds before finally hitting send.

Abruptly, she said to Halima, "You and Adnan are wonderful together."

Halima laughed. "How so?"

"You care for each other. That's always been clear, but it's even more apparent when I see you with the children." She had long had the sense that there were two types of men: spectacularly bad choices, and interchangeably mediocre ones. She only realized, now, how far she had come from that impression. There was such a thing as a happy marriage. Easy and generous love.

"You haven't met anybody special in Louisiana?"

"No."

"You never were a romantic," Halima said. "I don't mean that as a criticism. But I never saw you with anybody. At least, you never admitted to feeling anything for anyone."

"I've had a few flings. But they were mainly ill-advised." She was grateful that Halima didn't press further. Beyond her happiness for all of them—Halima and Adnan, Suresh and Rupa, even Shoba and

Mohan—was the realization that, if given the chance, she actually could love somebody. She could give of herself. The thought both settled and unsettled her. She sipped her tea, then said, "Tell me how it's been for you here. Honestly. Do you know any other families?" Halima shrugged. "I don't expect we'll stay long. It's best not to make so many friends." She adjusted the blanket over Safia's feet. "I've accepted that Adnan can't make a living in Pakistan. So, I'm happy to be in the States. But this place. It's not good for the kids. Not good for Karim, especially."

"In what way?"

"The children here tease. They make fun of his accent. One older boy, some time back, called him Osama. And now they use this name constantly. Osama. As though they even know what it is they're saying."

"Oh, Halima. I'm sorry."

"He's been fighting. He hit a boy in October. A boy teased him, and he punched back. And the teacher says, 'Oh, he's angry. Violence is never accepted in our school.' She won't understand he is only defending himself. Safia is so small. And she's a little girl. It's different for boys."

Vega wanted to counter that point—an instinctive reaction to any claim that life was harder for boys than for girls. But she had nothing to say. Safia seemed enveloped in the small and comfortable world of her family. Earlier that evening, she and Asha had made oatmeal cookies with Adnan's help, then she had given Asha a tour of her tiny bedroom, introducing her stuffed animals one by one. Karim had sat in the corner of the living room with his Legos, quietly assembling a series of black and gray towers.

"If we can move to a proper university town," Halima said, "something more cosmopolitan, then we can make a nice life." She took a deep breath, then wiped her eyes with her napkin, smearing a line of kohl across her temple.

"I'm sorry, Halima. I'm sorry for you and for Karim." She imagined Halima and the children trudging through Montclair, how wonderfully inconspicuous they would be in a town like that. How happy they could be.

Halima breathed slowly, steadying herself. "I don't blame Adnan. He's working so hard. I can't allow him to feel guilty, especially because there is no immediate solution."

They were quiet for a bit, then Vega said, "The children will become more comfortable here. For better or for worse, they'll become American."

"Maybe. I think about this so often. If we stayed in Lahore, I would be worried every time I went to the market or dropped the kids at school. And we would be living off paise from the university and at the mercy of student protests and faculty strikes. But in another way, we would be happy. It's an imperfect trade. It's always an imperfect trade."

The following spring, Vega was invited to present at a conference at the University of Michigan. She flew with Asha to Newark Airport, where she met Suresh to hand her off. He spun Asha around, then tugged her braid. "Your brother keeps asking for you!"

She giggled. "He can't *talk*, Appa."

"Oh, he can. He's a very smart baby. He keeps asking, 'Where is my akka?'" He zipped Asha's coat, then adjusted her hood. To Vega, he said, "I wish you had time to come home. Rupa hoped to see you."

"Next time I will. Please give her my love."

Her connecting flight didn't leave for another two hours, and she had hoped they could linger. She had woken up at four in the morning and desperately needed a coffee. But Suresh seemed to be in a rush. There was talk of an ice-skating trip when Tara and Veena finished school. Vega pictured him in his Dockers and button-down, making his way tentatively around a rink. She felt a peculiar urge to give him a hug. Instead, she kissed Asha goodbye and watched them disappear down the escalator.

Michigan was frigid. She had brought her winter coat, dug up from a box of clothes she reserved for trips to New Jersey, but the wind whipped through it. It tangled her hair and chapped her knuckles.

At the welcome reception, she made a cup of tea and searched for familiar faces. It was a pure sociology conference, and she knew not to expect Naomi. She saw Charles, her former colleague at LSU, who showed no interest in her casual updates from the department. He talked, instead, about his training for the Boston marathon. "People ask me how I qualified, because I came to running late in life, you see. They ask me, 'Charles. How did you pull this off?' You care to know?"

"Yes," Vega said. In a way, she was curious. She had never seen Charles look so animated.

"Eight-hundred-meter sprints. See, if you're a distance runner, that's counterintuitive, to practice sprints. But it's what you've got to do."

She ran into a cluster of Indian academics she had met or emailed over the years. Among them was a quiet woman named Nirmala, who slipped away from the conversation. Later, at lunch, she introduced herself as a former nurse who now operated a fistula clinic in Bihar. "It isn't politics-work," she said. Her English was shaky, and Vega would have shifted the conversation to Hindi if not for the two white women sitting at the table. "Our funding comes from aid groups, only. USAID, but then also church. American church, they will send checks. We sign form saying we do not have abortion, but that is no problem. Sometimes baby die because of labor problems, but not because of abortion. But we try, always, save mother and baby."

"You are, of course, pro-choice?" one of the white women asked. "As an organization, you believe in women's reproductive freedom?" In the calm of the table, the question sounded accusatory.

"Ma'am, yes. But church money is very easy for us because we don't have to write such big grants and then do so much reporting. So, of course, we must take."

"Right," the woman said. "I understand bureaucracy exists. But for you to sign away your right to perform abortion, aren't you undermining women's rights in other ways? I mean, as a feminist, which I

presume you claim to be, how can you allow your organization to grow
fat from donations of American churches?"

"Not fat, ma'am. We have a lean operation. If women want abortion, they can go elsewhere."

"I believe Nirmala is offering a perspective on fundraising that
American institutions don't have to consider," Vega said. "Certainly
not American universities." She wanted to offer a steelier defense, but
before she could say anything further, the woman threw her hands up.
"I mean, this has American hegemony written all over it."

Nirmala shifted in her seat. The other woman at the table opened
her mouth, then closed it. Vega thought of Emily, her constant stream
of fundraisers for inoffensive causes: childhood diabetes, cancer research, holiday toy drives. Sometimes Vega wanted to prod her to think
about the context of these matters. "It really is rooted in American agri-
cultural practices, isn't it? We really need to think about the problem of
air pollution and environmental regulation. It puzzles me that wages
can be so low in such a wealthy country. Does that ever puzzle you?"
But the effort never went far. In the end, Emily just smiled sweetly, and
Vega tossed in ten dollars.

The other woman broke the silence. "You provide care during recovery as well?" she asked. She had a British accent.

"Yes, ma'am. We don't send home immediately. Women stay for
full healing time. And then, if they have children, we have small school
where they can study and be with mother as she heals."

The discussion splintered into small side conversations. That evening, Vega was walking into the hotel lobby when she saw the British
woman sitting at the bar. She waved Vega over. "God, that was brutal,
no? That lunchtime conversation."

"I spoke to her afterwards," Vega said. "The woman, Nirmala."

"How is she doing?"

"I think, like any of us, she would have appreciated more respect
for the work she does." Vega paused and worked through her next
thoughts. "Americans don't always realize the compromises that organizations in the global South have to make. I'm not an expert on

Indian NGOs, by any means. But I sense that Nirmala is engaged in work that is difficult beyond the comprehension of anyone else who was seated at that table."

"I do realize that. I should have stopped Kate at the time, but I was so surprised by it all. She really is a reasonable person. And an excellent professor. We actually drove in together, a few of us. I was giving a talk at Oberlin, where she teaches. Anyway, I'm just rambling right now." She shook her head. "I'm Ellie."

"Vega."

"In any case, I don't know what came over her. I don't know her to be so abrasive."

Privately, Vega had a few theories, chiefly that a woman like Kate might feel license to be abrasive to a woman like Nirmala, though she would be nothing but collegial to a woman like Ellie. But she figured she had already made her point.

Ellie gestured to the bartender. "Will you have a drink?" she asked Vega.

"If you're having one."

Vega ordered a red wine, and Ellie a whiskey soda. As the bartender poured the drinks, Ellie said, "I'm an adoptive mother myself. So I can't speak to the trauma of childbirth. But we don't know how to talk about motherhood in academic circles, outside of dry policy talk."

"I'm the only mother in my department," Vega said. "Fathers abound, of course."

"It's not so bleak at Bryn Mawr, where I am. I can't really complain. Supportive colleagues, good health care, etcetera. And I'm a single parent, so every bit of that helps." She went on about conference travel, her mother who had moved from Liverpool earlier that year to help with the children, the politics of adoption and her experiences with Ethiopian agencies. Vega found it all interesting enough, but it was difficult to pay attention because a realization was slowly forming.

She took a sip of her wine, then asked, "How long have you taught at Bryn Mawr?"

"Forever, it seems. This is year ten."

"I lived in that area for a bit. In New Jersey. After my daughter was born, I completed a semester of coursework at Montclair State."

Ellie's face looked stiff. A forced calm. "I know that university well."

Vega's head was starting to hurt. She flagged the bartender, ordered a water, and drained it quickly. "So did you always want to have children?" she asked.

"God yes," Ellie said. "I always wanted to be a mother."

That night, Vega went down the well-trodden path of looking up Winston online. She read his syllabus and course reviews and studied his hundreds of Facebook pictures: vacations to Zagreb, Napa, Jamaica. At a conference at Harvard, smiling his impossibly white smile. And then, she found the one piece of evidence that confirmed her suspicion; it was an acknowledgment from an academic book published eight years earlier, when Winston was still married. *I'm grateful to Winston Kinney and Ellie Martin for the use of their beautiful home.*

# 31

One September morning, Asha declared she no longer wanted to go to school.

"What about all of your friends? They will be so sad if you don't go. What about Lila and Sophie? Who will they play with?"

"Each other."

"Your teacher will miss you. Who will be line leader?"

"I'm not line leader anymore. I was line leader last week."

She cried in the car and clung to Vega's hand at the door. And though she was calm in the afternoons when Vega picked her up, it seemed more a calm of resignation, as though her sadness had faded to a general malaise. Heartbreakingly, she often forgot what day it was. As soon as she woke up, she would ask, "Do I have school?" Vega dreaded the answer she had to provide five out of seven mornings.

Suresh came to town in October—a whirlwind forty-eight hours— and they sat outside at a strip mall café, watching Asha peel the layers from her chocolate croissant, everything ending up on her shirt.

"You seem tired," he said.

"Not tired," she said. How to describe it? Lonely? Detached? She didn't know the Tamil word for either.

"You'll tell me, no, if there is anything you need?"

"There's nothing, Suresh. Really." She had tried to tell him about Asha over the phone, but always stopped short. She didn't know how to find the right balance, how to sound concerned without being alarmist. And some days, Asha seemed better. Not quite happy, but not miserable either. Vega had emailed Asha's teacher, who reported there was no reason for concern. "She's happy as a clam!" she wrote. "She does her work and actively participates!" Why worry him if the problem would resolve itself?

On the night he left, Vega sat next to Asha on the couch and pulled her onto her lap. She kissed the top of her head. "You're ready for school tomorrow?"

"No."

"Asha. I don't want you to be sad. That isn't an acceptable way to be in life. Life has to be happy at least some time. *Most* of the time, really."

"I'm not sad all the time. Only at school."

Vega looked down at her. She looked older suddenly. She had been taking swimming lessons at the YMCA and her legs were longer and thinner, the hair on them dark and stubborn-looking, and she had started chewing her nails. Vega could already see the surfacing of the things Asha would spend her life trying to suppress. The habits she would try to break. The body hair she would wage endless battles against.

"There's a boy I hate," Asha said. "He touches me."

Vega felt her breath stop—an idiom she didn't realize was a literal possibility until that moment. When she regained it, it surprised her that she could speak.

"Asha. You need to tell me about this."

"I hate telling it."

"Have you talked about it before?"

"I told my teacher."

*That bitch*, Vega thought. *Happy as a fucking clam.* "Asha. Please talk to me. Where does he touch you?"

"With his finger and sometimes his pencil. He licks his pencil and touches me with it."

"I mean, where on *you* does he touch you? Where on your body?"

"I don't want to tell."

"Asha!"

Asha looked up, small and infantile again. "In my ear," she whispered.

Details trickled in. "He's *mean*," Asha said. "He calls people fat. He puts library books in his backpack but doesn't read them. He just takes them so nobody else can. He told Sophie he was going to come to her house and kill her cat."

"Kill her *cat*?"

"Yes."

There was a flurry of communication. Emails to the teacher, then formal responses with the principal copied on the message. At night, Vega lay in bed, unable to sleep, her image of Max growing more and more monstrous. She thought of the men on the campus parking lot years back. In her mind, Max was a smaller version of this—camouflage pants and a vacant stare. *Make us move. Mexican bitch.*

One rainy Tuesday, Vega sat in a conference room in the main office across from Max's mother and the school dean, Ms. Evans. Max's mother was skinny, freckled, and young, wearing flower-printed medical scrubs and snapping her gum fiendishly, looking in desperate need of a cigarette. "You understand the behaviors that concern us?" Ms. Evans asked. "We have a strict no-bullying policy in our school."

Max's mother picked at her cuticles and nodded.

"We're going to work on a plan," Ms. Evans continued. "I'll sign his behavior report every day, then he'll bring it home for you. In the meantime, of course, he'll be reassigned. To a new desk partner."

Vega repeated the word *reassigned* to herself. It sounded bleak and Communist and cruelly clerical. She imagined Max being sent off by train.

Outside, Max's mother told Vega, "I'll whip his ass when we get home. He knows not to touch a girl."

"I don't think that's necessary," Vega said. She thought to add that it wasn't the fact of Asha being a girl that concerned her, but there didn't seem a point. And, upon reflection, she wasn't even sure if that was true.

"His daddy's Honduran. He's your color. That's why Max wants to be gangster. He's back in Honduras. He has another wife and a kid. Max is telling me, 'I'm gonna go live with my daddy. I'm like, 'How the fuck you gonna get there?'"

Vega looked at her, horrified, unsure where to begin.

"I give him everything he asks for. He has Mario Kart. Nikes. I let him watch horror movies, but we have to watch them together, you know? But he just asks for his daddy." She stared straight ahead, then said, "That's what's fucked up about kids. The only thing they want is the one fucking thing you can't give them."

E llie sent her a warm and collegial note, asking Vega to get in touch if she were ever in the Philadelphia area. It was an invitation of friendship, and Vega knew she should send a thoughtful response, inquiring about Ellie's children and sharing an anecdote about Asha. Under other circumstances, Vega thought, they could have been friends. She waited a few days, then drafted a brief message, equally warm, but noncommittal enough to end the correspondence.

Instead, she connected with Winston over Facebook, intending not to write him but to let their virtual friendship simply exist. But before the end of the day, he had sent her a message: *Been too many years, my girl! Tell me everything.*

There was no reason to mention Ellie. She couldn't have suspected anything, and even if she had, she seemed to lead a full life. Two children, tenure at Bryn Mawr. She sent him a bland update on her courses and research. Then she added, "You remember I had a daughter? She's seven now."

Maybe he would commiserate. It was possible he and Ellie had adopted together and then divorced, that her two children were his as well. But he made no mention of fatherhood when he wrote her back.

*Come to New York and see me. Blow off some steam.*

O n the day before her flight, she dug up the three pairs of nice underwear she had bought during her brief interlude with Seth and drove to a threading salon housed in the garage of a middle-aged Gujarati woman. Rationally, she knew that she could not sleep with Winston, that it was morally compromising even to imagine it. But when she re-read his messages, she remembered the soft roll of his accent, the way he pronounced her name, the sandpaper-like feel of his hands. And it seemed ridiculous, self-punishing, to not at least plan for the possibility.

The woman at the salon waved her in without looking up. "You have special occasion?" she asked in a bored, nasal voice that suggested she asked this of all her clients and didn't particularly care about their answers.

"No," Vega said.

She waited her turn on a plastic chair next to two women, a mother and twentysomething daughter. "They seem so ill-*suited* for each other," the daughter was saying.

"You mean, because she is a very ugly woman?"

"Ma!" The daughter laughed. "That's not what I said."

Vega sat back and closed her eyes. She imagined an adult Asha, her thick American accent. *Ma!* If she spent another ten years here, that would be the span of Asha's childhood.

"You see," the mother said, "what happened is this. He was very fat when they were looking for a bride, so the family made the match accordingly. Then, he began jogging. All the time jogging. Five miles here, half marathon there. Now he has lost all the weight, but what to do? A match is a match."

# 32

Vega's flight arrived twenty minutes early, but Suresh was already waiting. Asha ran to him, and he and Vega hugged clumsily, as they usually did. In the car, she said, "Thank you for picking us up." It was a meaningless comment. Suresh's zeal for airport pickups had remained steady over the past decade. If she had been a perfect stranger, a friend of a friend, he would have been equally happy to retrieve her.

"You should have brought the baby, Appa!" Asha shouted from the back.

"He was sleeping, ma. He will be rested and ready to see you." To Vega, he said, "He's so different now. You won't believe."

"I can imagine. The pictures Rupa sent are lovely."

He smiled. "You're presenting at this conference?"

Vega had merged her visit to New York with a conference at Columbia entitled "Global Communication in the Twenty-First Century." It was a dull-sounding event, but she was able to register for free as an alumna, and the pretense of a work obligation made her feel better about seeing Winston. "Actually, I'm not. Attending only."

"A good break, then. An opportunity to listen and mingle. Enjoy visiting your old campus."

"I think it will be."

"You're welcome to stay with us. If you'd like, cancel the hotel." He had already said this to her over the phone multiple times. He was so Indian in this respect. Unable to understand why anyone would choose a private room over the company of family.

"I'm actually in the hotel only for the days of the conference. Over the weekend I'll stay in Margo's apartment. She's out of town." Years ago, she wouldn't have bothered sharing logistics, both because she found it tedious to explain these matters to Suresh, and because she found his interest in tedium to be depressing. This, she considered, was the heart of her dishonesty. She wasn't a chronic liar; in their three years of marriage, she had only kept one major secret from him. What she did was to keep from him the details of her life: how happy she was wandering New York or watching her students debate the content of her class. The coffee shop where she so often holed up with her books, and the bagel shop where she went for lunch most Fridays. Maybe none of this mattered. If anything, had he known her better, they may have divorced earlier. But she wished, nonetheless, that they had talked more.

"I'm meeting with a former Montclair State professor while I'm here," she said. "He teaches now at Rutgers."

"That's nice. Sociologist as well?"

"Public health, actually."

If he had asked her in that moment about the affair, if he had somehow suspected it and directly pressed, she might have admitted it. She may even have felt relief. But he just nodded. "Very nice. It's always nice to see old friends."

At the house, Rupa was moving briskly through the kitchen, holding Vikram on her hip and setting out plates for breakfast. "He looks just like Asha, no?" Rupa said. "Everybody tells us this."

Vikram looked nothing like Asha, but Vega smiled in agreement and took him from Rupa's arms. She held him by the window, holding out her finger for him to clutch. Over breakfast, he made the rounds, starting in his highchair, then moving from one lap to another. Both he and Asha had grown enough that she could hold him with minimal assistance, and the change delighted her. "He likes me so much," Asha said. "I'm his favorite."

They made sweet and dull conversation, ping-ponging between Rupa's medical school updates and questions about Asha's first grade class, which produced incoherent answers only Vega could follow. Periodically, she interjected to clarify: *Jillian is her teacher's name. Mr. Fox is a game they play at school.*

Vega washed dishes while Suresh and Rupa went into the backyard with Asha. She set Vikram in his highchair and poured some water in front of him—a trick that always entertained Asha when she was a baby. He looked puzzled at first, then banged the tray harder and harder, surprised every time the water hit his face. For a moment, he looked as though he might cry. Then he smiled, and Vega saw it. He looked just like Asha.

She woke up, disoriented, in Margo's Brooklyn Heights apartment on Sunday morning. She had forgotten how beautifully lit the place was, how pleasant just to make a cup of coffee and sit in Margo's plush, sky-blue chair, staring at the gray of the city. She and Winston weren't meeting until late afternoon, and she had planned to get some work done that morning. Instead, she lazed until ten o'clock, then wandered down Smith Street and into a boutique where she tried on a red dress. It was a shapeless, silk thing that hung off one shoulder. She stared at herself in the mirror for a few moments before taking it off. It was something an adult Ashwini might have worn, had she been given the chance to become an adult.

"It's a good color on you," the saleswoman said.

It was a good color. She could wear it now, under her coat. She and Winston could skip coffee and instead go back to Margo's place. It would be so easy to coax him, and so thrilling once they were there. But she hung the dress back. "If you change your mind," the saleswoman said, "we close at six."

She bought a sparkling water and copy of the *Atlantic Monthly* from the corner store next to the coffee shop, then settled at a table. After a few minutes, it occurred to her he might not come. Just as she was giving up, setting her magazine aside, there was a tap on her shoulder. "Vega."

Perversely, and also for practical reasons, she had wanted Winston to look terrible, but that wasn't the case. He was as lean and muscular as he had been before, with a bit of gray hair that added to his appeal. Still, when he bent to kiss her cheek, she didn't feel the sexual stirring she had expected.

"I see you have a book coming out," she said. "And you're tenured at Rutgers and everything."

"Yeah." He smiled. "I would have brought you a galley, but I hate doing that to people."

"Why? I would have liked it."

"Nah. Then you're under all this pressure. Next time I see you you'll have to pretend to have read it."

She laughed. "I would actually have read it. I'm not a good liar."

When they sat back down after buying coffees, he said, "Your timing is good. I spent last semester in Kingston. Just got back last month."

"You were on sabbatical?"

"Not quite sabbatical. My mother passed. I was with her for the last months."

"Winston. I'm sorry." Everything around them seemed to slow down. At the next table, a couple in their fifties or sixties was staring at each other, she looking angry, he indifferent. "Well?" the woman said, to which the man responded, "Well *what?*"

"It's alright, really. She was a hell of a woman. But she was near ninety, and it had been a long time coming. She was a sports journalist. Did I ever tell you that?"

"You didn't. That must have been uncommon for her time." It puzzled her, how differently he must have remembered their time together, as though they had the type of relationship that would have led to frequent discussions of their family lives.

"Oh, yeah. There were a few women who made names for themselves later, especially when Jamaican track-and-field became a thing. But she spent most of her career in a man's industry." He shuffled through his pockets, and Vega thought for a moment that he would procure an article she had written, but he pulled out a tube of lip balm. An endearing detail of Winston she had forgotten about.

"And she *traveled*, man. She covered the entire West Indies team, so she was *everywhere*. Trinidad, St. Kitts, Barbados. Australia, a few times. She went to South Africa in the late eighties. During apartheid." He laughed. "She stayed with a Black family in Cape Town. Gave them her per diem. She said, 'I'm not spending a cent in a white-owned hotel or restaurant.' And she stuck to that. She's actually been to India. I never told you that?"

"You didn't. I wish you had." She worried the comment sounded sarcastic, but she meant it fully. "We never really talked about things like that."

He sat back and folded his arms. "*We* never did?"

"We never did. These are lovely details. It's nice to learn about your life."

"You're going to tell me you don't know anything about me."

"Yes, I am going to tell you that. I know nothing about you."

"Where did I grow up? Give me country and city."

"Come on, Winston. Those are basic things. Jamaica. Kingston, I think."

"Correct. I have any siblings?"

"You mentioned sisters. You talked about this elaborate Sunday hair ritual, but that's the only thing I know."

"Older or younger?"

She laughed. "Winston, what is this? I was under the impression they were older, though I don't think you ever said."

"Correct again. Where did I spend my summers working?"

"The port. You were a tour guide. And you spent some time at the clinic near your house." He raised his eyebrows, prompting her to continue. "It was a malaria clinic. Can we stop now? I've taken state-issued exams I found less stressful."

"You want to play that same game with me?" he asked.

"I don't. Enjoyable as it was."

"I would fail spectacularly. Do you know why?"

"Because you never showed any interest in anything about me outside of your bedroom?" She realized she sounded hurt, and that part of her actually was.

"That's where you're wrong, my girl. You never told me a single damn thing about you. I know where you were born because I straight up asked you one time. I don't know about your family, aside from the few times you mentioned your daughter. You kept yourself all buttoned up."

"Winston, that is nonsense." There was something more honest she wanted to say, but it took her a moment to find the words. "If I had told you more, or tried to, it would have been apparent you didn't care." He opened his mouth, but she put her hand up before he could interrupt her. "I wanted more from you than you wanted from me."

He looked surprised. "It wasn't some arrangement where I held all the power."

"Wasn't it?"

"No. No it wasn't." He wove his fingers together and rested his chin on his knuckles. "I was confused at the time. And certainly, I was no saint. But I liked you. I had no doubts about that. If you had pulled me, I would have come towards you."

"You might be misremembering things."

"I'm not. Afterwards, after my divorce, I thought about getting in touch with you. But I assumed you had either found some happiness in your marriage or were happy outside of it. It seemed wrong to intrude, either way."

It shouldn't have mattered after all this time. And yet, the words seemed to reach inside her, quieting her, resolving an old hurt she had forgotten about. "I wish I had known that then," she said. "Even if nothing would have come of it."

They were quiet for a bit, then he asked, "Did your husband move with you to Louisiana?"

"No. We divorced. He stayed in New Jersey but comes down quite regularly." She looked past Winston to the middle-aged couple, the woman crying silently into her hand, the man dipping a biscotti into the contents of his mug. It was a particular brand of cruelty, Vega thought, to be so unfazed by someone's suffering.

"You didn't seem surprised to learn I'm not married anymore," Winston said.

"I'm going to tell you something strange. I was at a conference last spring, and I am fairly certain I met your ex-wife."

After a long pause, he said, "Ellie."

"Well. Now I'm fully certain."

"How do you know this?"

"We were talking, and I pieced it together. I never mentioned your name. I feel I should apologize, but I'm not sure for what."

"No. Of course not. Christ, of course you shouldn't." He shook his head and breathed out slowly. "Of the three people in question, I'm the only one who should apologize. I didn't behave kindly towards her. Or you, I suppose, based on the nature of the whole thing."

"She seems well, regardless. She has two children."

"I've heard. I've kept in touch through mutual friends. I was happy to know that."

"I remember you telling me that she didn't want children."

"I think I gave you an impression of her that served my interests at the time. I don't deny that."

They sat uncomfortably for a few moments. Vega watched the couple behind them. The woman had stopped crying and now looked hunched and exhausted. The man was still sipping his coffee. Vega wished the woman would leave. Collect what remained of her dignity and just walk out.

"I might be considering marriage again, though," Winston said. "Hopefully with more success this time."

"Is this a general plan? Or is there a particular woman in mind?"

"I met a woman when I was back home in Kingston. Vivienne. We've actually known each other for years, but we reconnected. She's a biologist. Younger than I am, and she wants to start a life together. She wants a family."

Vega expected to feel a sting of disappointment, but what came instead was the slightest hint of relief. It was a relief to like Winston but not want him, to enjoy his company without bracing for all the sadness that accompanied desire and sex. "And you're open to all of this?"

"More than open, actually. Something struck me in Jamaica when I was with my mom and sisters." He looked squarely at Vega. "You know, my sisters, right? The two of them?"

"The ones who are older than you?"

He winked at her. "That's them. With the Sunday hair ritual. Anyway, just spending time with my sisters and my nieces and nephews, and then their kids—the older two have babies of their own. I want a family. I want a legacy. You must feel that way, no? With your daughter?"

"That she's my legacy?"

"That you're raising the next generation. Leaving something behind."

"I hadn't thought about it that way. It's so consuming on a daily basis that I don't often think about what I want from motherhood. Aside from her happiness." She paused. "And maybe this sounds bleak, but I want her to live a long life. I worry all the time about her safety."

"I can understand that," Winston said. "I haven't even *conceived* these children yet, but I've already picked out the neighborhood I want to raise them in. I'd build a wall around them if I could."

Vega considered different responses, but she couldn't think of anything that was both honest and worth saying aloud. She didn't want Asha to grow up as she did—cloistered, privileged, sheltered from poverty and public institutions. But there were other walls she wished she could build around her. She wanted to shield her from every existential threat. She wanted an impossible guarantee that her daughter would live to be old. That she would survive.

On their walk to the subway, Vega asked, "So does this mean you might move back to Jamaica?"

"Perhaps. Vivienne's degrees are from the UK, and she's only ever practiced in Jamaica, so I worry she won't have the same job prospects in the States. I spoke with some folks at the University of the West Indies. It's possible they could create a position for me. It might take some finagling, but I could pull it off."

*So this is how it ends*, Vega thought. It dawned on her that she would likely never see Winston again. There wasn't enough history or affection between them to force a reunion.

"I hope it all turns out well," she said to Winston outside the subway station.

"Same," he said, squeezing her hand. "Enjoy your little girl."

She was hungry when she arrived back in Brooklyn, and there was a restaurant on Margo's block she wanted to try. But first she walked back to the Smith Street boutique and plucked the dress from the rack. She had no business buying it. Even on sale, it was nearly two hundred dollars and would probably languish in her closet, something she would try on and admire, but never actually wear outside the house. But it was so pretty, and it was so wonderful to feel pretty in something. She had another useless thought—an adult Ashwini, traipsing with her through Brooklyn, delighting in every handmade bracelet and overpriced coffee drink. *Please*, Ashwini used to ask Rukmini, who would give in every single time. *Please can we buy this?* There was some comfort in looking back and knowing that Ashwini—the youngest, the favorite—had been given all the small things she had asked for.

"Just this?" the saleswoman asked.

"Yes," Vega said. "Just this."

# 33

Vega remembered her father-in-law as an unsmiling man who dressed in sweater vests, even in the choking Chennai heat, and feverishly monitored the Indian Stock Exchange. Now, he sat on the floor with Asha, playing Snakes and Ladders. The two had spent the morning at the beach. He was wearing a Giants baseball cap that Asha had insisted Vega buy for him at Newark Airport on the way to their flight.

"He has talked about only this for six months," Kamala said. "Vikram and Asha, Vikram and Asha." She and Vega were in the kitchen, Vega hovering uselessly by the sink while Kamala stirred a pot of pongal. Originally, Vega had planned on a quick trip to Chennai, the focal point of which was Vikram's first birthday in late June, but Suresh had convinced her to extend her trip. He, Rupa, and the baby, as well as Shoba, Mohan, and the girls, would be there for the full summer, and he wanted as much time together as possible. Additionally, there was the matter of Asha's birthday at the end of July. "We can't celebrate one child and not the other," Suresh said. "How will she feel?" Vega couldn't argue with that.

She had some loose research intentions and had inquired about a slew of activities for Asha: Tamil lessons, morning yoga, a class on marine animal ecology, but when she called the phone numbers listed, they were either disconnected or went unanswered. There was an added challenge; the school year in Chennai had started two weeks earlier, and by the time Asha woke up each morning, the children of the city were already dressed in their school uniforms, trudging off to their various campuses. Vega managed, finally, to get in touch with the ecology course, but it turned out to be a grim affair, held in a windowless room at the local gymkhana, led by two dour-looking co-directors, and attended only by their combined set of five children.

"I have to find something to occupy her," she told Gayatri. Shoba and Mohan were supposed to arrive in two weeks, which Vega hoped would introduce some order to their lives. In the meantime, Asha had settled into a cossetted existence—only child, only grandchild—that brought to mind a character in a Frances Hodgson Burnett novel, a colonial brat being pampered by her ayah.

"Really?" Gayatri asked. "How do you think most children around the world are raised? Not in marine ecology programs, I assure you."

If Vega's work were more structured, if she had an office where she was expected to report every day, she could possibly leave Asha at home with either set of grandparents. Then, at least, whatever chaos unfolded throughout the day would be resolved by the time she returned. But her work consisted mainly of trying to figure out what her work even was. She spent hours in her father's study aimlessly researching, scheduling meetings with various NGO leaders that would invariably be canceled or postponed. Through it all, she could hear the adults downstairs pleading with Asha to take one more bite, giving into her requests for sliced mango or a bowl of ice cream, consenting to another walk along the beach—a walk that typically resulted in yet another ice cream. Asha, a conscientious kid at home, had started leaving her plate on the kitchen table for Vasanti to clear.

"You're spoiling her," Vega told Rukmini. She was particularly irritable that day. Kamala had come by earlier with a set of the Amar Chitra Katha comic books that Vega and her entire generation had been reared on, but that Vega now found cheap and disturbing. Militant re-creations of *The Ramayana* and *The Mahabharata* in which the demons were all dark-skinned and the heroes golden-colored, the men grotesquely muscular and the women all demure and large-breasted with impossibly small waists.

"They're only stories," Rukmini said.

"Okay, then. *Lolita* is just a story too. Perhaps she can read that next."

"The Russians are a different matter," Rukmini said. "There's no harm to Amar Chitra Katha. You and Ashwini read the same things."

"Yes, but they're crap."

"You loved them when you were Asha's age. Let her read them. Then, when she is an adult, she can decide for herself that they are crap."

*When she is an adult.* India had revived Vega's fears of Asha's mortality. The tragedies reported in the *Advocate* or the *New York Times* had terrified her, but reading the *Hindu*, she could scarcely comprehend the scale of every disaster. A train derailment that killed one hundred and twenty. A storm in West Bengal that decimated a village. She had hired a car for the first week, and on the night the driver, Muthu, picked her up from the airport, she had flown into a rage over the absence of a seat belt.

"I specifically requested!" she said. "I cannot drive fifteen kilometers without a seat belt for my daughter!"

"Madam, I'm sorry." Muthu pulled the seat forward and rummaged behind it. "It's here, madam. It's stuck, only." He couldn't have been older than twenty. Vega could feel Asha's eyes on her. She was tired from the flight but awake enough to be puzzled by this new side of her mother. On the ride home, Vega tried to overcompensate by talking too cheerily with Muthu. *When would he finish his B. Comm? How many siblings did he have? How wonderful that he helped to pay his sisters' tuitions.* Throughout the drive, as Muthu mumbled his terse answers, Vega imagined Asha's body flying from the crashed windshield onto the road.

On her fifth night in Chennai, Rukmini came into Vega's room. They had finally shaken their jet lag. Asha was already asleep, lying on a pallet on the floor, her damp hair matted around her neck.

"She's adjusting nicely," Rukmini said.

"Perhaps."

Rukmini sat on the edge of the bed. "What do you mean by this? Perhaps?"

"You don't need to give in to every one of her requests, Amma. Vasanti doesn't need to make poori and chole every day just because Asha asked for it."

"What's the harm? Vasanti doesn't mind."

It was a pointless argument, Vega knew, and she was in no position to make it. She had spent the past days being carted around by Muthu, leaving him on congested intersections in Egmore and Nungambakkam so she could take vapid meetings with NGO directors or wait in endless lines at the bank or consular office—errands that accomplished nothing, taking up a full afternoon but requiring her to come back the following day.

Rukmini gestured to the bag on the floor. "You did some shopping today?"

"I went to Kalpa Druma after my meeting."

"That's a lovely shop. Show me all you bought."

"They're just simple things. One cotton sari and a few skirts."

"Let me see, then. You used to love to show off your purchases."

It was Ashwini, actually, who loved to parade around in anything new, but Vega didn't bother to correct this memory. Rukmini reached into the bag and set the sari on the bed. "Indigo. Lovely color."

"I like it too."

"You're young enough to wear these block prints. It has a blouse piece, no? You can take it to Urmila. She's expensive, but she does a good job."

"Gayatri recommended a tailor in T. Nagar. He sews all of her blouses."

Rukmini refolded the sari and smoothed it with her hand. Then she pointed to the trunk on the floor where Vega and Ashwini used to keep their clothes. It was sealed shut. After Ashwini died, Vasanti had been tasked with organizing it, and Vega assumed it was empty.

"You have to take some time to sort through all of this," Rukmini said.

"The trunk? I thought Vasanti did that years ago."

"She washed and folded everything. But I don't know what to keep and what to donate. I couldn't do that on my own. And Asha might want some of it someday." They looked down at Asha. She was so small in her sleep. If there was any sort of a god, Vega thought, this was the gift it gave to mothers. To let them see their children, at night, shrunk back down to their infant state.

Rukmini fingered the edge of the bedsheet. "You're worrying too much about small things. She's fine. She's happy."

"I'm not worrying, Amma. I only ask that you don't spoil her. She's capable of putting her plate in the sink. I don't want Vasanti cleaning up after her."

"That is a small thing."

"No. It's a big thing."

"Fine. But what I'm saying now is something different. What she asks for is so small. Some sweets, some silly books. Games your father and P.N. play with her. Let her be. Let us give her these small things."


Vega's former professor at Hyderabad, Dr. Das, was now the chair of the Sociology department at Presidency College. To Vega's relief, she had a selective memory of Vega's time there, remembering the quality of her coursework but not her reasons for leaving. They exchanged a few emails and met for coffee at a charming but terrible bakery next to Triplicane Book House where, over dry pieces of chocolate cake, they discussed Vega's research, the rise of right-wing extremism in Gujarat, Barack Obama's prospects in the 2008 primaries. Vega assumed that it was a casual reunion, but at the close of the conversation, Dr. Das informed her of a temporary visiting scholar program that, as she put it, "would be going exceptionally well, except we are currently lacking a visiting scholar." Thus, two weeks after she arrived in Chennai, Vega found herself standing in front of a classroom at Presidency.

The campus delighted her. She loved the brick and terra-cotta build-ings with their arched entryways, the manicured lawns, the shocks of bougainvillea and hibiscus. She and her colleagues gathered at lunch-time and shared whatever food they had brought from home. One, a woman named Deepika, had two sons close to Asha's age. On Saturday mornings, they brought the children to campus and projected a film for them in the department's lecture hall while they caught up on grading. Afterwards, she and Deepika would sit on a bench with cups of tea from the canteen and watch Asha and the boys tear across the green.

"Students like your lecture style," Deepika said. "They talk about your class."

"I like them, too." She had anticipated a month of easy teaching, students so steeped in rote learning that they were eager for any devi-ation from droning lectures and high-pressure exams. But they were bolder and more energetic than she had anticipated. They debated anti-corporate activism, collective mobilization. They held internships with grassroots organizations she had never heard of: All India Net-work of Sex Workers, Intersex Justice Program. A small group of them had spent the previous summer in Pallur, assisting in the development of a rural women's farming collective.

"Even that has its privileges," her student Kumaran said. "If this work is based on volunteerism, then it is a privilege to challenge sys-temic inequity. What of our classmates who cannot afford to work for no wages? Are they not committed activists?"

There was a hum of agreement. The first paper Kumaran sub-mitted had been an examination of the masculinization of Dalit men, and Vega read one of his paragraphs over and over again, presenting it to the class for discussion. *There is a classic image we associate with Indian masculinity: working-class, dark-skinned and bare-shirted, sinewy and marked by labor. It is not unlike the hyper-masculine characterizations of Black men in America.*

"I'm an anomaly," Kumaran told her one afternoon. They were sitting in her office, drinking milky tea from the canteen. There was no formal practice of office hours at Presidency, but she had implemented what she called "Open Door Sessions," and they had become her favorite part of the week. "I'm an upper-class Dalit kid. My parents were both lawyers, so I had all the tangible advantages. Parochial schools. Tennis club. At school, all of my friends were these rich kids. 'Boat Club Brahmins.'"

Vega laughed. "I've never heard that phrase." She had taken swimming lessons at the Boat Club as a child and remembered it as an unremarkable place that served stale potato chips and imported juice boxes, where she sat shivering in her towel after another failed attempt at the backstroke. But it had been renovated since. She and Gayatri had gone at the beginning of the summer, lounging on wicker furniture and sipping mango cocktails and icy bottles of Kingfisher. It had been, she recalled guiltily, the highlight of her first few weeks at home.

Kumaran rapped his fingers on the arm of his chair, then glanced at his watch. He was a wiry kid with over-caffeinated tendencies, who seemed always in a rush to get to his next meeting. "My father used to say, 'Oh, you're lucky. When I was a boy, I would never have had access to such a place. Those people would never have sat at the same table as me, invited me to their private clubs.' I tell him, it's worse to be a novelty than to not be invited. My classmates love to be seen with me in public. 'Oh, we have one Dalit friend. Look how far we've come.'"

"There is an American sociologist I'd like you to read," Vega said. "Eduardo Bonilla-Silva. He deconstructs this notion of a post-racial society." She had recently suggested to Kumaran that he consider graduate work in the States. "You can get an excellent fellowship," she said. "I would be happy to write you a letter of recommendation." She pictured him at Low Library, surrounded by adoring classmates, with his shaggy hair and dog-eared copy of *The Annihilation of Caste*, dropping obscure facts they all pretended to know.

"Maybe," he'd said. "But mainly I'm interested in Hyderabad, or JNU in Delhi. Why leave if my work will all be based here?"

Another thought struck her. Had Sukumar Reddy been alive, had Kumaran wound up studying under him in Hyderabad, he would have fallen under Reddy's spell, trading in his ideas for words that simply sounded like ideas. For a stinging and shameful moment, she was grateful Reddy was dead. She watched Kumaran gather his papers, then bound towards his next meeting.

Suresh and Rupa finally arrived, weary from twenty hours on a plane with an infant. Suresh, despite his exhaustion, spun Asha around, then sat on the floor with her and feigned interest in her collection of chipped shells.

P.N. sat on the chair behind them, holding Vikram, staring at the baby's face as though trying to memorize his features. Three generations of males. Vega had never been moved by that sort of thing, the tenderness of grandfathers and fathers and sons. But maybe, she thought, there was something to it. Just as there was something particular to Rukmini's love when she rubbed oil into Vega and Ashwini's hair when they were girls, or when she sat next to Vega on the bed and stared down at Asha's sleeping body.

Later, Vega helped Kamala bathe Vikram in the kitchen sink. The house had been chaotic moments earlier but was now still and quiet. Asha was asleep on the pallet she shared with Kamala. Suresh and Rupa were getting ready for bed in the tiny guest quarters that doubled as Kamala's sewing room. Vega remembered the few nights she had spent there shortly after she and Suresh were married, staring at the rows and rows of framed embroidery: marigolds, peacocks, lumpy figures of Ganesha. She remembered the sound of P.N.'s hacking cough through the thin walls, how trapped and lonely she had felt. In the mornings, she would lie under the covers, pretending to be asleep, delaying the moment when she would have to get up and use the small, shared bathroom.

"You take him, kanna," Kamala said to Vega, wrapping the towel around Vikram. "I'm becoming so old, and he's so heavy now."

Kamala was hardly old. She was fifty-eight, four years younger than Rukmini, but her arthritis had aged her. She still embroidered, but she had been asking for Asha's help to thread her needles. At night, she coated her hands in Tiger Balm. And with this new condition, she seemed to have adopted other habits of the aged and infirm. She blasted Sun TV, glued to a new Tamil soap opera about a reformed gangster turned politician. She complained incessantly about crime and corruption and had recently voiced her support for Lal Krishna Advani.

"He's a religious zealot, Amma!" Vega said. Asha, sitting on the floor and sorting through her ever-growing pile of shells, looked up, and Vega lowered her voice. "He's made no apology for his actions in Gujarat. You've always been a Congress Party supporter. If Advani wins, how will you explain that to your grandchildren? How will you tell them, 'I voted BJP. I voted for a political party that was responsible for the murder of thousands of people?'"

Kamala had sighed, seemingly exhausted by the depth of this political discourse, and adjusted the plastic fan. "I am considering my options, only." Now, she made small lentil and rice balls and fed Vikram by hand as Vega held him on her lap. Her eyes were watery. "He eats well."

"You can tell from his cheeks." Vega kissed his head. "He's happy and healthy."

"I've wondered so often how your mother survived. To lose one daughter. And then you and Asha, so far away."

Vega had never spoken about Ashwini with her mother-in-law. For a ridiculous moment, it surprised her that Kamala even knew. "It's hard for them still," she said. "It always will be, I think."

"And for you, kanna," Kamala said softly. They were quiet for a while. Vega squeezed Kamala's hand.

"He wants some milk, you think?" Kamala said. "Do they give him cow's milk yet?"

"Rupa is still nursing. I don't know if they're giving him cow's milk also."

"Buffalo milk is very good. Easy for infants to digest."

"You should tell Suresh and Rupa. We can send for some tomorrow, if they want it."

Vikram was squirming and kicking his legs, jet-lagged and wide awake. The cloth Kamala had tied around his waist was now wet. Vega rummaged through Rupa's purse for a diaper, changed him, then set him on the floor. "You go to sleep, Amma. I can watch him."

"You have class tomorrow."

"I teach only in the morning. I can rest afterwards." Kamala lingered for a minute, looking doubtful. Vega recalled how Shoba had insisted on watching Asha when she was an infant, telling Vega, *She's like a daughter to me. Like my own flesh and blood.* She wished she had some of Shoba's emotional candidness, that she could somehow express to Kamala how much she loved Vikram, how good it felt to care for him. Instead, she lifted him so Kamala could give him a kiss. Then she sat up with him until nearly two a.m., when he finally began to doze off. She held him on her chest and lay on the couch, feeling him grow heavier and heavier until they were both asleep.

Shoba and Mohan arrived with Tara and Veena, and Suresh's parents' home acquired a happy but disorderly look—unzipped suitcases, the floor scattered with hair ties and little kid socks, abridged editions of *Treasure Island* and *Little Women*. Days later, Shoba and Rupa's parents, Janaki and Kumar, came from Coimbatore. They were a dull, devout couple who went daily to the Ganesha Temple and seemed overwhelmed by the relatively cosmopolitan buzz of Chennai, complaining about the traffic and clutching each other's arms as they walked down the street. But they were sweet with Asha, and for this, Vega felt kindly towards them. "I remember her when she was only a baby!" Janaki said. "Now look! Such a big girl!"

Vega was spending less and less time with her parents. At first, they were tolerant of the situation, sensitive to Asha's need to be with Suresh's side of the family, but this tolerance quickly faded. "I hardly see you anymore," Rukmini said. "What kind of divorce is this? It's as though you're married to your ex-husband, his current wife, and his in-laws."

Vega laughed. "That's nonsense."

"It isn't. And my granddaughter has practically become a stranger."

There was some truth to that. Asha had been devoted to Vega's parents before her cousins and brother arrived, but now couldn't be torn from P.N. and Kamala's house. That night, as she was helping Asha brush her teeth, Vega said, "Your paati and thatha are missing you. Maybe after I come from work, we can have lunch here. Then we'll go to Ruku Paati's in the evening."

Asha spit and rinsed her mouth, then looked up at Vega. "Tell Ruku Paati to come here. I want to all be together."

Asha still viewed her relatives as a morass of people who, because they were related to her, must also be related to each other. But her request was enough to coax Vega's parents. They began eating dinner all together, four children and eleven adults, the girls always finishing their meals quickly before running off to play, Vikram always falling asleep on somebody's lap. Kamala's former cook, Madhu, emerged from retirement, preparing industrial-sized pots of bisibeli or pongal and staying late to pack up leftovers and clean up the mess. Watching her, Vega was reminded of the constant cycle of cooking and cleaning that awaited her in Baton Rouge. She hadn't so much as picked up a dish towel since arriving in India.

One night, Vega and Suresh were the last ones left at the table. The rest of the adults had gone to sleep and the girls were sitting on the porch, where Madhu was serving them tiny bowls of ice cream.

"I'm going to declare an ice cream moratorium when we get home," Vega said.

Suresh smiled. "They only spoil her because we visit so infrequently."

There were other reasons too. In the States, Asha was a middle-class kid. A first-grader at Grant Elementary School. Nobody special. In Chennai, she was anointed by caste. If they lived here, she would eventually be steered towards St. Agnes or Rhodes. The Boat Club. Vega didn't want this for her. She was tired of the loneliness of Baton Rouge, dreading their return, but the thought of this cushioned life made her uneasy as well.

"I forgot to mention this to you," she said to Suresh. "Your mother is threatening to vote BJP. She's become a right-wing hardliner in your absence."

"She won't do it, in the end."

They stared at the girls. Tara and Asha sat with their legs stretched out, Veena with her arms wrapped around her knees. Then, Suresh said, "My mother is lonely. That's the problem, I think. It makes her act irrationally. It isn't a decent way to live. So far away from one's children."

"She can spend more time in New Jersey, maybe? She can be helpful with Vikram. And Asha and I can come home more often to be with her. Keep her company." He was still staring ahead, and she jostled him with her elbow. "If nothing else, you can ensure she misses the election."

He laughed thinly. Only later that night, as she was tucking Asha into her cot on the living room floor, did she realize Suresh wasn't talking about his mother. He was the one who couldn't bear to live so far from his child.

# 34

G ayatri's cousin, Sudhir, was coming to town. Vega hadn't seen him in two decades, but she remembered him as a gangly and bespectacled boy, aggressive about his knowledge of cricket statistics and World War II. The sort of kid who was endearing to adults but unbearable to other children.

"You'll like him now," Gayatri told Vega. "He's working as a journalist for Al Jazeera. Real sharp fellow."

"Excellent. I love sharp journalists."

Her words came out more bitterly than she had intended, and Gayatri looked hurt. "I'm saying only that he's an interesting man. In any case, he's based in Dhaka, so I'm not suggesting anything long-term."

They were sitting in Gayatri's flat in Santhome. It was three kilometers from the Presidency campus, and it had become a welcome escape over the past few weeks. Gayatri had given her a spare key, and Vega would often come during her afternoon break to make a cup of tea and enjoy the quiet of Gayatri's sitting room—a room blissfully empty of scattered toys or Amar Chitra Katha comics.

Gayatri had been pushing Vega to stay a bit longer in Chennai, to explore a permanent position at Presidency. Sometimes Vega daydreamed, looking up Montessori programs for Asha and browsing side streets in Annanagar and Nungambakkam—neighborhoods that would be too expensive for an Indian academic, but that she could afford if she offered a down payment in U.S. dollars. She should have felt some freedom. Instead, her former in-laws' house had begun to overwhelm her, with Kamala's flurry of cooking and feeding, and the constant chirp of the girls' voices. She craved time with her parents, but the moment she was with them, she found their presence grating. Rukmini kept pressing Vega to clean out the trunk, to take what she wanted of Ashwini's old belongings. At night, Vega stared at it—a wooden, leather-bound thing with a vaguely diarrheal smell that had belonged to her grandfather. She wanted nothing to do with the trunk. She wanted nothing to do with her mother. But in the mornings, when she left for campus, she felt the same aching loss that used to surface every time she dropped Asha at day care on Monday mornings. So desperate to be alone, then so lonely when she finally was.

The verandah door slammed. Gayatri came inside holding a pile of laundry and dropped it on the floor. Vega reached for a sari and started to fold. "You look lovely in saris. I wish I could pull them off."

"You could pull anything off, if you wanted to."

Vega set the folded sari aside and stared at Gayatri for a moment. They had always had an easy friendship, free of the small tensions of growing up together. After Ashwini's death, Gayatri had said to Vega, "You can yell and scream at me any time you need. Take out all your anger." But Vega could not imagine doing that. It would have brought her no comfort to hurt Gayatri.

"Hey," Vega said. "I'm happy to meet Sudhir. Really."

"There's no obligation. It was only a suggestion."

"I know. But I'm sure he's interesting. And if nothing else, if we all get together, then it will be more time spent with you." The kettle whistled. A few moments later, Gayatri returned with the tray of tea and set it on the floor. Her expression was still stiff.

"Gayatri. I feel there's something I should apologize for. But I'm not sure what."

Gayatri shook her head. "I was seeing someone. Just recently, I called it off. I'm upset, only. It will pass."

"You were seeing someone?" Gayatri's love life had long been a mystery to Vega. Among the girls they had grown up with, she was

the most open about sexuality, the first to talk casually and unapolo-
getically about men she had slept with. But as far as Vega was aware,
Gayatri had never been in a relationship. She remembered something
one of her Sri Vidya classmates had said of an anthropology professor on campus—a brilliant but aloof woman who published widely
on indigenous art but could never remember students' names: "She's
interested in *peoples*. Not as much in people."

"He's a typical Brahmin. Spoiled by his mother and won't move
from his parents' house. A few days back, he told me that his parents
still don't know about me. He thinks this is a joke. He says, 'My mother
is looking for a match for me.' Later, when I ended things, he told me
his mother would never have approved of our marriage because my
father is a Nair, and his family does not accept caste difference. As
though he's a little boy who needs permission."

"He sounds like a fool, Gayatri."

"Then I'm a bigger fool."

"That isn't true." But it puzzled her that Gayatri, who so easily saw
through the idiocy of Sukumar Reddy, could have fallen even briefly
for a man like this. "How long were you seeing each other?"

"Nearly a year. We met at a biology convention."

"Nearly a *year*? I'm sorry, Gayatri. I wish I had known."

"You're difficult to talk to sometimes."

Vega started to protest, but she knew there was some truth to this.
Gayatri called and emailed more often than Vega did. And when they
did talk, Vega didn't ask many questions, or probe beyond Gayatri's
casual updates on work, family, politics, the occasional weekend trip to
Kerala or Pondy. It wasn't that she didn't care. It just never occurred to
her to probe. For the two decades of their friendship, she had operated
under the assumption that Gayatri was doing just fine.

"I'm sorry if I don't express this well. But I miss you and think of
you all the time."

"I believe that, Vega. And I miss you. But sometimes, when we talk,
I feel as though I'm interrupting your thoughts. I don't know how else
to describe it. You've seemed so sullen and angry lately."

Vega squeezed her knee. "Come on, Gayatri. I've been sullen and angry my entire life. This is nothing new."

"Not your entire life. Just the past fifteen years."

Vega couldn't counter that. She had been a happy child, unaware there was anything to be unhappy about. Even as an abstract concept, she hadn't really understood unhappiness. She experienced it in the way characters in books did—fleeting disappointments felt in one chapter and resolved in the next. She hadn't been aware, until Ashwini died, of this deeper, lasting variety.

"I'm sorry about your relationship, Gayatri. I'm sorry it lasted so long, and I'm also sorry it ended."

"It's nothing."

"It *is* something. These losses hurt. And I know there is no sense in telling you this now, but you will meet the right man. And when you do, it won't be full of bullshit and casteism and moral compromises."

"I know. I really do know that. And I'm not interested in discussing him further. I've wasted enough hours." She paused. "There is something I want to mention, though. A few weeks back, when I stopped by your parents' place, I was sitting with Asha. She was showing me some of her drawings, and I told her, 'Your chiti used to be a wonderful artist.' She didn't have any reaction. Maybe I shouldn't have brought Ashwini up so casually, but I assumed that she knew. And it's been bothering me these past few weeks."

"You're bothered that you told Asha about Ashwini, or that you think I haven't?"

"Both, I suppose."

"I talk about her in front of Asha. And she's seen her photographs, of course, but she's never asked any questions. I realize how vague that all sounds. And if you're asking whether I have ever explained to her, 'I had a sister, and my sister died,' then the answer is no. How would she even make sense of that?"

"How does anybody?"

Vega distracted herself with a loose thread on her kurta. "Do you remember how much Ashwini used to love her music lessons?"

"Of course I remember. I remember everything about her. She was like my own sister."

That was true. In some ways, Gayatri's affection for Ashwini was simpler and easier than Vega's, uncluttered by the actual challenges of sisterhood. *Ashu*, she used to call her. Gayatri was always happy to let Ashwini tag along on their walks, happy to play endless rounds of carom or rummy or Twenty Questions with her. It hurt to remember this. Vega should have been the one to give Ashwini a nickname, to let her join for anything she damned well pleased.

"Do you remember that she insisted on continuing veena lessons when we came back from Cleveland? Her teacher's house was on 8th Cross. Where that restaurant is now. Zaytoon."

"I know, Vega. We walked her there a thousand times."

"Yes, but that was a long time ago, when we used to walk her together. When we came back from Cleveland, I would walk her to class alone. It was our ritual, for some reason. On her last class, she told me she was having difficulty breathing. I thought she was just fussing. But by the time we arrived, she was so tired she couldn't even walk up the steps. It was stupid of me. Why would I insist she go if she could hardly breathe?" She had replayed the details of this memory over and over, but she had never described it aloud. Despite logic, despite science, she believed if she had just let Ashwini rest that day, she might have survived another year. Or another five years. And what else was life but those small increments? Five years might have become ten. Fifty.

"You didn't know she was so sick."

"Of course I knew she was sick, Gayatri. We moved to Cleveland because of her condition. I was fully aware how sick she was. It's as though I were being deliberately cruel or something."

"That's really what you think of yourself? That you were deliberately cruel to your sister?"

"They took her to the hospital that night. And it was too late. Her lungs collapsed. She was dead after a week." At least that was how Vega remembered it, though it was possible her memory was incorrect. Maybe more than a week had lapsed, or maybe it was only a day or two.

What she recalled, with certainty, was that it was the last walk Ashwini ever took. The last afternoon she was fully alive.

"She adored you. You were good to her. And there was nothing you could have done to make her live longer."

"I want to scream sometimes, Gayatri. I don't know about what, or to whom. I just want to scream."

"Then scream."

"I can't. That would be ridiculous. Do I look like a child to you?"

Gayatri laughed, then she pulled Vega towards her and kissed the top of her head. "I want you to know something, Vega. You are among the best people I know."

"Then you need to keep better company."

"Vega. Shut up. You were a wonderful sister. You're a wonderful mother and a wonderful friend. You're even a good ex-wife."

Vega started to protest, but some part of her wondered if Gayatri was right. If she was, in fact, a good enough person. If, despite everything, she was doing just fine.

G ayatri had planned an elaborate evening out for them, but Sudhir's flight was delayed, so at ten o'clock on a Tuesday night, they sat at a plastic table outside of Rotiwalla Cafe, tearing into large, communal parathas. Sudhir had a relaxed, unshaven look. He was the kind of man who, were he a few years younger, Vega might expect to see on a layover at the Frankfurt Airport carrying a towering backpack, surrounded by an eclectic and international circle of friends. But he was also attentive and modulated, a good listener, curious about a dam safety review Gayatri was conducting in Orissa and asking detailed questions about Vega's students.

"It's a different generation, no, than what we were used to? I teach one graduate course at the University of Dhaka and the students actually give a damn. They're *curious*. I love it."

Vega was so attracted to him that it was jarring when he spoke to her directly, and she knew, even before she opened her mouth to respond, that whatever she said would come out as drivel. She was right. "The humanities field here is rethinking the model of rote learning and quantitative exams. Students seek professors who will assess them more holistically." What the hell was she talking about? *Assess them more holistically?* She hated herself.

"That's the work too, no? They say the problem with higher education is that the student body turns over every four years, but the professors stay for thirty or forty." Later, when Gayatri left to use the bathroom, his voice softened. "Gayatri tells me you have a daughter."

"Asha. She's eight years old."

"She's here with you in Chennai?"

"She is. She's with her grandparents. Soaking up the last few weeks of their attention."

He smiled and dragged a last piece of paratha through a smear of lime pickle. "I remember you when you were small. Rather, when we were both small. You had a younger sister, I remember."

"I did. She passed."

"I know. I'm sorry. That must have been a terrible loss."

"It was." Gayatri had returned from the bathroom but was lingering inside the restaurant, gathered around a television with a small crowd, watching what looked like an archery competition. It was something Gayatri would have had no interest in, and Vega was grateful for yet another small gesture of kindness. "I remember you were a sort of trivia whiz," she said to Sudhir. "You delivered some long list of facts about bauxite mining. I had never heard of it before, but it stayed in my head. I went to a World War II Museum a few years back and there was a large didactic plaque on the history of bauxite mining. I remembered you so clearly."

He smiled more broadly this time, and Vega felt something inside her open. The desire to touch and be touched. To discover a new body, a new sense of humor, a new worldview. But later that night, standing outside the gate of her parents' house as the rickshaw idled, the fantasy faded. There had been a good stretch, even after Asha's birth, when she felt alive and desirable. Now she felt both infantile and stale. A child living with her parents, and a mother bound to her child.

"How much longer are you in Chennai?" he asked.

"We leave in two weeks."

"Back home to Louisiana?"

"That's the plan."

He scratched his head, and she saw, suddenly, a trace of the boy he was. Bespectacled and antsy, always chewing his lip.

"I leave for Bangalore on Thursday morning. Just through Sunday. Perhaps we could see each other tomorrow. Or I can call you when I'm back."

She imagined seeing him tomorrow. Maybe she would wear the red dress she had no business buying. "When you get back, then," she said.

"What's the catch?" she asked Gayatri, later. "He's married, isn't he?"

"He isn't. He *was* married. Briefly. Perhaps you can bond over that shared experience."

"Any children?"

"No children."

"What is the story of his ex-wife?"

"Bloody hell, Vega. I met her only once. She's a photographer. Bengali girl. Dhina was her name. I think they parted on decent terms."

She thought about him constantly. On the nights when Asha slept at P.N. and Kamala's house, she touched herself, imagining his hands and his tongue. But in the mornings, she felt ashamed. What kind of adult masturbated in her parents' house? As promised, he called when he returned from Bangalore, but she demurred.

"I'm so busy wrapping things up," she said. "Packing and whatnot."

All around them were stories of movement. Ameya had accepted a tenure-track position in Boston. Halima's husband, Adnan, was joining the faculty at University of Maryland, and they had bought a house in Gaithersburg. Within a radius of ten miles were a mosque, a synagogue, and a Hindu temple.

"Goodness," Vega said. "How will you ever choose?"

"Idiot," Halima said. "But it's a sign, no?" Their green card had been approved, and she was a finalist for a position at Towson University. Shoba and Mohan planned to decamp to Coimbatore for the remainder of the summer. Even Gayatri was thinking of leaving Chennai. "There's a research institute in Bangalore," she said. "Might be good to have a change of pace."

Vega had been putting off packing, but when their final week approached, she lugged her black suitcase from the guest bedroom, wiped off the layer of dust, and left it open on the floor. Periodically, she would toss in something—the skirts she had bought at Kalpa Druma, the red dress she had brought with her and never worn.

"You'll be okay going back home?" she asked Asha.

Asha shrugged. She was quieter than normal and had resumed an old habit of chewing the tips of her hair. Vasanti had cut a mango for her, slicing a grid of vertical and horizontal lines across the halves and pushing it outward so it formed protruding squares. Asha stared down at the skins.

"Your Ashwini Chiti used to call that a turtle shell," Vega said.

"Why?"

"Doesn't it look like the pattern on a turtle's back?"

Asha looked more somber. "Does it make you sad thinking of her?" Vega asked gently. Gayatri had recently given Asha a small wooden loom and Vega had sat with her for a full afternoon, watching as Asha eventually produced a lopsided, woven rectangle. "We can put this in the pooja room, next to your chiti's photograph," Vega said, and she thought she detected a change in Asha's expression. A flash of interest, then a slow dimming.

"Asha," Vega said. She cupped her daughter's chin.

"I'm not sad," Asha said.

"Then what?"

Asha picked up the mango half and took a small bite. "I just don't like to think about eating turtles."

Vega hadn't meant to tell Suresh about Sudhir, primarily because there was nothing to tell. But as her departure date drew closer, she had a nagging feeling she was throwing something away.

"What's the problem?" he asked. "You have five days remaining. Ample time to get together with this fellow. You can arrange to meet for a juice."

Vega laughed at the suggestion of juice. Vikram's party had come and gone, and she and Suresh were at P.N. and Kamala's house. It was nearly midnight, and they were the only ones still awake. Shoba had spread old saris on the grass for people to sit, a style tip she had seen in *Vogue India*, and Vega was collecting and folding them. Suresh was crouched by the outside faucet, washing the last of the empty pots.

"I may have missed my chance. He called and I declined. Anyway, he lives in Dhaka."

"No harm in trying again." He set the pot upside down at the edge of the step to dry. "Rupa said something interesting some days back. She said when people visit from India, even if they come to Boston or New York City, they will make an effort to visit New Jersey only to see us. But if we live in the same place as somebody, we may go months or years without even crossing paths. We don't make an effort when we are close by."

"That isn't true of you and Rupa, though. You always make the effort." Suresh often updated her on visits to or from people she could scarcely recall. When Rupa was seven months pregnant, he had driven them to Pittsburgh to attend the first birthday of a former classmate's daughter. "Harsha's baby," he had said. "Naturally we couldn't miss." *Who the hell is Harsha?* Vega wanted to ask.

They folded the last of the saris and Suresh crouched next to her, looking pensive. He had an old-world way of squatting, on his feet with his knees bent, the way her grandfather used to sit. "One small question I've always had."

She raised her eyebrows.

"Is it difficult for you to see Shoba and Rupa together?"

She wasn't sure what question she had been expecting, but this certainly was not it. She stared at him.

"I know you care for them both," he said. "But they're such close sisters. And I think, sometimes, of your loss."

Her eyes burned and she was grateful for the dark. "I love Shoba and Rupa," she finally said. "I love seeing them, and I love seeing the children all together."

He nodded. He was still squatting. The sight of him made Vega's knees ache.

"I wondered sometimes if that is why you moved so far. So that you wouldn't be reminded of your sister."

She wiped her face with her dupatta. "I moved for a job, Suresh."

"There are jobs in many places."

"Not in my field. I was lucky to receive an offer anywhere."

They were quiet for a few moments, then he said, "I miss my daughter."

"I know you do."

He stood and began stretching. When they lived together, Vega had found it maddening how—apropos of nothing—Suresh would launch into a series of lunges or knee lifts or begin practicing his backhand. It seemed cruel now that she could have harbored such rage over something so small.

The light went on in P.N. and Kamala's bedroom. One of their middle-of-the-night bathroom trips, Vega figured. She thought again about how she should coax them to spend more time in New Jersey. Kamala's mind seemed to be unraveling, even beyond the sphere of politics. Earlier that week, Vega had asked her why she didn't see a doctor for her arthritis. "If it is God's plan for me to have this condition, then so be it."

"But you use Tiger Balm. Do you think God made Tiger Balm?"

Kamala had seemed surprised by the foolishness of the question. "Of course God made Tiger Balm."

The light turned off. Suresh finished his stretches and sat down. "Both of you," he said quietly. "I miss you both."

That night, alone in her bedroom, she opened the trunk. She was too tired to sort through it in the way Rukmini had asked, but with Asha away—sleeping at P.N. and Kamala's—she was able to turn on the light and force the latches open. They were both rusty, one slightly bent, and she had nearly given up when she felt them loosen.

Vasanti had wrapped everything in an old sari. It was a pink cotton that Vega peripherally remembered from her childhood, one of Rukmini's nicer daytime saris that had faded over the years to something she would wear only around the house. Vega opened the folds. Stacked on top was Ashwini's favorite silk pavadai, an eggplant-purple that had been sewn by Rukmini's tailor. Vega pulled it from the trunk and laid it on the floor, touching the fabric tentatively, as though it would fall apart in her hands.

She pulled out a dupatta, two skirts, and a ziplock bag containing Ashwini's old hair clips. There were a few T-shirts and kurtas, and the red harem pants Ashwini had begged for at the Mylapore Tank. Then she came across something yellow. It was a cardigan with wooden, heart-shaped buttons that Rukmini had bought at the mall in Cleveland, one that Ashwini wore constantly, and Rukmini used to hand-wash for her in the bathroom sink, always laying it to dry on a towel on their bedroom floor. Vega draped it across her lap. She ran her finger along the seam, the inside of the sleeves, the flower pattern embroidered across the neckline. She returned the rest of the contents to the trunk and carried the cardigan to bed with her, breathing in the mustiness of the wool, pressing it to her chest in the way she used to hold Asha when she was a baby.

# 35

Three days before Vega was to fly back to the States, she and Sudhir sat at the side of the pool at the Park Hotel. It wasn't the most inspired of locations, but she was grateful for the quiet. They had started their evening at a Turkish restaurant on the second floor of the hotel, which turned into a nightclub after hours—a fact unknown to Vega when she suggested they meet there. "There's a hint of the mystical harem at Pasha," Sudhir read from the dinner menu. He had found it all funny. The host dressed as a sultan, wearing an enormous gold fez, the belly dancer who wove between the tables. "I'm so sorry," Vega kept saying, though they could barely hear each other over the music. She wished she could have laughed along with Sudhir, but to her it was painfully embarrassing. At the table next to theirs, a middle-aged businessman gestured to the dancer, trying to coax her onto his lap. She and Sudhir left before ordering food, and now sat with their feet in the water, her red dress pulled up to her knees.

"I'm so sorry," she said again. "That really was hideous."

He laughed. "It was fine. I think you were more bothered than I was."

"I'm sorry I wasn't a better sport."

"You're a fine sport."

"I'm not, really. I've never been. When my sister was sick, there was a performing clown who used to come to the hospital every Sunday. I hated it. I would sit in the waiting room until he had left the children's wing. I couldn't even bear to look at him."

"Clowns are another matter entirely. Nobody can blame you for that."

Vega looked away, but she could still feel Sudhir's eyes on her. She wondered if her dress was ridiculous. She had been too self-conscious to wear it in her house, in front of her parents and Asha. Instead, she had employed the teenage trick of leaving the house in a kurta and jeans under the auspices of a night out with Gayatri, then had gotten dressed in Gayatri's flat.

"Where do you stay when you're in town?" she asked Sudhir.

"Sometimes Gayatri puts me up. Now I'm staying at this eco-hotel in Anna Salai. Rainwater barrels. Lots of Europeans. You can imagine the type." He went to collect their drinks. When he came back, he asked, "It seems silly to sit next to a pool and not jump in. I wish we had planned better."

"Do you know I can't swim?"

"Come on."

"Really. I took lessons at the Boat Club for years, but it made no difference. I used to think there was something wrong with my lungs or my bone structure." In truth, water made her so nervous that she dropped her feet to the pool floor each time she felt herself float. Her teachers didn't seem to notice, and she moved through the rungs of her coaching lessons through whatever blend of privilege or indifference led children to be mindlessly promoted. Sometimes she took Asha to the pool at the Baton Rouge YMCA, where the water never exceeded four feet. She stood in the corner, watching as Asha jumped from the side and swam to the surface, untouched by her mother's failures. She wondered if any language had a word for this: the knowledge that your child could do something you could not.

"There's a trick to floating," he said. "I taught my nephews. I could teach you in five minutes."

"I'm certain it wouldn't work for me. My sister was a good swimmer, though. So I can't even blame my parents for this particular failure."

"I remember your sister when she was a little girl. Maybe nine or ten years old."

"She wasn't much older when she died." She felt, as she always did when Ashwini's name hung in the air, two conflicting hopes: that they would talk about her, and that they would change the subject and never return to it. Sudhir opted for the former.

"You must have been a comfort to her when she was sick."

Vega thought about that. She could recall countless moments of comforting Ashwini, but always for minor losses and grievances: a fight with a friend, a middling exam grade. If they ever talked about death, Vega had no memory of it. "I don't think I was, actually. She was so young. I don't know if she ever fully believed she would die. I didn't believe it either."

He moved his hand closer to hers, but just let it rest on the ground. "Well. There's some mercy to that. For her, at least."

"Maybe. There's no way of knowing, though. Maybe she wanted to talk more openly about death but didn't know how. And our quiet on the subject didn't help."

Their food arrived—spring rolls and Thai curries—and they walked to their table. "Tell me about the last twenty years of your life," Vega said. "I lost track of you when you left Chennai." She was relieved to escape the topic of Ashwini, but the moment she did, she wished she could go back to it. She remembered Suresh, on one of the last nights they ever slept in the same bed. *You never talk about your sister.*

"What is there to say? My family moved to Delhi. I studied at Doon School, did my undergrad in the UK. At East Anglia. And then, I've moved around a bit through my position at Al Jazeera. I was in Cairo for a year, then Qatar."

"The famed Doon School. I hear it's a life-altering place."

"I think it can be. My mother was diagnosed with cancer and my parents were in the States for treatment quite a bit. So, maybe it was easier for me to be away. But sometimes I think it would have been better to have stayed with them. I didn't understand the gravity of the diagnosis until after she died."

"I'm sorry." She tried to think of something more meaningful or useful to say. Instead, she opted for honesty. "You may not have known the gravity of the diagnosis until she died, even if you had been with her. It's difficult to accept death until you have to."

"Maybe. Who knows?" He ate a spring roll, wiped his hands, then said, "It wasn't my intention to spend the evening talking about death."

"It wasn't my intention to lead you to a Turkish nightclub."

He laughed again, and Vega felt herself soften, give into him. "Are you in a rush to go home?" she asked.

"I'm not. I assumed you would be."

"No," she said. "I'm not."

An hour or so later, they stood in his hotel room, like children unsure how to initiate play. He spoke first. "We should swim."

"You're joking."

"I'm not. There's a pool downstairs. It's warm and shallow. In five minutes we can prove there is nothing wrong with your lungs."

"I have nothing to wear to swim."

"The hotel is practically empty. I have an extra T-shirt and shorts. That's all you need. What is the worst that will happen?"

"I will hate it, and I will embarrass myself. The night will end abruptly, and we will never see each other again."

"Five minutes," he said.

"All of that can happen in five minutes."

But Sudhir was already riffling through his drawer. Moments later, Vega stood in the bathroom, wearing a white T-shirt and his cotton shorts, the latter rolled up to fit her waist. That summer, staring at herself in the mirror, she had started to feel old. She was troubled by the wisps of gray—too few to conceal, but too many to pluck. There were slight wrinkles at the corners of her eyes and mouth, and she had taken to using Rukmini's anti-aging face moisturizer. But now, dressed in white, with her hair in a loose bun, it startled her to see how young she looked.

"You could still have another child," Rukmini had told her weeks back, unprompted. "You don't realize this. How many choices are still ahead of you." They were alone in the kitchen together, peeling almonds. Asha had gone for a walk with Vega's father and was no doubt off somewhere, eating more ice cream.

"I have a child."

"I said *another* child, kanna. I had two. It was a lovely number."

*And now we both have one*, Vega thought. To Rukmini, there was nothing more tragic than childlessness. Vega knew what she was implying, though neither of them would ever say it aloud. If you have one child, and you lose that child, you've lost everything.

"Do you want children?" Vega asked Sudhir. They were standing in the pool. The water reached her shoulders and her shirt ballooned around her. It had made her nervous when she'd first stepped in, but now she settled into it. Her face and neck felt cold compared to the rest of her body.

"I think I do. Meaning, I don't have a burning desire. But if I did become a father, I'm sure it would make me very happy. I enjoy doing fatherly things. Reading. Playing board games. Sometime back, I was making an omelet and thinking, 'If I had children, I would do this for them.'"

"You would make them omelets?"

"Sure."

His tone was so honest, so unrehearsed, that it made her laugh. "I imagine you would. Is Dhaka your permanent home?"

"I don't think it is. I don't have ties to the city. I like my work, and I have friends. But they aren't deep relationships." He exhaled slowly, and Vega recalled Gayatri mentioning that he had once been a smoker. She found this attractive—not that he had smoked, but that he had quit, that he was sturdy enough to remake himself. She listened as he talked about his years in Cairo, the city he had loved most aside from Delhi. "I had a flat overlooking the Nile. And there was a vendor who sold roasted sweet potatoes in the winter and that smell sometimes comes back to me. This was around seven years back, during the first Palestinian intifada, and there was a convergence of journalists in the area. We were together all the time. And then slowly, everybody trickled out. Before anybody left, we threw a party and said, 'Oh, we'll visit you in Beirut or Jerusalem or wherever,' but most of us have never even seen each other again. A few get togethers here or there, but never the large group." He paused. "There was a teenage boy who worked in the garage below the building. He loved Bollywood, and he would always sing these songs, but, you know, he would muddle up the lyrics. I used to give him small things. Cash during Eid, some old clothes that no longer fit. And then one day, he just disappeared. Somebody said his father had died, and the family went back to their village. But I think about him so often. These characters who just pass through your life, and then you never see them again."

"I know," she said. "I always miss people I never thought I would miss."

"I'm not the only one? I thought everybody else in the world was better at moving on."

"Of course not. Most people spend their lives and die in their native villages. Or towns or cities, or wherever. We don't let go easily. I was on the Columbia campus earlier this year and I went into the corner store where I used to buy tea during my graduate school days, and the family that ran the store was no longer there. The man working at the counter didn't know where they had gone, so I suppose it's changed hands a few times over the years. Who knows? But I felt so sad, you know, because there are people in your life from whom you drift apart, but they're retrievable. And then there are people you don't know well enough to keep in touch with."

"Right," he said. "They're just gone."

They were quiet for a bit. She tapped the floor of the pool with her toe, then said, "I don't know if that is statistically true, by the way, that most people stay in their native villages."

He smiled, and she couldn't tell if his look was pensive or flirtatious, or both. "What about now? Is Baton Rouge your final home?"

"No. It isn't." She thought of her house in Baton Rouge, the clutter of metal hangers, the stack of junk mail that would be waiting for her when they returned. How desperately she tried to distract Asha with small indulgences: Saturday picnics in the park, Sunday morning croissants, as though she could trick them both out of their malaise. Throughout the summer, Vega had been reminding Asha, "This is a holiday. After it's over, everybody is going back home." She was afraid Asha would think she was settling into a new and wonderful life in Chennai, surrounded by family, only to have it pulled from her.

"You're lifting your legs," Sudhir said.

"What on earth are you talking about?"

"When you lean back, your legs go up. Didn't you notice?"

"That's hardly swimming."

"But it is buoyancy. Could you do that on land?"

"Okay. I'll grant you that. Maybe there is nothing wrong with my bones."

"I'm going to tell you something. A small suggestion."

"Please don't."

"You can't say no before you even hear it. Just listen. Close your eyes, plug your nose, and go under. Your body can't help but float."

"Mine won't," she said. But she did it anyway, counting with Sudhir and going under the water. Then she lifted her feet and felt her body rise to the top.

Vega and Asha had been living in Montclair for three months, nearly to the date, when Rukmini arrived with the contents of Ashwini's trunk. "All utility items," Rukmini said. "Asha can wear them when she's older." She also brought with her the stack of Amar Chitra Katha comics Vega had intentionally left behind in Chennai. Now Asha was curled up on the couch, tearing through them.

"She is going to turn into a Hindu fundamentalist," Vega said. "And we will have only you to blame."

"Nobody becomes a fundamentalist by reading some small books."

"Actually, that is how many people become fundamentalists."

"You're a good mother. You'll see it doesn't."

At another moment, Vega would have kept the argument going.

Now, it didn't seem worthwhile. She took out the clothes, starched and tightly folded, those mundane reminders of Ashwini's short life. Rukmini was exploring the living room, running her fingers along the windowsill and jiggling the door handle with the precision of a housing inspector. "The curtains are quite nice."

"I know. Gayatri had them made for me. She sent the pillows and throws, as well."

"It's a good place," Rukmini proclaimed. "Small, but adequate."

They took Asha to the park that evening and watched her zip circles on her scooter. Rukmini was tired from her flight, a bit heavier than she had been last year, and she walked with a slight limp. She seemed much older than Vega remembered.

"You both appear settled," Rukmini said. "And she is happy."

Vega had accepted the position at Brooklyn College in April, and two months later, she and Asha arrived in New Jersey. "There's no need to find something immediately," Suresh had said. "You stay with us as long as you need." They set her up in a basement suite they had furnished for Rupa's parents, a blissfully cool room that smelled of eucalyptus. Suresh had moved a small desk into the corner. "For your studies," he'd said.

She split her days between research and house-hunting, sometimes alone and sometimes with Asha in tow. She visited a floor-through brownstone in Brooklyn that she loved, blocks from Margo, that was painfully out of her price range. She saw a dizzying series of identical suburban homes in identical New Jersey towns where she knew, the moment she stepped inside, neither she nor Asha would ever feel at home.

"You can always rent," Suresh said. "Then, if ever you need to move, you stay with us in the interim." But Vega didn't want to rent. She wanted to buy a home, however modest. She wanted to move in, then never move again.

"Call Dierdre," Shoba said. "Such a good lady. She won't take advantage. She loves Indians." Thus, Dierdre emerged, coiffed and eager, clipboard in hand. Days later, they stood in front of a two-bedroom

house with a small office, on a quiet street just off Bloomfield Avenue.
"You know the area?" Dierdre asked. "It's very multicultural."

Vega's stomach had lurched as they drove down Bloomfield, past
the coffee shop and used bookstore—both remarkably unchanged—
and past Café Abyssinia, then past an ice cream shop that Asha pointed
out from the back window. The house itself had its own charm. It was
the smallest on the block, white with blue shutters. On the sidewalk
were faint traces of a child's hopscotch game.

"I know it quite well."

"Good! Now, there is no backyard. Which is why it's been on the
market so long. But there *is* a park up the street. And, I always say, a
park is like a lawn you don't have to water." She went on about the
school district and the local Indian community, but Vega didn't need
any convincing. She had found where she wanted to live.


"What about when your fellow comes?" Suresh asked one
night. They had eaten dinner at his house, as they did most
Fridays, and were clearing the table. Rupa was bathing Vikram. Shoba,
Mohan, and the girls had come and gone, and Rukmini and Asha were
in the basement playing one of their endless rounds of Go Fish. In
three days, Rukmini was returning to Chennai, and Vega was beginning to feel the first surfacing of sadness. That morning, she found a
grocery list Rukmini had written on the back of an envelope and left
on the bookshelf: *cooking oil, bananas, brown bread.* She held on to it,
unable to throw it out.

"It will be good when I go," Rukmini had said. "It's good to have
your routine back."

It was true. Vega did like her daily routine. She liked walking Asha
to school, then taking that familiar commute into the city. On Wednesday and Thursday nights, when Asha slept at Suresh and Rupa's, Vega
stayed late on campus then went out to dinner, sometimes by herself,
sometimes with Margo. And then there were Fridays, when they ate at

Shoba and Mohan's or Suresh and Rupa's, always leaving late, Asha falling asleep in the car on the way home.

"You're prying, Suresh," Vega said.

"I'm not prying. I'm talking about logistics, only. Asha should stay with us that week. Easier for everybody."

She and Sudhir had been in close touch over the year, and occasionally one of them hinted at something more permanent. But beyond his visit in late November, they had made no plans for the future. Sometimes, the thought of being with him thrilled Vega. She imagined him moving to New York and getting to know Asha. In some distant way, she fantasized about having a child with him—a second sibling for Asha and grandchild for her parents. Other times, she was happy just as she was.

She spooned the last of the dhal and vegetables into Rupa's lunch container, then slid it into the fridge. From the bathroom, they could hear Vikram crying. A few weeks earlier, he had said his first word: *ball.* The language came steadily afterwards. *Amma, Appa, Asha, vroom.* Vega was reminded of Asha at that stage, the slow start and then the quick acceleration, the shocking realization of what she had been processing all this time.

"Rupa has to be at the hospital early," Suresh said. "She should go to sleep."

"Go help her. I can finish in here." Vega took the dish towel and wiped down the table. Then she went into the kitchen, washed the last of the pots, and set them in the rack to dry.

# Acknowledgments

Thank you to the MFA program at Boston University. To Leslie Epstein, Xuefei Jin, and Sigrid Nunez: I owe this book—and every future book—to your wisdom and generosity.

My agent, Judythe Cohen, and the entire team at Janklow & Nesbit believed in *Habitations* with the heart and tenacity that writers dream of. My editor, Carina Guiterman, along with Sophia Benz, Stacey Sakal, and Susan Bishansky, pushed me to sharpen this novel with every revision. I am also grateful to Kayley Hoffman, Megha Jain, Lewelin Polanco, Beth Maglione, Amanda Mulholland, Jackie Seow, Danielle Priellip, Hannah Bishop, and all of Simon & Schuster.

So many writers lit the path for me through the brilliance of their work and the warmth of their encouragement. Thank you to Deesha Philyaw, Mecca Jamilah Sullivan, Weike Wang, Pooja Makhijani, and the No Name Writers' Group of New Orleans: Adrian Van Young, Anya Groner, Jessie Morgan-Owens, Julia Carey Arendell, and Tom Andes. Thank you to my earliest writing teachers: Robin Coste Lewis and Matt de la Peña. I'm eternally grateful to Val Otarod and Victor Yang for the joy and camaraderie you brought to this process. How does anybody write a book without the two of you? Thank you to Katy Ancelet and Chital Mehta for sharing your precious time and incisive feedback, and to Aftab Ahmad for your guidance with Urdu translations.

To my colleagues and students at the University of Mississippi: It's a gift to work and write alongside you. Thank you also to the Bread Loaf Writers' Conference and the Barbara Deming Memorial Fund.

To my parents, Girija and Kalyan Sundar, and my brother, Arya Sundar: Thank you for a childhood filled with books and laughter.

To my family in India: Thank you for always opening your doors to me.

To my web of aunties and uncles in the States: Thank you for the decades of boundless love.

Thank you to the friends who have sustained me: Namrata Krishna, Devika Gajria, Abbey Marks, Mia Green-Dove, Faye Zemel, Kristy Magner, Asia Wong, Brett and Shiva King, Katy Ancelet (once again), Emily Maw, Jill Polk, and all the children and adults of my beloved Sunday Supper family.

To Toshan, Amara, and Sajan: You are the funniest, wildest, smartest, and most delightful people I know, and you have filled my world with wonder (and cats).

Finally, thank you to Aaron DeLong, the love of my life and my sharpest critic. You made every draft of this book possible.

# About the Author

Sheila Sundar is a professor of English and creative writing at the University of Mississippi. Her writing has appeared in the *Virginia Quarterly Review*, the *Massachusetts Review*, the *Threepenny Review*, and elsewhere. She lives in New Orleans with her husband and their three children. *Habitations* is her debut novel.